"The book crackled with sensuality. . . . The only thing I hated? That it ended."

—*Under the Covers Book Blog*

"Full of beautiful descriptions, vivid imagery, great characters, and humor. This isn't a run-of-the-mill, slapped-together erotica. This is engrossing, well-written literature that happens to be sexy as hell."

—*The Book Vixen*

"Intriguing, smart, super hot, and just plain well written have come to be hallmarks of Cole's writing, and it comes out full force in this new series."

—*The Brunette Librarian*

"The romance is lusty, HOT and HOT and did I say HOT?"

—*Clue Review*

"Grab a fan, the smelling salts, and keep the BP cuff on hand, this is going to have you panting for more! BEST CARDIO EVER!"

—*Tome Tender Book Blog*

"Five sexy CAN'T-WAIT-TIL-THE-NEXT-ONE, WHAT-AM-I-SUPPOSED-TO-DO-WITH-MYSELF-TIL-THEN stars."

—*Kayla the Bibliophile*

"A drop-everything-now MUST-READ! . . . Intense, ridiculously sexy, and thrilling the entire way through. . . . One of the HOTTEST series I have ever read!"

—*Shayna Renee's Spicy Reads*

"Can someone please hand me a chainsaw to cut this sexual tension?"

—*Guilty Pleasures Book Reviews*

THE
MASTER

KRESLEY COLE

POCKET BOOKS

New York   London   Toronto   Sydney   New Delhi

Pocket Books
A Division of Simon & Schuster, Inc.
1230 Avenue of the Americas
New York, NY 10020

Copyright © 2015 by Kresley Cole

All rights reserved, including the right to reproduce this book or portions thereof in any form whatsoever. For information address Pocket Books Subsidiary Rights Department, 1230 Avenue of the Americas, New York, NY 10020.

First Pocket Books paperback edition March 2015

POCKET and colophon are registered trademarks of Simon & Schuster, Inc.

For information about special discounts for bulk purchases, please contact Simon & Schuster Special Sales at 1-866-506-1949 or business@simonandschuster.com.

The Simon & Schuster Speakers Bureau can bring authors to your live event. For more information or to book an event contact the Simon & Schuster Speakers Bureau at 1-866-248-3049 or visit our website at www.simonspeakers.com.

Manufactured in the United States of America

10   9   8   7   6   5   4   3   2   1

ISBN 978-1-4767-9728-1
ISBN 978-1-4516-5010-5 (ebook)

Dedicated to the incredible Barbara Ankrum,
who dropped everything to beta read this book
(and *Dead of Winter*, and *Dark Skye*,
and *The Professional* . . .).
What would I do without your amazing vision?

THE
MASTER

"*They say I'm heartless and manipulative,*
that I amuse myself by playing with others' lives.
They aren't wrong."
—MAKSIMILIAN SEVASTYAN

"*A mal tiempo, buena cara.*
To bad weather, good face."
—ANA-LUCÍA MARTINEZ ~~HATCHER~~
(ALIAS: CAT MARÍN)

CHAPTER 1

Mi madre must be turning over in her grave right now.

As I rode the elevator to the penthouse of the ritzy Seltane Hotel—it'd taken two staffers to key me up to the fortieth floor—I chewed on a fingernail.

Was I really about to let some strange man have sex with me? For money?

The elevator arrived too quickly, forcing me onto a private landing with its own lobby and an elegant sitting area. An open newspaper lay on a coffee table, as if someone had recently left.

The entry—a pair of ornate mahogany doors—was just beyond, looming. Could I bring myself to ring the bell?

Apparently, this penthouse was one of the largest (more than ten thousand square feet) and the most expensive (thirty-two grand—a night) in Miami. Who in their right mind would spend that much money on a hotel? Clearly my first client was *loco*.

Other than that, I didn't know much about him. He was a Russian businessman, here in Miami for a week. He'd been not only vetted but vouched for by sister escort agencies all over the world. In other words, he was a *hobbyist*, a routine user of escorts.

Tempted to bolt, I pulled out my phone to call my hookup, Ivanna. She was a Ukrainian immigrant and high-class escort, making bank; I was her cleaning lady. She thought my current employment was a waste of my "spectacular figure and fresh-faced beauty." Yeah, yeah.

When she answered, I said, "I don't think I can do this." I began to pace the lobby, my stilettos silent on the plush beige rug.

"Of course you can. You don't understand how badly I wish I could be there. If this man is renting the penthouse for a week, imagine how rich he is!"

The Russian had booked Ivanna, but she'd had a reaction to Botox (she was only thirty!). She'd thought she'd be okay by tonight, so she hadn't called to cancel. A big no-no for escorts.

"If my eyes weren't swollen shut . . ."

"Ivanna, I'm not at this point yet." I'd been vacillating like crazy. Though I'd prepared to take a couple of dates—getting an exam and a waxing—I'd always suspected I'd balk. "I'm not *here*," I insisted. But wasn't I? Yesterday I could've sworn I'd seen Edward.

In Miami.

I'd been riding the bus home from a cleaning gig when I'd seen a tall, lanky blond stepping out of a bodega, striding toward a Porsche. The last time I'd seen him had been in the glare of headlights, his green eyes stark against his blood-coated face.

If he was here, then I needed to flee to a new city as soon as possible. But that took funds.

"You make this job sound so horrible," Ivanna said. "You're going to do great. You have the balls, and that's half the battle!"

Despite my upbringing—or maybe because of it—I was pretty shameless. Even with my, ahem, generous ass, I'd proudly strutted the beaches of Jacksonville in a micro thong bikini. I'd gotten hot and heavy with all manner of high school boys, doing everything but screwing, earning a reputation as a cocktease. When I'd started having sex with Edward, I'd studied tips and tricks, anything to tempt him. So I knew how to get a guy sprung.

Ivanna said, "You'll have inquiries from the agency site before you know it."

She'd gotten the web guy for *Elite Escorts* to toss up a makeshift page for me, by promising him an HR. Hand release.

I knew all the lingo, had chuckled as she'd recited acronyms, never imagining I'd be *using* the lingo. A BBBJ was a bareback blowjob. Swallowing was BBBJNQNS—bareback blowjob, no quit, no spit. MSOG—multiple shots on goal—meant the client could come as many times as he liked in the specified time limit. "You shouldn't have bothered with that web page for me." I'd told her I would only do this once or twice, but she'd just smiled and said, "That's what we all thought. Now pose for your site photo!"

"You only have a couple more minutes to be on time," Ivanna said. "Take a deep breath, remember my three key points, and you'll be fine."

First, I should look for a nondescript envelope of cash lying on a conspicuous surface—my "donation." I was to do nothing until I pocketed the money. And then? The name of the game was *upselling*, getting him to pay for services above and beyond the outcall, earnings that were all mine.

Second, since my client wasn't likely to inspire arousal—despite the fact that I hadn't had sex in forever and my libido was going crazy!—I'd need to figure out a way to furtively lube up. Most escorts did. Lube made for safer sex and limited VF, vagina fatigue. Of course, a condom was mandatory.

Third, the majority of clients that used Elite Escorts liked ingratiating, sweet dates; I was a cheeky smart-ass. So I would have to curb my personality to succeed.

Damn it, I should never be in the service industry—in *any* capacity.

But I needed this money to run! I had my own rules, and in three years I'd never broken them.

1. *Never say anything above and beyond what is absolutely necessary.*
2. *Never create links between you and anything else.*
3. *Never stay in a place longer than six months.*
4. *Never get soft.*
5. *Never attract undue attention.*
6. *Forgodsakes, never, never, never trust another man.*

Without funds, I was going to break rule number three.

"Trust me, Cat, with your business savvy, you're going to make a killing," Ivanna assured me.

How savvy was I? Although I had six houses to clean each week—including hers—five of the women beat me up on my fee, assuming I was an undocumented worker from Cuba.

"Just have fun," she said. "It doesn't have to feel like work. Your waxing was probably more uncomfortable than your date could ever be."

But . . . "It's been more than three years since I slept with anyone." And Edward's pitiful attempts shouldn't even count.

"That is . . . hmm. How strange," she said, as if I'd told her I liked to wear other people's skin. "We'll discuss this later. For now, remember: sex is like riding a bike."

I turned toward the elevator. "*Mierda.* I can't. This was a mistake."

Ivanna sighed. "I didn't want you to get your hopes up too high, so I never told you my record for one night."

"Are you going to now?" She'd been vague, saying the sky was the limit, but she'd refused to give me hard numbers.

"My record for a six-hour outcall is over twenty thousand in cash and jewels."

Twenty. Thousand.

Money like that could catapult me directly into the next phase of my life plan! When I regained the power of speech, I sang, "And we're off to fuck the wizard."

She laughed. "I hope he's a wonderful wizard. Oh, one last thing, Cat. You're going to have a gut-check moment, and when you do, ask yourself: would I have sex with this guy for free? If the answer is yes, then why not view the money as a bonus?"

"Okay, *muy bien*. I can do this," I said, psyching myself up.

"Go get 'em!"

Disconnecting the call, I turned to check my appearance in a lobby mirror. December was usually mild, but this year had been downright balmy, so I'd worn a wrap dress of forest-green silk. The style was understated, with a conservative neckline, in case he wanted to take me out, but the sides were held together by only a single bow at my hip. Stilettos gave a hint of naughty.

I twisted around to view the back. The thin silk was too tight across my ass, leaving little to the imagination. Nothing to be done for it now. I faced forward and eked out a smile.

I'd worn only lip gloss, mascara, and a touch of glittery bronze eye shadow. Ivanna said it brought out the vivid copper color of my irises, making my eyes look exotic, especially against my dark hair. I'd left the length of it down in long loose curls.

Makeup: *in place*. Hair: *best that can be expected*. Conclusion: *If I were a horny Russian lech, I'd do me*.

I checked my cell phone clock. I had less than two minutes to make an on-time arrival. Stowing my phone in my purse, I pressed the doorbell, then gazed around, battling my nerves. I glanced at that newspaper on the coffee table again. Would a guy this rich have a bodyguard or something—

The door opened, revealing my first-ever client. In escort slang, he was DDG.

Drop. Dead. Gorgeous.

He looked to be in his midthirties, with a full head of thick black hair and a built body. He was well over six feet tall. His blue eyes were hooded, his penetrating gaze roaming over me.

He wore a lightweight cashmere sweater, winter white, that molded over his rigid pecs. The color made the piercing blue of his eyes pop. Dark, tailored slacks highlighted muscular legs and lean hips.

If I was ever going to lose my "escort cherry," I couldn't imagine a more ideal client.

Yet the Russian glanced behind me, as if he expected someone else to be there.

"It's just me," I said, surprised my voice sounded so casual when my heart was pounding.

Without a word, he turned, heading into a living area. I followed.

Accent lighting illuminated the tasteful modern décor. Floor-to-ceiling panoramic windows offered what had to be the best view in the city. All the balcony doors were open, the sound of the waves reaching us even this high up. This place was huge, the size reminding me of my former mansion. Oh, to be rolling again . . .

He faced me. "I confirmed a woman named

Ivanna. Your agency suggested her when I sent in my preferences." His voice was deep and rumbly, his accent tingeing the words.

I was a sucker for men with accents. Edward's slow Atlanta drawl used to light me up. Until I'd found out he was from England. "Ivanna was supposed to come tonight, but she had to call in sick."

"I requested a tall, slender blonde, at least in her late twenties. Ideally from Europe. Perhaps her substitute could have matched *any* of my requests."

Instead he'd gotten me—twenty-two, five feet two inches tall, curvy, brunette. Oh, and one generation away from Cuba. Giving him a fake smile, I teasingly said, "Isn't variety the spice of life, *querido*?" Sweetheart.

He wasn't budging. "You're not what I ordered."

I, above all people, knew that you shouldn't have to pay for something you never asked for. I had a flash memory of Edward edging toward his gun, moments after declaring his love for me.

"Are you even of legal age?" the Russian grated.

"And then some."

He looked unmoved.

I'd read and reread *Getting to Yes*, and I thought I could finagle one night out of this guy. But then, was I really ready to take this step? "I can't change your mind?"

When his expression grew even colder, I was glad he was about to kick me out. I would make a better outlaw than I would an escort. *Outlaw? Give it time, Cat.*

In a stern tone, he said, "I never reverse myself on decisions."

I shrugged. "Okay, your loss." How confident I sounded! Like a working-girl pro. Relieved, I turned toward the door, sauntering away—

I thought I heard him hiss in a breath.

Mierda. Knowing my luck, I'd split the seam in my dress.

CHAPTER 2

"*P*erhaps I was . . . hasty," he said. "Stay for a drink."

Had my ass worked for me? Was I happy about this?

When I turned and traipsed back, he headed to the bar area. This was actually happening. I was going to have sex for money.

Over his shoulder, he said, "I'm Maksimilian Sevastyan."

I turned it over on my tongue, finding his name a mouthful. In my mind, I styled him *Máxim.*

"*Encantada.* Nice to meet you. I'm Cat Marín." I glanced around for my donation. Nothing. Which made me uneasy, but I gamely bellied up to the bar.

"Is that your working name?"

My alias. "That's what they call me." And that was what my fake ID said, whenever I was forced to use it.

I'd chosen my grandmother's name of Catarina, and her mother's name of Marín, and then I'd assumed the identity completely. Though I missed being Lucía, that life was like a distant dream.

"What do you drink?"

Good question. I couldn't remember the last time I'd had alcohol. Maybe beer after a 5K race? "Um, whatever you're having."

"Vodka martini?" Probably not a good idea. "You must have a preferred cocktail."

I was about to say something stupid, like "Sex on the Beach!" but instead said, "White wine would be great."

"You seem uneasy."

I admitted, "I'm a little new to all of this."

"Uh-huh. I've booked many escorts. Not one has ever said she's been at this awhile."

He thought I was lying. I was the world's shittiest liar. Early on, I'd realized that anytime I'd been put into a position to tell an untruth, I'd resented it so much, I would stew for days. So I'd just stopped doing it. "I'm not lying to you."

He waved my words away, turning to the wine collection.

As he investigated the offerings, I studied him up close. He was clean-shaven, with smooth skin that looked newly tanned, but he had no laugh lines around his eyes. Weird. No wedding-ring tan line either. At least he was single.

His lips were firm, his white teeth even. A wide masculine jawline complemented his strong nose and chin, his broad cheekbones. His hair was close-cut on the sides, longer on the top. What would it feel like to run my fingers through it?

"There's a cellar somewhere on this floor, but I think you'll like this wine." When he uncorked the bottle, his muscles moved beneath his thin sweater. He wore a diving watch that probably cost more than my rat-trap apartment complex.

The only thing that could compete with the view of him was the view outside. The wraparound balcony had small torches along its clear glass railing. Past an infinity pool that I would kill to experience, I could see the ocean. A nearly full moon hung heavy in the sky.

"Go take a look." He poured a glass and handed it to me. "I'll meet you outside."

I wasn't supposed to do anything until I got paid, but after a quick risk/reward assessment, I said, "Okay." As I strolled past the pool, steam rose from the heated water. In fact, the entire pool deck was heated. I crossed to the balcony rail and sampled the wine, sighing at the taste. I could see the appeal of drinking with this on tap.

A warm gust blew, and I inhaled the salty air. My eyes went half-mast at the sound of the ocean. I could almost imagine I was on Martinez Beach. Nearly a century ago, my father's family had bought a long tract of oceanfront property near Jacksonville, putting it into a trust, never imagining the fortune it'd be worth today.

Short of returning there, I would have loved to remain in this city. Unfortunately the only Miami in my future was M.I.A.M.I.: Money Is A Major Issue.

If I made bank tonight, I could reboot somewhere

as exciting, maybe LA or San Diego. I'd leave right after my last college exam, then get on with phase two of my reclaim-my-life plan: *Disappear Forever*. I'd buy a real fake ID (oxymoron?) and a social security number that would hold up under scrutiny.

Here I was dreaming about bank, when I hadn't gotten my donation, much less upsold him for more. I knew my hard limits, but other than that, I wasn't sure what I would do.

As I drank, I recalled the article Ivanna had made me read to help with my first date: The Top Ten Ways to Wow a Client. Suggestions included feigning breathless absorption when he talked, pretending affection, faking orgasms, and always telling him he was right.

Seriously?

Máxim joined me outside, with the wine bottle in one hand and his drink in the other. He set the bottle on a nearby table, then stood beside me. The moon bathed his face, lovingly highlighting all his chiseled features.

Though unpaid, I began to relax. Regardless of what else happened, I was presently in the Seltane penthouse with a client who might just give me the FOTC. Fuck of the century.

I took another sip. "Did you add crack sprinkles to this vintage?"

"I was fresh out of crack," he said in a derisive tone. "What do you think of the view?"

I grinned over the rim of my glass. "I suppose it's *adequate*. If you like this kind of thing."

At my attempt at humor, he tilted his head. "I

looked you up on your agency's site." Only a couple of the items Ivanna had listed about me were true—two-thirds of my measurements and my status as a CAN, certified all natural, with no surgical enhancements.

I recalled the fake bio she'd read to me: *I like dancing* (I hated dancing) *and yoga* (jogger here). *In my spare time* (as if I had any!), *I enjoy performance art* (no, *gracias*) *and shopping* (a form of torture).

"Your photo's unusual," he said.

"Is it?" Ivanna had taken pics of me on an out-of-the-way beach. I'd worn black boy-short bottoms that rode up my cheeks, no top, mascara only, and my hair piled up on my head. She'd chosen one taken from the back that I hadn't posed for.

My head had been turned to the side as I gazed off at something. My eyes had been distant, because I'd been deep in thought—*second* thoughts—about this entire idea. Oh, and cursing Edward as usual.

The blood arcing across our bedroom . . . those ugly sounds . . .

Shake it off, Cat.

The Russian said, "It's not your typical boudoir shot with flattering lighting and risqué lingerie."

"A hobbyist like you would know, huh?" I drank more wine, frowning when I reached the bottom of my glass. "I'm not really a simulated boudoir kind of girl."

Without a word, he refilled me. "What kind of a girl are you?"

A dogged survivor who believed in living to fight another day. But I told him, "A girl who believes in topless beaches for everyone. *Viva la revolución!*" I thought that was funny, but he just tilted his head again.

"Your photo makes a man wonder what you're thinking about. That was by design, no?"

"I didn't choose the one that was uploaded." I'd only allowed Ivanna to use it because I'd looked a world away from the last pictures taken of me, when I was still a teenager.

"You're twenty-six?"

Ivanna had inflated the number. "Old enough to know better."

Máxim peered at my breasts. "Measurements: thirty-five, twenty-three, thirty-*six*?"

"Thirty-four and a half on a good day. I didn't put that up either. I like my size." I could go braless if I wanted to, but could still produce cleavage when necessary.

His brows drew together. I got the impression he was trying to fit me into a box, and having unexpected difficulties.

I could've told him, *My ass won't fit, yo.*

"You have a marked accent. Not native to the States?"

"I grew up in a Spanish-speaking household." With *una madre loca*, Catholic to the core. Despite her refusal to learn English, she'd homeschooled me until high school and kept most people away from our secluded beach. I didn't like thinking about my childhood, much less talking about it.

"In Miami?"

I shrugged. Questions like this made me nervous. The less anyone knew about me the better. Connections to others were breadcrumbs. That was why I didn't date, didn't socialize. Not that I had time between scrubbing toilets and going to school.

"You don't care to talk about yourself?" He gave a humorless laugh. "That's a first."

"Oh, you don't want to hear about my boring life. I have an idea: let's institute a no-personal-questions rule."

"And you think you can keep yourself from digging about me?"

If it kept him from doing the same? "*Sí.*"

"Very well, then let's get down to business. I believe this is the part where you upsell me."

Busted.

"I'll only need you for an hour or so," he continued, "but I don't like to be mindful of such things, so I booked half the night. How much will it cost to let me do anything I desire to you?"

What would a guy like this—gorgeous, rich, condescending—want? "Some things aren't on the table."

A flash of anger. "Everything is on *my* table, little girl."

This was turning into an issue. *No, no, remember your mantra.* When faced with a difficulty, good businesswomen said, "It's not a problem," then went to work fixing it.

"Though I'd love to get to know your body better"— I gave him a brazen once-over that seemed to surprise him—"I can't provide some of the services you might desire. There's not enough money in the world."

"Such as?"

"BBBJ. In fact, bareback anything is out."

"I have no interest in that. You replaced another tonight—I'll expect you to do what she would have. What I ordered from your agency."

I recalled Ivanna's kink specialization: bondage, discipline, submission, and the like. She had gear all over her apartment. Had this guy requested her for more than her looks?

As a vetted hobbyist, he couldn't be *too* dangerous. If he offered me enough money, could I trust a strange man to tie me up? To make me helpless?

No, gracias. My ability to trust was broken, like a fractured limb that had never been set, now shrunken and useless. I even refused to trust myself when it came to men.

But I didn't want to lose out on this money. "Why don't we take tonight as it comes? See where it leads us?" *See where I can lead you.* "I promise we'll both be satisfied."

He narrowed his blue eyes, and it was like a blast of icy air blew over me. "Do not play games with me. And don't mistake my intent—I couldn't care less if you enjoy this or not, so don't pretend to."

What a dick! *Cállate la boca, Cat!* Shut your mouth—

"I won't tolerate feigned passion."

So much for Ivanna's article. Somehow I managed to say, "Understood."

"Then I'll pay you three thousand—and you'll be amenable to my interests."

My knees almost buckled. That much money would be life-changing! Yet words were leaving my lips: "Make it five, and we have a deal."

He stilled. Had I angered him? Blown everything? *Mima*, my island grandmother, had a saying: "Pigs get fat, hogs get slaughtered." I was about to be bacon.

"Deal," he said.

En serio? Wait, what had I agreed to? Amenable to his interests?

"I assume you'll want to be paid in advance."

Holy shit! "Yes, *por favor*."

"Follow me." He returned to the living room, heading toward a stylish briefcase on a console.

Once fifty bound Benjamins sat tucked in my purse, my fate had been sealed.

He took my empty glass from me, setting it down. I'd drunk that wine too? I might've been buzzed, but my nerves prevented it. Now that the thrill of the deal was fading, anxiety took its place.

He crossed to a suite, saying over his shoulder. "Come. I'm keen to see what five thousand buys me in Miami."

I stiffened at the reminder.

At the bedroom entrance, he turned to me. "What's your hesitation? Feigning shyness won't be tolerated either."

My thoughts were in a tangle. Two stood out. *You're going to be a hooker, Cat,* warred with *Five thousand dollars, idiota!* Gut check? Oh, yeah.

But Ivanna was right; I would have sex with this guy for free.

Besides, my situation demanded drastic measures. Nothing this man could do to me would be worse than what Edward would do if he caught me.

Since he was my husband, and I'd foiled his plan to kill me.

With that in mind, I joined the Russian in the bedroom. What I saw on the bed made me freeze in my tracks.

CHAPTER 3

A ball gag. A crop. Leather restraints.

Ni en broma! Not on your life.

No, no, surely I could figure out a happy medium. This man had to be interested in more than BDSM. "Explain what you'd do to me."

He coolly said, "Once you've stripped, you'll go to your knees at the edge of the mattress, buckling the gag on yourself. I'll bind your arms behind your back, and you'll lean forward resting on your forehead. Then I'll whip your body wherever it occurs to me to. When I'm satisfied with that, I'll fuck you from behind."

This sounded like a script. Like he did this with every escort.

He'd said nothing about kissing my nipples, nothing about petting me. In his scenario, we'd share the fewest points of contact possible while still technically having sex. He wouldn't see my face or hear my voice. He wouldn't even touch me to gag me!

I would be just a receptacle. Which he'd pretty

much warned me about. A faceless, voiceless receptacle.

I'm not there yet. So my options were to walk out or try to change his mind. Nothing to lose by the latter. Why not make this into a fantasy? I could be anyone tonight. A femme fatale, a man-eater.

I told him, "While your script sounds . . . interesting, I don't think that's what you really want."

His brows shot up. "*You* don't."

I turned toward the suite's sitting area. All the windows and doors were open in the softly lit room. Gauzy moonlit curtains fluttered. I sauntered behind the couch. When I patted the back cushions, inviting him over, his lips thinned.

Long, anxious moments passed as we stared at each other. *Heartbeat . . . heartbeat . . . heartbeat.* Then it seemed like curiosity forced him to stride over.

When he took a seat, I smiled, sidling around in front of him. I stepped forward until he had to make room for me, spreading his knees.

I played with the sash on the side of my dress. "Would you like me to take this off, *Ruso*?" Russian.

Curt nod.

I slowly untied the sash. Letting my dress hang open like a robe, I gave him a curtained glimpse of my provocative black demi bra and thong set.

I couldn't read him, couldn't tell if he liked the view or not. He looked so cold.

So why was I getting hot stripping for him? I glanced at his big, masculine hands. What would they feel like squeezing my breasts or cupping my bare pussy? My nipples were taut, my panties growing moist. I never wore lingerie like this, and I felt hypersensitive after my waxing a couple of days ago.

I shimmied from my dress, tossing it to a neighboring seat. When I faced him in my underwear, he casually draped his arms along the back of the sofa.

"Turn in place for me." He was so calm, detached even. This was like foreplay with a computer. A DDG computer. "Slowly."

I reminded myself that I was playing the femme fatale. My two glasses of wine told me I was doing *fine*.

As I turned, I could feel his eyes on my cheeks, exposed in my tiny thong. Which only made me wetter. Furtive lubing would not be a problem. In fact, maybe I should leave my panties on for a little longer? It'd been a while since I'd had the time or energy to masturbate. What if I lost control?

Like everyone else on earth, when my body got turned on, my brain turned off. But mine was a total factory shutdown, a labor strike. I needed my wits to handle this guy.

I faced him again. Had his breaths shallowed a touch? "Show me your breasts. Let's see if I like your size as much as you profess to."

I removed my bra, tossing it in the direction of my dress. I was secretly proud of my pert breasts. They fit my body but were plump, with jutting nipples that were not quite pink and not quite tan. My small areolas were raised, giving the peaks a slightly puffy look.

When I squared my shoulders, the Russian's nostrils flared—finally a hint of passion from him!

"Very nice. I hadn't thought the view from the front could compete with the back."

Wow. An actual compliment. My attention was drawn downward. A very large erection pressed against the material of his slacks. *Muy grande.* Maybe *too* big? For all my fooling around, I'd only had intercourse with Edward, and he was nowhere near as well endowed.

"Continue."

Strip totally? Deciding against that, I stepped forward, straddling him. I rested my knees beside his hips, my hands on his shoulders. A breeze from the ocean drifted in, mingling with his intoxicating scent—a blend of sandalwood and simmering man. His scent made me tremble—it was like an unfair advantage, used to drug new escorts.

When I lowered myself atop the thick ridge of his cock, I could feel his heat even through our clothes. My eyes went wide; his narrowed.

I'd be taking his length inside me directly. The idea no longer filled me with hesitation. I shivered with desire. My nipples puckered even tighter, right before his eyes.

I wanted this man, this stranger.

I could count on one hand the number of guys who'd gotten me off. Most times had been accidental when I'd been fumbling in the backseat with a boy or grinding one at a keg party. Edward had never gotten close. Not that he'd cared. But this Russian—

"I did *not* invite you to straddle me," he snapped. His body went tense—*angry* tense.

I froze with confusion. Most guys liked it when topless girls straddled them.

"You just assume I *wanted* you atop me?" He couldn't sound more cutting. He grabbed me, lifting me to the side—as if to fling my body off him.

Yet then he stilled. His hands were so big on me, his fingers covered a good bit of my ass. After a hesitation— when we seemed suspended in the moment—he began to knead me. When he lowered his hands to grip my curves, a low groan escaped him. But he still held me upright.

Again, something was happening that I didn't understand, as if some inner battle were being played out. In my lust-dimmed mind, I wondered if he tied women up and fucked them from behind because he didn't like to touch too much of them.

Just when I'd decided that was the case, I found myself settled back over him, the raised bulge of his cock directly between my legs. Had I won this round?

His anger seemed to have been put on hold, but he wasn't ready to concede defeat. "You still refuse to give me what I want?"

And he was going along with my refusal? Emboldened, I leaned in next to his ear. "I'm going to give you what you *need*, Ruso." The wine and my arousal were making my own accent thicken even more. My stiffened nipples brushed the fine cashmere of his sweater, which felt incredible, so I skimmed them again.

What would it take to get this man's mouth on my breasts? When I imagined him sucking me . . . a soft moan escaped my lips, my back subtly arching.

He clamped his hand over my nape. "What kind of escort brazenly denies a client? You're either starving at this job—or making a fortune. . . ." He trailed off when I rolled my hips, running my pussy over his cock, with only my moistened panties and his slacks between us.

I gasped at the sensation, breaths shallowing. My clitoris began to throb.

He drew his hands away, resting his arms over the back of the couch again, as if he'd made a conscious decision not to touch me. I got the impression that I was being tested somehow—or that *he* was. "Put your hands behind your back. Now."

He probably expected me to clasp my elbows. "Of course." Instead, I dropped my hands directly behind my ass, grasping high on his thighs to hold my balance.

He tensed again, but before he could say another word, I whipped my hips over his length. My head fell back as I moaned. I'd forgotten how irresistible sexual play could be, had forgotten about uncontrollable urges and the hardness of a man's body.

I faced the Russian, beginning to ride him. Though his gaze was rapt on our point of contact, he refused to move his own hips to meet me. No matter. The bulge of his zipper had lined up with my swollen clitoris, my soaked panties rubbing that bud. *Fricción!* Sultry, damp friction . . . sent me ever closer to orgasm. Soon I was panting, grinding him like a pole dancer.

He clutched the couch, his long fingers gone white-knuckled. "Is this what you think I need?" His voice alone could make me come. The husky timbre had only deepened. "To be ridden?"

"I think you need passion." I certainly did.

"Maybe if it wasn't feigned."

I nearly laughed. "Oh, I'm not feigning anything." How to tell him I would climax soon?

"Wait." He seized my shimmying hips, holding me still. "Up."

Confused, I put my hands on his shoulders and rose up on my knees. Was he kicking me off again? Then I followed his narrow-eyed gaze.

His slacks, which probably cost thousands, now had a damp spot over his groin. I'd wetted him through my panties.

I should have been worried about his reaction, but I was too far gone to care. I dropped as low as his hands would allow, wanting my pussy back atop his hot hardness.

He grated, "*Blyad'!*" Whatever that meant. "You're truly wet for me. Very wet. You've been using me to get off?"

"*Por Dios*, why are you talking so much?" I said between breaths. "Want to come, *Ruso*."

He blinked at me. The cool, detached Russian looked stunned. "Then by all means." He released his grip. "Continue."

"*Gracias*." I sighed with relief, letting my nipples skim his chest on my way down. If he'd allowed that . . . I threaded my fingers through his hair and leaned in to kiss his neck. When I gave a little suck over his pulse point, his head tipped back.

I lost the ridge of his zipper, so I writhed atop

him, hunting for it. Had his hips finally moved? Did he want that contact too?

I found the perfect spot. "*Ay, perfección.*"

When I set back in, he faced me, his blue gaze flicking from my eyes, to my lips, down to my tits and thong and back.

As I pleasured myself, his own lips caught my attention. They were as attractive as everything else about him. The fuller bottom one had a sexy dip in the middle. What would it be like to kiss him?

Ivanna said it bonded people too much, and that you had to save something special for a lover in your life. I had no lover, and no fear of bonding. Right now, hovering on the edge of orgasm, I had no fears at all! I gazed at his lips, licking my own.

"You think I need to be kissed?" His words were hoarse.

"Doesn't everyone—"

He bucked his hips hard, rocking his unyielding cock against my panties.

At last! "Oh! *Fricción* . . . Do it again, *por favor.*"

He did it again. And again. Soon he was groaning with each thrust, but the sound was pained, as if he were getting punched in the stomach at the end of each one—or cutting himself off.

I'd think about all this—later. "Don't stop!"

As he shoved against my pussy, I muttered incomprehensible things, switching from one language back to the other, struggling to communicate that I was on the verge. "Oh, my God. *Ay, Dios mío.*"

"You're about to come?" he asked in a strained voice.

"About to combust!" I clasped his face with both hands.

Our gazes locked. His was still defiant and angry, his chin jutting stubbornly—even as he met my undulations.

"No, no, *cariño*." Rubbing my thumb over his bottom lip, I whispered, "*No te pongas bravo conmigo. Don't be angry with me. We'll both feel good soon.*" I leaned down and covered his mouth with my own. His lips were firm and hot. I licked the seam of them, whimpering. My movements quickened until I was bucking over the Russian's cock.

He parted his lips; the tip of my tongue found his, the spark that set off—

Pleasure. Exploding. Electrifying me.

Currents sizzled through my veins to make way for . . . *fire*.

"*Mmmm!*" I cried out into his mouth. Bliss engulfed me, forcing my hips to gyrate on him. Lost, I rubbed my tits against his chest. I moaned, riding him like a toy as my pussy contracted over and over.

Only as sanity returned and the spasms faded did I realize he wasn't returning the kiss. I drew back.

He'd gone completely still. That strain within him only grew. "You kissed me. You *came*. That was not supposed to happen."

"It was the heat of the moment. *No te pongas—*"

He wrapped my hair around his fist, forcing me closer till our lips met.

When I gasped, he set in with a fervor. He kissed

as if he hadn't taken a woman's lips in years, as if he'd only been storing up need. I panted; he heaved breaths. His hands dropped to clench my half-bare ass.

A growl sounded from his chest. An actual growl. The idea of inspiring that kind of lust turned me on so much, my arousal returned multiplied. I held his face between my hands and sucked on his tongue. He groaned, his fingers digging into my curves as I started grinding on him again.

I broke away for a breath. "What are you doing to me?"

"I could ask you the same," he bit out in a baffled tone. "I detest surprises. I don't tolerate them. And yet . . ." His brows drew together. He looked . . . not *calculating*, but something akin to that—as if he were working out the angles of a problem. "Still here," he muttered to himself. He yanked me close, burying his face against my breasts, lips seeking.

I arched to his mouth.

"The moment I saw these pouty nipples, I feared I couldn't let you go until I'd sucked them."

Feared? Why would he . . . My thoughts grew dim when he turned his head to take a nipple between his lips, dragging his tongue over the sensitive peak. When he suckled it with a groan, I cried out, "Finally!" I was on fire again! Raw inside. Needing *more*.

He turned to the other one, muttering, "So sweet and plump. They tease my tongue." Once he'd left that one wet and aching as well, he pulled me back to face him, excitement in his expression. "All of this is acceptable."

"I-I certainly think so."

"*Very* acceptable."

Okay? What was going on here? I sensed in him a seething need for me, barely contained—and building. Another woman might fear it; I drank it in like wine.

"Ah, little Cat." A gleam shone in his wicked blue eyes. "You're about to get fucked. Hard."

CHAPTER 4

He laid me back on the couch, looming over me, predatory. Without warning, he grabbed both of my ankles in one of his hands, lifting my body up as he snatched my thong off and tossed the silk away.

"Spread your thighs."

Confused by this turnaround, I tentatively did.

Eyes riveted to my pussy, he licked his lips. "So lush. I can *see* your need. Did you enjoy the orgasm you stole?"

"Stole?"

He knelt on the couch, reaching between my legs. He ran his forefinger along my lips, spreading my moisture, then rubbed me right over my entrance.

My lids went heavy as I watched his face. His gaze was keen with fascination as I grew even wetter for him. I got the impression that he hadn't fingered a girl in forever. Of course, his "script" hadn't called for it.

He teased my opening until I was squirming, about to shove myself down on his finger. "You just get wetter and wetter. I could make you come again, only from this."

Yes, but I'd lose my mind! "*Más.* Give me more, Máxim."

He narrowed his eyes. "You call me Máxim?"

"I'll call you whatever you want if you finger me more." My toes were curling in my stilettos.

As he probed deeper, inch by inch, I moaned from the filling sensation.

"Your little clit's so swollen. Do you want me to rub it?"

"*Yes!*"

"Or do you need to be fucked?"

"Both! Either! Anything . . ."

Yet then he frowned. "Your pussy's tight. *Very* tight."

Would he know that I hadn't had sex in forever? *Need to distract him.* "I'll be this tight around your cock, *querido.*"

He pumped his finger inside me. "Tell me you want it." He laid his free hand over one of my breasts, thumbing a nipple.

"Yes, I want your cock!" My thighs quivered. I tripped toward another orgasm, and he hadn't even touched my clit. I'd never felt so much pleasure with a man; I *loved* being an escort!

He pinched my other nipple. "Then I won't give it to you yet." He stilled the hand between my legs. "Fuck my finger." Again I sensed a surge of anticipation in him, as if he were a kid with a new toy.

Shameless with need, I began to move against his hand, sending his finger in and out of my pussy. I was already about to levitate when his thumb made contact with my aching clit. "*Ummm!*"

He rubbed it with slow circles while fingering my core.

My eyes rolled back in my head, and I arched my back, stiffened nipples pointed at the ceiling.

"You're about to come again?" he asked in disbelief. "Look at me."

With difficulty, I raised my head.

"You don't come without my permission."

Qué? I had no control.

"Ask me for my permission. Say 'Can I come for you?'"

Confused, I whispered the question.

I didn't realize I'd spoken in Spanish until he rasped, "In English, beautiful girl."

"Can I come for you?"

"Not until I tell you." He wedged another finger into my core, screwing them into my tightness.

The fullness sent me over the edge. "*Máxim!*" The fire was back, searing every inch of my body. As I thrashed my head, I dimly heard him telling me he could feel my pussy squeezing, that I'd been bad, and he'd punish me for coming without permission.

But all the while he thrust his big fingers and circled his thumb, drawing out my orgasm, forcing me to ride each mindless wave, each delicious spasm. . . .

When he withdrew from me, I moaned with loss, still not sated. For some reason, I was even hornier than when we'd started.

His smoldering gaze raked over my naked body,

taking in my glistening pussy, my flushed chest, my swollen breasts—even my hair fanning out wildly from my head. He reached forward, grasping a lock. "You're so fucking sexy," he grated, and immediately frowned, dropping my hair. Was he surprised that he found me sexy—or that he'd told me? "You want me too."

"Want? *Estoy desesperada!*"

He stood to undress. "Desperate? Don't worry, I'm about to give you what you need." He removed his shoes and socks, then he pulled his sweater over his head.

As he revealed more of his body, I shivered with appreciation. His wide shoulders were muscled, his pecs rigid with dusky nipples, his arms brawny. He had sculpted washboard abs, and a tantalizing black goody trail that I wanted to nuzzle. His tanned skin sported a few raised scars over his chest and arms, but they didn't detract from his hotness.

His expression grew stern. "You disobeyed me. You came without permission."

I stretched my arms over my head, loving his gaze on my tits. "I regret nothing."

He unbuckled his belt, his movements menacing. So why did I feel no fear of this strange man? He snagged a condom from his pocket, then unzipped his slacks. As he worked them over his massive erection, I gasped.

His cock was a work of art. Distended, damp-tipped, with a plum-colored crown and a thick veined shaft. I wished I could explore every inch of it at my leisure. I'd never been a fan of head, but I licked my lips to imagine my tongue flicking that bulbous tip, teasing it. My mouth nursing that length . . .

He stood nude before me, his body the most mouthwatering I'd ever seen. All I could think: *Best job ever!!!*

He wrapped his big fist around his shaft, giving a stroke that rendered me breathless. More moisture beaded the slit. As he rolled on what had to be an extra-large condom, he said, "Show me what I'm soon to enjoy." There was no mistaking his tone. He'd given me a command.

Beautiful arrogant man.

I would follow his order, but I'd do it my way. I lifted one foot onto the couch back, resting the stiletto heel against the sofa's piping, then let my knees fall wide. I undulated in this position, taunting him with my spread pussy. "How do you like variety now, *querido*?"

His cock pulsated in his hand, and he muttered something in Russian that sounded like a curse. He returned to the couch, kneeling between my legs. The difference in our sizes struck me. He made me feel tiny and fragile—while he was all hard edges and power.

He leaned over me, using one hand to restrain my wrists over my head. With his other, he gripped his shaft and aimed it. When the crown slipped down my slickened lips, he hissed in a breath. "So fucking wet for me."

As he prodded that broad head, I had my first worry.

I was soaked, but he was *big*—

He shoved inside to the hilt, yelling with pleasure.

Too big! "Ow! Hold up!" I strained against his grip. "*Mierda,* give me a minute."

Lips parted, he released my wrists and drew back on his knees, leaving me pinned on his cock. "'*Ow?* Hold up?'" This was the second time he'd flashed me that expression of shock/amazement; I termed the look *Máximo shockeado.* "You're determined to enjoy your fucking?"

I guessed other women had let him shove away. "Let me get used to your size." The fit was so tight that I could feel his dick throbbing with each of his heartbeats. "Can you do that?"

He held himself still, shuddering from the effort. His skin began to dampen with a sheen of sweat. He grated, "*Somehow.*"

Tentatively, I rolled my hips, sending his shaft in and out of me.

In . . . out . . .

In . . . out . . .

In. Out.

In.

Each time I could accept his length more readily, my body accommodating his. Pleasure subdued the pain. My lids grew heavy again.

"Good girl." His gaze was fixed between my legs. "I see you taking me, *dushen'ka.*"

When he leaned over me once more, I threaded my fingers through his thick hair. At my ear, he murmured Russian words, then he took my mouth. He'd liked it when I'd sucked on his tongue, so I did it again—

He growled into our kiss, his hips shooting forward between my legs. It didn't hurt this time, wrenched a moan from me. He withdrew, then sank even deeper. And it was . . .

Increíble! I broke away to cry, "Yes, yes! *Más, Máxim!*"

Leaning on his forearms, he began to surge into me. His black hair was mussed from my frantic grip, his eyes hooded. He stared down at my face, brows drawn, as if I'd confounded him. "You're making me lose control."

Did I appear as lost to lust as he did? "I don't want you to hold back," I panted, spellbound by him.

His gaze narrowed, as if I'd challenged him—or was giving him lip service. He withdrew, then rammed his hips forward, taking my breath away.

But I loved his strength, his intensity. "That's all you've got, *Ruso?*"

He went to his knees again and gripped my hips. "That was a warm-up." Seeming to use every muscle in his body, he yanked me close as he shoved. "*Uhn!*"

I cried out, lifting up to meet his next thrust. He rocked into me; I rolled up to him, the pressure hitting my clit each time. Once the two of us were in sync, our bodies moving together, he pistoned between my legs, railing me as I'd never been fucked before.

Fuck of the century? Try millennium! I was holding on for dear life, hovering on the very verge of orgasm.

"So *tight,*" he grunted, his jaw set as he pounded away.

Ay, Dios mío, he could move! Each time he

snatched me to him, his biceps bulged. His pecs flexed, hard slabs of muscle beneath sweat-lathered skin.

Just watching his toiling body pushed me closer to the brink. He enjoyed watching as well, was transfixed by my bouncing breasts.

The tension gathering inside me was about to release—if he kept up those long, deep thrusts. So close . . . so close . . .

Accent thick as gravel, he bit out, "I love your nipples, your tits, your gripping pussy. The way you watch me with those stunning eyes. You like to watch me fuck you?"

"Yes! Máxim, you're going . . . to make me come . . . hard!"

"Fuck. *Fuck.*" He swelled even more, until it was too much! "Can't hold on! My cock's about to explode!" The lines of his face grew tight, as if he were in misery. Then his body stilled.

No, no, no! *No, keep moving!*

His look of misery vanished, ecstasy lighting his face as he began to ejaculate. He threw back his head and roared to the ceiling, his throat working, tendons bowstring-taut. He gave a brutal stab of his hips, then another, bellowing, "It's . . . so . . . fucking . . . *good!*"

His shattering thrusts hurtled me over the brink. "Yes, yes, YES!" I screamed, my vision blurring. My back bowed, my tits slipping across his sweating chest.

"*Blyad'!* I feel you!" As my core clenched him, he bit out, "Your greedy pussy's milking my cock. You'll have every last—*ahh!*—fucking drop out of me!"

Hot. Wet. Bliss.

Continuing on and on and on . . .

Just when I could take no more, he shoved into me one last time. A long satisfied sound rumbled from his chest. His lids slid shut, and he collapsed over me.

I lay boneless beneath him, my limbs splayed. I moaned when his cock twitched inside me; he groaned when my pussy continued to squeeze his shaft.

As if our bodies wanted more of each other.

He nuzzled my neck, his exhalations tickling my damp skin. His heart thundered against my chest.

By the way he'd reacted, I began to think I might've given *him* an FOTC.

CHAPTER 5

I patted his ass, sighing, "Not bad, Máxim."

With a half frown/half scowl, he withdrew, revealing a condom filled with more semen than I'd ever seen.

"*Un hombre viril.*" I stretched out on the couch, grinning from ear to ear, finally understanding the term *fuck-drunk.*

Rising, he yanked off the rubber and dragged on his pants. "You're pleased with yourself."

"Pleased in general."

"I don't *ever* lose control like that. I never come until I'm ready to." His harsh tone was accusatory, as if I'd done something unforgivable.

Qué cosa? Huh? "This took me by surprise as well." I rose to look for my clothes.

"You don't make a habit of getting off with your clients?"

"No."

Again, he clearly didn't believe what the hooker was saying. "Something about me in particular must be 'special' and 'different' among your clientele. I suppose coming with each of your dates, all day long, would be an occupational hazard."

Wouldn't know. By the time I'd collected my clothes, he was already in the next room. Shame. I'd wanted to see him from the back.

I heard the shower running and had no idea what I was supposed to do. Leave? Get ready for round two? I donned my underwear, then grabbed my phone, ringing Ivanna.

After I'd given her a rundown of everything, she sputtered, "Maksimilian Sevastyan?"

"Yes. You've heard of him?"

"Of course! He's a politician and a *billionaire*!"

The former interested me more than the latter. My father had been in politics too. Not that I'd ever tell the Russian. And not that he'd ever believe me if I did.

Ivanna continued, "He's one of Europe's most eligible bachelors, but no one can land him. Damn Botox! Is he as gorgeous up close as he is in pictures?"

"He's DDG."

"Have you talked about me at all?" she demanded.

I rolled my eyes. "Tell me what I do now!"

"The payout was excellent, so upsell him for the whole night. You're already at his place, have spent money and time on clothes, makeup, and transpo."

The kids in my business courses had nothing on Ivanna the Escort's expertise. Or mine, for that matter. "You're right. Sunk costs." Economics informed the decisions I made every day.

"Act as if he rocked your world," Ivanna said, the

phrase almost comical with her accent. "Like he is the best lover you ever had." *He is!* "Make him think he's the only one you'll give your private number to. They eat that shit up."

"But it *is* private." I hadn't even allowed her to give it to the agency. "I don't want anyone else to have it."

"We'll get you a new number this week. For now, your job is to play to his ego and get him for the rest of the night—or to snag a future date. Though that isn't likely to happen."

"Why not?"

"He's never booked the same woman twice. Oh! I could still get a date before he leaves town! Maksimilian Sevastyan, can you imagine?"

Yes, Ivanna, yes, I can. She was going to have sex with a guy I'd screwed. She'd know his mighty body, would get high on his scent. At the thought, my emotions, which had been up and down all night, took a header.

When the shower stopped, I hung up the phone, hurrying to the bedroom. I leaned against the doorway of the suite. Pulling my hair over my shoulder, I acted all alluring.

He exited the bathroom with a towel wrapped around his hips. *Por Dios*, that body. How could one man be so utterly blessed?

Before I could say anything about another go, he scowled. "You're still here?"

My lips parted. He'd expected me to let myself out, without even saying good-bye?

Yes. Because my purpose had been served. He was

looking at me like he might look at a used condom. Oooh, this man got my back up! He'd been all excitement and passion before; now the icy chill was back.

He sat on the edge of the bed, casting me a disgusted look. "I suppose you remain in the hopes of upselling me for the rest of the night. Maybe even offering me your *private line*?"

Although that was precisely what I'd been advised to do, I gave him a haughty smile. "I'm good for the night, and my private line stays private, *querido*. I'm just on my way out."

When he dropped his towel and climbed into the high bed, I turned to find my dress. From the bedroom, he gazed out into the sitting area, rising up on an elbow. I caught him ogling my body, actually tilting his head for maximal viewing.

Keep looking—last time you'll ever get to see it.

Once I'd gotten my dress on, he lost interest and shifted over on his back, bending one brawny arm behind his head. I'd been so affected by what we'd done, while he behaved as if he'd just completed a bodily function.

It hurt. I wanted to hurt him back. "Apparently I need to remind you that tips aren't included."

In a forbidding tone, he said, "There's cash on the dressing room console."

I found a gold money clip filled with hundreds. Maybe two grand's worth. "How much?" I called.

"Take whatever you think your performance deserves."

Performance? What a dick! I'd come my brains

out, and so had he! So I took it all, including the god-damned money clip. Passing the bedroom door, I said, "Thanks for the tip, *pendejo*." Asshole.

"I'm surprised you aren't acting ingratiating." He was still talking to me, engaging me?

I turned back to him.

Mocking sneer in place, he said, "You're supposed to tell me how I moved heaven and earth for you. You're supposed to fawn over me, increasing your chances that I'll book you again."

I gave him an *aren't you adorable?* smile and purred, "Oh, baby boy, don't you know statistics? Chances can't be improved from one hundred percent."

CHAPTER 6

*O*n the long cab ride home, I took stock of myself.

Catarina stock had taken a beating in today's trading. Even as I gave a bitter laugh at the double meaning, my fists clenched. While my body felt well-loved, a little sore, the rest of me felt cheap and used. He'd *made* me feel that way.

Before he could say anything more, I'd pivoted on my heel and left him, heading downstairs to face the real world. By the time I'd reached the lobby, I was shaking. Bright lights had accused me; it'd seemed all eyes were on me. Like everyone knew what I'd done.

When I'd asked for a cab, a gap-toothed bellman whistled one forward, but he'd smirked as he opened the door. "Madam." I'd almost popped him in the groin, but refrained because of rule number five. *No undue attention, Cat.*

One measly paid sex act had netted me burning humiliation.But the money! Five grand and then the two I'd lifted. Seven thousand dollars! I could probably pawn the money clip. I had plenty to get out of town. Yet even my windfall couldn't cheer me.

Dinero sucio. Dirty money, for dirty deeds.

I could now add hooker and thief to my rap sheet. I took a deep breath, trying to shake off this feeling. *A mal tiempo, buena cara, Cat.* To bad weather, good face.

When my cab was a few blocks from my apartment, I told the driver, "You can stop here." Rule number two: never create links. If I didn't take precautions, this cab's route would link my home to the hotel.

He raised his brows. "Drop you in this hood?"

Nothing here could be as dangerous as what had lurked within my former Jacksonville mansion—my husband.

I paid the cabbie, and he peeled off. I crossed a murky abandoned parking lot in my stilettos, dodging a minefield of broken bottles, tires, rusted mufflers, and weeds growing amok.

My spirits sank even more as I came upon my shady apartment complex. I didn't need the busted street-lights to see peeling stucco, rust stains, and duct-taped windows. Fat vines grew along the walls like tentacles claiming the building for the deep.

The interior was much, much worse. I felt fifty years older as I climbed the cracked cement steps to my studio apartment.

While I worked to unlock my door—it always stuck—movement to my side caught my attention. Mr. Shadwell, my creepy apartment supe/manager, stared at me with his buglike eyes.

He was one of those Florida rednecks who should never have left the swamp. He wore a sweat-stained wifebeater that showed off his puny arms and furry shoulders. He didn't even offer to help me as I struggled with my lock.

In our last conversation, I'd asked him to fix my leaking roof. He'd propositioned me again. So for now, I kept pots all over my studio.

Already, he'd been hitting me up for "protection deposits." My need for anonymity meant I didn't get to do anything about it. Basically, I paid him not to attack me—as he did the vulnerable single moms, prostitutes, and undocumented workers in the complex, those who would never go to the police.

Shadwell was the reason I hadn't saved money to move. Which was why I'd screwed the Russian.

"Busy night?" The pig smirked, flashing his hit-or-miss teeth. His love of filterless cigarettes had left the remaining ones discolored.

I considered and discarded answers—girls' night out? Bachelorette party? But this insect of a man wouldn't force me to lie. My lock started to give way.

Before I could get inside, he rubbed his paunch, then lower. Too low. "We'll be *seeing* you real soon."

I couldn't help but think I'd just received a warning.

After dead-bolting my door behind me, I leaned back against it. Coming from the Seltane penthouse to my cramped studio was like a slap in the face.

In my kitchenette, the stove didn't work, nor the little refrigerator. I had a miniature microwave for canned dinners. A large bowl contained apples, bananas, and oranges to eat on the run. Strategically placed pots littered the floor. I'd moved my pitiful sagging bed into the center of the room, under the largest area of non-leaking ceiling.

Dinero in hand, I wended around the pots to reach my "safe," my window AC unit, non-working of course. I used my Swiss Army knife to unscrew the filter, revealing a cranny. I added the money to my own meager operating fund: two hundred and fifty-seven dollars. Also inside were my fake ID and my one valuable: my mother's rosary. It'd been passed down through my family for generations and was the sole thing I'd taken from home.

The sight of Sevastyan's stack of cash next to the rosary made nausea churn in my gut.

Why had he turned something good into something dirty? I hadn't thought I could hate anyone else as much as Edward, but Maksimilian Sevastyan had made the podium.

What was it about me that men found so . . . disposable? Three years ago, Edward had planned on the ultimate disposal.

After fleeing him, I'd moved every six months, living in Arizona, Texas, Louisiana, and New Mexico. Half a year ago, I'd dared to return to Florida, figuring this would be the last place Edward would expect me to go. I'd headed to Miami, optimistic about getting lost in the sprawling city—and getting work without papers.

Was he here even now? Had I made a bad calculation?

I replaced the AC vent, screwing it into place, then

sank down on my creaky bed. I lay back atop rough thrift-store sheets, replaying my Edward sighting. When that burst of recognition had hit, my muscles had tensed to run.

If that man was him, then the last three years had altered him. He was now gaunt with bitterness etched into his face. No more angelic good looks to recommend him.

I'd been seventeen when we'd had a "chance" meeting over my summer break. He'd told me he was an attorney from Atlanta who'd moved to Jacksonville to start his own practice. He'd also told me he was twenty-five, too old for me. I'd thought, *Forbidden fruit!*

He'd already seen the world; I'd never traveled far from home. He was a sophisticated gentleman; I'd been proud of my keg stands. He spoke four languages, though strangely not Spanish.

Despite our differences, we'd had an uncanny amount of things in common—we'd liked the same movies, music, sports, pastimes, and foods.

My mother had seen right through him, saying he was a sinner with the face of an angel. So naturally, I'd *had* to have him.

When she'd died and her strict rule had ended, I'd suddenly had no counterbalance to my own strong will. I'd floundered, grasping onto Edward for stability. Utterly naïve about men, I'd accepted his heartfelt proposal of marriage, inviting him into my life, my home, my body.

Lightning flashed through my threadbare curtains, thunder shaking the building. Storms always reminded me of that last night with him. I'd come home early from a half marathon in nearby Savannah. A tropical depression had been blowing in, and the race had been canceled. I'd rushed home to help him batten down the hatches.

As I stared at my water-stained ceiling, my eyes lost focus, the memory overtaking me. . . .

A strange car was parked behind the house, a Jaguar. I almost hoped Edward was having an affair. It would explain so much, confirming my new suspicions. It would make my decisions going forward easier.

In one year of marriage, we'd gone from two people who had everything in common and finished each other's sentences to strangers.

I entered quietly, creeping up the stairs, hearing voices coming from our bedroom. I paused in the upstairs foyer. When my mother was alive, the walls had been covered with crucifixes and gloomy old portraits of our ancestors. After her death, Edward had hired a decorator, telling me, "You'll never move past her if you're constantly reminded. Let's make a fresh start."

I'd thought at the time, If you don't like mi madre's *home, then why are we living here, instead of in your own mansion? The one I'd yet to see.*

But I'd stifled that question, because it would open the door to so many other ones—a pulled thread that would unravel the blanket that I still occasionally slept with.

I'd agreed to the decorator, anything to repair the sudden rift between me and him, the one that'd appeared directly after our hasty courthouse wedding. He'd

*stopped calling me Lucía, insisting on Ana-Lucía (what
my mother had called me when I was in trouble). He'd
stopped flirting with me. We rarely had sex, and only at
my urging.*

*I stepped closer to our room, avoiding the groaning
spots in the wood floor. I knew their exact locations, had
been sneaking out of this house since I was twelve.*

*At the door, I detected perfume and heard my hus-
band and a woman speaking.*

"This is taking too long," the woman said.

*"You have to be patient and trust me." That was my
husband's voice—but now he spoke with a British accent.*

*Who the hell was in my bedroom with my husband,
and why had his accent changed? My fists clenched, my
unruly temper about to blow. My first impulse was to bust
inside and start cussing, but somehow I forced myself to
bite my tongue and listen.*

*"I usually am patient," the woman said, her accent
also British. "But you can't let her leave for these races,
Charles." Charles? "You need to be working on her constantly."*

Working on what?

*"Her training is the ideal cover, darling," my hus-
band continued. "Poor Ana-Lucía's going to collapse after
one of her long runs."*

*I rocked on my feet. They planned to . . . kill me?
These motherfuckers were going to kill me.*

This. Is. Not. Happening.

*"It will work seamlessly," Edward said. "Oh, if only
my poor wife hadn't taken amphetamines while marathon
training in this heat."*

Amphetamines? He'd given diet pills to me, saying, "Maybe you should lose a pound or two. Honestly, Ana-Lucía, your clothes scarcely fit across your backside. It's only fair, since I do make an effort to keep myself in shape for you."

I'd nearly told him I would lose weight in my ass as soon as he gained weight in his dick, but he loathed curse words. I used to admire that he was such a gentleman. It'd gotten old.

Edward said, "With that combination, no one will suspect another drug."

"Will she take them?" the woman asked. "She might be young, but she isn't malleable like the others."

The others? They'd done this before?? Serial killers were in my room, like snakes loosed inside!

"Give me more credit than that," Edward said. "Once I work my magic, she'll be choking them down. Julia, I vow to you that I will be a widower by the holidays. Shall we go to Aspen to celebrate?" *He had a smile in his tone.*

A horrific thought struck me. Por Dios, *had they killed my mother? She'd had a degenerative disease, but her actual passing had been sudden. The floor wobbled.*

Had they killed my mother?

Had they killed her?

This Julia *wasn't swayed yet.* "If she suspects you . . ."

"I always have an ace in the hole, darling. A pressure lever. If there's one thing I know about my wife, it's that she would do anything to avoid prison—"

Lightning flashed outside my apartment, thunder rattling the window. I was jolted back to the present before I got to the confrontation about his ace in the hole, before I recalled too vividly the feel of blood coating my face and body.

Maybe that was a good thing. I didn't want to spur even more crimson-drenched nightmares.

The storm intensified, rain pouring. My roof would soon leak like a colander. Depending on the duration of the storm, I could be up all night emptying the pots. If I didn't, my apartment would flood.

I pinched my temples. Edward had been right about me—I *would* do anything to avoid prison; even live in this shithole.

CHAPTER 7

"Listen up, folks, the final is next Monday at seven sharp," Ms. Gillespie, my econ instructor, told the class. She was a tall, graying brunette, with a no-nonsense demeanor. "And yes, I know it's cutting into your holiday break. Take it up with the active hurricane season."

Three classes this fall had been cancelled due to tropical storms; with each storm, my apartment had taken on water like a sinking ship—just as it had last night.

After no sleep, an early morning run, and a hard day of work, I'd had to drag myself to class. Despite my windfall, I'd been coerced by Mrs. Abernathy to clean her mansion. When I'd tried to quit, she'd told me she would report me to Immigration if I wasn't there. My no-undue-attention rule forced me to show.

"We'll spend tonight and Friday reviewing," Ms. Gillespie said. "So let's get started. I'm going to give you terms that might be on the exam. Define them and imagine real-world scenarios."

Luckily this was a lower-level econ course. I'd done all the heavy lifting for my degree in my first two years; all that remained was this last straggler class.

I took out my notebook and pen, determined to focus on this—and not on the Russian. For the past two days, I'd tried to put him from my mind, as he'd so easily done with me.

Ms. Gillespie started writing on the board, and I dutifully scribbled my definitions.

Final goods: products that end up in the hands of consumers. (Like my breasts. If I continued as an escort.)

I stifled a chuckle, earning a look from a few of my classmates, among them two guys who'd asked me out. Unfortunately, I'd had to turn them down, but their interest had puzzled me; I always showed up to class in to-the-knee cutoffs, old 5K T-shirts, no makeup, and my hair plaited into two braids. I wore clunky running shoes and usually reeked of Pine-Sol. A far cry from a glamorous escort.

Deflation: a sustained and continuous decrease in the general price level. (Or what would happen to an escort's rates with age.)

Economic mobility: the ability of an individual, family, or entity to improve or lower their economic status.

Edward had targeted me to improve his. I'd signed any document my lawyer husband had put in front of me, unknowingly transferring my home and my inheritance of millions to him. But he couldn't get my family's beach, the prize he'd truly been after.

As long as I remained alive, his mobility had flat-lined.

<u>Human capital</u>: a measure of the economic value of an employee's skill set.

I was increasing mine by continuing my education at this community college. Heart in throat, I'd enrolled, using the fake ID I'd bought from a source near the Texas border. If I ever reclaimed my life, maybe I could figure out a way to transfer all my stray credits back to my ritzy private college in Jacksonville.

Completing my coursework had become the holy grail to me. On her deathbed, my mother had begged me for two vows: to break up with Edward and to finish college.

I'd only given her one vow. She'd used her last breaths to say, "Run from that evil man!" Phase one of my life plan was to complete my credits to atone for not listening to her. I was one exam away.

So why was I thinking about Sevastyan more than my class? At least he hadn't blown the whistle about my theft. Hey, he'd specified no amount for my tip! And how valuable could that money clip be?

I'd been nervous about him ratting me out, which pissed me off. I was a closer; if something went unresolved, that meant I didn't have the power to settle it and could assign no endpoint.

This unsettled feeling sucked. I already had enough loose ends in my life.

I'd talked to Ivanna several times since that night. She went way back with Anthony, the owner of Elite Escorts, so she would have heard if Sevastyan complained. So far, the Russian hadn't contacted Anthony about my heist—nor had he booked me.

Ivanna had told me, "Don't take it personally, Cat! It happens to the best of us."

I didn't even *want* to see Sevastyan again. At all. Not whatsoever.

"You need to get back out there. Come in and talk to Anthony. Sign on officially. He's a schmuck, but they all are."

"I was thinking about heading out of town for a while."

"Nonsense! I'll let you take a break, but then we'll get you back in the saddle. You can't let yourself get down about Sevastyan. He wasn't even in the realm of possibility."

Then she'd related all the gossip she'd learned about his dating life from her friends at sister agencies. He only booked one escort at a time, and he always overpaid. He was never cruel to his dates—though he wasn't particularly kind either. He hired a new girl every other night, but never for parties or events. Then he just took a famous actress or model.

I'd wondered why a guy like that would need to hire escorts at all, then thought back to his script. I couldn't shake the feeling that he didn't like to be touched. So why had he let me? I'd climbed him like a jungle gym.

Today Ivanna was supposed to get a callback with even more dirty laundry—so I'd turned off my phone and gone about my job and school.

I'd decided three things about him:

His nastiness was directly proportional to his obscene wealth. (Why? When I'd been rich, I'd always been nice.)

He'd affected me exponentially more than I'd affected him. (I was merely *what five thousand had bought him in Miami*.)

No one should be that sexy. (Yesterday, I'd gotten off while fantasizing about giving him a BBBJ. Then I'd been disgusted with myself, blaming my run for making me horny.)

Though I'd sworn to Ivanna that I had no further interest in him, I'd broken down today, slipping off my cleaning gloves to Google him on Mrs. Abernathy's computer.

Between laundry cycles, I'd learned that he'd grown up in Siberia, but had gotten a business degree in record time from Oxford. He had two brothers. His net worth fluctuated between nine hundred million and just over a billion, depending on how the market was doing.

Though only thirty-one, he was a powerful politician—a member of the State Duma, or something. There were rumors of a *mafiya* connection. Maybe I was only attracted to criminals? The thought depressed me. At least his business dealings focused on real estate and government contracts all around the world.

In almost every picture of him, he'd been flashing a movie-star smile, with a tall blond beauty on his arm.

Why had I tortured myself researching him? I'd never see Maksimilian Sevastyan again. Would never know his touch again.

Good riddance.

Once class was over, I hefted my backpack, dreading the long bus ride home. All I wanted to do was microwave a can of soup, soak in my spackled tub for a decade, and *not* think about Sevastyan. Or how he'd be booking a new girl tonight.

Which I didn't care about.

As I waited at the bus stop, I turned on my phone. It beeped like crazy. Eight messages from Ivanna?

Mierda! The only reason she'd call that much was if the icy Russian had ratted me out! With a shaking hand, I dialed her. "Uh, hey?"

"Sevastyan's been calling Anthony like mad! Apparently, he is one scary-sounding man."

Why now? I'd thought I was in the clear! "I know. Listen, I can explain—"

"I had to do some quick thinking since Anthony didn't know he'd hired you yet. By the way, if he asks, you were an independent, a platinum-level producer out of Tampa."

If you say so.

"Anyway, the Russian wants you to return to the Seltane. Now."

Maybe the money clip had sentimental value? A gift from an ex-lover?

"Oh, Cat, he wants to book you! Do you know

what this means? You're the first girl ever to get a call-back."

"Wait, *book* me?"

"*Da*, for tonight. Anthony was calling me, and I was calling you. And when Anthony couldn't confirm you . . . well, let's just say that Maksimilian Sevastyan is used to getting what he wants."

You have no idea.

"The man kept offering more and more money. Finally he demanded to buy your personal number. Anthony just called me for it."

"Which you would never give him, right?"

At that moment, I got a text chime from a strange number: waiting

"Ivanna, we talked about this! There are boundaries."

"We did talk about your number, about changing it. I held out for longer than even I would've expected, but when Anthony told me Sevastyan offered ten thousand, I caved. We're to split half. There's twenty-five hundred for you at the agency." *More* money? "By the way, Anthony thinks your vagina is full of rainbows—and dollar signs. Aside from the Russian, you've gotten requests online! He wants your 'upskirt magic' working on other clients."

I didn't have magic. Sevastyan simply wanted his money back, or his clip. Or he planned to punish me for stealing from him. Maybe with a crop? "What else did you tell Anthony about me?"

"Nothing else. Mainly because I know so little. Other than the fact that you scrub toilets for a living—

which might cool a billionaire's ardor, if that got back to him. Cat, listen to me. I think you could *land* Sevastyan, so I'm going to do everything I can to help you, and then you'll take care of me forever."

"I'm not going, Ivanna." And walk into a trap?

While she blustered, I texted Sevastyan: no dice, querido. have plans xoxo mwah

He wrote back an instant later: this isn't a request

The man thought to intimidate *me*? He'd have to do better than this! Gritting my teeth, I texted: the money's gone. regret nothing

He replied: then you'll be needing more

There was only one way to meet this problem. Head on. I hung up on Ivanna's tirade and dialed the Russian's number. I opened with: "What's your game, Sevastyan?"

"What do you think it is?"

Ay, his voice. My lids nearly closed. Then I remembered what a dick this guy was. "I think you're pissed, and you want to teach me a lesson."

"You did steal from me," he said. "I had to buy a new money clip yesterday."

"I procured a well-earned tip." I could hear ice clinking in a glass. Having a cocktail while waiting for his cocktease?

"I would think the pleasure I gave you—three times—was its own tip."

"Then by that reasoning, you shouldn't have to pay for it at all, *pendejo*."

"I looked that word up. Not very nice of you to call me an asshole. Twice. I think you're the first woman in my adult life who's refused to fawn over me. Right now, you sound as if you could take me or leave me."

"Guess which way I'm leaning, *Ruso*."

He chuckled at that. The sound was warm and rumbling, seeming to stroke me from the inside. What had happened to the icy Russian?

"Come over, Cat, and I'll make you glad you did."

Maybe he *had* liked sex with me that much? Had I thrown one over on the billionaire? Didn't mean I would let him off the hook. He'd treated me like shit, left me hanging for two days, then barged into my life with all the finesse of a tidal wave. "Couldn't find a tall blonde? I thought that was what you really wanted." What if he *hadn't* waited a day to request another girl? What if he'd screwed someone last night, intending to switch back to me? "Or maybe you booked one last night to fill your quota?"

"I didn't book another date."

It worried me how much that relieved me.

"No one is more surprised by these developments than I am. I told you I never reverse myself. Yet I have concerning you."

My heart raced. I *had* affected him just as much as he had me.

"It seems you know me better than I know myself; you were one hundred percent certain I'd call. Here I am." His voice had grown huskier. "Now, tell me you wouldn't want a repeat."

Merely thinking about him got me wet. "That's all you want?"

"*All* I want?" He sounded amused. "A repeat would be a lot to hope for, no?"

What if he got all ice-cold again? Would it matter if he paid me as well as before?

Yes. He'd hurt me.

Even worse, what if he *didn't* get ice-cold? *Que Dios me ayude.* God help me.

I did a quick risk/reward analysis. Risk: erosion of self-worth and possible infatuation. Reward: more money, and therefore more security. I'd be closer to a new identity. Great sex wasn't *un*welcome.

I just couldn't allow myself to get caught up in him. I would put up a wall between us, keeping him at a distance.

Logistics . . . Getting from my apartment to the Seltane took nearly an hour. I'd cleaned today; no way I could forgo a shower. "I can't be there until nine, and I can't stay very long. Not that this is a problem with you." I laughed. "A nanosecond after you nut, you'll be wondering what I'm still doing there. I'll start reaching for my clothes as soon as your balls tighten. It'll be like a fire drill."

He murmured, "*Amazing,*" as if he were a safari guide encountering an unknown creature. "Now you ridicule me?"

"Only because you make it so easy."

"Where have you been that your own agency can't get in touch with you?"

"Here and there. If you wanted to see me, you should've scheduled. Why, you could've booked me when I was with you Monday night! Oh, but you were too busy being rude as hell."

As if I hadn't spoken, he said, "You were out on another date?"

Surely I imagined that subtle hint of jealousy in his tone. "Remember our no-personal-questions rule?"

Silence. Had I pushed too hard?

"I want you here in the next fifteen minutes," he finally said. "How much will it cost?"

"Nah, *no es posible.* In the future, book often and book early."

Another bout of silence.

At length, he grated, "Wear something sexy."

CHAPTER 8

At the door to Máxim's suite, I removed the long lightweight jacket I'd worn to conceal my racy dress.

He'd said sexy, so I'd gone to Ivanna's, uncaring if I was fifteen more minutes late. She'd brought out the tiniest dress I'd ever seen, gifting it to me because, as she'd put it: "My breasts are too big to wear this since I got enhanced."

The cream-colored confection was short and backless. Two narrow bands of silk made a halter to cover my tits—somewhat. Side-boob galore. The "skirt" was about eight inches long and displayed the cleft of my ass, but the hem was trimmed in a fringe of slinky strands, making for a peekaboo situation whenever I took a step.

A braided gold cuff on my upper arm, chandelier earrings, and fuck-me stilettos rounded out the ensemble. I'd worn my hair in a loose knot to show off my bared back.

She'd even given me a beaded purse to go with

the dress. Ivanna's last instructions: "Land him, Cat. Whatever you did—do *more*."

What had I done that other women hadn't? Well, I'd kinda been a bitch at times. I'd refused to "fawn." I'd insisted on my own pleasure.

Three things I could definitely repeat! With that thought in mind, I pressed the penthouse doorbell.

"You're late," he snapped when he answered. "You said nine . . ." He trailed off as he raked his gaze over my body. "Fuck. Me."

"*Hola.*" I hoped I sounded casual, but he looked even hotter than last time. He wore a sharp gray suit, with the collar of his crisp white button-down open. "*Qué pasa?*" I sauntered past him into the living room. Stopped in my tracks.

Another man was here, a giant. Burly and even taller than Sevastyan, this guy had a bald head, a brick-end chin, and a bulldog jaw shadowed with rough stubble.

My heart tripped with panic. "I don't do that."

"Do what?" Sevastyan frowned.

"Two men." Instinctively, I retreated a step—then realized with a start that I hadn't taken a step toward the door; I'd taken a step closer to Sevastyan.

"Ah. Vasili's my head of security and right-hand man. Has been for over a decade."

Relief sailed through me.

Vasili grated something in Russian. Sevastyan responded. I couldn't understand the words, but there was no mistaking Sevastyan's *do not fuck with me* tone. He looped his arm around me, drawing me close, which seemed to surprise Vasili.

More evidence that Sevastyan didn't like to touch or be touched? Or he hadn't in the past?

In English, he said, "Vasili was just leaving."

The man shot me a cutting look as he passed.

When we were alone, I said, "He certainly doesn't like me."

"He's suspicious because he can't find information about you. Anyone who comes in contact with me more than once would have an inch-thick dossier by now."

That sounded risky, but I'd only be here for another hour or so, then *adiós*.

I set down my jacket and purse. "I don't appreciate being strong-armed into a date at the last minute. I do have a life, you know."

"In my experience, most escorts don't have to be 'strong-armed' into dating billionaires."

"Oh, baby boy"—I gave him an *embarrassed for you* wince—"you weren't quite a billionaire today, now, were you?"

His lips curved. "Bad day in the markets. So you looked me up? And you still give me shit?"

Growing serious, I said, "I didn't appreciate you violating my privacy. I meant what I said Monday night: I wanted my line to stay private."

"You're really angry about that? I know something that will cheer you." He crossed to his briefcase, offering me a stack of hundreds, bound with a currency strap. "Five thousand. I assume you won't try to haggle for more after our first night."

I followed him, accepting the money. This would

be twelve grand in two nights! Plus the phone number fee! Still, when I thought of how miserable I'd been over the last two days—and his high-handedness today—I found myself saying, "No haggling. With the late-booking fee, it's *ten* thousand. Or I take the party in my tiny dress somewhere else."

I knew I'd aimed too low when he handed me another stack—as if I'd asked him to pass the salt.

My anger faded. I could afford to get another number. Wasn't like I would need to update my contact info with all my friends and family, since I had neither. Once I left town, I'd toss the phone anyway.

As if in a dream, I floated toward my purse to stash my windfall.

When I returned, his gaze raked over me in a way that made me want to fan myself. My nipples were already straining against the silk.

"I thought I told you to wear something sexy." A joke out of the Russian? "Why didn't you dress like this last time? I only turned you away because you appeared almost . . . wholesome. At least from the front."

"I wasn't sure if you would take me out. Now I know you won't."

He crossed to stand in front of me, seeming to make a visible effort to keep his eyes on my face. "Perhaps I would if I had no time limit."

"You're the one who called at the last minute."

"I began calling late this afternoon."

I tapped my chin. "Then that sounds like a *you* problem."

"Where were you tonight?"

"I told you. Here and there."

"Do you have a standing date?"

"Boundaries, Sevastyan. That's none of your business."

"It's my business when your schedule affects my plans."

His plans consisted of depositing sperm into a condom, then dozing off. How nice life must be for him.

"And following another is not my style." He stalked even closer.

"You aren't, okay? Not that you'll believe me. I haven't had sex with anyone but you in a while."

"Have you thought about me?"

"Fleetingly."

His lips curled again. Not surprisingly, he had a sexy grin. Everything about him was sexy to me. When charming and warm like this, he was a different man. One I found myself dangerously attracted to.

He pulled me closer, lowering his head. His scent washed over me, sending shivers over my body. "I think you missed me, Katya."

Oh, my name in his accent made my toes curl!

Right at my ear, he said, "I think you replayed what we did, and it made your soft little pussy wet."

His rasped words turned me on so fast and so hard, I gasped. His mouth descended over mine. I tasted a bite of vodka as he gave me sensuous flicks of his tongue.

So much for my wall and boundaries. I welcomed his kiss, lapping back. Just like that, the fire raged, and my fingers dug into his shoulders. When he clamped my thigh to his hip, I rocked my hips to him.

He broke from the kiss to ask, "Did you miss this"—he thrust his hard cock against me—"for two days?"

I moaned, nodding, grinding back.

"It wouldn't take much to make you come, would it?" He nuzzled my neck. "Rub your sweet clit with my thumb and you'd go off."

"Try me—"

My stomach growled. Loudly.

He drew back, releasing my leg. "You haven't eaten dinner?"

I shook my head.

Seeming to wrestle with a huge decision—which involved peering at my legs, my lips, my hard nipples—he sighed and said, "Let's go down to the bar for some food."

Why not call for room service? "Are you wanting to feed me, or show me off in this dress?"

"Maybe both."

CHAPTER 9

$\mathcal{I}$n the elevator, his towering frame and palpable energy took over the space. He trailed the backs of his fingers up my spine, making me shiver again. "So sensitive."

Downstairs, as we headed to the outside bar, he kept a proprietary hand on my back. Taller than all the other men, he walked with his chin up and his shoulders squared—utterly arrogant. Which I kind of enjoyed, when it wasn't directed at me.

The Seltane's outdoor area was breathtaking, with giant palms, multiple small pools, and luxurious seating nestled in romantic alcoves. He squired me away from others, closer to the ocean. Though two sofas wrapped around the candlelit table, we sat on the same one.

Our server—*Tiffani!*—was a tall blonde with a striking face. I expected Sevastyan to drool over her, but he was very attentive to me. He selected a white wine, a specific vintage that must be expensive; Tiffani raised her brows. He ordered a vodka martini for himself, telling her, "We need something to eat, something quick. Have the chef surprise us."

As we waited for drinks, I relaxed back on the sofa, determined to enjoy the lavish setting. My lids went heavy as a breeze wafted over us, dancing with the table's candle flame. Palm fronds fanned above. The now full moon was tinged with yellow and painted the waves.

While I was gazing at the ocean, he'd been gazing at me.

"What?"

"I can't figure you out. I can figure *everyone* out. I've met spies less secretive than you." Spies? As a politician—or *mafiya* heavy—did he mean that literally? "Are you so secretive because you fear another besotted client? I'm sure you've had your share."

I teasingly said, "Should I be worried about you?"

"You looked me up online—what do you think?"

"Your long trail of brokenhearted blondes tells me your heart is bulletproof. Just like mine." I said this so confidently, but I *could* see my interest in him deepening—if he stayed warm like this.

Tiffani returned with our drinks.

After she'd gone, I sipped more crack ambrosia. Over the rim of my glass, I said, "You have excellent taste in wine for someone who never drinks it."

"Nothing but the best."

So I'd figured. I was beginning to suspect he'd preferred tall blondes because they represented cachet. He'd had no problems with my looks Monday night or tonight.

"Back to the subject at hand," he said. "Could I tempt you to tell me about yourself if I paid—"

"*No.*"

He raised his brows. "I'm to ask you zero personal questions, but you can read whatever you like about me?"

"Should I believe everything I read?"

"Absolutely not." He shook his head. "You know my net worth, yet you continue to treat me as if I'm an aggravation."

"Monday night, I was delighted with you—but then you were cruel to me."

He opened his mouth to say something, closed it, then tried again. "That night was . . . different." He gazed out at the water as he said, "I expected you to do the escort spiel and resented it. I wanted nothing to color the experience."

What did he mean by different? Surely he expected me to ask. So I didn't. "I do know your net worth. You should pat yourself on the back for a good job. But it won't affect my behavior."

He faced me. "Oh, really?" His words were tinged with ice.

The man thought I was cozying up to him for his money. The irony! "Your wealth is an abstract—it's leprechaun gold to me."

Why would I dream about his money—instead of my own? There'd been a few million liquid, but Edward had probably blown through that much searching for me. He still had the mansion, but not Martinez Beach.

Each decade, the strength of the land's trust eroded; in time, a lawyer like him could figure out a way to circumvent the trust. With resort encroachment on both sides, its value would be through the roof.

Others had had the same idea. Developers had hounded my mother constantly, one reason she'd become a shut-in.

"I could almost believe you," Sevastyan finally said. When I shrugged, he asked, "How much of your online bio is true?"

"Not a lot."

"You don't like dancing, yoga, and shopping? What do you do for fun?"

"I can't dance, I scoff at yoga, and I despise shopping. I'm a runner, and I don't have spare time for fun."

A muscle ticked in his wide jaw. Of course he would take that to mean: *I'm always on my back.* "I have little time myself. Most of my life is dedicated to business."

"Hmm."

"Hmm, what?"

I ran the pad of my forefinger around the rim of my glass. "You could've had fun Monday night. You missed out on the time of your life."

"Did I? Tell me what we would've done."

"The party would've begun right after you screwed my ever-loving brains out on the couch. Instead of getting rid of me when I patted your ass, you would've laughed. Maybe even tickled me. Wrestling would've ensued, and I might have let you win. Then we would've had another round of drinks and gone swimming." I fake-examined my nails. "If you must know, seeing me dive naked would've been life-changing for you."

"Would it, then?" His blue eyes grew lively. His charisma was off—the—charts. "Continue."

"We would've had sex again. In the water. Then, after more drinks, I would've ridden you on a lounge chair until your eyes rolled back in your head."

He groaned low. "MSOG?"

Multiple shots on goal. "Sometimes I forget what a hobbyist you are."

"The hobbyist and his courtesan. How long have you been doing this?"

"Would you believe me if I told you that you were my first client?"

"*Nyet.*"

"Wow. Don't even want to think about your answer?"

"I 'strong-armed' an escort into a date and purchased her private line for ten thousand dollars. Before that, I downloaded her goddamned picture to my phone. If I'm to be brought this low, it shouldn't be at the hands of a rank novice."

My pique passed. "Is there a compliment in there?" Had he truly downloaded my picture?

"You fuck too well to be anything but a pro."

"Thanks?" Maybe he liked the idea of me being a professional. If I convinced him I wasn't, maybe the thrill would be gone for him.

And did it matter when I'd never see him again?

"Is Cat short for Catherine? Or maybe Catarina or Catalina?"

"I'm just Cat."

"Tell me your real name."

"That's not even on the table."

"Like I said, everything's on my table. I'll get it out of you sooner or later."

How long did he think this arrangement was going to continue? "You better hurry. You return to Russia soon, no?"

"I've decided to stay until the twenty-eighth. My older brother is getting married in Nebraska that weekend, so I'm remaining in the States till then."

Could *I* have had something to do with his decision?

He sipped his drink, waiting for me to reply. And waiting . . . "This is where you angle for multiple dates, telling me you'll show me the town."

Angle? That was something Edward would do. I gave Sevastyan a tight smile and patted his shoulder. "I'm sure you'll get up to something. Have fun."

His lips parted. "I gave you an in, and you didn't take it. I find you a very singular creature."

I laughed. "*I'm* singular? Psst, I'm not the one who gets off on whipping strange women."

He gave me that DDG smile. "This is precisely what I'm talking about. You know what I'm worth, but you still give me lip. It's incredibly refreshing."

For once my sass (as my mother used to call it) was working for me!

"Unlike every single other escort I've been with, you didn't try to upsell me after sex; you simply *took* my money."

I jutted my chin. "You deserved that."

"Maybe I did," he conceded. "And you didn't feign passion. In fact, you insisted on your own pleasure."

"You're a good-looking man. I find it hard to believe that no one gets turned on when they're with you." I glanced down. When had we gotten so close together? We now sat thigh to thigh.

"They have their reasons. Some have admitted that they keep that part of themselves separate from their clients. I've observed others so busy thinking about upselling me, or even landing me, that they don't relax."

And I'd told him, "Ow! Hold up." I had to stifle a laugh.

"Or else an escort bills herself as a submissive, when she's anything but. I've had many who swear they enjoy discipline and bondage, yet then I would see no evidence of it."

Ivanna had told me that she initially enjoyed it. But one day she'd had five outcalls, had been tied up and whipped by five amateurs. Her experience had soured her on it.

"It's not easy to find a true submissive," the Russian continued. "One who's beautiful and available would be snapped up." He peered at me keenly.

Though I was beginning to suspect that kink with Máxim might just blow my mind, I wasn't ready to sign on. "How did you discover your interest in that?"

He leaned back, glass in hand. "I'm in the business of information. For many years, I've brokered in it. I was investigating a particular man—one I thought I knew well—when I learned of his darker . . . leanings.

I wanted to understand what drew him to that type of life. The more I learned, the more curious I became. I tried it and found it suited my needs."

He didn't sound like a man who'd discovered a secret passion and reveled in it. He talked about BDSM almost mechanically. "So you enjoy it."

"It suits my needs," he repeated.

"Then what made you decide to call for *me* today?"

"I was at a yacht party yesterday, hosted in my honor. Many businessmen attended, and even more escorts. As I had no intention of calling you again—and proving you right—I gravitated toward my usual." He swirled ice in his glass. "But the blondes weren't doing it for me. Figuring my tastes had changed, I approached a petite Latina. Didn't work out either. Still I fought the impulse to call you. I made it to this afternoon. When I pulled up your picture, I decided I'd have what I truly wanted."

Had he slept with the Latina? Me on Monday, her on Tuesday, me on Wednesday night? "So you had a taste test of sorts. I guess I outperformed her in bed?"

"I didn't fuck her or anyone else there."

I exhaled, relieved once more.

"And no one at that party was using a bed."

"It sounds like an orgy." *Dios mío.* "Do you often attend them?"

"I wouldn't say *often*." He turned my question back on me. "Do you?"

"I've never been to one." I was open-minded about sex, but an orgy would never be in the cards for me. "That's not my speed."

"Have you ever slept with more than one man at a time?"

"I've never had sex with more than one man." He'd think I was talking about *at one time.* And he would still disbelieve me. "I don't want to."

"Earlier, you balked hard. That's unusual in your line of work, no? Still, I can see it."

"Why?"

"I'll wager your clients can barely handle you, much less another added to the mix."

"Thanks. I think." I drank.

"Have you ever even tried BDSM?"

I shook my head. "I wouldn't want to be struck."

"There's more to it than that," he said. "Whipping a woman is not a favorite aspect of mine."

"Then why was a crop part of your script?" Maybe because it limited touch even more?

"If you've never tried any of it, then how do you know you won't like it?" He'd deflected my question.

Because of my ineptitude at lying, I dodged and deflected, bobbing and weaving, and I was attuned to similar tactics in others. "I liked Monday night," I told him, dodging his own question. "I liked how the weight of your body pressed down on mine, and our skin touched all over, and I could feel your big muscles flexing." I leaned in, wanting closer to the heat emanating from him. At his ear, I murmured, "When your chest rubbed over my nipples while your cock plunged, I came until my vision blurred."

He inhaled sharply. "We should return. *Now.*"

"We'll ditch—"

"Here we are!" Tiffani said, tray in hand. She was probably puzzled when we both scowled at her.

My scowl faded once she uncovered the dishes. Lobster salad with citrus dressing, and langostinos accompanied by truffle-butter risotto. The bottle of wine sat at my disposal.

I moaned with my first bite. I was indulging in a meal like this—when I'd planned on nothing more than a can of soup. "*Está como para chuparse los dedos.* This is delectable."

"I wasn't hungry before, yet now . . . I think you increase *all* of my appetites," he said, his words loaded with innuendo. But when he met my gaze, I got the feeling he was telling me something more. Between bites, he asked, "Aside from jogging, what are your other interests? And that shouldn't count as a personal question."

What *had* I enjoyed doing before my life had changed so drastically? "I like to cook." My mother had taught me. It seemed we only got along when we prepared dishes together, neither talking, soft Cuban music playing on the radio. Though I looked so much like her, we'd been opposites in every way. She'd rarely smiled or laughed, yearning for the religious life she'd given up for my father. "I love swimming, reading, and hanging out with friends." Past tense. I missed having friends.

I'd had a great group in Jacksonville—loud and ballsy, each one. I missed swapping dirty jokes. I missed laughing and confiding.

When I'd gotten married, I'd grown apart from

them. To bury my head in the sand about my disaster of a marriage, I'd buried myself in school, racking up twenty-one credits a semester, over and over.

"What are you thinking about?"

Edward, Edward, Edward. I shrugged.

"I can't stop wondering what's going on behind those beautiful eyes of yours."

"*Nada.*" He'd called my eyes *stunning* last time.

"You truly don't enjoy shopping?"

"I hate it. This dress is a loaner." *Gracias, Ivanna.*

The only fun I had each week was cleaning her condo. As I washed windows, she would paint her long nails and tell me stories about escorting. I got a weekly earful about debauched nights, bizarre clients, and tried-and-true techniques.

But I never told her anything about myself. She had family back in the Ukraine that she was desperate to bring over. If she saw a reward for information about me, she would choose her family over me. I didn't begrudge her, but I also didn't share anything unnecessary.

Sevastyan asked, "Would you want to shop if I said we could go pick up a bauble right now? Get a store to open for us?"

Now he was just screwing with me. I wondered if he did that with other people. "Delaying sex for food is one thing. For dinner *and* shopping? Silly *Ruso.*"

"You make a valid argument."

By the time Sevastyan and I had finished eating, I'd had two glasses of wine, commanding myself to take it slow on my third.

"I don't have to ask if you enjoyed the meal," he said. "You got a blissful look on your face with each bite."

"That obvious, am I?" It couldn't have been helped. Whenever I was with the Russian, everything felt amplified. The taste of wine. The texture of food. The feel of his fingers tracing my back. The pleasure in a kiss— or a climax.

"I like when I can tell what you're thinking and feeling, *dushen'ka*."

"What does that word mean?"

"It's a way of calling you 'dear.'" He stretched his arm behind me, and I found myself curling up against his chest. An unexpected sense of ease bloomed between us. Almost like déjà vu, as if I'd been with him before.

The last thing I needed was to become infatuated. We were in a transactional relationship—which was going nowhere. *Boundaries, Cat. Build the wall.*

He trailed his fingers over my arm. "I never thought I'd meet a woman with more secrets than I." His voice was low and relaxed. "And you ask so little about me."

"What should I be asking? What would you ask if you were me?"

"Why I was in Miami in the first place. For politician or *mafiya* business. You must have read about my syndicate ties."

"I don't think I want to know about the dealings of *la mafia Rusa*."

"Are you certain?" His tone was coaxing, as if he dangled bait. *Screwing with me again.* "I'm open to talking about my activities."

I was only going to be with him for another couple of hours, so what did it matter?

"I've never been with a date who didn't dance toward the subject."

Those actresses and models? Or the paid help? I drew back to cast him a bored look. "No thanks. I watched *The Godfather* once. I'm sure you can't improve on that."

He canted his head. "I guess that disproves Vasili's suspicion."

"Which is?" I reached for my glass, taking a sip.

"He believes you're a plant, paid for by my enemies or the tabloids to dig up information. I think I'm too proud to tell him that you have very little interest in me."

I frowned. Edward had made my pride *sing* with pain. I remembered yelling at him: "How can you be married to a woman you don't desire? Why won't you go to counseling with me?" Without looking up from his computer, Edward had said, "I'm so sorry, Ana-Lucía—are you *still* talking?"

So I told the Russian, "I'm not *un*interested, Máxim. But I'm a very private person. The less I ask of you, the less you'll ask of me."

He got a stubborn look in his eyes. "I want to know something you've never told another client. Something that no one else knows. I won't let you go until you do."

What to say? *I'm an only child of only children, and everyone's dead, so I have to look out for myself. For the last three years, a very sick man has been hunting me.*

He'll stop at nothing to kill me because I drew blood. So much blood . . .

Yet he'd drawn it first.

I opened my mouth to decline, but Sevastyan said, "Just one thing."

Was I so starved for interaction, so lonely, that I'd break a rule? Did I need it this badly? As long as I didn't reveal anything that could be used to track or identify me. Words were leaving my mouth. . . . "I'm obsessed with economics."

"Slang for money? I kind of figured that out."

"No, *econ*. As in, the study of. I read everything about it that I can get my hands on." I had since I'd taken my first course in the subject at nineteen. The professor had harped on incentives, making me wonder what had incentivized a rich, older, and sophisticated man like Edward to marry me.

My speaking Spanish gave him a headache. He wanted me to diet away my ass. He made fun of the freckles on my nose. He didn't even like sex with me, never responding to the moves that used to drive guys crazy. Though squeezing my ass had made more than one high school boy spontaneously come, Edward never touched me there.

Only one glaring answer could be supported. He was in it for the money.

Which meant he had none. Which meant he was a con artist.

Which meant my mother had been right about him. I'd discovered him and Julia together not two weeks later.

I faced Sevastyan. "One day I had this epiphany." My words came faster with my excitement. "I realized that economics are the building blocks of life."

"I thought that was DNA."

"Then you need to get more imaginative. On our two dates, you and I have played out several economic scenarios."

"Explain." When I hesitated, he said, "I want to hear this."

"You asked for it," I muttered, before saying, "By singling out tall, kinky blond escorts, you possess a *complete preference*, the ability of a consumer to fully identify his desires for services. Although I could argue—based on your reaction to me—that tall blondes are *positional goods* for you, sought only to increase cachet. When I showed up at your door, you experienced *supply shock* because an unexpected event changed the supply of a commodity, resulting in a sudden variation in its price. I might have employed *profit maximization* with you, because I had *market power*."

His lips parted.

"And Monday night, when you were wondering why I was still in your presence—though you were done fucking me—and giving me the same look you'd give a used condom, you'd reached *satiation*, a level of consumption where the consumer is fully satisfied in a given period of time."

His dumbstruck look deepened. He didn't reply, just stared at me.

So I twirled my hair like a bimbo, lisping, "And I like long walkth on the beath."

Nothing.

"I was joking about that satiation part. Almost mostly."

He muttered, "*Blyad´*." Another awkward silence followed. His relaxation was gone, and I didn't even know why.

"See, this is why we shouldn't talk. We do better with body language, no?"

He almost seemed . . . wary. "Do you have a degree?"

"No, I don't." This could get dicey.

"But you went to college?"

Bob. "It wasn't a prerequisite for my current employment." *Weave.*

He was about to ask me more, but Tiffani returned with the check, saving the day.

I told him, "I'll just go run to the ladies' room." I grabbed my purse and hurried off, the tassels of my skirt tickling the backs of my thighs.

When I passed the outdoor bar, guys gawked, knowing what I was. Or thinking they did.

In the bathroom, I stared into the mirror. Cat Marín, escort.

A far cry from my onetime goal: Lucía Martinez, tycoon. From an early age, I'd played with the idea of taking over the world, maybe going into politics like my late father. Even as I partied in high school, I'd gotten straight A's, earning tons of AP credits. I'd planned to graduate college at age twenty-one, with a 4.0 GPA.

Yet the harder I worked, the further I got from my dreams. Which wasn't exactly incentivizing! At least the GPA was still within reach. All I had to do was make an A on my last final.

Ever since I could remember, my mother had told me I wouldn't need a college degree because I would marry and have children. Once Edward had come into the picture, she'd suddenly gotten hip to the times: "Girls like you should be too busy in college to date! In this strange country, it's expected that you will have a career, and marry in your thirties. That's simply how it is here. Finish your degree."

She hadn't instilled much of her Catholicism in me, but I did get the concept of penance. School was mine. Each credit was like one of those medieval indulgences you could buy to wash away your sins.

With a sigh, I smoothed a curl behind my ear and tugged down the hem of my dress.

By the time I passed the bar again, the men were prepared. Three guys tried to press business cards into my palm. I held up my hand. "No, *gracias*."

The men were all wealthy-looking and fairly attractive, but I wouldn't call any of them. This career would begin—and end—with Sevastyan.

When I returned, he looked furious. "Whenever you're with me, you do not canvass for more business."

"I wasn't!" With a glare, I sat. "I was surprised by their cards."

"You wear a dress like that in a Miami hotel bar and are surprised when men want to pay you to fuck? They know what you are—you might as well wear a sign."

And that sign did *not* read: Tycoon Walking.

Which pissed me off. I was buzzed enough to say, "Brilliant. I'll model my sign after a cabby's: Vacant, Off Duty, Taken."

"Tonight you're definitely taken." He cupped my nape, drawing me in for a kiss. His lips were so firm, and God, he knew how to use them.

Soon we were at each other's mouths, ravenous, kissing for everyone to see. My nipples hardened almost painfully against my halter.

I startled when I felt his palm on my inner thigh. His hand climbed higher. Higher. My dress would provide no barrier, the hem nearly reaching my thong.

Then . . . contact. Against my mouth, he growled the word: "*Wet.* You're practically vibrating for it."

I squirmed in my seat.

He drew back until our mouths were inches apart. "I'm going to pretend that you aren't like this with your other clients. That I alone make you feel this way." He slipped his forefinger past the silk to trace the seam of my damp lips. My thighs and pussy obediently parted for him. "Purr in your accent that it's true, and maybe I'll believe it."

I leaned forward. "I'll whisper it in your ear." When he tilted his head down, I nipped his earlobe, *hard*. "You make me this way, you arrogant *pendejo*."

"Little witch." He was grinning when he took my mouth. Sinking a finger inside me, he kissed and kissed me until I was riding his hand. I neared the point of no return when he broke away from me.

His eyes were hooded, his hair mussed from my hands.

I could only imagine what I looked like. Panting, I squeezed my thighs around his hand. "Why'd you stop?"

He gazed down at me with those penetrating blue eyes. The color of sunstruck ocean. "Do you need me inside you, Katya?" His voice was so husky it made me tremble.

For some reason, this felt like a turning-point moment. So again, I asked myself, *Would I fuck him for free?*

My answer: "*Absolutely.*"

CHAPTER 10

$\mathcal{I}$n the elevator, Máxim maneuvered me against the wall, his body looming.

I turned to him, jutting my breasts and hard nipples for attention. His raised his hands, only to drop them, fists clenched. "Camera," he muttered, stepping back. Then he cast me a look of resentment, as if I were the cause of his current discomfort.

As if *I* wasn't just as bad off as he was. If I didn't feel him inside me soon, I was going to climb the walls!

He stormed from the elevator. In the lobby, he yanked me to him. When I hopped up to lock my legs around his waist, he caught me, growling his approval, his hot hands gripping my ass.

Between kisses, he said, "I've thought about you ever since you left. Couldn't concentrate on business, on *anything*, for two fucking days."

I moaned, absorbing his words. Was it bullshit? Hazily, I realized he had no incentive to bullshit me.

He was guaranteed to have sex with me. For all he knew, I owned absolutely nothing.

How . . . freeing. "I couldn't stop thinking about you either, Máxim."

"I love it when you call me that."

"I'd rather have a mouthful of you than of your name."

He groaned. "I vowed to myself I wouldn't book you. I told myself there could be no such thing as a body like yours."

Against his lips, I said, "I vowed to myself I'd hate you forever."

Balancing me, he managed the front door, closing it behind us. Then he set back in to our kiss. Soon it was burning out of control, our bodies moving and thrusting together. When he broke away, I hungrily followed his lips, panting for more.

"Still! I'm losing control. You do this thing with your mouth—"

I leaned in and did that thing with my mouth. With another groan, he used his free hand to rip the top of my dress, and I didn't care. I wanted him to bare my body, anything to get his lips back on me. He fondled my tits until my nails dug into his shoulders.

But then he drew back, giving his head a hard shake. "Wait, *dushen'ka*. We're going to relax and take this slowly. I have a matter to discuss with you."

I barely listened to him. My nipples were rubbing across the material of his shirt, driving me crazy. "Discuss *after* you're inside me." I tightened my legs around him.

"I'm not going to fuck you on the couch again."

"Then fuck me against the wall! Please, please, please."

"Damn it, Katya," he grated, digging in his pocket to snag another condom. "I don't want you to hurt."

"I won't. It'll be good." I leaned forward, teasing his mouth, sucking on his tongue.

How he managed to put on a condom, hold me up, and kiss me at the same time, I'll never know—but I felt the crown at my entrance.

When he inched inside, I had to stretch to take him, but it wasn't like Monday night. No pain, just exquisite fullness as he sank ever deeper. Once he'd seated his cock as far as he could go, he seemed to force himself to go still. "Did I hurt you?"

"No, Máxim!"

He bit out, "I am officially . . . booking you . . . for the rest of the night."

"I am officially dying to fuck you again. It's so good. So good inside me. Don't hold back!"

He pulled my hair loose, tangling his free hand in the curls. "You need more?"

"*Por Dios*, yes!" I sucked on his neck, moaning over his pulse point.

"Then I want my cock covered in your wetness. I want to stir myself in it." Only then did he draw his hips back, giving me a measured thrust.

The pleasure was so intense my breath caught in my throat. Another withdrawal and pump made me moan low. He alternately shoved his hips, then languidly stirred them.

He took my mouth, delving his tongue in time with his cock. My legs had eased down, my calves resting over his rock-hard ass. I could feel his taut muscles moving as he worked my body.

His determined thrusts were sending me closer to orgasm. "Harder, *querido*!"

Clutching my ass with splayed fingers, he wrenched me up and down with more and more force—until my teeth clattered with each landing.

I bucked to him, spurring him with my heels. He went wild, surging up inside me. "Come on me, Katya!" His face was an agonized mask, his body wracked for release. "I've waited two days for you to milk my cum again."

I hissed in a breath at his gravelly voice and accent, his dirty words. At that moment, I wanted to give him anything he desired. "I'm so close!"

He clasped my nape, his palm covering it. "Yesterday, I jerked off to fantasies of you. Even late Monday night I fucked my fist, replaying what we did."

When my core clenched in reaction, his eyes widened.

I confessed, "When I imagined sucking you off, I started finger-fucking myself. In my mind, you fed your cock between my lips. You came in a flood, and I drank you down."

His hands started to shake. Brows drawn, he rasped, "*True?*"

"True. It was *mi fantasia*, just a fantasy. But as I orgasmed I was licking my lips for more."

Máximo shockeado. At that, his shaft thickened

until he could barely move. "It's my fantasy too. Woman, the things you make me think . . ."

Those tremors began deep inside me. "You took your cock away from me, and I've wanted it back ever since." One more hard thrust, and I'd be gone.

"I'm going to give it back to you all night long." He withdrew to the tip, then slammed home—

"Yes, yes, *yes!*" My climax ripped through me; I threw back my head and screamed his name.

He went motionless, snarling words against my neck: "Your tight little pussy—*uhn!*—hot, wet . . . greedy!" He began to pound me, bouncing me on his cock, forcing my heart-stopping climax to continue. "You're taking my . . . *cum!*" He bit out a broken yell as he ejaculated.

With each emptying thrust, he shuddered and groaned, pumping and pumping . . . until he was spent at last.

As we caught our breath, he clasped me possessively, both arms locked around my body. "Yet again, I didn't make it to the bed."

I couldn't stop pressing appreciative kisses over his cheek, his lips, his neck. "You regret that?"

He lowered his forehead to mine, seeming to bask in my kisses. "Never."

We met gazes when he began to stiffen again.

"My satiation didn't last long." With a muttered curse, he eased out from me, setting me on my feet. He removed the condom, zipped up his pants, then headed to the hall bathroom to dispose of it.

That was *too* good. I needed to get out of here—before I fell deeper under his spell.

When he returned, I'd already put on my coat, belting it over my ruined dress.

"What the hell are you doing?"

"I told you I couldn't stay for long."

"Oh, no. I meant what I said. I'm booking you for the rest of the night." His tone was all commanding: *So says the king.*

He strode to the bar, selecting a bottle of champagne.

"Celebrating something?"

"*We* will be. You're going to show me fun."

I hesitated. I could stay here, toasting champagne with him, or return home, tripping through murky parking lots to reach my pathetic apartment.

An entire night with him? *Boundaries. I can do this.* I'd still leave town next Monday. I'd *have* to. I'd never break my third rule to stay on the move. I believed that was the only reason I was still alive.

Besides, Sevastyan would make this easy for me. After a whole night together, the player would grow tired of me and send my ass packing.

"Ah, you've decided to stay," he said, reading me so well.

"I worry though. I don't know if you can handle my brand of fun."

His full, open smile was *devastating*. Better than in pictures. "One way to find out."

I slipped off my heels and jacket. I unzipped the

remains of my dress, stepping out of it. He appeared enthralled as I wriggled from my thong.

Naked, I sashayed in his direction, breasts swaying. On my way to the pool, I trailed my finger over his chest. "Your life's about to be changed." I ran and dove in.

When I broke the surface of the water, he was still groaning.

CHAPTER 11

"You're not drinking as much as I am," I told him from the shallow end. "Are you trying to take advantage of me?"

He sat nearby at the edge of the pool, feet on the top step, wearing only his unbuttoned shirt and gray boxer briefs that highlighted the strength of his legs and his erect shaft. For some reason, he'd stopped undressing after his pants.

"I'll pay you a thousand dollars if you tell me something more about yourself."

I turned on my back, floating, savoring the heated salt water. "Like what?"

"What do you want out of life?"

So much! Phase one was atonement, and phase two was disappearing. Phase three entailed getting a career and friends and a social life. Maybe once I had a new identity these things would be possible. World domination was a distant phase four.

I faced him again, smoothing my hair back. "A

house. A yard. A dog to run in the yard. A kitchen with tons of spices, all organized how I like them."

"Demanding creature, aren't you?"

"Ha." I wished hourly for some way to free myself from Edward.

"No man in that scenario?"

I never yearned for a relationship, since I was always preoccupied with survival. Plus, once burned, twice shy. Yet even before Edward had turned murderous, I'd been so disenchanted with men—and stunned by my own bad taste in them.

The love I'd thought I'd felt for him disappeared so totally, I doubted I'd ever loved him at all.

I swam closer to Sevastyan, settling on one of the steps. "Any man in my life would have to like my house. And my dog would have to like him. I would have a very discerning dog."

He chuckled. Oh, I enjoyed that sound. "Stringent requirements."

"And you?" I asked.

"I used to want only power. Now I'm not sure. My political term is ending, and I'm letting it."

"Why?"

"It requires me to be in Russia more than I'd prefer."

"Don't you like it there?"

"In winter? I despise it," he said, the words seeming to skim the surface of what he was thinking. "I might stay in Miami, buying and selling this town. I like it here."

He would move here right when I was leaving? How unfair. *Cool yo jets, Cat!*

"You could teach me Spanish."

Okay, now he was just playing with me. "Sure. Say *cállate la boca*."

He repeated the phrase. "What does that mean?"

"Shut up."

"You're teaching me how to tell you to shut up?"

"*Por Dios, no.* You must understand when I tell *you* that."

He laughed out loud, reaching out to pull me forward till I was standing between his bent legs. "I enjoy your humor, your playfulness. You're like a *kotyonok*, a little kitten—"

Vasili suddenly appeared on the pool deck, gaze alert, hand on the gun in his holster.

Máxim twisted to conceal me, and I sidled up to his back. Another laugh rumbled from his chest. "So unused to the sound of my amusement, he comes running."

"He could hear us?" I whispered.

"He must be making the rounds. I've booked the two stories below for him and his men. Vasili oversees all three floors."

"Oh." A small army of *mafiya* henchmen must be nice. All I had to protect myself was continual movement, a dead bolt, and a prayer. "Do you need this much security? Or is this more of an entourage situation?"

"I don't think I'm under an acute threat right now. But the show of might deters some foes, and extra men always come in handy." Sevastyan said something in Russian, and Vasili left. "Did seeing the gun bother you?"

"I don't know." My sole experience with one had been horrifying.

Bent on uncovering Edward's ace in the hole, I'd retrieved my father's commemorative pistol, a gift from the Cuban government. I'd loaded the accompanying bullets, planning to shoot the ceiling to get Edward's attention, like they did in movies. I'd also grabbed my mother's rosary and donned it for courage.

At the end of the night, I'd been drenched in blood, fleeing a madman.

I swallowed. *Shake it off, Cat.* I told Sevastyan, "It must be reassuring to be so protected. . . ." I trailed off. I'd dampened the material of Máxim's shirt and could make out marks on his back. Unable to stop myself, I tugged his shirt from one shoulder.

Muttering something that sounded like, "*Get this over with,*" he yanked it off.

I gasped. Scars covered his back from his neck down to his hips—crisscrossing lines of them, as if he'd been whipped—repeatedly. What the hell had happened to him? Who could have done that? No wonder he had issues with touching!

He rose and turned with his shoulders squared, a dangerous glint in his eyes. He grated, "Ask me what happened."

I was the last person in the world to ask about something so personal. "That isn't my business." Sometimes I wanted to strangle people who stuck their nose in my own. "If you want me to know, you'll tell me, and I'll listen."

He narrowed his gaze. "Only a handful of people

have ever seen my back. If you find out the story behind the scars, you could sell it to a tabloid. Make a lot of money."

I rolled my eyes. "Now you're just pissing me off, *pendejo.*"

He tilted his head. He'd probably expected me to clasp my hands to my chest and tell him *I would never sell a story!*

"Look, Sevastyan, I don't mind problems—I handle problems—but I *hate* when they're unnecessary. So don't do this with me."

"You're not going to make the observation?"

"What observation?"

"That I whip women because I was whipped."

"That's not why you do it."

He raised his brows. "Thrall me with supposition."

I said nothing.

He stabbed his fingers through his hair. "It drives me mad not knowing what's going on in that head of yours."

I couldn't take his pain away, but I could acknowledge it. I could let him know he was still gorgeous to me. "Then I'll *show* you what I'm thinking." I climbed out of the pool and crossed to him. "Turn around, please."

He hesitated. When he finally turned, I could tell he was holding his breath, wondering what I'd do.

Standing on tiptoe, I pressed a tender kiss to the highest scar, then lightly grazed my cheek against it. On a shuddering exhalation, he murmured, *"Dushen'ka."*

I kissed and nuzzled the next line and the one

below it, all the way down to the small of his back. When I got to his muscled ass, I pantsed him. I nipped one flawless, sculpted cheek, then started back up.

He turned, gazing down at me with his brows drawn. "Singular creature."

I told him what I told myself whenever my guilt grew too painful: "It happened. It hurt. Better things await you."

"Like what?"

"Like pouring champagne down my chest to drink from my nipples? While I ride you? That's in your future if you want it."

He swallowed. "A bright future for me, then. I'm long overdue for that." He retrieved another bottle from the bar. . . .

While I rode him on a lounge chair, he drank and drank.

More champagne . . .

We made toasts to each other. He tickled me. When I tried to escape, he pinned my wrists above my head and played with my breasts till I writhed. "In case I haven't told you," he rasped, "I like your size as much as you do." Then *he* rode *me*.

More champagne . . .

Room service arrived with pan-seared diver scallops, Wagyu beef tenderloins, and Beluga caviar. As we fed each other, he blamed me for how famished he was.

"Caviar is decadent!" I told him.

"I can't believe you've never had it." Voice gone gruff, he said, "There are many things I could show you."

More champagne . . .

I lay on a float on my front as he pulled me around the pool, our faces close. We discussed books and business theory till the pads of my fingers pruned.

More champagne . . .

We reclined side by side on a double lounger, sharing a blanket, gazing up at the full moon and stars. I was *seriously* buzzed. But I liked the faint feeling of spinning; it made the sky twirl for me.

"I've divulged more about myself than you have," he said, his voice rumbly with relaxation. "I can't tell you how unusual that is."

"Ask me light questions, and I'll answer."

"Very well. What was your first pet? A dog?"

"A goldfish. I never got to have a dog."

"If you want one, why don't you have one now?"

I stretched an arm over my head. "Ah, to be Máxim Sevastyan for a day. What you want, you get."

"I want more answers from you, but I don't get them."

Bob and weave. "What was *your* first pet?"

"A gelding."

"I've never been horseback riding." There were plenty of farms on the coast, but my family's mansion was isolated. I'd been secluded till I'd gone to high school. After that, all I'd cared about was partying.

He looked at me like I'd grown two heads. "That's unacceptable. None of your clients took you? A lover didn't?"

I shrugged again.

"I'll take you. You'll enjoy riding with me."

I was sure I would. And yet it would never happen. I drained my flute, raising it for more, and he poured. I could drink this stuff till eternity. "Do you often take lovers out riding?"

"Lovers? I've never had one." His voice turned chilly as he said, "My previous relationship was with a blond escort and lasted one hour. I wish her all the best." Dipping even chillier, he added, "I'd ask when your last relationship was, but I have no doubt you're currently in one."

"What? I'm not."

"A couple of times tonight I caught you staring off at nothing. I've found that usually means a woman is thinking about a man."

I had been. About Edward. What if I'd been mistaken about seeing him in Miami? What if I gave up more nights like this, fleeing for nothing?

Or, what if he *was* here to make good on his last vow to me?

"I'm not in a relationship, Máxim." How could I ever trust another man? I'd always think he was using me. I jokingly thought, *Unless he's a billionaire.* Then I chastised myself. *Jets. Cooled. NOW.* "What about you? Do you want one?"

"It would depend on whether I found the right woman." He turned on his side to face me. "What's your earliest memory?"

I had vague impressions of my father. He'd been an attaché to Cuba, with a ready laugh. Sometimes I could remember hazel eyes that crinkled at the sides and the smell of cigars. "My most fully formed one? Helping my mother and grandmother make paella. I got to toss a handful of spices in, and I was beaming. My mother warned me to watch my pride."

If she hadn't been able to extinguish it, a year of Edward's inexplicable disdain couldn't have. My pride had merely lain dormant for a short while, bouncing back with a vengeance, roaring to life.

And yet I'd chosen to disappear—instead of fighting back, a decision I still struggled with. Was I being shrewd?

Or cowardly?

Máxim asked, "Are you close to your mother and father?"

"My father died a while ago." He'd been in a car accident in the Cuban countryside, far from any hospitals. "I wish my mother and I could have been closer before she passed away."

She didn't "pass away," Cat.

I'd never forget the way my stomach had plummeted when I'd learned for certain that she'd been murdered. The rage I'd felt. . . .

"You're so sure that Ana-Lucía will keep quiet?" Julia asked Edward. "She's an impulsive troublemaker."

"What could she say to the police?" he asked. "That she suspected I had something to do with the old bat's death? I've been a model husband for over a year, and I've snowed everyone she's ever come into contact with. I play tennis with her lawyer. Who would believe her? And even if her mother was exhumed, the case is in Ana-Lucía's safety-deposit box, the one she obtained by herself, in her name."

He'd asked me to secure it for a coin collection, giving me a locked case to store. Mierda, *he had the key! What was actually in it? What was his ace?*

Edward continued, "No one but her has ever accessed it, and her fingerprints are the only ones on the case. She fought constantly with her mother and was the sole heir to a fortune. Means, motive, opportunity, and a murder weapon. One word to the police, and Ana-Lucía's done."

They'd killed my mother; they'd framed me for it.

When they'd stopped talking and started kissing, I'd decided to get answers, one way or another—

"Katya?" Máxim was studying my face, as if trying to read my thoughts.

I forced a smile. "Just thinking." *It happened, it hurt. . . .* I shook away my memories and said, "My mother was very strict."

"So you rebelled? Is that how you got into escorting?"

No, that was how I'd let a monster into our lives. I cleared my throat. "A story for another time. Are you close to your parents?"

His gaze slid away. "Both died when I was a boy."

"I'm sorry," I said. "What's *your* earliest memory?"

"My mother singing. She rarely did, but she had a lovely voice." Changing the subject, he said, "Did you do well in school?"

"Straight A's. I couldn't get enough math, used to do puzzles for fun. What about you? What was your favorite subject?"

"Debate."

"Already a politician?" I turned on my side, facing

him. Now our conversation seemed even more inti-mate.

"But no longer. Maybe I'll go into business with my older brother, if he'll have me."

"Why wouldn't he?"

"We were estranged. He left home when I was young, and I resented him. For years, he's suspected that I had malicious intentions against him. I can't say that I didn't at the time."

"That's sad. But no longer?"

"We're speaking, which is an improvement. I'm close to my younger brother," he said. "Do you have any siblings?"

I hesitated. Sometimes I imagined tidbits of my information being fed into a search engine. It would spit out my name if given enough variables.

Sevastyan already had several: Spanish-speaking female, approximately twenty-six, no college degree, deceased parents.

Would I now add *only child*? "I'm sure my family is boring compared to yours. Let's talk about something more exciting." I raised my flute again. Downed so soon?

He readily poured. "Like what?"

"Sex?"

"I'm going to make a blanket statement: I like ours. I'm fairly certain you do too. Tonight, you've repeat-edly touched my back. You even scratched it earlier."

"*Perdón!*" I'm sorry! "Did I hurt you? I forget my-self with you." *Factory shutdown.* "What if I do it again, Máxim?"

The left corner of his lips curved up. "I didn't say I wanted you to stop. I thought it would bother me, but it doesn't. I knew you'd forgotten yourself, and I relished every fucking second of it."

I exhaled. "You scared me. I thought you were going to have to put mittens on me."

"That's your worry?" He reached for me under the blanket, laying a casual palm over my hip, his thumb lazily stroking. "I expected the scars to bother you."

"They don't. I'll grow accustomed to your back— but I will *never* get over your ass."

He gave me that glorious full smile of his. I reached over and placed my hand on his face. "I love your smile."

"Everyone says I'm charming, but I don't smile or laugh naturally. I think to myself, *Would now be a normal time for someone like me to show amusement?* Then I force myself to react, as people do when a camera turns to them. But with you, it's unconscious. I just respond."

"Truly?" His smile in person *did* look different from the one I'd seen in pictures. Those never engaged his eyes. I leaned forward to kiss him, but when my lids slid shut, the world went off-kilter. I drew back. "Whoa. I think I need to cool off." I rose, swerving on unsteady feet, then dropped into the pool.

He followed shortly after, caging me in, with my back against the infinity edge. Steam rose from the water, flickering the lights, making the ocean blue of his eyes glow. "The way your hips and ass move when you walk . . . it's like a revelation."

I swallowed, my hands landing on his shoulders, my legs wrapping around his waist.

He slowly rocked into me. "Why can't I stop touching you?"

Wordlessly, we stared at each other as he took me. Something was occurring between us. More than sex. Something I'd never experienced. I wanted to come; I wanted to cry; I needed to smooth his brow and ease his own thunderstruck look. "Máxim?"

He could only nod slowly, acknowledging . . . *something*. Never speeding up his pace, he told me, "Say my name in your accent."

I rubbed the side of my face against his, murmuring, "Máxim."

"Say you need me to fuck you like this."

Between panting breaths, I whispered, "I need you . . . to fuck me . . . like this, Máxim."

"Tell me I fuck you better than any man before."

"Máxim, you fuck me . . . better than any man before." And then he proved it. Even as I buried my mouth against his neck to muffle my screams, I wondered if I could fall in love with someone in one night.

CHAPTER 12

The sun was coming up when I woke against a man's chest.

I blinked, disoriented. What the hell—

My eyes went wide. I was in the Russian's bed! And everything from the night before was a fog. I stifled a groan, swearing I would never drink again.

I rose up on an elbow to look at him. He slept on his back, one brawny arm around me, the other over his head. I nearly whimpered. *Un hombre magnífico.*

How would Máxim be with me this morning? Would he act like nothing unusual had happened? Be embarrassed that we'd been drinking and oversharing? That I'd seen his scars?

What if he looked at me the way he had our first night, waking up to sneer, "You're still here?"

I cautiously rose, finding a robe in the bathroom, then crept out of the bedroom suite. The housecleaner in me cringed at the mess in the sitting area. We'd hit this place like a hurricane.

I scuffed to the kitchen and found orange juice. Guzzled. Then I took another full glass out by the pool.

I drank it down too, then frowned at my empty glass. I'd thought I'd be a hundred times more hungover than this. Wasn't too much champagne supposed to mess a person up? I felt *great*. Maybe because we'd eaten?

Or maybe I was still drunk?

I shrugged, concerned with more pressing matters. Though my memories were foggy, my emotions were pinging clear. I was infatuated with Maksimilian Sevastyan.

No, I hadn't wanted a relationship. But being with this sensual man in this romantic setting made me wonder what it'd be like to live with and love someone like the Russian.

Seemed my heart wasn't bulletproof.

Yet I'd also thought I'd loved Edward. Obviously, I was *not* to be trusted.

I stared out over the ocean. A storm was rolling in, backlit by the rising sun. I hated storms.

Was Edward even now in the city, watching this very sunrise? I exhaled a gust of breath, memories of that last night with him overrunning my thoughts.

Gun in hand and rosary around my neck, I'd reached for our bedroom door, prepared to brazen my way into some answers—I had to know what was in the case. When I entered, my husband was screwing Julia, more impassioned than he'd ever been with me. . . .

"So I'll be dead by the holidays, cabrón?"

He jerked out of her, scrambling from the bed to his

feet, his dick bouncing. "Ana-Lucía! I can explain every-thing!" His accent shifted from British to Southern mid-sentence. He pulled on his pants, and I let him. "Please, calm down! And for goodness' sake, put the pistol away."

Lightning flared, matching my mood. I finally un-derstood the phrase "seeing red." I pointed my gun at the woman frozen on the bed. "Who the hell is she?"

Edward raised his palms. "Talk to me." He didn't like my attention on Julia? "She's an old friend who was passing through town." His blond brows drew together as he gazed longingly at me. "This didn't mean anything. I just missed you so much, darling—I was momentarily weak. I was so stupid. But we can work this out. You are the one that I love."

He was good.

Julia stood, wrapping a sheet around herself. She was tall and slender, with long sandy brown hair and porce-lain skin. "May I get my clothes?"

Lightning flashed again. "No. You move closer to him. NOW, bitch." I waved the gun, and she hurried to his side. Even in this situation, they somehow looked dignified together, a sterling couple.

I turned to Edward. "If you lie to me again, I will shoot you in your scrawny dick. How did you kill my mother?"

"What are you talking about! Have you lost your mind?" His green eyes appeared stunned, as if I'd sprung this information on him—out of nowhere. "Your mother died of natural causes. You know that."

How could he be so believable? For the tiniest in-stant, I thought to myself, Well, I did know that. I shook my head. "*Natural causes? Weren't you going to make* my *death look natural?*"

Edward was aghast. "*You're accusing me of murder? When I've never raised a hand to you? I've never even raised my voice. Everyone knows how much I adore you. All our friends talk about my devotion.*"

In other words, if I cried, "Murder plot!" no one would believe me. "*What's in the case in that safety-deposit box?*"

"*Case? Now what are you going on about, darling? How did we go from my—admittedly stupid—screwup to murder?*" There was that reasonable voice again.

How much had he been gaslighting me in the past? "*I heard you two,* cabrón. *No one's celebrating my murder in Aspen this year.*"

Julia was unraveling. "*I told you this one was trouble!*"

I sneered to her, "*With a capital fucking T, Julia.*" Back to Edward. "*How did you kill my mother? And what's in the case?*" I cocked the pistol, movie-style, and aimed it at his groin. "*Try lying to me again.*"

He narrowed his eyes. "*You won't shoot me. If you do, all your money—now my money—will go to my heir. You signed over everything to me a year ago.*"

"*Then you're right. It doesn't make sense to shoot you.*" I turned the gun to Julia. "*I should shoot her. She'd be your heir, no?*"

"*Ana-Lucía!*" His breath left him, his voice scaling higher as he said, "*Don't hurt her.* Please.*"

The most shocking revelation of the night? This monster truly loved her.

"*Don't make me hurt her! Answer my questions.*"

Staring down a gun barrel, Julia said, "*I will answer

them for you. We can talk about this. In the case, there's a syringe. It was the last injection given to your mother. She was dying anyway, but we hastened it."

My lips parted. Julia had confirmed murder.

She continued, "We targeted you for the land. Charles—Edward—knows how to break the trust."

Shock muffled my thoughts, but I needed to stay sharp. What incentive did Julia have to admit these things? I gazed at them through watering eyes. The two were farther apart from each other. While she stalled, he'd been sneaking closer to his dresser!

He must have a gun in there. "Stop where you are, Edward." Keeping the pistol trained on them, I sidled toward the dresser. "You got a gun? I'll be taking it, as well as the key to that safety-deposit box."

I pulled open the top drawer, taking my gaze off them for a split second—

Lightning blazed; he threw a lamp at me. Everything happened so fast.

I deflected with my arm. The old pistol went off.
BOOM!

A dark spray arced across the room toward me, splattering my face and chest. Blood? From Julia's throat??

Her hands clamped her neck to stem the spray, but it kept welling up in spurts. Her body collapsed.

Edward dropped to his knees beside her, frantically clutching the wound, as if trying to put the blood back in. Coated in crimson, he yelled over his shoulder, "What have you done?" Dimly I realized his accent had changed again. "You bitch! What have you DONE?"

Julia made ugly, wet sounds. Until she . . . didn't.

Dead.

I just killed someone. I just killed someone. *Six hours ago, I'd been hoping it would stop raining so the race wouldn't get canceled.* I am covered in someone else's blood. *It dripped from my jawline and fingertips, from the gun. I had to swipe my sleeve over my eyes.*

He howled with grief, rocking her head in his lap, sobbing. "She was everything *to me! She was my LIFE! You KILLED her!"*

Edward had already been prepared to take me down for one crime. Now he would see to it that I fried for two murders.

I backed away from the gruesome scene. As I ran from the room, he bellowed, "Prison's too good for you!"

I stumbled, nearly falling down the stairs. Still clutching the pistol, I bolted to my Mercedes. I laid the gun on the floorboard like it was a live bomb.

As I reversed past Julia's Jaguar, my headlights caught Edward's face. A nightmare. His crazed green eyes were stark against his own mask of blood. Trickles of it ran in the rain.

He raised a gun! Shit! I couldn't back down the winding drive. Three-point turn. Shit, shit!

He shot at me! Missed. My scream was loud in the confines of the car. He bellowed, "I will BUTCHER you! I will cut you into pieces while you live!" *He aimed again, missed.*

Forward, forward! *My tires spit up the pea gravel, spinning in place. Before I could speed off, I heard him yelling,* "Go to the police, and you go to jail! COMING FOR YOU, WIFE—"

Lightning forked out over the ocean; I blinked repeatedly.

I wasn't back there. My sweating palms weren't white-knuckling a steering wheel. I was safe up here in this tower, with a powerful lover and bodyguards. In time, I caught my breath, and my pulse leveled out.

When Edward had vowed to butcher me, I'd seen the madness in his eyes. I'd seen my future if he ever got to me.

That night, once I'd calmed down enough to think, I'd weighed scenarios. Best case: He turned me over to the cops to fry for two murders. Worst case: He made good on his vow.

The only path open to me? Living to fight another day. So I'd disappeared.

Vanishing from the grid was easy—all you had to do was cast aside any possession you ever valued, expect nothing to replace it, shed your identity, and sacrifice any connection you'd ever made.

By the time I'd gotten to Texas, I'd started to wonder if I should fight for my life back. Though I'd always considered myself brave, I was letting my mother's murderer *live in her goddamned house*?

I should at least know what my options were. So I'd pawned my watch and my simple gold wedding ring to get a decent lawyer. The lady had been perplexed by my story. There was no warrant out for my arrest. No missing persons report on me. No death of a woman named Julia. Edward had covered it all up.

He truly was coming for me.

My prospects had been grim. To try to reclaim my

inheritance, the attorney required a fat retainer. To divorce Edward, I'd be forced to create links. I wouldn't be hidden from him—the well-respected closet serial killer who was bent on revenge.

Plus, there was the safety-deposit box. He couldn't access it without me; I couldn't without my ID and the key. I imagined it as a land mine we both circled.

My risk/reward analysis said: *You're fucked. You'd better come up with some rules to try to stay alive. Good luck with that.*

I shook my head hard to dislodge the memory of that night, just for a little while. Just until the next storm.

It happened. It hurt. Better things awaited me. One day. Hey, maybe I'd outlive Edward.

I took a deep breath, then returned inside, grabbing my phone out of my cash-filled purse. After unlocking the code, I checked my messages. Ivanna never texted—her long red nails made it impossible—but she had left a voice mail: "Call me! I'm dying!"

Anthony had left several: "Hi, Cat, it's Uncle Anthony! Welcome to the agency, sweetie. Call me about tonight." "Phone Uncle Anthony, girl." "Still waiting on a call. . . ."

I'd have to deal with that later.

There was also a threatening message from Mrs. Abernathy. "Cat, you need to confirm for cleaning on the thirty-first. I'm having a party, and I'll need you. None of this nonsense about quitting, or I will make that call."

INS. *Bésame el culo, puta.* Kiss my ass, bitch.

When I passed the coffee table in the sitting area, I frowned at the sight of Sevastyan's briefcase. Hadn't he and I sat on that couch, looking at papers, sometime late last night? My eyes went wide. He'd shown me test results that said he was all clean. My own all-clean results had been right beside his. Fucking e-mailed to him.

Ivanna had insisted I go to the "agency physician" for my exam. I'd thought it was cheaper or something. But why should I expect privacy when I was a paid-for thing? I'd never felt more commoditized.

Sevastyan had said, "This is what I wanted to discuss with you. I want us to be able to do anything to each other, whenever we want, with no barriers between us. I'm dying to taste you. Will you let me?"

"I don't know," I'd said, drunk and annoyed. "I'll need to think about this." But my annoyance had disappeared when I'd realized I could give him head without a condom—and utilize all the tricks I'd picked up in high school or read about or learned from Ivanna.

BBBJNQNS? *Gracias*, yes.

Now my face flushed. I think I'd told him, "I really want to taste you too. If there was ever a cock that deserves to be tongue-worshipped . . ." Then he'd pulled me in for a kiss, and my thoughts had gone on hiatus.

I tried to recall more, but all I managed was the start of a headache. So I used a guest bathroom to wash off, brushing my teeth with a complimentary toothbrush. I was tempted to sneak away and not deal with the aftermath of last night. But when I crept back to his bedroom, I found Máxim had turned on his side, arm outstretched—as if reaching for me.

I crawled back under the covers with him. In sleep, he wrapped an arm under me, covering both of my breasts as he pulled me close. When he held me like this, my will dissolved, my worries, my blood-coated memories. . . .

Sometime later, I woke again to his husky words in my ear: "I now understand the appeal of waking to a lover." With a long exhalation, he slid inside me.

CHAPTER 13

"*I* slept for *five* hours?" After sex, he'd risen, frowning at the clock. "This is a record. I feel like a new man."

"You look ten years younger," I told him as I stretched. "Now I'd put you at mid-twenties."

"I just turned thirty-one."

"Yes, but you looked thirty-five before."

He raised a brow. "You won't ask why I don't sleep? I've had insomnia for decades."

I sighed. "Why *wouldn't* you? You're in a high-pressure job—which might be dangerous—and you're running a billion-dollar empire."

He chucked me under the chin. "I don't know if I'll quite be a billionaire today, *querida*." When he strode to his closet, the lines across his back saddened me anew. He returned wearing broken-in jeans, with an undershirt for me. "Here. Arms up."

I hopped from the bed, raising them, and he pulled the shirt over me. It swallowed my body.

He grinned down at me. "Almost as fetching as you were in that dress."

"The smirky attendant downstairs ought to have a field day with my appearance now. Fuck knots in my hair and a T-shirt hem under my coat."

"You're not leaving."

"Pardon?"

"I've decided to book you until the twenty-eighth."

Stay here with him for ten days? A vacation in paradise with a sex god?

No, no, no! I'd be breaking rules one, three, four, and even six to a degree. "Oh. That's a lot to decide." Besides the fact that I was leaving town on the twenty-second, I feared growing used to hooded blue eyes and mind-blowing sex.

While he was enjoying a regular piece of ass, my infatuation would be spiraling out of control. Afterward, the hobbyist would wash his hands of me, and I would be devastated. "Can't we take it one night at a time?"

"*Nyet.* I want to know that your luscious little body is mine alone." He dragged me over to sit across his lap, more aggressive than he'd been last night, even more proprietary. "I expect a heated negotiation—I welcome it—but this *will* happen, Katya."

"I had some things planned over the next week."

"Like what? Tell me, and I can be reasonable."

Disappearing. I shrugged.

His eyes darkened. "You still won't reveal a thing?" Yet then he seemed to make an effort to keep things light. "What are you—a wanted fugitive?"

"Ha. That sounds exciting."

"Then what is it?"

"You realize Christmas is coming up?" Wouldn't he have somebody else to celebrate with? His brothers?

Comprehension lit his face. "You already have plans with another. Of course you would." He sounded casual, but his expression tightened.

I had no idea what my holiday would be like. I'd be fresh off the bus. Starting over. Knowing no one.

The thought exhausted me. Maybe I could remain here till the twenty-second, earning more of a safety net? With that money, I could hit the ground running in California.

But to stay with Máxim, I'd need to go home and get some things—without him learning where I lived. Tomorrow night, I'd have to figure out a way to sneak to class.

Unless I skipped. *No penance?*

He set me away, then stood. "Is a regular client taking you skiing? Or maybe a partner is bringing you home to meet his family?" There was no mistaking his jealousy now.

"I don't have either," I said. "I'll come back to-night, and then we'll work out a schedule, okay?"

"What do you have to do that's so important? Another date you don't want to break? You intend to go from my bed to another's, then back to me? Unaccept-able."

"That's not it."

"Then tell me."

"I have a private life, Máxim. Even if I don't book

dates—or have a boyfriend—I still have things to do. You just assume I have no life outside of this."

"How much money will it take for you *not* to?"

I glared. *En serio?* "This can't be taken from my life." I was almost tempted to tell him about school, but I held off.

For one thing, I didn't *know* this guy. Not really. And I'd paid *dearly* for my lesson never to trust another man. If I broke that rule, then I would've paid in vain. Not to mention rule number two; if there was ever a place that linked things in my life, it was my community college.

"Tell me what's so important—or cancel it."

Cancel? Maybe I could skip that one measly review period on Friday. It wasn't even a regular class. As for the exam, I could call Ms. Gillespie and try to reschedule it for after Máxim left. She might let me.

Risk/reward. Risk: my interest in him deepening too much. Vasili snooping around. Reward: money. Again, great sex. After last night, that particular reward was even more pressing.

I didn't like extending my time in a place where Edward might be, but figured I would be safe here with Máxim. "I have to make a call, then." I crossed to the dresser and grabbed my phone, unlocking it.

"Smart girl."

"In private." When he didn't budge, I said, "You've won this round. You're getting your way. Please leave."

"I'll go. But only because I need to speak with Vasili."

Once he left, I rang my instructor. "Hi, Ms. Gillespie, I'm so sorry to bother you, but is there any way I could reschedule Monday?"

"I suppose you won't be there for the review period either?" In a stern tone, she said, "I will make a *single* exception for you, Cat." The only time she had available was the afternoon of the thirty-first at two.

I'd be in Miami much longer than I'd anticipated. Máxim would be gone. Still, I agreed. On New Year's Eve, I'd leave town to the sound of fireworks.

As I disconnected the call, I disbelieved I was postponing the holy grail. I'd have to hit the Russian up for so much *dinero*, it'd be worth it.

I walked out of the bedroom, saying, "Okay, we're all settled. Heated negotiation to commence . . ."

He was in the middle of an angry exchange with Vasili. They both turned to me, accusation in their eyes.

"What?" Alarm trickled through me, and I had the impulse to bolt.

Máxim strode toward me. "Are you on birth control?"

I bit my lip. "Why would you ask that?" Was that information in the records they'd e-mailed?

"You have to be on something."

"I'm going to be." The doc had told me to wait until after my next period to start, and that wasn't for a couple of weeks. How long would the pill take to work? "I have a prescription. It's not a problem."

He stabbed his fingers through his hair. "Are you telling me you only work three weeks a month?"

What did that have to do with birth control?

"Again, it's not a problem." Though this should have been a private conversation, Vasili looked on stonily.

"You think to entrap me?"

"Entrap? What are you talking about?"

"You told me to come in you!" He was all but yelling.

I had? My gaze darted. "And you . . . *did*?"

The arctic blast was back. "Half a dozen times. As if you don't remember!"

My lungs contracted. He might have knocked me up! *Preñada*? Pregnant? "I-I don't remember that!" I remembered pleasure and closeness. But we'd been in the pool so long, and then things had really gotten foggy. "I wouldn't have told you that!"

"If you think to trap me with a child, you could not be more mistaken."

The fucking nerve! "*Now* it's a problem. I don't want a kid, much less your kid."

"Then tell me this isn't a good time for you to conceive. When was your last period?"

I swallowed, my mouth gone dry. *Por Dios*, I was about to ovulate. Or I already was.

Sevastyan read my expression. "*Blyad'!*"

Vasili said something in Russian, but I repeatedly heard a word that sounded like *prostitutka*.

I considered this situation from their point of view. A hooker, who was ovulating and not on birth control, had gotten Europe's most eligible bachelor billionaire to come in her.

Six times.

Sevastyan grated a reply to the man in Russian, and Vasili hastened out of the room.

To me he said, "Other women have plotted the same scheme! Congratulations, you've come the closest to success." Despite the early hour, he strode to the bar and poured a vodka.

"I understand how bad this looks, but we can fix this." My eyes widened. "A morning-after pill! I can take one!"

He wasn't listening to me, beginning to pace. "The first time in my life I relax my guard enough to fuck without a condom, and you pull this move."

I was being accused of trying to cheat someone out of money. *Me!* I covered my mouth with the back of my hand to contain hysterical laughter.

He kept pacing. "A play on a Russian mobster? What were you thinking?"

I bit the inside of my cheek to keep from yelling, "I don't *do* the swindling—I *get* swindled!" How much longer could I muzzle my runaway mouth? One day, I was going to blow, like a seething boiler.

The thought horrified me; I mentally renewed my allegiance to rule number one.

"I thought you were smarter than this," he said. "But then, you are greedy."

A greedy prostitute. That's how he saw me. I was so out of here. I'd go get my own pill, putting this all behind me.

When I strode toward the door, he blocked me. "You think I'm letting you leave? When you could even now be pregnant with my child?"

"I'm going to get a morning-after pill."

"And I'll just take your word for that?" Clamping my arm, he forced me back into the bedroom. "We're going to fix this, then see about teaching you a lesson." He snatched my phone from me.

"Give that back! What the hell are you doing?"

"A doctor is coming this morning."

"To do *what*?"

Sevastyan just gave me a menacing smile, then locked the door.

CHAPTER 14

$\mathcal{F}$or the next two hours, I sat stewing, getting more and more nauseated. I *had* still been buzzed all morning, and now my hangover hit me with the force of a freight train.

I'd banged on the door, calling out, "I'm sick, Sevastyan! I need to take something." He hadn't come. So I could do nothing more than curl up on the bed, stomach roiling. I was mustering the energy to go hold vigil at the toilet when the door opened.

Sevastyan said, "He's here."

I sat up, and the room started to spin. I half-heaved. "I'm sick."

"Uh-huh. Of course you are. And right when the doctor arrives? How fortunate that we can get him to take a look at this other ailment." He grabbed my arm, forcing me to stand.

I tottered. "*Sevastyan . . .*"

He gazed down at my face, scowled. "Fuck." He released me. "Go."

I sprinted for the toilet, and skidded to my knees just as I started vomiting. The bastard was right behind me, leaning in the doorway.

"Go away!"

The champagne smell made me heave again and again, until I felt like I'd thrown up bottles of the stuff.

Finally he left.

I emptied my stomach till I was too exhausted to do more. Somehow I made it to my feet and flushed the toilet. I used his toothbrush, then threw it away. I felt grimy, and I couldn't lose that sickly sweet champagne scent.

If I tried to take a shower, would I fall asleep under the water? I *should* fall asleep there.

I tossed a towel to the floor, turned on the rain showerhead, then sat with my knees to my chest. This was working! My nausea eased as sleep stole over me. I leaned my head against the wall, and I was out. . . .

"What the hell are you doing?"

I blinked up at Sevastyan. How long had I slept? He looked furious, as usual.

He turned off the water, plucking me from the shower. He roughly dried me off, then dressed me in another T-shirt. "Get this over with, then I don't care what you do."

"*A*re you happy now?" I demanded of Sevastyan when the doctor left.

I'd agreed to let the Miami "Gyno to the Rich" administer a morning-after shot *and* insert an IUD to prevent fertilization. Was that the Russian's idea? He was that paranoid?

He calmly sat on the living room couch. Though rain threatened, he had all the doors and windows open. "Happy? No. Satisfied that your plan won't work? *Da.*"

Having some strange man examine me was bad enough, but Sevastyan had stayed in the room! He'd been there when the physician had said things like, "Definitely could've conceived," "Somebody certainly had a vigorous night," and "What a tiny cervix; this will hurt."

Sevastyan hearing that stuff was worse than the pinch of insertion. To add insult to injury, the two men had talked privately afterward. About my body!

I held out my palm. "I want my phone back. I wish I could say it's been nice knowing you. . . ."

"You don't get off this easily. I've mitigated the damage, but now you'll pay for your crimes. You'll stay here until I decide what to do with you."

"You can't just *keep* me!"

"Watch me. A deceitful little girl like you needs to learn not to fuck with a dangerous man like me."

"You know what? Consider the phone a parting gift." I grabbed my purse, coat, and shoes and bolted for the door, yanking it open.

In the lobby, Vasili spoke with two other suited men, holsters visible.

Though I expected them to stop me, I reached the elevator call button, pressing it repeatedly.

Nothing happened. I pressed it again. I had a sinking suspicion I'd now need a key to get off this floor. I turned to the stairwell, shoving on the door. Locked?

In broken English, Vasili said, "No leave." The other two were impassive, like statues. Zero help there.

I marched back inside to Sevastyan. "You can't do this!"

"Why not?"

I hurried to one of the room's phones, pressing nine for an outside line. "I'm calling the agency. Anthony won't allow this!"

"None of these phones will call outside the hotel. No Wi-Fi, no Internet. No communication for you. Oh, and *Anthony*? He couldn't sell your body to me fast enough."

"*En serio?! Hijo de puta cabrón!*" I pinched my brow. "I'll figure out a way to get free of you. Unless you plan to chain me up twenty-four/seven."

He grew very still. "Do not forget that I possess the means—and the inclination—to bind you in my bed."

His script equipment. "What will it take to make you believe I didn't try to deceive you? I would never have a child with someone like you. Much less plot to do it. And I would never scheme to get my hands on someone else's money!" To myself, I murmured, "This isn't happening." I paced. "Look, you need to understand some things about me."

He leaned back against the cushion. "I can't wait to hear this."

"I've never had so much champagne and didn't know it would hit me like that. I don't remember what I said, but I wouldn't have told you I was on birth control."

"Why weren't you?"

I stopped pacing, deciding to reveal part of the truth. "I haven't had sex in a long time. You're my first client."

"If you wanted me to believe you were a novice, then you shouldn't have acted like such a professional. When you spread your legs to me, purring, 'How do you like variety now, *querido*?' I wondered if even *I* might be out of my league with an escort like you."

"You *are* my first! Ask Ivanna! She'll tell you. She sent me here in her place because she had a reaction to Botox, and I needed the money. I almost backed out."

He gave a bitter laugh. "You mean your first client—in Miami? I hear from your agency that you're a pro from Tampa! Not to mention that Anthony had you booked into infinity before I bought you."

"You can't buy me; I was never for sale!" Spanish left my lips, every vile curse word I knew. "If you didn't want to get trapped, then why did you come in me? Why not protect yourself?"

"I wanted no barriers. Which I discussed with you in advance! I should've known something was off when you didn't try to charge me extra!"

Burn. I balled my hands into fists. "What will it take to make you see reason?"

"Your name."

I sucked in a breath. "*Jamás.*" Never.

"Then prepare for a stay."

"How long?"

"In my world, when someone tries to steal from another, they are punished severely."

In my world too. At least with Julia.

"You'll remain until I'm satisfied you've paid for your greed."

Sevastyan would probably get tired of me in a day or two, tops. The novelty would wear off. But if it didn't, the most my captivity could last was another ten days. He was leaving town, then going back to Russia.

To bad weather, Cat. On the bright side, I was safer from Edward here than practically anywhere. Now that I was stuck in Miami till New Year's, the tower began to feel like a bastion.

Never would I have imagined that staying with a Russian mobster and his armed henchmen would be my safest play. Not only that—I'd be staying in the most expensive hotel room in Miami. No creepy supe rubbing himself while leering at me. No cans of cheap soup, leaking roofs, and rough thrift-store sheets.

My biggest fear had been that I would fall for Sevastyan because the sex was so great. Now that he was showing his true colors, that wouldn't be a problem.

I narrowed my eyes at him and thought, *Oh, no, Ruso! Don't throw me in this briar patch!*

I decided then that this would be my retreat—in both senses of the word. I'd bide my time and recharge.

This problem had an endpoint to it, was on its way to being settled. Which meant I could handle it.

"It looks like you've got me," I said airily.

He frowned at my change in demeanor. Sevastyan had just acquired a "prisoner," and the joke was on him.

CHAPTER 15

$\mathcal{I}$ sat in my new room—adjoining his, naturally—trying to recall more. No matter how drunk I'd gotten, I wouldn't have told him to come in me; was he making it up as an excuse to keep me?

Right before the shit had hit the fan earlier, he'd been pissed that I'd had other things to do, supposing I was about to go away with another man. Then all of a sudden Sevastyan had a reason to keep me indefinitely? *Qué coincidencia.*

But I couldn't remember last night, and attempting to only made my head hurt worse. Though I was no longer nauseated, I was wiped out, my temples pounding.

This pillow-top bed was like a cloud, the thread count of the sheets astronomical. I lay back and tugged the fluffy duvet close, gazing out through the wall of floor-to-ceiling windows at the ocean. In minutes, I drifted off.

I dreamed I was lying out by the pool while Sevastyan's hooded eyes watched the sun darken my skin. . . .

When I woke, I was curled against his bare chest, my bent leg stretched over his thighs. Staring out at the water, he lay tensed, with his hands behind his head. He reminded me of our first night, when he'd kept his arms over the back of the sofa, struggling not to touch me.

The sun was setting? I'd slept the day away? Tentatively, I eased up. No headache? No stomachache? I stretched my arms above my head.

He shifted as well, sitting up against the headboard. "You slept for hours."

As if speaking to a child, I said, "Because I was recovering from being *blackout drunk*. A condition I found myself in because *you* kept pouring champagne. I trusted my older-man date and got trashed with him, and the next thing I know, I'm on the wrong end of a speculum, getting an IUD shoved inside my body—after being informed I'm a prisoner."

"Funny you should mention my being an older man. The doctor said you were probably in your early twenties."

"I never said I was twenty-six."

"You looked young, but your confidence made me believe you were older." He pinched the bridge of his nose. "Tell me you can legally drink in this country."

"Relax, Father Time. You're not going to jail for serving me alcohol—only for everything else."

"You're twenty-two, aren't you? When *I* was twenty-two you were thirteen."

"That sounds like a *you* problem." Then I frowned. "Why did you get in my bed?"

He let the other subject drop. "Because I can."

"Is that why you pulled me against you?"

"*I* didn't. You moved toward me, clasping me close, because you're used to sleeping with your partner."

Whatever. "You put your arms behind your head because you were tempted to pet my hair, weren't you? Hmm? Hmm? You enjoy petting my hair."

He didn't answer.

"I'll bet you've been replaying our night, and it's got you sprung. This just proves my theory."

He narrowed his eyes. "Which is?"

"That you like me more than I like you. You'd rather kidnap me than let me go." I stretched again. "Will I be fed during my captivity? I'm starving. In prison, I'd get two hots and a cot."

Glowering at me, he picked up the phone and dialed room service. "What do you want?"

I scrambled over him and snatched away the phone, enjoying his shocked expression.

"*Hablas español?*" I asked the woman.

"*Sí.*"

Inwardly I wore an evil grin. In Spanish, I told her, "I need pizzas. Six of them. Big. Macaroni and cheese. Lobster bisque and whatever else you have with lobster. Basically lobster piled on lobster. I want Cokes. Not diet, but real ones. In glass bottles, if you can find them. Also, if you bring up ten Cuban midnight sandwiches, with extra pickles, Mr. Sevastyan will tip you extravagantly. Please put that gratuity in with the total.

Excellent. Thank you for your help!" As I hung up, my stomach growled in readiness.

"I suppose you always sleep the day through," Sevastyan said, his tone snide. "Occupational necessity."

I sighed. "You keep thinking you know things about me. Yet you are always so wrong, it astounds me."

"Then give me an example."

The bilked heiress accused of bilking another! "You'd never believe me. You'd laugh in my face. But one day, when all this is a distant memory, I'll send you a postcard—with a *list*. Once you verify everything, you'll cringe with embarrassment." He opened his mouth to reply, so I abruptly rose to go to the bathroom.

The spacious area was bigger than my studio. For as long as I was in Sevastyan's tower, I'd enjoy free toiletries, unlimited hot water, and all the towels I could possibly use. With no visits to the laundromat. The life!

I knotted my hair atop my head, then washed my face. I brushed my teeth with another complimentary toothbrush.

I passed him on my way out, not deigning to speak to him. With nothing to do but wait on my gourmet feast, I took one of his business journals to the pool deck, my prison yard. I stretched out on a sofa directly under a heater.

I noticed that everything had been cleaned—by someone who was not me. For once! Talk about a gilded cage.

When I heard the doorbell, I rushed inside, uncaring what I looked like. Three waiters were pushing laden carts into the living room. They made a valiant effort not to look at my braless breasts under my T-shirt.

Sevastyan had put on a shirt. He scowled at my chest, then said, "What is this?"

"You didn't specify what I should order. And don't we have to feed all of our bodyguards? They can have whatever I don't eat. *If* there's anything left over."

Once the platters had been spread out and the men had departed, Sevastyan said, "This is ridiculous."

"Since I lost out on the big bucks, dinner is my consolation prize. Are you going to begrudge me one paltry, very large meal, when you foiled my plan for millions? *Millions!*" I bit my knuckle theatrically.

"You think this is funny?"

"Someday you'll see the humor like I do. I only wish I could be around to see the look on your face." I started hunting for my sandwich. "Ah, there!"

He grudgingly said, "What is that?"

I smelled it. "*Medianoche.*" Midnight sandwich. Eaten after clubbing.

He retrieved one, tasting it. "Good." He took another bite.

I tried mine. Not as good as I made, but it'd do. "Dibs on anything with lobster." I grabbed a Coke, opened the bottle. Drink and plate in hand, I headed back out to the pool.

He could keep me prisoner—ha!—but that didn't mean I had to spend time with him. I returned to my sofa to eat.

Over my meal, I concluded that I should be thankful for this rift between me and the Russian. I'd liked him so much that I might have done something stupid like *really* trust him. I would've told myself that since he was in the *mafiya*, he could help me with my legal problems—and would never judge me for the blood I'd shed. Now I realized that he could use my precarious situation to manipulate me.

Sevastyan's behavior proved that I had the shittiest taste in men. If I started to develop feelings toward a guy, then he should be on an FBI watch list, and I should run the other way. This was as undeniable as science.

All for the best.

Once I'd finished eating, I lay back and closed my eyes. As I delved into my memories from the night before, more details surfaced of conversations we'd had. On the topic of sex secrets, I'd told him I'd never deep-throated before or had anal, though both were fantasies of mine.

He'd revealed that he'd been older when he lost his virginity—like older than I was now. He'd told me he'd never had sex without a condom but often wondered what it'd be like. He'd also admitted to fantasies of having his cum swallowed, which made me shiver (then and now). No wonder my masturbation fantasy at the beginning of the night had turned him on so much.

He'd said something else about oral sex that had blown my mind. What was—

Sevastyan had never gone down on a woman!

"Why would I have?" he'd asked. "I never gave a damn about another's pleasure. But I'm ready to make up for lost time. In fact, I have a matter I want to discuss with you. Come with me to the living room. . . ."

So that was how he'd teed up our discussion. Nice segue, *Ruso*.

My eyes went wide. Over the night, he'd gone down on me, three earth-shattering times! I lay back on the sofa, reliving the first time.

He'd nuzzled my thighs, spreading them, pressing openmouthed kisses higher and higher. Right before he licked me, his eyes had been keen with curiosity. With his first taste, his lids had slid shut. I'd whimpered as he'd muttered to himself, "Never get enough of this." Then he'd set in, tonguing me greedily. Grinding his cock against the cushion, he'd groaned, vibrating my sensitive clit. I'd come, wantonly bucking to his mouth. Once it was over, I'd tried to push him away, but he'd captured my wrists. With a low growl, he'd licked my orgasm clean.

My cheeks reddened when I recalled my frenzied reaction. I'd shoved at his chest until he'd laid back, then I'd *devoured* his cock. I'd sucked on his balls, licking everywhere, moaning around his shaft while he'd grunted, "*Fuck, FUCK!*" over and over. He'd told me, "Take my cum into you! Drink it, *dushen'ka*." Our gazes had been locked as I'd consumed spurt after spurt. Once he'd finished ejaculating, I'd pumped him for more. "*No más?*" I'd pouted while he gaped. *Máximo shockeado.*

"Better than fantasy," he'd grated between breaths. "And I'll only need a couple of minutes to give you more. You make me *insatiable*."

I remembered smoothing leisurely kisses over his dick until he'd swiftly grown rock hard again. Then he'd pushed me back on the lounge chair, looming over me. He'd laid his cock between my legs, rubbing that unyielding flesh over my clit.

I'd been on the verge of factory shutdown, caring about nothing, thinking about nothing, but coming.

As my head thrashed, he'd told me, "I want to fuck you like this. Everything's on my table."

Back arching, I'd begged for his cock, crying out for him to shove it in.

Oh, he had. Without a condom.

I recalled the wonder in his tone: "Your pussy"—thrust—"gets so"—thrust—"hot!" As I'd moaned, he groaned, "It's like fucking a little forge."

So that was how it'd happened. Yes, I should have told him earlier that I wasn't on the pill. But it wasn't as if I had lots of experience with this. In fact, I'd only had that conversation once before, when I was *seventeen*.

Sevastyan had sat me down to discuss things between us going forward, but I'd been stupid and drunk—not only on champagne, but on *sex*. I'd been too preoccupied with the possibility of sucking him to pay attention.

Winds blew over the deck, ruffling my hair and grazing my pebbled nipples through my T-shirt. As if I'd been trained over the night, I immediately thought of Sevastyan's mouth sucking them. How could I still desire the man who was holding me prisoner? I *must* be close to ovulating, which meant I was basically in heat.

I would take another shower—and manually take the edge off. When I returned inside, each step made my breasts move against the T-shirt, the material skimming over the hard peaks.

He remained on the couch. Leaning over the coffee table, he rifled through papers. When I entered, he stilled, saying nothing.

Just looking at his gorgeous face made my breath hitch. I traipsed past him, in a daze. Whatever he saw in my expression made his body tense, his nostrils flare.

I gazed away, couldn't meet his eyes.

A dark laugh. "Now who's been replaying what we did? It's gotten you as wet as I was hard. But I warn you now, little girl, do not pleasure yourself—even to thoughts of me—or there will be consequences."

To thoughts of him? The nerve!

"You'll follow two rules when you're with me. You do not lie, and you do not touch yourself. Unless I've commanded you to for my entertainment."

I whirled around. "Such ego! How do you know I wasn't imagining another man? My *partner*? Also, be aware that anyone who's ever tried to 'command' me has failed miserably." I left him, heading for my room.

In the shower, I kept seeing him in my fantasies. He was right—if I got off, it would be to thoughts of him. I refused! Ignoring all the aching parts of my body, I washed and dried off.

I stole another T-shirt of his, then climbed up into the guest bed, turning on the TV. Though years had passed since I'd watched it, I stared blankly at the screen as a night's worth of memories returned.

The way he'd thrown back his head and roared as he'd ejaculated inside me.

The addictive taste of his cum.

The possessive way he'd licked my pussy, as if someone was about to take his favorite treat away and never give it back.

With a curse, I surrendered to my lust, bunching the shirt to my waist as my hand dipped. I was arching to my fingers when I heard: "You really are in heat, aren't you?"

CHAPTER 16

Mierda!

"Couldn't hold out?" He knelt on the bed and seized my wrist. "If you have these needs, you call *for me*." He brought my hand to his mouth to suck my middle and forefinger between his lips.

As he licked them, he closed his eyes. I shook from sensation, feeling each pull of his mouth in my nipples and core. Could I come like this? I wanted to tell him to leave me alone, that this wasn't part of the deal. But those memories . . .

He took my wet fingers and returned them between my legs. "Pet yourself."

I hesitated until he peeled off his shirt and opened the fly of his jeans, his dick proudly jutting, hard as steel. The tip was moist, taunting my tongue.

Game over. I had to experience him just one more time. My fingers got busy.

When he was naked, he started jacking that thick shaft as I masturbated faster. His big fist. His huge cock.

"You like to watch?"

I nodded breathlessly.

"I might let you later. For now, I want more of your taste."

Grabbing my ankles, he yanked me across the bed. "Spread your legs." When I did, he stared at my pussy. "This is mine now." He met my gaze, telling me, "I *own* it. Just as I own you. I'm your master now, Katya."

How could that arouse me so much? I was independent, not about to be *owned*—

He buried his face between my legs, groaning against my lips.

"*Ruso!*" Even as my knees fell wide, my gaze locked on his length, on the bead glistening atop that plump crown. "I need your taste too."

"You want to suck me?"

"Yes!"

Another dark laugh. He maneuvered around to kneel above me, aiming his shaft to my mouth.

Though I'd never sixty-nined before, I eagerly parted my lips for him, tonguing the tip. He continued kissing me so sensuously, but I had to lift my head to get any of his length. Why wouldn't he give me more? "*Más, Ruso.*"

"You said you've never taken a cock deep," he rasped between licks. "You want your fantasy?"

"I don't know. . . . Maybe I could try?"

He released me, then moved to stand beside the bed. He pulled me bodily until my head hung back off the edge of the mattress. Then he stepped over me, positioning my head between his muscular thighs. With the height of the bed, this put his cock and heavy balls just above me.

"Máxim?"

As he guided his shaft down to my open lips, he said, "Take breaths between my thrusts."

Qué?

He fed his cock into my mouth, then cupped his hands behind my neck.

Oh! I knew this position. Ivanna had called it the "throat swab." Like this, his dick slid in at a much better angle. Deeper than I'd ever taken one.

But when the crown went too far, I tensed at the sensation, jerking back. My legs drew up defensively.

He pulled out. "Relax, *dushen'ka*. You can take me," he said, and he stroked my cheek with his thumb.

For some reason, that random touch—amid all the dirty sex of the last twenty-four hours—affected me so much. When he sank in once more, I ordered my body to relax.

"Good. That's it." He pulled out. "Breathe." Once I'd inhaled, he slowly thrust again.

We did that twice more, with his hands cradling my neck. His thumbs lightly rubbed my throat, guiding me, coaxing . . . until the crown breached deep.

I was doing it! This way was so much easier! Or was it because of the man?

"You're deep-throating me, Katya." He sounded proud, which messed with my mind—and aroused me to a frenzy. I moaned around him.

"Taking it so good." He withdrew, widening his stance. "Breathe."

I inhaled, greedy for more. On his next thrust, I swallowed him even deeper, reaching behind me to grip the muscles of his ass. Soon we had a perfect rhythm between his thrusts and my breaths, in sync again.

"Take it . . . take it . . . such a good girl . . ." He was teaching me, praising me, and I grew ravenous for him. "My cum will shoot straight into you."

I moaned again.

"You like this. I can feel your moans as well as hear them. Breathe, baby."

I dimly remembered a trick Ivanna had told me drove some men crazy. As my throat received Sevastyan and my hands cupped his ass, I dipped my fingers between his cheeks.

"*Dushen'ka?*" In a hoarse voice, he said, "Are you going to be wicked with me?"

I circled my forefinger at his center. To the sound of his groans, I prodded and prodded.

I penetrated—

"*Uhhhn!*" His mighty thighs quaked around my ears. "You're taking my cum before I'm ready!"

I moaned again, and he bellowed, "*Katya!*" Against my tongue, his shaft began to pump. With a growl, he fucked my mouth, shooting creamy torrents inside me.

I drank while his thumbs helped his cum down my throat, his grip on my neck possessive but . . . tender.

Then came a last shudder. A final spurt of hot seed.

A long ragged groan . . .

He pulled out of my mouth, drawing away to return to the other side of the bed. Between breaths, he said, "Now it's your turn." Again, he seized an ankle and dragged me to him. As he leaned down, his harsh exhalations heated my jutting clitoris, my swollen lips, and the sensitive opening between. "You're already on the verge. Deep-throating me got your pussy even wetter? Or maybe you liked exploring your master's body? Ask permission to come."

Despite my need, I wasn't going to obey. "Can I come"—I bucked up, offering myself—"is what I'm supposed to say. But don't you want to make me orgasm?"

Accent thick, he said, "I'll punish you for that later. You *want* me to, don't you? For now, I'm going to lick your needy little clit." He lashed it with his tongue—once, twice, three times—and I screamed as my climax began.

Coiled tension exploded. I fisted the sheets and thrashed my head. Mouth hot and tongue hungry, he forced my aching pussy to contract again and again. . . .

He kept kissing me. Too sensitive! Too much! I had to twist my hips before he released me.

He sat on the bed and collected me in his arms. Claiming my lips, he gave me my taste, taking his own, our tongues lazily twining.

I was soon primed for round two, but he drew back. He affectionately tucked a curl behind my ear, making me sigh. "You just sucked me off, and you didn't negotiate a price. I think you're beginning to like me."

"*Pendejo!*" I disentangled myself from his arms.

"Should I start a 'donation' tab?"

"*Bésame el culo!*" I stormed into the bathroom. Inside, I gazed at my reflection, attempting to process what had just happened.

I'd never felt safer with a man—or cheaper. How could he be so tender, so praising? Then so cruel? Everything with him was an extreme. The *pleasure* was extreme.

As was my love life. Between my two lovers, I'd gone from "I plan to murder you at my earliest convenience" to "I *own* you."

The latter of which aroused me *insanely*. Why? Why? Why?

I sensed, with a sick feeling in my chest, that Sevastyan was the only man who could make me feel this passion and intensity. In my limited time with him, maybe I should ignore his dickish comments and explore my sexuality? Experience as much of his heartstopping eroticism as I could?

To last a lifetime.

After washing off, I returned. He was on the bed, gloriously naked, with a shiny metal contraption in his hands. "You touched yourself against my command, and you came without permission."

I swallowed. "What is that?"

"Your descent into BDSM."

I backed up a step. "You're going to hurt me."

That angered him. "I am not a man who would *ever* hurt a woman."

"Then what is that?"

He rose, stalking closer. "It's a chastity belt. To keep you from coming."

"Are you joking?" How archaic! "You just had that lying around?"

"Hardly. I couldn't have cared less if a partner got

off or not. Plus, I never would've been around one long enough for it to matter."

The glimmering metal captivated my eyes. "Where did you get it?" And why couldn't I look away? *Intrigante.* So intriguing.

"From the maker. A rush order."

"Why me?"

"Because I own your body now. I bought it, and I'm owed it for what you did. I want control over it."

My back met the wall. "You mean control over my sexuality."

He planted a hand above my head, leaning in. "*Yes.*" I was about to tell him where he could shove that belt, when he said, "It's only fair since you control me to this degree."

"What are you talking about?"

"You make me hard at a glance and have me dripping pre-cum like a randy lad, though I never did before. *You* do this to me. Minutes ago, I shot down your throat till my eyes rolled back in my head, and yet . . ." He jerked his chin at his rebounding erection. "Why would I not want to control you in turn?"

My lips parted at his admission. *I* was affecting him like this. Me. A man of his experience, who'd known so many women all over the world, found something special in me.

Just as I did him.

"I'm going to put this on you, and you're going to like it." The wicked promise in his eyes made my heart race with excitement. He sounded so confident, as if he knew something about me—something that I *didn't*.

After a hasty risk/reward assessment, I decided to try it for a bit. I could always take it off.

"Spread for me, *dushen'ka*," he said, reading me so well.

As I stared up at his face, I found myself spreading my legs.

The strap he ran between my thighs was wider in the front, tapering to a G-string in the back. Cushioned on the inside with inflexible metal on the outside, the belt fitted over my clit, leaving part of my lips exposed, then slipped between my cheeks. Both ends of the strap fastened into a circle of metal around my waist. I was surprised by how tight it was, by how seamlessly it fit me.

He jostled the belt to make sure I couldn't get out of it. Before I could protest, he'd secured a small padlock on the side.

"You devil, you didn't tell me it'd lock!"

"And I keep the key." He looped a thin leather lead around his neck, a key dangling over his chest.

I sucked in a breath, rocked by how sexy I found the lock and key. It was like an erotic locket for two that intertwined when put together.

Suddenly I needed to come like crazy. With access to my clit barred, all my thoughts instantly focused on that area of my body.

"I own every one of your orgasms, Katya. I'll bestow them upon you as I please." He returned to the bed, to *my* bed, then stretched out beneath the duvet.

"You're sleeping the night with me?"

Without opening his eyes, he said, "That is non-negotiable."

"I'm supposed to keep this on till morning?"

"If you want me to remove it, I'm sure you'll figure out a way to convince me." With a laugh, he said, "Sleep well."

CHAPTER 17

$\mathcal{O}$nce his breaths grew deep and even—insomnia, my ass—I cupped my palms over the front of the belt and rocked, desperate for friction. I felt only a slight increase in pressure, not nearly enough to come.

Heat emanated from his body, his scent intoxicating me. And that leather lead around his neck got me so horny, my pussy quivered in its cage. *This—is—agony!* I turned over on my front, grinding the mattress, stifling a moan.

When I finally passed out in frustrated exhaustion, sizzling dreams of the Russian tormented me even more. I kept seeing the lost look in his eyes when he'd licked me for the first time. Kept hearing his husky words of praise when I'd taken his length so deep.

I woke after dawn with my clit throbbing, my nipples like arrow-points against the sheet. And a bounty of a man was right beside me. Nearly six and a half feet of muscle and power and latent sexuality.

Over the night, he'd turned on his front, drawing

a knee up. Biting my bottom lip, I tugged the duvet off him. As predicted, I was growing used to the scars on his back, but not the rest of him. I moaned at the sight of his ass, those rigid muscles with sharp indentations on the sides. He lay so his shaft pointed back. His heavy testicles looked warm and relaxed.

Mouthwatering. I'd wondered if I should experience as much of him as possible. Seeing him like this, I found the answer so obvious. *Of course* I would. Why was there ever even a question?

I slipped between his legs. Laying my palms on his ass, I dipped down to drag my tongue over the firm head of his cock. He awakened with a groan. The slit beaded pre-cum, so I lapped it up. Another bead appeared; *más para mí.*

His dick hardened until he had to turn over. "I can't tell which of your personalities I like better—the fiery Cat who comes out claws bared, or my sweet Katya, who steals between my legs so she can lap at my cock for a treat."

I rose up on my knees, shamelessly fondling my breasts. "I can't take much more of this, Máxim."

"Then, congratulations, your tongue enticed me to free you." He removed his key, unlocking me with such carnal anticipation, I gasped. I might have been willing to suffer all these hours again just to see that primal, masculine look. By the time he'd unstrapped me, I thrummed with need.

He lay back once more, his expression filled with intent. "Ride me." The Russian looked very focused on what he was after.

I sighed with relief. *Happily.* But when I moved to straddle his cock, he said, "I can't be inside you yet. You're not to have more of my 'vigorous' fucking until tonight."

The doctor had told him that? So what was I supposed to ride?

He seized my hips and pulled me to straddle his face.

"Oh!"

He reached up to cover my breasts with his big hands, fingers pinching my sensitive nipples. "Show me where you ache."

With a whimper, my hands dipped, and I spread my pussy above his mouth. This was part of my punishment for "deceiving" him? *Más, gracias.*

Running his face against my thighs, he abraded me with his morning stubble. He moved my fingers, replacing them with his own.

He opened me wide. I felt his hungry gaze inside me. "You ache here?" He licked the rim of my entrance.

I almost went off. "Ah! Yes, *Ruso! Mmm!*" I moaned against the back of my hand.

"What about here?" His strong tongue snaked over my throbbing clitoris.

"*Oh—Dios—mío!*" I arched my back.

He paused, seeming to make a decision. Without warning, he suckled my clit between his lips.

My eyes flashed open in surprise, my lungs emptying on a scream. "Máxim! I'm coming!" In total abandon, I gripped his hair as he tugged at my bud, sucking me off. His mouth was merciless. After a night of torture, I mindlessly writhed atop his face.

Over and over and over.

Once he'd wrung every moan from me, I tried to rise, but he held me fast and licked at my orgasm.

"No, let me go!" My thighs trembled around his head as he feasted. "Too much!"

He ignored my cries. As if he were in an agony of pleasure, his eyes closed, a growl sounding from his chest. Then he set in with a frenzy, forcing me toward another climax. A graze of his teeth . . .

"Too much!" I clawed at the headboard, struggling to escape.

His brawny arms curled over my thighs and clamped me against him. Once he'd locked my pussy to his mouth, he stiffened his tongue—and fucked me with it.

"*Ahh!*" Helpless, I surrendered, settling my entrance over his mouth to take his hot tongue-fucking.

His arms clenched my thighs too hard, as if he'd forgotten himself. The idea that he couldn't control his reaction to me only ratcheted up my need.

"You're going to make me come again, *Ruso*. Can't stop it." Sensations inundated me. The rumble of his growl against my pussy. His forceful tongue breaching my core over and over. The bite of his stubble against my vulnerable lips. "Make me come, make me . . . want it so *MUCH*!"

Even more powerful than the first, this climax overwhelmed me. I clasped his face as I melted against his tongue, grinding my flesh against it.

Once the tremors ebbed, I begged, "Please, Máxim, no more. *Por favor*."

He released me. Boneless, I tumbled over to my side.

With heaving breaths, he rocked his hips, his rampant cock thrusting at air. "You wanted to watch me?" He took that veined shaft in his fist and began to masturbate it. Licking his lips for my taste, he jacked himself, his biceps bulging, his heavy balls bouncing with each stroke.

I curled up next to him, my face on his torso for front-row viewing. I'd never seen a man masturbate to orgasm before.

As he neared the edge, his knees drew up. His torso muscles rippled under his sweat dampened skin. "Unless you want me . . . to come on you . . . slide your mouth over my cockhead."

I eased down and wrapped my lips around the crown. With my nails digging into his hips, I sucked while he pumped.

"Is my beautiful girl going to take every drop?"

I moaned my assent.

"I'm going to empty my cum in you. Fill you in every way." With his free hand, he palmed the back of my head, holding me steady for his release—as if he feared I'd change my mind and get away.

Sounding out of his head, he bit out, "When you ground your sweet pussy against my mouth, my cock almost went off right then. You rode my fucking tongue, didn't you, Katya? Just to make me insane. You rode it till you came on it."

I whimpered around the crown. Wanting to try something I'd read about, I straightened my tongue and dipped the tip into his slit. I tasted his pre-cum before it beaded.

"*AH!* You can't even wait for it? You drive me fucking mad!" He thrust his shaft between my ravenous lips, against my busy tongue. He bellowed, "*Drink me, Katya!*" He dug his heels into the mattress, his back bowing as he erupted. "*Take it . . . take it . . .*"

I drank his offering, consuming his cum as greedily as he'd licked mine. Again and again and again . . .

He grated Russian words as his shudders eased. When he pulled me away, my lips had so much suction, they made a *pop* sound.

"I never thought to hear that." He gave a strained laugh as he dragged me up to his chest. "Never thought to possess a woman so greedy for my cock, I'd have to pry her still-sucking mouth off me."

Wrapping an arm around my neck, he trapped me to him. His other arm was over his face, his heart thundering against my ear.

Why would he admit to these things, those sexual things, if he was still angry with me? Maybe he couldn't help himself. Or maybe we were easing back to where we'd been the night before?

As soon as the thought occurred, he moved me off him. Leaving me in a tangle of sheets, he rose without looking back.

I was still sitting there in confusion when he returned, showered, shaved, a towel wrapped around his waist.

"As much as I've enjoyed feeding you your dinner and breakfast—straight from the tap—you need to eat actual food."

I shot him a glare. "And now you turn back into a dick. It's all pumpkins and carriages with you, *Ruso*. What will it take to convince you I didn't set out to deceive you? I'm not interested in having a kid, not yours or anyone else's—not for years and years. Maybe if I live to be your age, I'll consider it then."

"So the exact timing was coincidence?"

"*You* called *me*, forcing me to come over!"

"And you took advantage of my weakness! I know I'm only one client among many. Your night with me was merely one in a stream of them. But you'd have me believe you were so careless? When this is your livelihood?"

I wanted to scream that it wasn't. Yet hadn't I accepted two paid dates with him? "And it's your life! The day I have a child with someone like you . . ." I trailed off. "That day will *never* come. The problem with all your wealth, Sevastyan, is that *you* come with it."

"Sell that somewhere else. I'm a rich, good-looking male in my prime. You're already addicted to my cock."

"Maybe I am. That doesn't mean I want to be tied to you for the rest of my life." My temper was close to redlining. "And why would you want to be anywhere near a woman you think so badly of? You're accusing me of using a baby—a *baby*—as a payday."

"Maybe I deserve a woman as deceitful as I am scarred. Maybe I'll keep you indefinitely. You'll be my sub, and I'll be your master. At least until I'm done with you."

"*En tus sueños*, you paranoid prick!" In your dreams!

He made a grated sound of irritation. "Do you think I want to be so paranoid? So jaded?" His voice rose with every word, until he was almost yelling. "Do you know how bloody frustrating it is knowing everyone wants something of me? And I can trust no one?"

"*En serio?* Everybody wants something from everybody else!" I yelled back. "That's how the world works! Do you think you're unique in not trusting? I—trust—no—one! You poor little rich boy, you don't have more problems because you're rich—you just have different ones!"

"What problems do you have to equal mine? You're young and beautiful. You suck and fuck for a living. Do you strain yourself picking out what nail polish to wear on your dates?"

"You have no idea! *No tiene idea!*"

"Tell me!"

Muzzle it, Cat! "You don't get my secrets! You don't deserve anything from me—much less a child!"

"No? Then all I know about you is that you decided to solve whatever problems you *think* you have—by selling your body. Bravo. Great idea."

My jaw slackened. "*Hipócrita!* You're going to give me shit about being an escort, when you've kept the entire industry afloat with your dick? Baby boy, do I need to teach you the law of supply and *demand*?"

"I know I'm a man with vices, but you're young

enough . . ." He scrubbed his palm over his face. "You could have gotten another job. You could have applied for scholarships or loans, gone to school. America is the bloody land of student loans! If you needed money, you could have borrowed from a relative or a friend until you'd saved up. Anything other than sell yourself!"

"Amazing. You think you've got me all figured out."

"How many men have known your body? A hundred? Two hundred? A thousand? There had to have been an alternative."

I feigned a look of surprise. "Why, I never explored alternatives to hooking!" Resuming my glare, I demanded, "Where is this coming from? It's not like I sprang this on you."

"No, you sprang a paternity play on me!"

"I know why you're keeping me here, and it has nothing to do with entrapment. How fortunate for you that you could cook up this accusation. You'd do anything to have me here for your pleasure. *Specifically* me."

"What are you talking about?"

"You hired escorts and had your script because you didn't want to touch another. You don't use a crop on women because you were whipped; you do it to *avoid touching them*." That muscle ticked in his jaw. Bingo. "Yet then I came along, climbing all over your body, and you could tolerate it. Even *liked* it. I'm unique to you. Something about me has your cock pointed due north. No wonder you want me more than I want you—I do things for you that no one else can."

He crossed to me, clamping my nape with his hand. The feverish look in his eyes should've unnerved me.

Yet I never felt threatened for an instant. "Do you deny that, *Ruso*?"

"I don't. I knew I was fucked from the moment I first got close to you." He tightened his grip on me. "I saw you had freckles on your nose and your eyes were the color of new pennies. You smelled like pleasure itself."

I exhaled a breath.

He dropped his hand. "So I'll keep you as I please, until I can shake this." Because of course he *would* shake it. "If you think you have me by the balls, you're mistaken."

In the haughtiest voice I could manage, I said, "I've got a monopoly *on me*—I control the supply of something you demand. So actually, I do have you by the balls! Oh, *querido*, the weight of them in my palm is making my hand tired."

"I *will* be done with you," Sevastyan vowed. "Just give it time."

CHAPTER 18

*A*fter our fight, I turned up the radio on the deck and hit the pool in my bathing suit—or rather, my thong.

I'd found it in a little hotel bag, freshly laundered. The silk had a solid front on it and could pass for a bathing-suit bottom. No top? I'd pretend I was European.

For over an hour, I swam laps. Without my daily grind of running, scrubbing floors, and sprinting for buses across town, I had way too much energy.

Plus rule number four—I couldn't allow myself to get soft. Rebooting in a new city was always tough. I'd be ready.

Unfortunately, I was still turned on, which meant that my nipples were hard. Without a bathing-suit top, water streamed over them, making me even hornier and more keyed up. A vicious cycle.

"Keeping your figure for all your sugar daddies," Sevastyan observed as he strolled onto the pool deck.

He wore a crisp charcoal-gray suit and an expression that said: *I command all I survey.* "Admirable." He turned down the stereo volume with the waterproof remote.

"Who knows when you'll be done with me?" I treaded water. "You might toss me back to my daddies this very day, into their frenzied, pawing clutches."

His jaw clenched, that muscle ticking. Jealous, *Ruso*? "I'm leaving, won't be back until after dinner."

"What am I supposed to do all day?"

"Contemplate the many things I could've done for your punishment."

"Is gulag an option? Maybe the place where they kept Pussy Riot? Sir, I'd like to be transferred to gulag, please."

Ignoring that, he said, "Will you go against my command and touch yourself when I'm gone?"

Would I masturbate? As primed as I was from this morning's cataclysmic oral sex, not to mention the belt all night? And then with nothing to do to distract me?

Hell yes.

There was that wicked gleam in his eyes. And there went my heart racing from the thrill. We both knew I'd get myself off, but he thought I was about to lie, to avoid the belt.

Though chastity had maddened me, I already kind of . . . *craved* it again. I craved the carnal excitement in his eyes when he'd locked me in—and when he'd freed me.

It might torment me, but I believed it would torment him too. I suspected the Russian would obsess all day about the woman he "owned," about the lover he'd left trapped and yearning in chastity.

His *first* lover.

That leather lead would circle this powerful man's neck—as if I'd placed a collar on him. The metal key would sear his chest.

With that in mind, I lifted my chin and said, "I plan to spend the day leisurely finger-fucking myself."

Máximo shockeado. His fists clenched, his nostrils flared, his eyes . . . delighted.

I'd just made the Russian a very happy man.

"*You little witch!*"

"*You fucking devil!*"

When Sevastyan returned just two hours later, we collided in our haste to grapple each other, kissing, both of us snatching at his clothes.

Before he'd left, he'd added a short, fat dildo to the strap of my belt. It didn't go deep enough to get me off, just far enough to make me *crazed*.

Against my lips, he bit out, "Couldn't think of anything but this."

"You didn't warn me what that dildo would do to me!"

"Cut my bloody meetings short." His accent was thicker than I'd ever heard it. He kicked his shoes off. When he yanked at his socks, I almost strangled him with his tie.

"I rolled on your bed in agony, trying to come from pinching my nipples."

He groaned as he sucked my bottom lip. "I nearly jerked off in a bathroom stall."

"I humped your pillow for a solid hour."

"*Fuck!*" With his shirt over his head, he ordered, "Get my goddamned pants off!" I yanked them down his legs. When I saw the wet circle on his gray boxer briefs, I shivered, tugging them down too.

Naked, he grabbed the key and reached for my shaking body. Once he'd unlocked me, he eased the dildo from inside me, then tossed the belt to the bed. My fingers flew to my aching pussy; his did too. We met gazes, both stunned at how wet and swollen I was.

He raised a shaking hand to his mouth. As he licked his fingers, his cock pulsed, bobbing on its own, straining for my flared lips. Moisture slicked the head. I reached for him, rubbing it with my thumb.

"Witch." His fingers returned for a second helping.

"Devil," I gasped, panting for him.

"Tell me you don't need to be owned."

"As soon as *you* do. I wore your lock. But you wore my key, didn't you? How many times today did you touch it?" I grabbed his dick, leading him to the bed, which clearly thrilled him.

But then his big hands covered my hips to lift me off the floor. He tossed me onto the mattress, as if I weighed nothing. Standing beside the bed, he grabbed my ankles, pulling me toward him till my ass was at the edge. "Spread for me."

I drew my knees up, letting them fall wide. My hands dipped between my legs, my fingers parting my lips until cold air tickled me inside. "Is this where you want to be, *querido*?"

He shuddered with need, and his voice broke lower as he grated, "Your pussy is *krasavitza*. Beautiful. Tell me it's all mine."

I couldn't catch my breath. "It's all yours." I moaned when he fitted his cockhead against my opening.

As the crown nudged, I undulated on the tip. I could come like this. In a few seconds, I would. I'd been tormented, driven mad for sex. His cock—searing and pulsating and ready to pleasure—was heaven compared to that dildo. "Don't make me wait, *Ruso*!"

"Play with your tits for me. Pinch those plump nipples some more."

I cupped my breasts, tweaking my tender nipples, arching to my own touch.

He made that growling sound that drove me wild. "Look at you." His hooded gaze raked over me. "There is no such thing as your body." He clamped his big hands around my ankles, raising my straight legs in a V. He ran his face against my calf, then kissed my inner ankle.

I moaned with wonder, had never known how sensitive the skin was there.

Then he bent his legs, as if he were about to lift something—or shove into me with more leverage than ever before.

I swallowed. "You're going to fuck me with all your might?" Anticipation made my toes curl.

"I am. And you're going to take it." His big body

surged forward, ramming his cock into me to the hilt. "*Uhhhn!*"

I cried out, "*Ah, Máxim!*"

"*Baby?*" he groaned. "Already?"

As pleasure exploded inside me, my cry pitched to a scream. "*Oh, my God!*" My core-deep tremors clenched him.

"Feel you!" He gnashed his teeth. "About to . . . *follow* you." He stopped thrusting, instead grinding between my legs, stirring his cock.

As I moaned and writhed, he drew out every wave for me, sending me soaring again and again. Slowly, I came back down. Through heavy-lidded eyes, I watched him struggling to hold back his cum.

His muscles rippled, his grip on my ankles constricting. "When you come, I need to *thrust* into that grip. . . ." He trailed off, as if just talking about it would set him off. He shuddered, and his dampening torso flexed against the backs of my thighs.

He shook his head hard. Tense moments passed before he regained control. I could swear I almost felt his semen receding down his length.

"You didn't ask permission, Katya." He brought my legs together, coiling his arm around them. He lifted me bodily, till my pussy was the same height as his cock. Only my shoulders and head touched the bed.

When he'd positioned me how he wanted me, he pulled his shaft out to the tip, then used his entire body to shove back in. Over. And over. His groin slapped my raised ass with each assault.

Blood rushed to my head, my arms falling back.

I could do nothing more than lie there and take his lusts. Could only receive and accept and feel. Shivers broke out over me, and I stretched back, euphoric.

He rasped, "You're smiling, beauty. You're enjoying your fucking?" His hips were like a piston! "Does my cock make you happy?"

I moaned, "*Yes.*" The motion and my helplessness, his intensity and the sight of his muscles toiling—all combined to return me to the brink. I tried to arch into his movements, hastening my orgasm.

"You're about to come again? Ask me for permission, Katya!"

I thrashed my head. "No!"

With a brutal shove, he commanded me, "Ask me the goddamned question!"

"I'll ask, I'll ask . . . How many times did you touch that key today?"

"Disobedient witch!" To punish me, he hauled up on my legs and gave me his hardest thrust yet.

"*MÁXIM!*" I hurtled over the edge. White-hot bliss shattered me, radiating through every inch of my body. With each spasm, my pussy convulsed around his shaft, beckoning him once more to follow my pleasure.

"*AHH!* You're fucking *wringing* it from me! Can't resist you this time! You'll have it from me—"

His back bowed sharply, his torso muscles straining. He threw back his head to yell, "*Katya!*"

Semen shot so forcefully into my sheath, I whimpered; liquid heat bathed it like a balm. I watched his violent throes, spellbound by the chiseled planes of his body, those whipcord tendons. His hoarse bellows erupted from his chest and boomed off the walls.

Rocked by what had just occurred, I stared at him and breathed his name.

But once our orgasms subsided, he started to move again, still erect as he plunged into our mingled cum. He was just getting warmed up.

He lowered the weight of his body over me, pressing my knees into my chest. Gaze boring into mine, he said, "I touched that key *constantly.*"

CHAPTER 19

$\mathcal{O}$n the fifth day of my luxury incarceration, the hotel cleaning girl smuggled in a burner phone from Ivanna. Luckily, Sevastyan was away for business.

I called Ivanna at once. "I could kiss you!"

"So it's true? Sevastyan won't let you make calls?"

"He's holding me prisoner." With a permanent marker from the study, I'd drawn five slashes on the mirror above his sink, as though counting down days in prison. Sevastyan had been pissed: "Other women would kill to be in your position!"

Wearing a T-shirt, with nothing to do, and locked in chastity?

He'd put me in the belt again this morning. Then he'd assured me he *would* make it through all his meetings, and he would *not* return before sunset. He hadn't realized that he fingered the key around his neck even as he spoke.

Ivanna asked, "What happened to cause your, er, imprisonment?"

"He's totally paranoid! He thinks I tried to trap him by getting pregnant." He still thought that.

"Why on earth?"

I cleared my throat. "Because we had unprotected sex when I was close to ovulating, and I'm not on birth control. *Yet.* I admit, it does sound bad, but I would never trap anyone. I'd never had that much champagne before—I was crazy drunk." I rubbed my temples. "I didn't specifically tell him he could come in me, but I didn't tell him he couldn't either."

"It's okay, Cat. I have many escort friends who've 'accidentally' had a condom break—after they ran a pin through the client's condom packs."

"*En serio?* That's sick."

"It's not common, but when you reach my age, and you realize you only have two or three good years left . . . It's not as if I've been going to trade school, or saving up a pension. If I don't wed a wealthy man, I'll have to live off my savings—instead of bringing my family over."

Still I gaped. "*You* would do it? Trap a guy?"

"If the circumstances were right."

"No, you wouldn't. Don't say that!"

"Don't judge me, Cat. I have a seventeen-year-old sister and a sickly mother living in poverty, who go to sleep each night to the sound of gunfire. For them, I'd do *anything*. Trap a man? In—a—heartbeat. What wouldn't you do for those you love?"

I exhaled. "I'm sorry I was *criticona*. Judgmental." I'd once read on a T-shirt: *The judgiest people are the ones who've lived the least.* "But for the record, I did not set out to get *preñada*."

"It's still an option, you know. There's always next month."

The idea nauseated me. "Ivanna, when I thought I could be pregnant, it was like someone punched me in the throat. I never cry in front of others, but I was about to. I kept telling myself *Morning-after pill, morning-after pill* like a prayer."

"So that's how you addressed it?"

"No, a doctor came to give me a shot *and* insert an IUD—to be really, really sure. Each method is ninety-something percent certain. Add those two together and it equals: one paranoid Russian. Still, I was relieved. Getting knocked up would be one of the stupidest things I could do. Sevastyan must think I'm stupid."

I defensively pulled my knees to my chest. For some reason, it was imperative to me that he not believe that. "Why wouldn't he? I guzzled bottles of alcohol and let down my guard with a strange man. I *never* let down my guard. I won't ever again."

"Apparently, he let his guard down as well. Have you ever considered why he's so paranoid? He's a mobster AND a politician—is there any man more incapable of trust? Surely he's learned that faith in another can invite punishment." *Only always!* "Perhaps you have an IUD right now because Sevastyan wanted to enjoy you regularly?"

I narrowed my eyes. It wasn't as if *I* had asked for the thing. "Then maybe he's less *paranoico*—and more *manipulador*—than I'd thought."

"Speaking of manipulative, you should know,

Sevastyan's man of affairs called me, asking questions about you."

Vasili! "What did you tell him?"

"As little as possible, because that's obviously what you've been doing—and it's working! Count on me *not* to deviate from this plan. Though I don't know much anyway. I told him that you don't have a car, and you sing a lot. I informed him that when you eat one of those cuppy containers of flan, you are in heaven and smile for the rest of the day. I also mentioned that you adore me and have promised always to take care of me."

I exhaled with relief. "Thank you."

"So, what's it like between you and Sevastyan? Since you're essentially living together?"

"We fight a lot." After sex, as soon as we left the bed—or the couch or the shower or the floor—he would grow ice cold again.

Once we'd recovered from our frenzied fuck yesterday, he'd dragged me into the study, dumping me into a seat in front of a computer. No Internet access, of course. "Make yourself useful." A fifteen-page document in Spanish had been pulled up on the screen. "Translate it, then print a copy. You've got three hours."

The document had been about the Panama Canal. I began to suspect he was in Miami to take advantage of the upcoming canal expansion. Interesting.

Three hours later, I'd found him in the living room on the phone with his brother Dmitri.

Whenever he talked to his younger brother, his mood plummeted, and nothing ever seemed to get resolved. Yet he talked to the man *a lot*. Sometimes I could even hear Dmitri yelling, but Sevastyan never raised his voice or got angry in return. If I were Máxim's girlfriend and I gave a damn about him, I'd try to limit those calls.

When I'd dropped my printed report onto his lap, he'd ended the call. As if it were a chore to read, he'd exhaled and turned the cover sheet to the first of fifteen identical pages:

FUCK YOU FUCK YOU   FUCK YOU   FUCK YOU
FUCK YOU FUCK YOU   FUCK YOU   FUCK YOU
FUCK YOU   FUCK YOU   FUCK YOU
FUCK YOU FUCK YOU   FUCK YOU   FUCK YOU
FUCK YOU   FUCK YOU   FUCK YOU
FUCK YOU   FUCK YOU FUCK YOU
FUCK YOU   FUCK YOU FUCK YOU

I'd turned on my heel and sauntered back to my room.

Ivanna said, "It can't all be bad."

"No, it's not. Sometimes, I like it here with him." Between Sevastyan and the floors of gun-toting *mafiya* guards, I felt safer than I had in years. Up in his tower, I was getting used to luxury, to not scrubbing toilets, to gourmet food, to views that went on forever. When I looked in the mirror, I saw a changed woman—skin glowing, eyes clear, dark circles gone.

I was officially recharged and heading toward . . . bored. I hadn't been bored in three years!

I'd hit the penthouse library (because ten thousand

square feet of space meant it had a library). I'd finished novel after novel by the pool. Then I'd discovered on-demand video. I'd found a yoga class. Somehow I got through it. I would never scoff at yoga again.

"Is the sex amazing?" Ivanna asked.

"He puts me . . . he puts me in a chastity belt." Normally, I'd never tell her about this, but I had to vent.

She gave a throaty laugh. "How unexpected!"

"You aren't outraged for me? It's archaic! And I don't have any clothes. I either wear a shirt of his or go without. So basically I'm left naked and available for his use whenever he wants me."

"Your accent just thickened, and your voice grew husky. He's not the only one enjoying your situation."

I lay back, staring at the ceiling. "All I can think about is him. His body. It's like I'm drugged. My brain goes on a loop, replaying things we've done, imagining things we'll do. I walk around in this lust-fueled haze."

"It sounds enchanting."

"Have you ever had a man put you into chastity?"

She sighed. "I've never had one who cared enough to."

Care? He'd assured me he would toss me out as soon as he was *done using me*. And where would that leave me? Crushed. "I don't think that man's capable of caring. Ivanna, he can be so cold. *Por Dios*, I'd get whiplash if I tried to keep up with his moods."

And yet . . . he could also be a dream. This morning when he'd made love to me, he'd pinned my wrists over my head. But then he'd threaded his fingers through mine, locking our hands together.

Lock and key. Intertwined.

The pleasure he continued to give me was indescribable. And in those sweet twilight moments after sex, he drew me like no other man before. Earlier, as we'd caught our breath, he'd confessed, "I have little control with you. Stranger still, I'm making peace with it." Yet then he'd grown chilly once more.

Ivanna said, "Despite his moods, it seems as if you like him."

If I was honest with myself, I'd say that I did. I enjoyed his tricky mind and his intensity. His passion. But only an idiot would get attached to a guy like that.

Besides, if I developed feelings for him, then that meant he was trouble. Any impulse I had to like him or trust him should be taken as irrefutable evidence to do neither. *You can't argue with science.*

I told Ivanna, "I just want my freedom."

"Could you fall for him?"

"I . . . maybe?" *Idiota!* "I don't want to find out! Which is why I need to get away from him as soon as possible!"

"Why *wouldn't* you want him? Cat, are you already involved? Do you have a man?"

One hunting the city to kill me! I gave a humorless laugh. "Yeah. You could say I'm involved with another man."

"Do tell!"

I sighed. "Another time maybe."

"Very well. Then let's think about your end game.

With as much access as you've been given to Sevastyan, have you learned any scoop to tell me about his past? His deep dark secrets? We could sell such a story."

"His deep dark secrets? Those are the kind I keep best."

"So you won't tell me what he's doing in Miami?"

If I had to guess, Maksimilian Sevastyan was buying up as much of the city as possible. From what I could glean, Miami was the closest ultra-deep port to the Panama Canal, which meant tons of new shipping traffic for the city—traffic that would demand warehouses, infrastructure, and rail spurs.

Yet I told Ivanna, "He's here to work on his tan?"

"I see," she said in a knowing tone. "Chin up. Now that you have a phone, you can call others. Maybe another friend could do more than smuggle in contraband?"

"You're right. I'll burn up the wires, dialing everyone I can count on. . . ."

After we'd hung up, I threw my arm over my face, tempted to fling the phone across the room.

I was still friendless. Still trapped in this belt. Trapped with a man who looked forward to the day when he could discard me. I was about to scream with combined frustration when I shot upright, remembering Mrs. Abernathy's threatening message. *Mierda!* If she called INS . . .

I dialed the woman up. "Hi, Mrs. Abernathy, it's Cat. I'm confirming for the thirty-first. *Sí, señora.* I'll be there at nine a.m. sharp. *Gracias.*" My jaw dropped when she started a lecture about work ethics.

Work ethics. From someone who didn't have a job.

I'd just hung up and hidden the phone in the guest room closet when I heard Sevastyan return.

Already? The sun was still high in the sky. I smiled when he bellowed, "*Fucking come to me, witch.*"

CHAPTER 20

Knowing how much it would piss him off, I'd added a sixth slash to Sevastyan's mirror this morning.

Not long after, he found me in the pool, doing topless laps to music as per my usual. As per his usual, he was dressed to the nines. His tailored dark blue suit lovingly fit his broad shoulders and lean hips. His sunglasses made his hotness catapult off the charts.

He always looked flawless—except on those occasions when I could muss his hair. He picked up the remote, turning down my tunes.

"You and your clothes, *Ruso*. How much did that suit cost?"

"In U.S. dollars? Ninety or so."

I gaped. "Thousand?"

"A Dormeuil Vanquish suit doesn't come cheap." He jerked his chin at me and said, "I always pay for quality."

Thanks for the reminder. He was as hot and cold as

ever, but his overall mood deteriorated with each day I remained here.

So why hadn't he kicked me out of his tower? Though I was thinking more clearly today—he'd decided I could use a night's uninterrupted sleep without my belt—I couldn't figure him out.

And when exactly had *the* belt become *my* belt?

"I'm leaving for the morning, then holding meetings here from three on. You'll need to stay out of the common areas."

"Why? You don't want your associates to see your prisoner walking around braless in your T-shirt?"

"I don't need to give you a reason why. This is what I want from you." *So says the king.*

"If you have to hide me, then why don't you just send me packing?"

"You'll remain with me until I'm done with you."

Ooh, that burned me up! I wanted to slap him. At times like this I actually missed my shitty existence. Though I felt safe and had spare time, and had eaten so much lobster I was nearly sick of it, I did yearn for things.

Like having an occupation and running. I even missed attending class. "Oh, I see. Poor Sevastyan is *still* wanting this ass." I gave a theatrical sigh. "I suppose if I'm going to be your quote-unquote *prisoner* for another day, then I'll need things. I know you like to keep me barefoot and not-pregnant, but my uniform is getting old."

"Give me your address, and I'll send someone to fetch whatever you need."

"I can't give you that kind of information. You know why, *chulo*? Because I *do* fear a besotted client, and we both know that you want me more than I want you."

His shoulders tensed up. All arrogance, he said, "Then it's fortunate that I don't give a fuck if you want me or not. Don't test my patience. This week I'll have little enough of it."

I'd hit a chink in his armor! "Speaking of this week. Tomorrow is Christmas Eve."

"Do *not* remind me." Arctic blast. *Somebody doesn't like Christmas?* "Your partner will have to miss your smiles for the holiday. Never forget, *Cat*, you're here for my use—at my disposal."

Spanish left my lips, insulting him and all his ancestors. Yet then I grinned evilly, planning to shove seven figures' worth of his suits into the hot tub. To begin with.

He did a double take at my expression, then stormed off, barking something to Vasili on his way out. Probably: "Watch her."

I stewed for another thirty minutes, deciding how else to screw with Sevastyan.

In the shower, I lit on an idea. I couldn't dial out on the hotel phone, but I could dial down.

I dressed in one of his T-shirts for the last time, then called the concierge. "I'm Maksimilian Sevastyan's girlfriend," I told him. "And I'm going to need some things brought up to the penthouse and billed to the room."

"Of course. My name is Alonzo, and I'd be happy to be of service."

Muy bien. "Do you have a pen and paper?"

The man didn't miss a beat when I ordered bathing suits, cover-ups, lingerie, slip-on beach sandals, dresses, Louboutins, makeup, and my favorite brands of toiletries. I ordered multiple pairs of running shoes, athletic boy-shorts, and sports bras.

To go with all my workout wear, I kind of bought a treadmill.

When boxes began arriving, Vasili, the hulk of Russian bodyguards, scowled at me from the lobby. Three new security guys were with him, now searching the boxes. They were as impassive as robots, their holsters and guns visible—because they were ready to *drop* anybody not authorized to be on this floor.

Ha! Do your worst, Edward.

The treadmill delivery made Vasili's scowl deepen, folds appearing on his bald head. "Not smart."

"Sevastyan shouldn't have taken on the responsibility of a new pet if he didn't have time to watch her. My breed is very destructive."

In broken English, he said, "Boss not type of man to fuck with."

"I'll let you in on a secret. I'm not the type of *woman* to fuck with." Everyone always underestimated how tough I was. I kept getting knocked down, but I also kept rebounding, every—damned—time. During this enforced vacation, I would run miles in addition to swimming laps, getting even stronger.

I directed the deliveryman to set up the treadmill in front of the wall of windows in the guest bedroom. Ah, a view of the water for my jogs.

After that, I opened packages and tried on my swag for hours. The bathing suits alone were amazing. I'd told Alonzo to get a shopgirl to pick out "crazy sexy," and in Miami, that wasn't a phrase to be taken lightly.

I ate my room-service lunch, then moisturized with a light oil that made my skin shimmer. I changed into a scarlet micro-thong that had a little bell on the back. Love! My skimpy black bikini top barely covered my areolas.

On my way to the pool, my boudoir heels click-clacked, accompanying my bell.

Once I'd made sure I had a tan line over my ass to taunt Sevastyan, I rang up Alonzo for a hair stylist to come trim my hair. A manicurist as well. Vasili had glowered at them when they arrived, but he'd let them through.

While Sheila and Vera worked, we three enjoyed room-service piña coladas with ground nutmeg on the top. The cocktail was so delicious I called down to the bar manager to pass on my compliments, or rather, the Russian's. "All the drinks for the hotel are to be put on his tab today. Tell everyone *Salud* and *Feliz Navidad* from Mr. Maksimilian Sevastyan!"

I tipped the girls in Louboutins and dresses that were too big for me.

They departed not long before Sevastyan and his business associates arrived.

I was just returning inside myself. *Qué coinciden-cia!* Naturally I tugged down the back of my thong so that the tan line was visible.

The group looked like European businessmen—

with an edge. For every man in a suit, there was a tougher, less polished bodyguard.

And still, Sevastyan looked more dangerous than all the others put together.

When they caught sight of me, they stutter-stepped at my getup. Even Vasili raised a brow.

Máxim's piercing blue eyes promised revenge. So why was I never afraid of him?

In a purring voice, I told the men, *"Buenas tardes, señores."* I made a show of turning and shutting the sliding door, knowing how my ass would move, how that little bell would go off.

Ring ring ring . . .

I heard stifled groans behind me and gave them a *silly me* smile over my shoulder.

"Who is *this*, Sevastyan?" one asked.

He bit out, "Katya was just going to her room."

I narrowed my gaze. *Oh, it's on, Russian.* Now I was really going to fuck with "boss." I sashayed away.

In my dressing room, I rummaged among all my drawers of new clothes. I chose a tight black sports bra, pulling it on. My hot pink boy shorts surrendered to the cleft of my ass. I donned running socks and shoes, then pulled my hair up in a high ponytail.

I definitely needed to get water out of the kitchen before I tried out my new treadmill. *Hydration is important!*

I sauntered out. Though Sevastyan had his back turned and hadn't seen me yet, he must've noticed his associates' brows-drawn looks of lust, because his shoulders bunched with tension. Vasili stood by, shaking his head at me in warning.

"So sorry," I told the men. "I needed something to drink. Tanning makes me parched."

On my way back from the kitchen, one of them said in English, "You don't have to hide her away, Sevastyan. It looks as if there is *plenty* to go around this table."

Another said, "Share the wealth, man."

A few of the other men made sounds of agreement.

I'd just reached Sevastyan, so I paused and draped myself over his back. "Oh, there's no sharing. I'm Máxim's alone. Isn't that right, *mi tesoro*?" My treasure. "I'm his baby-mama. Or I *would've* been. So close," I sighed to the men, my words heating Sevastyan's ear. His muscles tensed against me. "You see, I'm not very bright. Someone like me wasn't able to discern the manifest economic *in*utility of a woman my age getting pregnant with a strange man's kid." I giggled. "As my island grandmother always advised, 'Don't use your brain, *mi preciosa*. Use your uterus.'"

Between gritted teeth, he bit out, "Are you done, Katya?"

"*Por ahora.*" For now. I whispered at his ear, "Have fun in your stodgy meeting. And know that once I've logged my miles, I'm going to finger myself *furiously*." I nipped his earlobe, smiled at the men, then traipsed away.

CHAPTER 21

"*Pleased with yourself?*"

I whirled around in the shower.

"Sevastyan!"

He was leaning against the doorway in the bathroom, watching me bathe. "I like it better when you call me Máxim." He wore only an opened shirt and his slacks.

"What are you doing? You said you had an afternoon of meetings." Scarcely an hour had gone by.

He gave a laugh. "I'm in Miami to be courted. I need none of them. When I heard your new treadmill stop, I simply called the meeting and rescheduled." He began unbuttoning his shirt. How could he make that act menacing? "You disobeyed me, *kotyonok*."

Even as my heart tripped, I squared my shoulders. "When bored, this *kitten* hops the fence."

He bared his muscular chest. I wanted to sink my nails into his sculpted pecs. Running had made me as horny as ever.

"You've ensured that my enemies—and my brothers—will find out that I've finally taken on a woman." He unbuckled his belt. "Evidently I was quite generous with gifts to her today. In fact, to the entire hotel."

I asked innocently, "Baby boy didn't like my little bell? No?" Hardening my expression, I said, "I regret nothing."

"You never do." He stepped out of his pants. "For someone who doesn't like to shop, you did well enough."

"I didn't *shop*. I committed retaliatory consumerism. I could've gone for jewelry, really putting the hurt on. Also, I debated washing all of your expensive suits in the hot tub."

As if I hadn't spoken, he said, "I wasn't quite ready for others to know about you yet." He pulled his boxer briefs over his dick, making it bob. "So now I'm going to discipline you for disobeying me."

"Oh, are you?" I'd meant to scoff. Instead, I sounded intrigued. "How's that?"

He entered the large shower enclosure with me. "I'm going to spank you." He yanked me close, his cock trapped between us.

More BDSM? "I don't want that. I'm not going to let you abuse me."

"Abuse is one-way, with the intent to hurt. What I do with you is for shared pleasure, and it is a two-way interaction. I'll be assessing your response, as usual."

"What does that mean?"

His mesmerizing eyes pinned my gaze. "I watch

for your pupils to dilate, a sign of surrender that means you'll let me do anything to you. Sometimes I hold your wrists to take your pulse and learn what makes your heart race. Even if I'm not touching your pussy, I can tell when you start to get wet; you get a pink flush from here"—he touched the left side of my chest and ran his finger in a straight line across my skin—"to here." Dropping his hand, he grazed the backs of his fingers over one nipple. "This sweet little peak always hardens a moment faster than the other."

I exhaled a shaky breath.

"All this golden skin." He traced the tan line beside my areola. "If I lick your flesh, will I taste the sun?"

Shivers coursed over me.

"Turn around and hold on to that bar." He indicated the metal towel rack. "Prepare for your punishment."

Was I really going to try another type of BDSM? I'd relished the belt, but that hadn't *hurt*.

"Don't fight me."

"*Por Dios*, just wait."

"For what?"

"I'm doing a risk/reward analysis."

He froze, a gust of breath leaving him. "Indeed? The courtesan who hardened all the cocks in that meeting would now like to perform an analysis?"

Shouldn't I brave this out for a few minutes? Just to see what all the fuss was about? Hadn't I decided to experience as much of his mind-blowing sex as I could in my limited time with him? To explore my sexuality?

He *was* looking into my eyes, studying me. Would my pupils truly flare now that I'd surrendered?

He gave me a cocky smirk. "There it is." He grabbed my hips and turned me around. "Hold on to that. And do not let go, or I'll deepen your punishment."

With a swallow, I reached for the towel bar, bending over, baring myself to him even more.

I could feel his gaze on my ass and pussy. "Risk/reward," he muttered. "I don't know whether to kiss you or whip you harder."

Positioned like this, I felt utterly vulnerable. So why was I having a hard time keeping my hips still?

Especially when he followed the tan line across my ass with a reverent finger. "You made sure I saw this, revealing it in a room full of men. But it was for me."

"Maybe—"

He slapped one cheek.

The sound was loud in the enclosure, startling me as much as the hit. "Whoa!" No warning? It stung—until he began kneading me with his big hands, transforming the strike into . . . *heat*.

His cock pulsed against his leg just before he slapped the other side of my ass. The rap echoed off the tile.

"Look at your ass moving with my strikes." Again, he kneaded me, generating that sublime heat. "For days, this flesh has begged to be chastised." A harder slap. More massaging. "I can *see* how wet you're getting. You were made for this."

I was beginning to think he was right. That bloom of heat spread from my ass to my thighs and pussy, to low in my belly.

With his next slap, I turned my head and moaned against my arm. He massaged me so perfectly.

"If you make me jealous, Katya, you play a dangerous game." *Slap.* He was breathing more heavily. "When those men leered at you in that thong, I had the impulse to tear off that bell with my teeth and fuck you in front of all of them—so they'd know who makes you scream."

His jealousy hit me like a drug. I shook.

"*I* am fucking you. No one else. I alone own your body." *Slap.*

I should be appalled by what he was saying; I could listen to his dark musings for days.

"You are my prized possession, and they coveted you." Did he just call me a possession? "When other men covet what's mine, I want to punish them. And you." *SLAP.*

The fiercest one yet. I hissed in a breath through my teeth. But right when I raised my ass for another, the devil stopped.

"Why did you quit?"

"Because now I need to fuck this"—he rubbed his cock along the wet lips of my pussy—"more than I need to chastise your ass. Spread your legs."

I eagerly did, and he pressed the crown to my core. With his heated palms, he clutched my hips. Without warning, he shoved forward and snatched me back at the same time.

The thrust ripped a cry from my lungs and sent me up on my toes—but I was slick, ready for his invasion.

"I knew you would love that." He reached his hands around, cupping my breasts. Then he pinched one peak, hard.

I gasped, and when my pussy clenched in reaction, he made a pained sound. "This as well." He seized my other nipple, tweaking both between his merciless fingers—so why was I arching for more?

"I'm going to clamp these, *dushen'ka*." He squeezed them as he thrust. "It will drive you crazy. We've got time."

When he released my nipples, I moaned as blood returned to them. I gazed down, marveling at how engorged they were, how lurid a sight. I could feel my own breaths fanning over the hypersensitive tips.

While I hung on to that bar, he poured some kind of bath oil over my ass, continuing his massage. One hand gripped my hip to hold me steady. With his other hand, his seeking fingers dipped between my curves. Would he touch my ass as I had his?

Even expecting the contact, when he stroked me dead center, I jerked, trying to tuck my hips.

His laugh rumbled. "You really are a virgin there. Your other man doesn't play with you like this?"

I didn't bother arguing.

"His loss." Sevastyan resumed his exploration, circling me with the pad of his slickened thumb. "Do not release your grip on the bar. No matter what I do." He dipped his thumb down, pressing. Was he going to penetrate me?

The pleasure was unknown to me, peculiar—but no less intense. I arched my back down, sending my ass even higher. He pressed and oiled, pressed and oiled, while I shook from the onslaught of sensation.

Then, *inside*. I moaned, dazed by how good it felt.

He groaned, "So goddamn tight."

I peered over my shoulder at Sevastyan's face.

His blue eyes were transfixed on my ass, on his finger penetrating me. His expression was possessive, as if he gazed at something he was proud to own. "I'm going to be the first one to fuck your beautiful ass."

"N-now?"

"Not yet. You'll anticipate it."

"Devil!"

Another low laugh. With his other hand, he reached around me, his fingers roving over my pussy. "Ah, my Katya's sweet, needy little clit." He rubbed it as he began thrusting his cock, his thumb still wedged inside me.

I was overloaded with pleasure, couldn't decide if I wanted to shove my ass back at him or rock my hips to his sinful fingers. "So . . . good . . . so good."

"I'm going to own every part of you," he rasped. "Your eyes, your lips, every inch of your body. Your complicated, too-clever mind. Your pussy is already mine—even you'll admit that." He thrust his thumb harder, wrenching a cry from me. "Soon I'll claim your tight little virgin ass." He pistoned his hips, our skin slapping.

I couldn't think. Shutdown.

"I'm going to work my cock inside you here, and when I pump my cum in you, I'll own this ass."

I pushed back on him, answering him with insensible sounds. Too much stimulation.

"There you go. . . . I feel your pussy tightening up on me, about to release. *I* make you feel this way—no other man—because you belong only to me. You're going to scream my name, aren't you, Katya?" He thrust his cock and thumb at the same time.

"Oh, my God!"

"When pleasure makes you mindless, you think of only one name. *Mine.*" His words tipped me over the edge.

I screamed, "*Máxim!*"

His fingers moved even faster, sending me into a frenzy, the waves of my climax overwhelming me. I clutched the bar for dear life, writhing, gyrating my hips.

"That's it, baby, that's it. Take your pleasure from me."

I did. Over and over.

My cries slowly dwindled. Once I was hanging limply, my body a quivering mass, he withdrew his finger to grip my hips.

Holding me in place, he stretched over my back and shoved hard inside my pussy. In a hoarse voice, he said, "I could fuck you forever, beautiful girl. I want you to come on me again." As he brutally surged into me, his balls slapped my clit. He railed me with all his might, going deeper with each thrust. I could only hold on for the ride.

He opened his mouth over my shoulder, almost biting me, like an animal. The touch of his teeth to my flesh—

My scream ripped through the enclosure. His cock was so swollen, my spasms could barely squeeze around it.

He snarled against me, driving harder. He released my shoulder to bellow, "Taking it from me! *AHH!*" He roared to the ceiling as he began to ejaculate, his fingers digging into my skin. His shaft, his legs, and his hips rammed into my body.

One savage shove. Another. And another.

Until a satisfied groan sounded from his chest.

Gradually, his shudders eased, but he remained inside me, as if reluctant to leave. He coiled an arm around my waist. "Let go, *dushen'ka.*" With difficulty, I made my fingers release the bar, and he pulled me up against him.

His breaths tickled my damp neck. His heart thundered against my back. One of his hands lightly covered my throat. He filled his other palm with a breast.

He was content to rest like this—as if being with me were the most natural thing in the world.

As if I were his long-term lover, his girlfriend. When he nuzzled my neck and pressed kisses to my shoulder, I found myself wishing I could be.

*H*is phone rang yet again as I dried off and donned my new silk robe.

"My brothers." He sighed, wrapping a towel around his waist. "I hope you're happy. Mobsters gossip worse than old women."

"I always heard that old women gossiped worse than mobsters." In front of the mirror, I combed out my hair, trying to act casual about what he'd done to me. He'd told me he owned me. For that space of time, he *had*. Máxim continued to give me fantasies—ones I hadn't even known were *mine*. "What will you tell your brothers about me?" I met his gaze in the reflection.

"That I've purchased a young Miami woman, enslaving her in my penthouse."

Ha. "And what will they have to say about that?"

"My older brother won't believe me. My younger will see absolutely nothing wrong with this—as long as I don't get attached." Dmitri. The one who brought him daily bouts of grief.

"While it's all fun and games to brag that you've purchased a woman, surely you're done with me by now. You *did* say you would shake this."

As if I hadn't spoken, Sevastyan left the bathroom, returning shortly after. "Before I forget . . ." He held up the chastity belt, modified once more.

I gasped. This time there were *two* plugs.

CHAPTER 22

*S*evastyan was setting me up for a crash landing. And I resented it.

As I changed into my new running gear, I recalled awakening this morning—cocooned by his warmth, his arms like a shield around me.

Before him, I'd been cold and alone and wary. Guess what Catarina was returning to in four days.

It'd be all the worse because I'd tasted a different life. I'd tasted the wickedest pleasures.

Yesterday, he'd kept me in the belt for only a couple of hours, both of us too miserable to deny ourselves for much longer. I'd been on fire, and he'd been more than my match, taking me four times over the afternoon and night.

His shower play and the second addition to the belt had left my bottom sore today—but the constant reminder of what he'd done to me turned me on anew.

A brilliant, gorgeous, billionaire sex god shouldn't amuse himself by playing with a woman's feelings.

Maybe I'd made an error deciding on this retreat. He would let me go on the twenty-eighth—of that I was sure. If the boundary between our bodies had fallen, somehow I had to maintain the one around my heart until then.

With that thought in mind, I snagged the marker I'd hidden in a shoe box, then marched to the master bathroom to add one more slash.

Beside my marks on the mirror, the bastard had written: *It's so good you should be paying me.*

I could all but hear him saying that in his seductive devil's voice, and it made me tremble. How dare he take over the mirror! That was my gig! Narrowing my eyes, I drew a seventh slash, then wrote: *You're gonna miss this ass when it's gone.*

I left the marker by his toothbrush—*your move, Ruso*—then marched to my treadmill, intending to make a racket. He slept on, arm stretched out, again as if he reached for me.

My chest went *pang*. My mind went *pendejo!*

He'd probably be pissed that I woke him so early on Christmas Eve day. His mood had continued to go downhill—hourly, it'd seemed. But I didn't care. If he was bothered, then he should sleep in the master suite—instead of getting me used to his big, warm body spooning me all night!

With the room's remote control, I opened the curtains, revealing the ocean. Today was a Miami stunner. Early morning sunlight glimmered over the ripples on the water's surface, making them look like diamonds.

Now that I'd feathered my gilded cage, the tower

was a dream. Here, I had running, swimming, business journals delivered every morning, a new wardrobe, and an endless supply of decadent food.

Oh, and a dream lover. Except for the fact that he would soon return to Russia, leaving me behind.

I was all but teed up for a crash landing, might as well dive from this tower myself.

With a series of beeps, I angrily set up my workout and the heart-rate monitor. When I started a walking warm-up, I *felt* his gaze on me.

"Why didn't I buy you a treadmill on day one?"

I glanced over my shoulder.

He was in no way pissed. He sat up against the headboard, hands behind his head, with that *I command all I survey* expression. The left corner of his lips curved. I'd noticed that side tilted up when he was amused—*and* his tricky mind was engaged. "I want to wake up like this every morning," he said. "Ah, the views go on forever, Katya."

Facing forward, I started my run, determined to think of anything but his eyes on my body. *Ignore him.* I needed to get into my runner's zone, that focused headspace I craved.

After my first mile, I glanced over my shoulder again, found his gaze transfixed on me. He regarded me as he might a gift he planned to unwrap. A distinct bulge tented the cover, but he appeared to be biding his time.

I started to sweat, breaths shallowing. Halfway through, I glanced back. One of his arms had snaked under the cover, that bicep flexing rhythmically. *Por Dios*, he was stroking himself as he watched me.

I stutter-stepped, the heart monitor beeping like crazy.

The devil knew what that sound meant. He chuckled.

No headspace. I was hyperaware of everything around me. My skin pricked with chills, even as I was burning up inside. I felt every drop of sweat trickling over my body. My nipples strained against my bra.

Running always made me horny. Running with him watching? Made. Me. *Loca.*

Any time I tried to take a break and process everything that was happening, he invaded my thoughts. All I could see, hear, or feel was him—as if he'd gotten a foothold in my mind and heart and had started swinging elbows.

With difficulty, I finished my miles. As I started my cool down, I wondered what I would find when I turned again. Maybe he'd already jacked off. Maybe he'd leave me alone. When I stepped off the treadmill, I found him sitting on the edge of the bed, his swollen cock jutting. My pussy clenched for it.

But I forced myself to head toward the shower. As I passed him, he caught my hand.

"You're going to have a seat." He used his other hand to pat one of his thighs.

"I'm dripping sweat."

His lids went heavy. "I *know.*" He reached forward and yanked down my boy shorts. Before I could step out of them, or my shoes, he'd lifted me over his lap as if I weighed nothing.

With my back to his chest, he tucked his cockhead

against my entrance. Grasping me behind my knees, he held me open atop his rod. "I'll give you this slow."

My arousal slicked the way as he sensuously . . . inch by inch . . . allowed me to glide down . . .

A gust of breath left him. "Your pussy's searing me. Is my Katya still in heat?" His shaft thickened near the base. My core had to stretch to swallow his girth. "Or does running arouse you?" He yanked up my soaked bra. His hands wandered all over my damp belly, breasts, and sex.

"Running," I gasped out. With my shoes still on, my shorts around one ankle, and my bra hiked up, I arched to his touch. "But knowing you watched me, the *way* you watched me . . ."

He kneaded my sweat-slicked tits and pinched my nipples, ruthlessly, as he had in the shower. "You get me harder than I've ever been. For an hour, I wet the sheet with pre-cum, my balls laden for you."

When he tickled my clit, I moaned, beginning to grind on him. I undulated, impaled, using his shaft.

He pressed his lips to the spot where my shoulder met my neck. With an openmouthed kiss, he licked my sweat, rasping against my skin, "*Mine*."

Ay, Dios mío, it is *so good!* The message he'd written was true. *Too good.* I needed my boundary!

As if he knew I wanted to resist him, he commanded, "*Surrender*," as his fingers covered my clit, rubbing side to side, fast, hard.

My eyes slid closed, my mind shutting down, almost like that headspace I'd craved.

Sensation ruled me.

I was aware of his cock, his hands—and his rumbling voice. I held on to the sound of it, as if he were leading me home. I moved on him like I'd never moved, keening his name. I craned my head back to get his mouth on mine, knowing he'd share the taste of my sweat and brand my mind with memories.

When I came, I was shaken, my cry against his lips plaintive. *Don't do this to me.*

In answer, his warm cum flooded me, as if to repeat, "*Mine.*"

For how long . . . ?

His body quaked with after-shudders, his arms locked around me. He clutched me tightly, as if I were a treasure he'd never part with.

"That merely took the edge off." He nipped my earlobe. "I'm nowhere close to satiation." There was a smile in his voice. Someone was having a great morning.

Setting me up for a crash. I disentangled myself from his arms, levering myself off his still hard dick.

He hissed in a breath. "That was . . . abrupt."

Without looking at him, I stepped from my shorts, toeing off my shoes and socks. I made my way to the shower.

Denying my escape, he joined me under the cascade, dragging me close. He peered down at my face, but I gazed away.

"Ah. I think you enjoyed that *too* much. I know I did. Does it make you uneasy?"

"Why do you have to sleep with me?" I demanded. "You don't even like me. You keep your things in the master bedroom. Why don't you keep yourself there?"

"Hmm. Maybe we should both sleep in my room, the *master's* bedroom. Perhaps I'll have your treadmill and your things transferred."

I'd wanted separation—not more closeness! "You said you'd be done with me. Why aren't you? How long will you keep me?"

His hands dropped to my ass, palms covering my curves. "I've observed that you're much more affectionate with the belt—"

"Not today!"

"Why?"

"I need to think."

"Then I'll have to coax your affection myself?" He leaned down and pressed his lips to mine so tenderly, kissing me and kissing me and kissing me . . . until I was docile in his hands. He soaped my body, bathing me, exploring. Every touch was its own seduction.

Why was he bothering to seduce me? I was here at his "disposal." What was his game now?

Soon I was trembling for it again.

He lifted me. "Wrap your legs around me." With a forearm under my ass and an arm looped around my shoulders, he worked me on his cock.

When we came, with our foreheads together as we shared breaths, I wondered, *Why fight this . . . ?*

Once we'd dressed, an extravagant breakfast spread awaited us on the pool deck. He'd ordered in advance, what looked like every item on the menu.

"To discover which are your favorites," he explained.

When he smiled at me, I realized he was responding to my own grin. Dick. *Why fight?*

Yet then his phone rang. Sevastyan answered with a resigned exhalation. Soon his expression darkened. Must be Dmitri.

I got the impression that Máxim had lost himself for a while this morning, and now was being harshly reminded of . . . something.

He looked increasingly angry—*at me*, as if I was the one who'd distracted him, from whatever it was he should never forget.

I sat on the couch, reading as a breeze fluttered the curtains and teased the curls around my face. I'd noticed that Sevastyan preferred the doors and windows open whenever possible, so I'd opened the line of them facing the pool.

Since that phone call, he'd been distant, his mood clearly depressed.

All morning, he and I had passed each other, gravitating toward one another, yet saying nothing. He'd read this same business journal by the pool while I was swimming. Or he'd *appeared* to. In reality, he'd been very interested in my bathing suit—a white one-piece woven from thin strips of material. His fascinated gaze had followed the webbing as it moved with my body.

Now he sat on the other couch with a newspaper open, but he didn't read it. His ocean-blue eyes were grave as he stared out at the matching water. What was he mulling over?

I could swear he struggled with a decision.

He checked his phone, texted something, then

abruptly stood. He looked at me, parting his lips. Thinking better of whatever he was about to say, he turned toward the door. "Vasili will be outside." Then he left me.

Qué? I was going to be alone on Christmas Eve? Yet another miserable, lonely one.

If he was teeing me up for a crash, I should at least get the benefit of company today.

For the last three holidays, I'd been undergoing the hard task of rebooting. The Christmas before those, Edward had left me to go on an "unexpected business trip." Probably a vacation with Julia that I'd unwittingly funded.

I thought back to the last Christmas I'd enjoyed. I'd cooked with *mi madre*, a traditional *Nochebuena* dinner.

Maybe I should cook today? I rose and strolled to the kitchen, checking pots, pans, and equipment. There were four convection ovens, warming drawers, two microwaves, and a steam oven—all brand-new and hi-tech.

I hadn't been in a fully functioning kitchen in ages—had never been in one as modern as this—and I missed cooking. I could order ingredients through Alonzo.

Preparing a meal would relax me, setting my mind right. That was the only reason I would do it. Not because I wanted to show off for Sevastyan.

He probably wouldn't even return until late. I'd known he would want to spend the holidays with someone other than me!

His loss. I'd treat Vasili and his battalion of body-guards to thank them for their protection.

I called Alonzo, listing all the ingredients and equipment I needed asap, everything from mint sprigs to a rolling pin, from food processors to meat ther-mometers.

An hour later, when several attendants arrived with bags and boxes, Vasili furrowed his bald head at me again.

I shrugged. Turning the surround sound to a Ha-vana station, I tied on my new apron.

To bad weather, good face.

I fried bacon, peeled sweet potatoes, and sim-mered brown sugar with anise seeds. I toasted almonds. I rolled dough and cut circles for crab *croquetas*. I chopped mint for mojitos. The entire floor smelled incredible.

I was singing "*Fuentecilla Que Corres*" as I put a spiced pork roast into the oven.

"What's this?" Sevastyan asked, making me jump.

I almost dropped the roast, one of three I was cooking. "A Cuban Christmas dinner." He'd returned!

"What's on the menu?"

"*Lechón asados,* pork roasts drenched in *mojo; lan-gostinos con salsa rosa,* prawns with pink sauce; *arroz congri,* beans and rice; *tostones,* fried sweet plantains; and crab *croquetas.* For dessert, I'm making *buñuelos,* fried sweet dough; *turrón de Navidad,* nougat almond candies; and *boniatillo,* sweet potato pudding."

He smirked. "So now you'll cook to get back into my good graces?"

I pressed my fingers to my chest. "I'm sorry; did you think any of this was for you?"

"You're preparing enough for an army."

"*Tengo mucha hambre. Es todo para mí.*"

"You're very hungry? And it's all for you?"

While he was picking up Spanish at lightning speed, the only Russian I knew was *blyad´, prostitutka, dushen'ka,* and *kotyonok.* "All for me. You couldn't handle my food. Dessert alone would make you have an orgasm *espontánea.*" To taunt him, I sampled a flaky *croqueta* I'd just fried up.

Before I could stop him, he'd snagged one, taking a bite. His lids went heavy, and he chewed slowly. "I'll expect dinner at seven. Do not be late." *Croqueta* in hand, he turned to go.

Ordering me? "*Pendejo!*" I tossed a handful of toasted almonds at the back of his head.

He paused, then continued on.

With a roll of my eyes, I got back to work. Though I kept the music going and I sang as I cooked (with a voice that no one would write home about), Sevastyan remained near the kitchen all afternoon, even when talking on the phone and reading business proposals.

Over the day, he relaxed by degrees. A time or two, I caught him doing nothing but staring at sailboats. His piercing gaze had been at ease, his complicated mind lost to daydreams.

In contrast, I grew nervous, as if I had a date later—when in fact, he'd simply commanded dinner. At six, he'd headed to the master bedroom without a word.

I'd finished everything, stowing dishes in the warming drawers, and I'd even packed heavy boxes for Vasili and his guys. When I called the man inside for pickup, he'd eyed my offering warily.

Speaking slowly, I assured Vasili, "This food is one hundred percent not drugged because I couldn't find any drugs."

He grated, "*Spasiba.* Thank you."

One more word in my Russian lexicon. "There are written instructions inside. If you put pink sauce on anything other than prawns, I will kick your Russian ass, *comprendes?*"

He exhaled, grudgingly saying, "Christmas no good for boss."

"What does that mean?"

"Boss want keep you. Okay. You keeped. Now fix Christmas."

That's all he would say.

CHAPTER 23

Fix Christmas? In the shower, I mulled over that curious exchange. Some people hated the holidays. I should.

This would explain why Sevastyan's mood had been deteriorating. When I'd brought up the subject of Christmas, he'd snapped, *Do not remind me!*

The idea of him in pain bothered me. *Really* bothered me.

Because I was an idiot.

He'd told me he would keep me till he could shake what he felt for me; while he worked to recover from his interest, Catarina was sinking deeper into infatuation.

Why else would I take pains with my appearance? After my shower, I donned a strapless red dress, along with the only jewelry I had: my earrings and arm cuff from my first night here. I wore my hair up in a loose knot and applied eye makeup and lip gloss.

Feeling silly for taking the trouble, I frowned into

the mirror. This was just a meal between a mobster and his prisoner (one he considered to be a lying *prostitutka*).

Still, I got to the dining room early, lighting the many candles inside and the torchlights on the adjoining balcony. I carted dishes to the table, then opened the room's doors and windows for Sevastyan—allowing in the sound of waves.

When he joined me, I smiled to see he'd worn slacks and a blazer, dressing up as well. That meant a lot. I told him, "I've decided to share some of my food with you, because I didn't get you anything else. I was debating a tall, blond blow-up doll—or a goldfish."

"I have a closet full of blond blow-up dolls, and goldfish travel poorly on airplanes. Dinner was a wise choice."

I grinned. "Mojito or wine, *Ruso*?"

"Vodka."

"Not on your life. Obey my playground rules, or take your balls elsewhere."

Raised brow. "Mojito."

I poured him one. When he sampled my concoction, I could tell he liked it. We sat, and I served him from the many dishes, detailing the main ingredients in each.

With his first bite of roast, he seemed to be stifling his reaction. "And on top of everything else, you can cook. Did you learn only from home, or did you have schooling too?"

"Only home."

He ate everything on his plate, so I served him seconds. But when he pushed his plate to me for thirds, I said, "There's a lot of dessert."

His first taste of *turrón* made him groan. Once he'd eaten that and a helping of pudding and two *buñuelos,* he said, "I didn't come spontaneously, but it was touch and go for a while."

I laughed over the rim of my mojito.

"You could be a chef," he said.

"That would be exciting. But I think I'd prefer your job as mogul, so I could dominate the world."

"You think you could handle my job?"

"I think you'd be surprised."

He rose, crossing to the sideboard. "I doubt that. I know how smart you are." He returned to his seat with a bottle of vodka and two shot glasses. "Cuban dinner, Russian after drinks." He poured.

Oh boy.

"*Za zdoroviye,*" he said. "To your health."

"*Salud.*" I drank my glass, coughing.

As he poured for us again, he asked, "Whose meal did I enjoy?"

"Pardon?"

"You would've cooked this for friends or family over the holidays. Maybe the lover I took you from." He shot his glass.

"The kitchen inspired me." I drank mine, with another wince.

"What's so remarkable about it?"

"The appliances." They worked. Also, the pots

weren't dedicated to flood prevention. "Why are you so convinced there's someone else?"

"You respond to two things: money and pleasure. I give you both, yet you hold yourself back."

I frowned. "There's got to be more than that."

"Why *wouldn't* you have a partner? If you didn't choose a man from outside your work, then one of your clients would have snapped you up."

"You sound so certain."

"When you fuck your clients"—that muscle ticked in his jaw—"you . . . affect them. But you would have me believe that not one has kept you?" He poured another round. "I see you, hear you, smell you, *feel* you. You should be haunted by men."

I almost gave a bitter laugh. If only he knew.

Edward had been on my mind more and more. Though he'd acted the gentleman, never using bad language, never raising his voice, he'd been eager to murder me. Now that he'd nursed his rage for years, what would he do?

Sometimes I swore I had an animal sense that he was closing in—

"You're doing it even now!" Sevastyan slammed down his glass. "Your eyes go distant whenever you think of him! That drives me insane!"

"I am in no way thinking about a lover."

"Why should I believe that, or anything you say?" He poured more vodka.

"I suppose you shouldn't. You have no reason to believe me."

"Are you being sarcastic? Ridiculing my inability to trust? I didn't simply wake up one day and decide to be like this. The last time I trusted someone's word, I was cursed to pay for the rest of my life."

"What does that mean?" How had he paid?

Silence.

How exactly did Vasili expect me to "fix Christmas" when Sevastyan wouldn't talk to me? "Fine. Forget it." I rose to clear the table.

"And you clean as well?" His tone was half-cutting, as if he intended to be rude but didn't quite commit.

"Oh, I'm a real *pro* at cleaning." When I'd finished with the dishes and had stored a mountain of leftovers, I returned.

He remained in the dining room, peering into his drink. Had he polished off the first bottle and started on another one?

I sat beside him. "You're hurting. I don't like it."

"Ah, the escort with a heart of gold."

I narrowed my eyes at him. Was insulting me *his* way of putting distance between us? Like the boundaries I was failing to maintain? "*Por Dios*, it's all pumpkins and carriages with you."

"You think me moody?"

I'd just told Ivanna about his hot and cold moods. "Yes, I do."

My answer surprised him? "All the world considers me a silver-tongued charmer—except for my Katya."

"Tell me what's on your mind, *Ruso*."

It took him a while to reply. "Ghosts of the past. You don't want to hear my drunken ramblings."

"Try me."

He pushed my vodka shot toward me. "How old were you when you had that memory of making paella?"

Random question. "I was almost four." I downed the glass, wincing less.

"What time of year was it?" Another pour for each of us.

Where was he going with this? "Right after Christmas. I remember because it was before the 'red scarf war.'"

"What was that?"

Between the mojitos and the vodka, I found my tongue loosening. Or maybe the candlelit room and the sound of the ocean influenced me. Maybe this man did. "*Mima*, my grandmother, knitted a red scarf for me, and I loved it to death, smugly wore it everywhere. I even slept in it. My mother wanted to take it away, believing it was a symbol of my pride. She often assigned meaning to things, said nothing happened by chance." In that, I might agree with her.

"Go on."

"Though I was so young, I somehow knew I was fighting for more than the scarf. I could not lose that battle." I sighed, glancing up. "I'm boring you. Your life is far too exciting for my silly story to be of interest."

He met my gaze, all intensity. "You will tell me the rest, Katya. Now."

Well. I cleared my throat. "I ran from her, threatening to sail away and never come home. I hid outside past dark. *Mima* was terrified. I only weighed about thirty pounds, and it was cold that night. She intervened with *mi madre.* When she called out that I could keep it, I came home and slept in it that night. Years later, my mother told me she regretted not taking it from me— she was convinced she could've curbed my pride right in that moment. She could've made me meek and dutiful."

"Then if you'd lost the war, I never would have met you."

If not for my pride and rebelliousness, I never would've latched onto Edward. Though I do believe my mother had suffered from a degenerative disease— she'd presented symptoms before Edward and Julia had descended upon us—I didn't know how much longer she could've survived. "True. My life would've turned out very differently."

"Do you wish you'd lost the war?"

"I don't think I'll know that until my entire life has played out." I just hoped that wouldn't be in my early twenties.

He rotated his glass on the table. "I would've been thirteen at that time."

"What were you doing? Riding horses and chasing girls?"

It was like a pall fell over him. "Not at all."

"Then what?" He didn't answer. "Sevastyan, I've told you something. It's your turn to talk."

He finished his drink, pouring us another round. "My older brother is marrying an American girl. Roman—excuse me, he goes by *Aleksandr* now—hasn't known her that long. Their wedding is very rushed."

I let Sevastyan get away with the change of subject. "How do you feel about that?"

"I understood his motivations to secure her for his own. Natalie's lovely and kind, speaks Russian fluently, and was a PhD student. Also, she's wealthier than I am."

While Máxim was screwing around with the broke-ass, fugitive hooker.

Oh, to be rolling again. Though my family had never come close to having a *billion* dollars, the worth of Martinez Beach continued to skyrocket.

"Aleksandr has changed for her. For the better." Máxim sounded contemplative, like his words only skimmed the surface of what was going on in his head. "I didn't think it was possible for men our age to change. What do you think? It's your job to know men."

"If the incentive is strong enough, I think some can change." Just not a sociopath like Edward.

"You make it sound so simple. Aleksandr wanted her more than he wanted his old ways, so he cast them aside?" He drank his shot.

I joined him. "Maybe it is that simple."

"He told me that he'd revealed everything of himself to her. The good and the bad. He unburdened himself, is now free of secrets." Máxim poured yet again. "I envied him bitterly. He also told me he knew—within a day of seeing Natalie—that he would love no other woman. That she was it for him. Do you think it's possible for a man to know such a thing so early?"

What a strange turn for this conversation. "I think you can have that feeling. But I don't know if it will last."

"If you saw the two of them together, you'd know they will stand the test of time," he said. "Just before I flew here, I visited them in her home state of Nebraska. He'd invited me there to ask me to be his best man."

"Did that surprise you?"

"Utterly."

"Is he in the *mafiya* like you?" I asked.

"In the years we were parted, he became a gunman, and I became the head of my own operation. Not quite rivals, but certainly not allies."

"Gunman? As in a hit man?"

"He'd probably prefer the term *enforcer.* He was basically a soldier for his boss, fighting against a rival syndicate. But no longer."

"And you want to go into business with him."

"The more I get to know him, the more I see he is ruthless but honorable. For all his faults, he's an honest man. The idea of partnering with someone I could actually trust is mind-boggling to me. Together we could take over Russia. But he doesn't trust *me* yet. Two months ago, he feared having his fiancée in the same room with me."

"Why would he ask you to be his best man?"

"At Natalie's prodding, I'm sure."

"Why did he feel that way about you?"

"He heard I'd turned into a callous man who enjoyed playing with others' lives. He believed I had grown up to take after our father—or at least the coldhearted, scheming side of him. We despised our father."

Had that man whipped Máxim's back? "Was Aleksandr right about you? Being scheming and coldhearted?"

He gave a humorless laugh. "Yes. It's called being a politician. Though I do admit to goading Aleksandr. When he thought me a danger to him, I gave him no reason to disbelieve it. Not for many years."

A danger? "Why?"

"Maybe because it amused me."

Por Dios. "Why were you separated from your brothers?"

He skirted the question, saying, "Only from one. Dmitri and I remain close."

They talked often enough.

"With Natalie at his side, Aleksandr improves. But Dmitri . . ." He trailed off.

"What?"

"He's angry and damaged by events in the past. I struggle with accepting that he always will be."

Those same events must have something to do with Máxim's scars. Did Dmitri bear similar ones? Did Aleksandr? "I'm sorry."

"I sit in the middle between two brothers. One tells me the future can be bright, and the other tells me the past will darken all of our days. What do you have to say about that?"

"Both could be right. It all depends on what kind of man *you* are."

Quiet.

"Máxim, what if Dmitri turned his life around, despite his past? A sword has to know the anvil and hammer just to be born, no? What if he realized that if he could overcome whatever makes him angry and damaged, the victory could be the very thing that makes him stronger?" I could only hope this for my-self. *Better things await you. . . .*

"Understand me," Sevastyan grated, "I would do *anything* for that."

"Would you? Then why don't you do it first, then show him how?"

A gust of breath left his lips. "You led me right into that, didn't you?"

I held his gaze. "Somebody needed to."

He stared at me, silent, for what felt like an hour. Then he abruptly rose and left the room.

"You're welcome for dinner," I muttered. "So glad you enjoyed it. Same time next year?" Furious with myself for thinking we'd been making progress, I headed to the torchlit balcony.

The air was as warm as on our first night in the pool. At the balcony rail, I gazed out.

Somewhere down the beach, a band played Latin music, soft strains reaching me. Sailboats dotted the dark water, their masts alight for Christmas.

I heard him joining me. Without a word or a touch he stood behind me, so close I could perceive the heat from his body.

We stayed like that for long moments. The tempta-tion to sink back against him and tug his arms around me grew irresistible.

Movement. I blinked down. He'd draped a breath-taking string of pearls around my neck. Each pearl gleamed in the torchlight. The strand must have cost a fortune. Why would he give me this?

His lips brushed across my nape in the tenderest kiss.

This was what he'd been debating all day! He'd vacillated about whether to give the escort a present, then left to pick it up.

When he turned to go, I caught his hand. "Why?"

He pulled away, but I heard him mutter, "Because this is the best Christmas I've ever had."

CHAPTER 24

"*H*ere," Sevastyan said gruffly as he handed me a state-of-the-art laptop.

It was Christmas morning, day eight of my retreat, and I'd been reading a business journal on the couch when he approached. "Another gift?" I was happier that he was talking to me than I was over the new computer.

Last night, before I could ask him anything, he'd left the hotel in a T-shirt and shorts, coming back two hours later, sweating and sandy. I'd been disappointed to miss a chance to run with him on the beach. Then he'd introduced me to aggressive, teeth-clattering, sweaty-man sex, and I'd forgiven him.

"Yes, another gift," he said.

"Then *spasiba*, Máxim." Oh, I could tell the Russian liked that.

"*Pozhaluysta.* You're quite welcome. But it comes with a catch. There's a folder of real estate proposals that have been submitted to me." He sat beside me, all casual, setting up his own laptop. "I'm going to assess them. If you like, you can look at them as well, and give me your take."

"You want my opinion?"

"As long as I have you here, I'll take advantage of your brain."

As long as he had me. How long, how long, how long? That reminded me of our ongoing mirror messages. In answer to my *gonna miss this ass* note, he'd written: *Good thing I own that ass.*

I'd replied: *The door will hit it on my way out.*

Though I'd tried to sound like my heart was still bulletproof, I could see myself *falling* for this guy. Not just an attachment. The real deal.

No, no, Cat. In three days, we'd be going our separate ways; I only had to resist him till then. Besides, my impulse to fall meant I should do no such thing. *Science!* "You know this computer has Wi-Fi. You're trusting me not to send out an e-mail SOS?"

"*Da.*"

What had brought about this turnaround? "We're going to . . . work together? Vetting proposals?" I couldn't stop the grin spreading across my face.

"You're happier than you were the day you ordered all your new things. The prospect of work trumps your bout of consumerism?"

"Absolutely."

"You'll look at them, then? And you won't give me fifteen pages of *fuck you fuck you fuck you*?"

My grin deepened. "I will look at these, just to keep you straight. After all, if you lose your fortune, I'll have nothing to swindle from you."

The left corner of his lips curved. "Have your fun. Then do your bloody work. . . ."

For hours, we read as a breeze blew in off the ocean. By midday, I had a pencil in my bun, his hair was mussed, and my feet rested on his thighs. Again I felt that strange level of ease with him, that sense of déjà vu. I still made a valiant effort to keep up my last boundary, but being with him like this was a battering ram to any wall I tried to maintain.

At lunch, we took a break, enjoying sex, leftovers, and coffee, then set back to work. I was able to go online and look up rents and property taxes, liens and foreclosures.

By sunset, there were printouts all over the floor, and I'd decided this was my best Christmas Day ever.

"Did you make any headway?" He rolled his head on his neck.

I slid him a cocky grin. "I completed cursory determinations on all nine proposals, *querido*. I was about to play solitaire while I waited on you."

"Let's see them."

"You want to read them? Now?" I was suddenly nervous.

He snagged my computer. "Now."

As he scanned my assessments, I studied his face. At times, he raised his brows. What did that mean? Wait, was that an unconscious nod? Damn, he read fast. Once, that left corner of his lips tilted for an instant.

Now that I'd been given the chance to impress him, I wanted to succeed! He'd liked my brain—wanted to take advantage of it. Would he still?

He raised his face and turned that penetrating gaze to me. "We matched on all but one," he said, impressed.

Even as my toes curled with pleasure, I fake-examined my nails. "Oh, did my baby boy get one wrong?"

His eyes grew lively in that way I loved. "You didn't ask me questions; you simply assessed proposals. Did you learn from all those econ books you read?"

My finance minor had actually been of more help today. "I learned a lot from those books." Bob and weave.

"But why did you recommend moving forward on the fifth proposal?" A block of run-down apartment complexes. "These aren't class A, B, or even C. I'd deem them class S for 'shithole.' That gulag you wanted to visit probably has more amenities."

Bingo. My bus route to one of my cleaning gigs passed those apartments, and they reminded me of my own.

"The numbers are marginal at best," he said. "Tell me your reasoning."

The Shadwell Theory. "Gross mismanagement." Emphasis on *ooh, gross*. "The managers are probably shaking down the tenants each month and under-reporting the rents collected. If you got even a semi-honest crew in there, you could lower rents, increase repairs and maintenance, and you'd still make more. Tenants are happy, owners are happy."

"*Lower* rents." He was looking at me in that keen way of his.

"It's just an idea." I bit my lip. "The property is in foreclosure. Banks like to clear their books of bad debts by year's end, so if you offered cash this week, you could steal it. Or so I've heard. There are tax implications as well—oh, wait, *la mafia Rusa* probably doesn't worry about taxes much."

His keen expression deepened.

You're talking too much, Cat. Muzzle it. To distract him, I said, "Can I see your takes?"

He handed over his own computer.

I read his notes and determinations, and nearly orgasmed at how his brain worked. *Boundaries!* "Not bad for a rookie."

"Glad you approve."

I was about to suggest we take "*un cafecito*," a coffee break for caffeine and sex—not necessarily in that order—when he stood and stretched.

As he headed toward the kitchen, he tossed over his shoulder, "You're going to the wedding with me."

"*Qué???*"

CHAPTER 25

*H*eart in my throat, I followed him.

He was at the leftovers again. "Are we out of the almond candies? Who ate all of them?" He glanced up from the fridge with a dark look. "Vasili, you prick." He turned to me. "It's your fault you fed him. Now he'll be like a stray dog coming around for our handouts."

"Sevastyan, let's be reasonable. Of course I can't go to the wedding." Did he expect me to wait in the hotel room while he went to the ceremony and festivities?

"You can, and you will." He took out the prawns, licking pink sauce off his thumb. "Now that my Cat's out of the bag, there's no reason for you not to be my date."

Date? Excitement filled me. Then realities weighed in. "It's not just a wedding. It's your brother's. If anyone found out what I am"—a *prostitutka*—"they'd consider it a slight."

And how would I fare at a wedding—when the

last one I'd been to was my own doomed courthouse ceremony?

He pulled out two plates, setting them down. "What you are? You're a beautiful, intelligent young woman."

Was he finally looking past my being an escort?

As soon as the thought occurred, he said, "I expect a heated negotiation." He grabbed me by the waist and plopped me onto the counter. "What will it take? Cash and jewels? You'll need clothes to wear." He wedged his hips between my thighs.

Confusion. "What are we doing here, *Ruso*? Why this turnaround? I'm your quote-unquote prisoner, re-member?"

"You can still be my quote-unquote prisoner in Nebraska."

"You hate me except for when we have sex."

"When we read proposals, I like you okay. When you sing and cook, I like you."

"You're teasing me?" The whole reason I'd been able to handle this time with him was because it had an expiration date! All I'd had to do was guard my heart for a little while longer, and I'd be free. I could avoid the inevitable crash. Now he was talking about extend-ing my time—and deepening things between us.

He really wanted to introduce me to his family?

No, that didn't matter! He might feel a connection to me, and I might even be unique to him. But his in-terest would fade. At heart, the hobbyist was a player, could have any woman in the world. Soon enough, he'd get back out there.

I crossed my arms over my chest. "I'm not going. When you leave, so do I. It was always our unspoken agreement."

He gave a laugh. "Was it?"

"On the twenty-eighth, *I* am going home. You are going north. That's my final say in this."

"Hmm. I can be very persuasive, Katya."

"There is absolutely nothing you can say or do that will change my mind on this."

The look in his eyes said *challenge offered, challenge fucking accepted.*

"*W*hat the hell is this, Sevastyan?"

"Shouldn't it be obvious, *dushen'ka*?" The bastard was tying me up in his bed.

After we'd eaten, he'd told me, "You're moving to the master bedroom tonight."

"Why?"

"That's what I want."

We had talked about it before, so I hadn't been suspicious. I *should* have been suspicious. Because half an hour later, I lay naked with my arms secured over my head.

He'd started with kissing, stripping me and getting me mindless. By the time he'd drawn back and I'd blinked open my eyes, my right wrist had been encircled by a black leather cuff with shining buckles and a metal ring. I'd slapped at him with my other hand, but he'd chuckled at my attempts, easily buckling the thing on my wrist. Then he clipped the ring on the cuff to a strap attached to the headboard. With even more ease, he'd forced my left arm over my head.

He'd wanted me in this room because he'd prepared the bed for bondage. The *master's room*. I'd never seen it coming.

Now he was going for one of my ankles. Two more straps snaked out from the footboard.

I kicked at him and twisted. "I didn't agree to this! Why do this?"

He snatched my ankle. Though I fought him, he cuffed it, buckling it. "I'm going to persuade you to go to the wedding with me." He pinned my leg down, fastening the cuff to its awaiting strap.

Even as I struggled, I gazed around for that crop, dreading it. The devil would probably make my whipping pleasurable, but I didn't want him to do to me what he'd done with all the other escorts. "Untie me! Damn you, I don't want to be cropped like the others."

He snagged my other ankle. "What we do is so far removed, Katya. You might think of them, but I don't." He buckled the last cuff, then secured it. "In any case, we're trying something new."

I was now spread like a starfish, black leather around my wrists and ankles. Immobilized.

"Look at you bound up for me." He grasped a lock of my hair from the pillow. "So beautiful."

I couldn't believe this was happening! Yes, I'd said I would explore my sexuality, but this was *una locura!* Crazy! "If you aren't going to whip me, then what will you do?" Maybe I could tolerate it if he lost the crop.

"I had an acquaintance who tormented his subs in this manner. I never comprehended the appeal before." He raked his gaze over me. "Now I completely understand."

Torment? "The appeal of what?"

"Forced orgasms."

"Wh-what are you talking about?"

"Sexually tormenting you. Just the idea gets my cock so hard." It was a rigid line in his pants.

"I didn't agree to this!"

"Have I steered you wrong yet?" He swiftly undressed. As he moved to the top of the bed, his huge shaft wagged, catching my gaze and making me want.

I bit my lip.

"You'll enjoy it." He flashed white teeth. "Eventually."

Chills raced over me.

He leaned down to kiss my forehead. "I'll be right back." He left the room, returning with a small bag and a magic wand—a plug-in electrical vibrator. I'd seen one at Ivanna's. She'd told me the vibrations were so intense they could make your teeth chatter.

Forced orgasms. With a magic wand. I squirmed. "You just had one of those lying around?"

"When I ordered the belt, I got carried away, buying all kinds of things for you. The belt distracted me for days, but I see now that I need to break out more *acute* tools."

"L-let's talk about this, *Ruso*."

"You can stop me at any time. All you have to do is agree to go to the wedding with me. Very simple."

"You devil! You can't do this! You're taking away my free will—again!"

"I didn't have to ask. I do own you now. I could compel you in other ways to go with me. But I want to hear you tell me *yes*."

"Hear me? You won't gag me? Like all the others?"

"No. Never. You're mine—which means I want to catch your every whimper, sigh, gasp, moan, and scream." He plugged the wand into a bedside outlet, turning it on and off as he raised his brows. "Powerful. And this one is unique—it has a range of different settings."

I jutted my chin. "I can take whatever you dish out, and I still won't go with you, *chulo*!"

At my renewed challenge, his cock pulsed, and a glistening drop appeared on the head. "We'll see." From that bag, he removed a roll of something that looked like electrical tape, then positioned the wand along my thigh—bulbous head *up*.

Realization. "You're going to strap this to me?"

"Uh-huh."

I flailed that leg as much as I could. "No, no!"

Despite my efforts, he taped several loops around it, forcing the bulb against my lips. I gawked at the menacing thing.

From the bag, he removed lengths of black rope.

"What's that for? There's nothing left of me to tie!"

"To secure your toy." I bucked my hips, but he successfully knotted rope around the wand, then up around my waist, cinching it tight. The bulb pressed seamlessly against my pussy, the top edge hitting my clit. "I don't want this getting loose, no matter how hard you struggle."

"Struggle?" Even as I said this with dread, my nipples hardened into tight points.

Of course he noticed. "They want to be sucked." He leaned down and wrapped his lips around one, flicking his tongue all over it while I fought not to moan. Then to my other nipple. Then back to the first. He licked and sucked and ran his stubble over them, the edge of his teeth.

I whimpered when he released me.

"They couldn't be harder. You're ready."

"For what?"

From that cursed bag, he withdrew a silver chain—with *clamps* on each end. "For these."

"No, no!" When he reached for me, I tried to make my chest concave, but he grasped my right breast, holding it steady.

"If it gets to be too much, just say *yes*. That's your safe word."

I narrowed my eyes.

"That's what I thought. My fiery Cat's back—to take anything I can 'dish out.'" He carefully applied the clamp to my nipple, close to my areola. I trembled with dread, but he didn't release his grip all at once. He slowly allowed it to tighten, the pressure increasing by degrees. "There you go. Relax into it."

I promised myself I would scream if it got to be too much, but I still hadn't by the time he let go of the clamp. I sucked in a breath. "*OW!*" My toes curled, my fists clenching. "Too tight!" It hurt, a lightning intensity focused right in my nipple.

But I was . . . taking it?

"The pain will get better, love. Breathe through it."

I released a shaky exhalation, and soon the pain did dull to a more measured pressure. I watched him preparing my other breast, readying its clamp.

Que intrigante. How intriguing. The shining metal in his hand dazzled me. What my body could handle amazed me. The sound of the slinky chain turned me on.

What was happening to me?

When he began affixing the second clamp, I gritted my teeth. "Ow, ow, ow!" I hissed in another breath, fists clenching again.

"Do you want me to stop?" He started letting up his grip.

Did I? This focused intensity was kind of . . . mind-blowing. But still, it *was* pain.

"All you have to do is say *yes.*"

"*Pendejo!*" I kicked one leg against its strap in frustration.

He released his hand.

"*OW!* They hurt, Máxim!"

He tucked my hair behind my ear. "Do they both?"

The first was growing numb. Oh. They both would then.

"Look at yourself," he said smugly. "How do you like variety now, *querida*?"

I peered down at my body. Damn him, the view shouldn't arouse me this much. The sight of my clamped nipples lit a fire in me! To reclaim the initial bite—and to wipe that smug look off his face—I shimmied my quivering, adorned breasts.

His lips parted on a stunned groan. "Do that again. Show me your new chain, *kotyonok*." His gaze was rapt.

I shimmied once more, showing off.

He rasped, "You're proud, aren't you? You should be exceedingly proud."

"You like me clamped and tied in your bed?"

"Right now I like you very much." He trailed the backs of his fingers down my body toward the wand.

Oh, no, the clamps had distracted me from the threat of that machine, just like they'd distracted me from the fact that I was taking part in *bondage*!

"Remember, one word stops this." He kissed my thigh . . . then turned on the wand.

I'd never felt anything like it! The thing was *increíble*!

Sensations bombarded me—the vibrations, the pressure of those biting clamps, the sound of the leather creaking as I pulled against my bonds. I shivered with awe. "What are you doing to me?"

In a devil's voice, he said, "You love your toy, don't you?"

I couldn't stop myself from nodding dreamily. "I *love* it."

"But you'll hate it soon too."

Reminded of his intentions, I fought to hold out as long as possible. Perspiration dotted my skin from the battle. Need mounted, building . . . building . . . "Oh God, oh God!"

He looked transfixed, delighted. "You're about to come for me in your bonds and your clamps. It's good, isn't it?"

Building . . . building . . . "Yes!" My head thrashed, my hair whipping.

"I am giving you pleasure. You're about to scream—for me. Never forget that."

Building . . .

The bastard plucked at the chain—

I shattered. I levitated. "*Máxim!*" Deep and wet and consuming, my orgasm made my back bow. My bonds snapped tight as my tits shook and my chain rattled.

I dimly heard some of his hoarse words: *abandoned . . . lust . . . slave . . .*

Once I'd regained lucidity, I bit out, "I will kill you for this when I get free!" Had he really said *slave*?

Breathing heavy, he grated, "Not quite what I'd hoped to hear." He reached for the wand, dialing it up a degree.

"*No!* P-please give me a minute." I came down from that first climax, only to hurtle toward one even more powerful. Sweat now slicked my skin, dampening the hair at my temples. "Just a second, *Ruso!*" My clit felt like it was on fire. Pressure coiled low in my belly. "I can't . . . I can't . . . not so soon . . ."

The pitiless devil said, "You can. You *will*."

My next orgasm hit me in blinding waves. "*Ahh!*" I yelled from the strength of them. Over and over, my core clutched emptiness. Every time I thrashed, the clamps pinched my nipples anew.

Gradually some of the tension left my body, but not all. I cried, "*Por favor*, why do this?"

"To make you crave me as much as I crave you," he bit out, his expression dark, his eyes fierce. No longer did their color remind me of the ocean. This blue was like the hottest part of a flame. "I'll steal you from the other. Seduce you from him."

"I-I don't understand."

He turned up the setting again. The vibrations were torture/ecstasy. I'd never been more *aware* of my pussy, of my flared swollen lips, of my throbbing clit. If I worked my hips, the bulb thrummed against the inner rim of my entrance. Could I come *again*? I surrendered to it with a moan.

"That's it, *dushen'ka*."

I met his gaze as I began to grind the slick head, undulating wantonly for him.

"Does it feel good, baby?"

In a dreamy voice, I said, "It's making my pussy feel so good, Máxim."

"*Fuck*. You love the things I do to you."

I nodded earnestly. "Uh-huh."

"I pleasure your body better than any man ever has."

"You do!" I worked the head of my toy.

"That's why you'll keep giving it to me."

I closed my eyes, nodding.

"Look at me, Katya."

When I did, that wicked gleam in his gaze set me off—

"*AHH!*" I came with a desperate scream. The

chain rattled as my sweating body convulsed. I was shameless, turning my knees inward as far as they'd go, my hips humping the toy.

"*Blyad'!*" His hooded eyes went wide.

When the spasms had eased to merely electrifying, I bared my teeth at him. "What do you WANT from me?"

He clasped my face, bringing his own close. "Everything." He briefly tongued my lips. "And I'll have it out of you. Thirty-one years of misery is lifted. I'm *owed* you!"

"Wh-what does that mean?" *Can't think. Insensible.* "Please let me go!"

"Some masters would leave a submissive like this, disregarded to suffer on her own."

What? Disregard me? I had no barriers, no wall— just my vulnerable underbelly, ripe for a slice.

"But I can't." He eased his towering, naked frame down beside me, the head of his cock painting precum across my thigh. "I can't leave you." He petted my damp hair from my forehead, tenderly kissing my mouth. "I suffer with you."

"Ah, *gracias*, Máxim." Now I was thanking him? For making me weak? For putting me through agony?

But he was in agony too. His cock was swollen, veins and shaft bulging. I sensed he was just preventing himself from yanking the wand out of his way and plunging into me to end this.

I caught his gaze, pleading with mine. "L-let's both come, Máxim. I'll be good. *Por favor, mi amor?*"

He rasped, "You are utter sweetness, aren't you?"

He traced the edge of the bulb, soaked from my pussy, then offered his finger to my mouth.

I met his eyes as I sucked it lovingly.

"Utter—fucking—sweetness." He returned his finger to the bulb, then back to my lips. He kissed me at the same time, both of our tongues twining his finger—a wet, filthy kiss to trade my cream between us.

Another orgasm struck. "*Mmmm!*" I screamed against his lips. I had to break away as I writhed, my limbs snatching at my bonds.

"*Stunning.*" His breaths came even quicker, sweat lathering his own skin. "Now, what do you have to tell me, baby?"

"I can't!"

"Tell me *why* you can't. Or tell me *yes*."

"No! No! No!"

"Very well." He rose on his knees, reaching for the clamps.

"Oh, wait, wait!" I wriggled my chest, but he caught me by the breast. I shook my head wildly.

"This will hurt." He gradually released one clamp.

Blood rushed back to the peak. Currents of pain sizzled up and down my body. I went light-headed, almost passing out.

"Stay with me, Katya."

My nipple was engorged, more sensitive than it'd ever been. "Ah! N-not the other! I can't take it, you devil!"

He was merciless, hand poised over the clamp. "Tell me what I want to hear. No?" He eased the metal apart.

"No . . . leave it . . . don't!" Too late; he'd removed it. My nipples felt like they'd been *branded*. I babbled in two languages. I arched toward him, shoving the aching peaks at him for succor, for anything! "Please, PLEASE!"

"Do you need something from me, *dushen'ka*? I understand the feeling. *I* need you to say yes."

Before I gathered my wits enough to curse him, he dialed up the wand. Then he leaned down and blew on my nipples.

I shrieked and my eyes rolled back in my head . . . as I came and came and came for him. . . .

When I could focus my eyesight again, I saw him above me. His neck and chest muscles flexed, his skin sheening with sweat.

He spread his knees and began to jack his cock. "You like to watch me, don't you?"

This vision of him only increased my agony—as he well knew. "Can't—no more—*por favor*."

His legs quaked as he fucked his fist. With his other hand, he cupped his heavy sac, kneading it roughly. "Be a good girl, and tell me what I want to hear." He released his balls to reach for the wand. "Don't make me do this, baby."

"N-no, *por favor!*"

"Then tell me! Why are you so bloody determined?"

"Máxim, why do you push me??"

"Woman, you will tell—me—why!"

"Because!"

"Because why? Damn it, answer me!"

"When this ends, I want to be left in one piece!" There. I'd said it.

"Your heart in one piece?" His gaze was almost inhuman, his piercing blue eyes full of fire. "Too fucking late. You might as well enjoy the fall." The crash. He turned the dial up to the highest level.

Instant orgasm.

Relentless.

Bone-melting.

As my back bowed sharply, I screamed, "YES! I-I'll go! I'LL GO WITH YOU!"

My words were cut off by his brutal yell. He began to ejaculate, pumping semen over me.

I screamed louder as his hot cum landed like a whip over my body. He striped lashes across my belly, my toy and swollen lips, both of my breasts. My abused nipples. As I writhed beneath him, semen pooled in the dip of my collarbone and mixed with my sweat. "*Mercy!*"

He lunged for the wand's cord, yanking it from the socket, then collapsed over me.

Between heaving breaths, he said, "We leave the morning of the twenty-eighth, Katya. You have shopping to do."

CHAPTER 26

*A*fter selecting several pieces of jewelry, including pearl earrings to go with my necklace, I vacillated over a gold pair that were crazy expensive—as in *could also buy a luxury sports car* expensive. They were dangly, with the tiniest padlocks and keys at the ends.

The older male jeweler polished his glasses and said, "Take your time, dear."

Today, while Sevastyan had been making last-minute tweaks to security for his brother's wedding (how much security could one wedding need?), he'd had vendors come to the hotel. "I know you loathe shopping," he'd told me, "but you'll have to suck it up." So said the king.

After I'd been *persuaded* to attend the wedding, I'd done a risk/reward analysis. Reward: more life-changing sex, traveling, seeing snow for the first time. I would get to meet his family and friends and learn more about him. I wondered how he would introduce me, how he would act around others.

Risk: the crash. Yet I'd worked to convince myself that I couldn't possibly fall so quickly. A little over a week? It was crazy even to think about! Right? I could go, enjoy the wedding, and my heart would be just swell.

In any case, I had no choice about attending; *to bad weather* . . .

This jeweler was the last of the vendors left. He'd displayed his wares across the long dining room table, atop a roll of black velvet. Earlier, Sevastyan had strode by on his way to the study. "She'll take them." He'd waved at the entire collection.

I hastily assured the jeweler, "He's joking!"

"Of course, dear," the man had said, but we both knew Sevastyan had *not* been joking.

At Máxim's insistence, I'd filled two closets. When the stores came to you, shopping was a completely different experience. I had more shoes than I could count, luggage, boots, skirts, blouses, sweaters, snow gear, purses, an unforgettable full-length dress for the night wedding—and drawers of lingerie.

Trying on bras had been a chore because of what he'd done to me the night before. This morning, my nipples had remained swollen, and my body had felt battered. To get through my run, I'd had to pop Advil and tape my nipples with Band-Aids. Sevastyan had watched me running again (*avidly*, a lion to my gazelle). Once I'd finished, he hadn't even waited for me to pass the bed; he'd nabbed me directly off the treadmill, forcing my legs around his waist. He'd tugged up my bra, asking, "What's this?"

"Tape." I'd gasped as he yanked my shorts aside and thrust into me. "They're t-too sensitive."

"You poor thing," he'd said, but his eyes had been gleaming.

Throughout the day he'd pulled me into our room to kiss them better—sweet, gentle kisses all around my nipples. Which had just made them worse!

To add insult to injury, he'd taunted me with his mirror message. I'd last written about the door hitting my ass on the way out. His reply?

How far will you get tied to my bed?

Fucking devil! I'd replied: *Baby boy, all the way to Nebraska.*

The mirror was huge, but we were already running out of room.

Now he returned from the study, ending a phone call. "What's the hold up?" he asked me.

The money you're spending! Keeping a tally had been challenging since there were no price tags, and I had to ask each time. But I could swear he'd spent close to—I swallowed—half a million dollars on me. Whenever that figure had robbed me of breath, I'd imagined his outlay as a teeny-tiny percentage of his wealth. Everything was relative, right?

Sevastyan's gaze flicked over the earrings, and that gleam returned. He told the jeweler, "She'll absolutely take those. . . ."

Once the man had gone, Máxim said, "I've seen your take for the day. Your results were meager."

"*Por el amor de Dios.* Seriously?"

"If you don't dress to the nines, it reflects upon me. You'll begin again tomorrow morning."

"Máxim, I don't need this much! And I'm worried about your spending. If you make a market return on your billion, then you've spent more than you earned today."

In the same tone I often used with him, he said, "Ah, does my baby girl think I only have a billion liquid?"

My jaw dropped. Unreported *mafiya* income. Then I burst out laughing. "I like your sense of humor."

"I have one?"

"You bring down my house." I petted his chest. "I can't shop tomorrow anyway. I have a date with this Russian guy."

Raised brows. "Oh, do you?"

"He's really rich, so he's taking the day off to play with me."

His eyes grew lively. "What are you two going to do?"

"Spend the afternoon by the pool, grilling out on the deck. Later, he'll take me running on the beach. I'm making margaritas. And more *turrón*. He's like a bear after honey with that stuff—"

Máxim swooped me into his arms and strode for the bedroom. "Fine. You're excused from shopping." He reached around and spanked my ass while I squealed. "I won't buy you another bloody thing—it's so goddamned unpleasant."

I wriggled. "What are you going to do to me?"

"All this talk about *turrón* and honey has my mouth watering for my favorite treat. . . ."

A couple of hours later, I'd been grinning, stretching on the bed when he'd tossed me a wrapped present.

"What is it?" I tore into it. I swallowed.

He'd gotten me . . .

A red scarf.

"*I* can't believe I'm going to see snow!" I said when Máxim's jet was forty thousand feet over central Florida. I smoothed my fawn-colored skirt behind me, then sat beside him on one of the decadent leather couches. "I will, right?"

From behind a business journal, he said, "If I had a dollar for every time you checked the forecast . . . I vow to you that there will be plenty of snow. If there's not, I'll have some made."

"It blows my mind that we're going from a play-date in the sun to Nebraskan winter."

Yesterday with him had been sublime. We'd wrestled in the pool, and he'd chased me around, and I'd let him catch me for sex.

Later when I'd prepped marinade for grilling and cooked dessert, he'd stayed in the kitchen to help. He'd asked me to speak more Spanish around him. Easy enough to oblige. But did he have to pick it up so quickly? He'd been reading food packages in Spanish.

Last night he'd taken me down from the tower to go running on the beach. I'd been uneasy at first— until I'd remembered what my running partner was.

Nearly six and a half feet of hard-bodied Russian ruthlessness.

The only thing that could make me hornier from running? Covering miles with him. Luckily, I'd been rewarded with another hit of aggressive, sweaty-man sex. On the beach. Behind a palm tree.

Life could be sweet.

But I remained confused about what was going on between us. How much longer would we be together? My being a weekend date was one thing. Returning to Russia with him was outside the realm of possibility.

So why had he spent so much money on me?

This morning's message on the mirror had only confused me more. He'd responded to my *all the way to Nebraska* quip with a cryptic reply: *Why stop there?*

Máxim lowered his paper. "So you've obviously never lived where it snows. Already I know you grew up on the coast."

I forced a smile. "How's that?"

"Children in Iowa don't often tell their mother they'll sail away." The search engine had two more variables. "Perhaps you are from Miami. Or the coast of Texas. Maybe Southern California?"

When I shrugged, my new bra rubbed my nipples, and I shivered at the contact. They were still sensitive days after he'd clamped them. Since then, the peaks were constantly hard, visible even now against my red cashmere V-neck.

The devil noticed my reaction and grinned. I told him in Spanish that my revenge would be sweet and unexpected.

He set away the journal. "You should know, I called Vasili off from his investigation of you. He was very disappointed."

Máxim had? "That explains the man's behavior earlier." When he'd driven us to the executive airport in Sevastyan's Bentley Mulsanne, the bodyguard/driver/right-hand man had glowered at me. As we'd boarded the jet, he'd cast me another surly look before he'd adjourned to the cockpit. Ever protective of "boss."

I'd asked Máxim, "What will it take to get a smile out of that man?"

"Your real name and ID. That's all he wants out of life. And possibly almond candies."

Now Máxim said, "Before then, Vasili had men turn Tampa upside down. You never lived there, did you?"

"I never told you I did. Why did you call him off?"

"Because you'll confide in me. Soon."

"You sound assured." Over the last two days, he'd been making me wonder: what if I recruited Máxim's help against Edward? This morning in the bathroom, I'd gazed into the mirror to practice what I'd say. I'd attempted to murmur the words, "I'm married to a murderer who wants me dead," and only air passed my lips. My lungs had seized up, as if a weight pressed down on them.

Máxim said, "I am assured. You're learning to trust me."

What if I . . . *did*? The level of faith that would require . . . I didn't know if my withered up trust was capable of reaching that level. How could I be expected to run on a limb that was shriveled and broken?

His gaze met mine. "I want what's best for you. You can trust me."

I glanced away. That was exactly what Edward had told me when I'd said, "I don't understand why I have to sign all these papers."

For so long, I'd followed my rules, trusting no one. I'd remained alone—and alive. I'd been silent—and hidden. How could I fly in the face of that?

Over the years, I'd learned to equate secrecy with survival. In my mind, to willfully break a rule was to call Edward down upon me.

I knew it was crazy. That didn't make it any less real to me. Had my psyche been damaged by my predicament? I don't see how it couldn't have been. No one should have to go through life imagining what a knife wound would feel like. . . .

"Katya?"

"*Qué cosa?* Huh?" Clearing my throat, I changed the subject. "Vasili is very loyal. How did you meet him?"

The look Máxim gave me told me he'd allowed me off the hook. "Vasili was about to be executed for a mob hit I knew he didn't commit."

"*Por Dios.* How did you know?"

"I was blackmailing the man who ordered the hit. I struggled with the decision to save Vasili or not. It was my first major blackmail scheme, and I was poised to collect many favors from a powerful man. In the end, I anonymously mailed the evidence to Vasili's advocate. Then Vasili turned around—and somehow tracked down *me,* pointing out my vulnerabilities. Hat in hand, he asked to work for me. How could I say no?"

"That doesn't seem very heartless."

"Perhaps scheming, then? I saved his life once, and he's protected mine ever since. Forfeiting my gain was the best investment I ever made." With a heated glance, he said, "At least until you came along."

"Ha. *Qué cómico.* Speaking of investments—what are you thinking for a wedding gift?"

"A stallion for their stable. One that wasn't for sale."

Of course.

He opened his ever-present briefcase, pulling out my phone. "You get this back." He handed it to me.

"Did you break my code and read everything?"

"Code-locked phones are surprisingly secure. I could have cracked it, but I would risk damaging all your data. And again, you'll confide in me soon anyway."

I shielded the screen, entered my code, then reviewed my texts with him. I'd had no idea how much this man was going to mean to me. I added him as a contact: M Sevastyan, then I checked my voice mail. Mrs. Abernathy had left a reminder that I'd confirmed cleaning on the thirty-first.

I was listening to a message like that while flying on a private jet. *Joke's on you, Abernathy.*

I asked Máxim, "Did I earn this for good behavior?"

"In case we get separated over the weekend, and you need to call."

"When will we be separated? I thought we were all staying at the same place." A lodge built around some historic manse, a location chosen by Natalie's mother.

Máxim said, "You might go into the nearby town with Natalie and her best friend, Jessica. They're your age. I suspect you're about to make new friends."

"Non-escort friends?"

"You said it; I didn't."

"Are they stiff? Or snobby? What if they don't like me?"

"Natalie is very warm. I met Jessica on my last trip to Nebraska and found her to be . . . colorful. They're going to love you."

"Dmitri won't be there?"

"*Nyet.*"

"I got the impression that he is pissed about this wedding." The man had been blowing up Máxim's phone as usual. Over the last two days, whenever Máxim had talked to him, he'd dragged me into his lap and stroked my hair, which seemed to soothe him. That close, I could hear Dmitri yelling in Russian, sounding enraged. Máxim would talk to him in a monotone, trying to calm his disturbed brother.

"He wants nothing good for Aleksandr," Máxim said. "Marrying the lovely daughter of a legendary billionaire is quite a favorable turn for our older brother. But I've set my mind to mending the breach between Aleksandr and Dmitri. Someone recently told me I should lead by example."

"I don't know who said that, but she sounds like the smartest person in the world."

"I'm beginning to suspect so."

I tucked my boots under me on the couch. "How did Aleksandr meet Natalie?"

"Her father, Pavel Kovalev, adopted him when he was young, becoming my brother's beloved mentor."

"Aleksandr was adopted because he was separated from you and Dmitri?"

Máxim nodded, but still wouldn't expand. "Kovalev never knew he had a biological child until Natalie searched for her birth parents. When the man discovered she was his, he dispatched Aleksandr to Nebraska to watch over her."

"Why would she need to be watched over?"

"Kovalev was embroiled in a war against another *mafiya* boss, Travkin. The man learned of Natalie just when Kovalev did. Travkin put out a contract on Kovalev—and his birth daughter."

What was I walking into? Had I jumped from the frying pan into the fire?

"Two weeks after Natalie arrived in Russia, a distant cousin decided to cash in, bringing a machine gun into Kovalev's home. Desperate to protect Natalie and Aleksandr, Kovalev tried to talk down the man. The gun went off, spraying bullets. Aleksandr could have saved either Kovalev or Natalie."

"He had to choose?" I understood how quickly a pistol could go off. I couldn't imagine a machine gun.

Máxim nodded. "Aleksandr tackled Natalie to the ground. Kovalev died in front of her."

"She saw him die? And she only got to know him for half a month?" That poor girl! Though I only had impressions of my father, for two decades I'd known that I was loved by him. "What happened to the contract? Is she still in danger?"

"Not at all. My brother walked into Travkin's favorite haunt, right in the middle of all the man's muscle, and shot the fuck in the face."

"You realize you couldn't sound prouder."

"I *know*."

Máxim would have *zero* problems with what I'd accidentally done to Julia.

"Any man who would target an innocent girl like Natalie deserved what he got and worse."

Máxim, meet Edward. "Is there worse than being shot in the face?" As soon as the words left my mouth, I regretted them. I *knew* the answer. What was worse than being stabbed? Being butchered.

Máxim stilled, his tone growing icy. "You have *no* idea."

I almost shivered at his expression.

"After that, Kovalev's billion-dollar syndicate was in chaos, and Aleksandr didn't know who he could trust among Kovalev's men. He took Natalie into hiding, calling on me to help secure her father's lands and operations in Russia," Máxim said. "If not for the man's death, I would not be at this wedding."

"Why?"

"In a time of trouble, I was a ready resource. Aleksandr saw that I could be an ally, and that I hold no true malice toward him."

"I don't understand why you would. Just because he left home?"

"It's not a pretty story. One best told at another time." He pinned me with his gaze. "Are you having second thoughts about this weekend?"

"I recall having *first* thoughts, but was a victim of your 'persuasion.'"

His lids went heavy, the bulge in his pants growing. "Don't remind me. I can't touch that memory without getting hard as a rock." He exhaled. "Too late. Have you ever been fucked in a plane?"

"No," I said breathlessly. "But I think I'm about to be. . . ."

CHAPTER 27

"How goddamned quaint," Máxim grated as we wandered through our suite.

The space was large and luxurious, with a sizable bathroom and dressing area, but there *were* some kitschy touches. The mobster looked so out of place in a room with plank wood floors and Quaker quilts. Doilies covered the tops of oak tables.

"Quilts." He smirked. "Charming."

I hopped on the bed, giving him a pouty lip. "Oh, does my baby boy suffer without his Four Seasons?" There'd been a display in the lobby made out of cornstalks and a wide red ribbon. Nothing brought to mind the holidays like cornstalks.

I stretched out and made snow angels on the bed. "Just think, we're going to have to snuggle here for warmth. We'll have to build up friction." I widened my eyes. "To preserve my very life, you'll have to fuck me all night long."

"If I must. But only to save your very life."

A faint motion in the window drew my gaze past him. "Ah! It's snowing!" I leapt up and scrambled to a window seat. I'd seen it *everywhere* on the ground during our limo ride from the airport to the lodge, but hadn't seen it falling. And I still hadn't been out *in it*. "Máxim, it is *actively* snowing." Every now and then, a flake would dance by! "*Pero quién sabe por cuánto tiempo?*" But who knows for how long? "We have to go before the snowfall stops."

"I'm not sure that would count as snowfall. Once we get changed, I'll take you out—"

I started ripping off my clothes. "When will our bags get up here?"

"Our things are already here."

I tripped in the direction of the dressing room, then yanked open a closet. "All our stuff is unpacked."

"I bring a valet for events. And now we have a maid for you as well. They're currently pressing anything that needs it."

No wonder he always looked impeccable.

"Wear layers," Máxim called. "The waterproof snow gear and warm socks."

"Got it."

In minutes, I'd rifled through my stuff and changed into a red turtleneck, snow-white ski jacket, black ski pants, mittens, and boots. The pants were surprisingly thin and fit like tights. As with all pants on me, they were snug across the back. Fact of life. I had my red scarf, of course, and a cap to match it.

Once I'd dressed, I decided to tease him with my

new outfit—just a little. I skipped back to the room. "Hey, Máxim, will you look at something?"

"Hmm?" He was unbuttoning his shirt.

I turned and leaned over the bed, innocently asking, "Do these make my butt look big?"

"You little witch." He lunged for me, but I scampered over the bed. "I don't think you want to leave this room."

"No, no! I'll be good."

He hesitated, then pulled off his shirt, his expression telling me I'd been let off with a warning.

I manned the window. "The sun looks like it's about to come out. Won't the snowflakes go away? Come on, Máxim!"

"You try changing with a raging cockstand," he said, his voice husky. "Those pants of yours aren't even fair."

I turned to him. "I need to touch snow!"

He'd removed his slacks, revealing gray boxer briefs and a very swollen erection. "And clearly"—he waved at his dick—"I need to fuck you. Yet again."

"What we did on the plane barely tided you over?" I'd joined the mile-high club with a scream. Sauntering over to him, I reached down to rub the wet spot on his briefs. "Can you fuck me in the snow?"

"I like the way your mind works, Katya." He swiftly dressed in jeans, a fleece pullover, and a black ski coat.

I grabbed his hand, pulling at him to hurry down the stairs. I'd seen a sign for a "winter wonderland trail" pointing toward the back of the main lodge. "*Si me haces perdermela, no te lo perdonaré!*" If you make me miss this, I'll never forgive you.

He groused, but I could tell he was having fun.

At the exit, I turned back to scold, "*Vámos! Apúrate, Ruso*—"

I ran into a chest. Gazing up, I found a blond giant peering down at me. He had a couple of friends with him. They all looked like Nebraska farm boys. Or possibly Paul Bunyan and his brothers.

"*Disculpe*. Sorry!" I'd been chattering away, not looking where I was going.

The first one murmured, "Ma'am," with undisguised interest.

Máxim's hand tightened on mine. As we passed the trio, I glanced back to see him giving them a lethal look, which the men didn't notice because they were still gazing at me.

Outside in the courtyard, the Russian seethed. "Those fucking farmers were staring at you? Is it not obvious you're with me?"

"It was my fault for running into them."

He scanned me.

"What?"

"This is going to keep happening."

"No, no! No more locking me up, *Ruso*. Remember, this Cat's out of the bag. Weren't we going to do a cab sign . . . ?" I trailed off when a flake wafted right in front of my face.

At the edge of the courtyard was a snowy yard, beyond that a vast leafless forest. White drifts piled up against trunks and blanketed limbs. The sun was coming out, but I forgave it; icicles in sunlight were spell-binding, like diamonds on the ocean. "Oh!" I hurried into the yard, and my boots crunched!

Máxim followed me, retrieving black gloves from his pocket.

"It's . . . it's so amazing." It *was* a winter wonderland.

He frowned, as if we were looking at two different scenes. "If you say so." His phone rang.

"Dmitri?" I asked.

"*Da*. Look around for a bit. I'll try to keep this short." He turned from me to take the call.

His shoulders tensed up, all relaxation gone. As he would say: *unacceptable*. Scooping up a big handful of snow, I made my very first snowball and beaned him in the back of the head.

He stiffened even more, as if his body disbelieved. A couple of barked words ended his call. He shook out his hair as he turned to me. "*Run*."

With a laugh, I did, sprinting toward the trees. My heart raced when his footsteps crunched behind me.

I'd just made the tree line when he seized my waist, swinging me up, and we went tumbling into a snowdrift.

"Is that any way to treat your man?" He maneuvered on top of me, pinning my wrists above my head. As I caught my breath, he gazed down at me. "You are so bloody beautiful."

I grinned. "I've seen *less* handsome men." Amid all this white, the blue of his eyes was even more piercing, his smile even more glorious.

"Have you, then?" He used his free hand to tickle me, making me squeal with laughter.

"I should never have mentioned tickling to you!" I squirmed, trapped.

"As if I wouldn't have found out eventually."

Eventually? How long, how long, how long?

Soon his touches turned less playful. His lips slanted over mine. He slipped his tongue into my mouth, deepening the kiss into a thorough taking. . . .

Yet then he broke away.

"Why'd you stop?"

He levered himself to his feet, helping me up. "We have an appointment." He brushed snow off my back, then adjusted his jacket to conceal his erection.

Hand in hand, we started on a path that meandered along the forest's edge. "Where are we going?" We were heading away from the lodge, cresting a small rise.

"Patience, *solnyshko*."

"What does *sol-neesh-kah* mean?"

"An endearment. You need to start learning Russian."

I parted my lips. Why would I? Unless? *Cool yo jets!* Still, I was about to ask him to expand on his comment when I spotted a stable down the hill. The building was enormous, with red painted walls. Corrals flanked it. "Oh! Can we stop at the stable?"

"I suppose."

As we neared, I said, "Am I going to get to pet a horse?" My eyes went wide. "I—can—*hear*—them, Máxim. I want to pet all the horses!"

He chuckled as he ushered me inside. "You heard them, did you?" The air smelled like oats and leather. "We're going riding."

"*En serio?*" I clapped my mittens.

"Look at your excitement. For my Katya, snow trumps a private jet. Horseback riding trumps jewelry. Singular creature."

Pleasure still coursed through me whenever he called me *his Katya*.

"I don't know how to ride, but I don't care." Laughing, I said, "Shove a helmet on me, *Ruso*—let's do this."

He was grinning. "We will go together. They ride Western here, so I'll put you in my saddle."

"Where are we headed? To an igloo? To the North Pole? To a place where St. Bernards serve brandy?"

He laughed, looping an arm around my waist. "Not far. I'll give you a taste, or else your thighs will be sore all weekend."

I quirked my brows. "Don't hold back on my account. I've been riding you like Seabiscuit at least twice a day for over a week."

The stable hand, a bearded older man, chose *that* moment to appear.

He cleared his throat, even more red-faced than I was. Oh, but he was leading the most striking chestnut horse! "What's her name?" I crossed to pet her.

The man said, "Chestnut, ma'am."

"Of course!" Love!

Máxim talked with the guy about the trail and some sights; I wasn't listening, too busy petting the horse and crooning to her: "*Poni bonita. Mi yegua castaña. Yegüita . . ."* Pretty pony. My chestnut mare. Horsey.

Máxim turned to me. "Are you ready?" He grabbed my waist. "Up you go." He lifted me, helping me into the saddle (which felt much higher up than I would've expected!), then mounted right behind me. Snug fit.

He put his arms around me, grasping the reins. With a click of his tongue, we started from the stable. I was officially riding a horse! I savored the scents— Máxim's sandalwood, the leather of the saddle, the new-to-me smell of horsehair.

He directed Chestnut along a path, leading even deeper into the forest.

I stroked the horse's mane, telling Máxim, "You're really comfortable with this."

"She's a very gentle mare for a leisurely ride. At my estate in Russia, I have a stable full of spirited mounts. There are many horses to pet."

Why tell me things like that? "And you have a closet full of blow-up dolls—by your own admission. *Pervertido.*"

He nipped my ear. "Smart-ass."

"I can't believe I'm on a horse. In Jack Frost's hood."

"You could almost make me enjoy winter again," Máxim said. "Horseback riding and snow, two firsts of yours I get to claim. You claimed another of mine earlier."

"How?"

"I was about to fight a stranger over a woman. I was very jealous when those men ogled you. I've never known jealousy like I continue to feel over you."

My toes curled in my snow boots. "They look at every girl they pass the same way."

"Not like that. And they have no idea what you're like. If others knew the pleasure you bring a man, I'd spend all my days fighting over you."

I was glad he couldn't see the wide grin that spread over my face. "Well, I'm sure you're going to be very popular with the women this weekend."

"I'll smile at them, and you'll see how it's different from how I smile at you."

When a deer bounded across the path, I cried, "Oh, look! Admit it, you paid to have that deer run in front of us. Come clean."

Sounding furious, he said, "I cued the deer ten minutes ago. What kind of outfit are they running?"

I burst out laughing, sinking back against him.

"I like hearing that sound. You laugh like you do everything else—wholeheartedly." He rested one of his gloved hands high on my thigh, and I could have sworn the heat of his palm burned through our layers.

I was growing aroused for him, though this was not the time or the place. We were horseback riding! In snow! I adjusted my seat, which made it worse.

Yet then he tucked me even closer to him, and I felt the unmistakable outline of his erection.

"Ohhh." I was about to schedule *un cafecito* for when we returned, but we emerged from the trees, coming upon a covered bridge. I'd never seen one up close. "*Lindísimo!* So cute!" The structure was small and narrow, stretching over a frozen creek. The roof had a coating of snow atop it, and the walls were rough-hewn. "This is like a ride at Disney World! Are we going inside?"

"We should take a break. Get out of the wind."

"What wind?"

"Work with me."

"Ah! I'm freezing." I leaned forward, wriggling my ass against the ridge of his dick. "Must go . . . inside for . . . warmth."

He snatched me hard against him, grinding me. "Little witch. That's the last time you'll tease me before I fuck you."

The horse's hooves clipped over the wood, echoing in the enclosed space. Halfway through, Máxim hastily dismounted and tethered Chestnut, then held his hands up for me. As he lowered me, he clamped me close to him. His lips covered mine, cool compared to his flicking tongue and the breaths we shared.

Only when I moaned did he set me down and release me. With that intent look in his eyes, he removed his gloves.

"*Aqui, mi amor?* In front of Chestnut?"

He peeled down my pants and thong to my upper thighs. "Here." He turned me toward the wall.

I heard his zipper going down, and my body grew even wetter with anticipation. I spread my legs as much as I could.

He covered me, bending down to wedge his cock against my entrance. When he straightened his legs, his shaft surged upward into my wetness. "*Unh.* My Katya's always ready for me."

He drove me up on my toes. "You devil, you make me this way!"

"I'm the only one who gets to." As he thrust, his bare hand cupped my mons. When he covered my lips, his cock moved between his fingers. "This is *mine*." He jostled me, and I whimpered. "It belongs to me." His grip was like iron, the heel of his palm grinding against my clit. "I own this. I own you."

Possessive, *primal.*

I melted for him.

As he worked my body with short snaps of his hips and that hot, possessive hand, he nuzzled my ear. "If I were a cunning man, I would've trapped *you* with my child." His other hand flattened over my belly. "I imagined it. You big with my babe. These breasts full of milk." He squeezed one, then the other. "My cock grew so stiff, I came in three strokes."

"*Máxim!*" He'd masturbated to that fantasy about me? The mere idea made my sheath tighten around his length. "*Dios mío, Dios mío.*" With a cry, I ground my clit against his iron grip.

He bucked into me and jostled that maddening hold on my pussy. "You're close, aren't you? I want you to come hard for me."

He removed that palm—"No! I need that, Máxim!"—only to return it with a cupped *slap.*

"Oh. My. God!"

"There you go. . . . That's it, baby. I can feel your wet pussy readying." *SLAP.*

The sound echoed around us as I tumbled over the

edge. As heart-stopping pleasure coursed through my veins, I drew a breath, *needing* to scream lungfuls.

He put his other hand over my mouth. "Scream for your man."

I did. Again and again and again.

"Greedy as ever!" He fucked harder and harder, shafting me with savage, animalistic thrusts.

He yanked up my scarf to bare my neck. A bite at my nape made my eyes roll back in my head. Right when I felt his heat spurting inside me, he snarled against my skin, *"Belong* to me!"

Violent shudders wracked his massive body. One after another. Until he'd spent all his cum in me. . . .

With a last groan, he lowered his forehead to rest atop my head. He lazily stirred himself in our wetness, wrapping both arms around me. He squeezed me hard, but I loved it.

Slowly we caught our breath. "*En un sueño.*"

"A dream?" Nuzzling my ear again, he murmured, "You're falling for me."

My core quivered around his semihard shaft.

A low laugh. "You can't hide that, can you? What are we going to do about this?" He'd said nothing about his own feelings.

I swallowed. "Get through this weekend?"

"Then we'll have a long talk. Agreed?"

"Agreed." Wait, what was I agreeing to? My head was still in the clouds.

"This is going to pain me, but I suppose we can't be late for the festivities." With another groan, he pulled out.

A shock of cold hit my pussy and ass. "Oh! Oh!" His damp dick must be freezing, but he sweetly tugged my ski pants and thong up before tucking himself back in.

He gave me a swat on my ass. I swatted his in return. He helped me into the saddle, mounting behind me. When his arms wrapped around me again, I lazed back, sighing in contentment. "*Me podría acostumbrar a tí.*" I could get used to you.

"This is why I'm in such a hurry to learn your language. You speak Spanish in my ear during and after sex."

And he spoke maddening Russian.

"Even when you sleep, you murmur in Spanish."

I talked in my sleep? *Mierda!* "You're learning too fast. I'll have no secrets before long."

"That's the plan."

I bit my lip, feeling like a countdown clock had started. Again, I thought, *What if I trusted Máxim?* Maybe I wouldn't be calling Edward down upon me. Maybe I needed to recognize a superstition for what it was.

Might it finally be time for me to recruit a teammate? A partner? Could any man be more qualified than Máxim to take on Edward?

By the time we'd reached the stable, I began to relax again. I didn't have to decide anything for two days, and I was determined to enjoy this man, this place.

After we'd returned Chestnut, we walked back to the lodge hand in hand. As we approached the entrance, he said, "In case those farmers are still hanging around, I'll show them who you're fucking." He grabbed me, tossed me over his shoulder, and carried me inside.

I was squealing with laughter, pounding my mittens on his back, when I heard a man say, "*Maksimilian?*"

CHAPTER 28

*W*ith a laugh, Máxim turned, which put my ass—in tights—on display. "Ah, Aleksandr."

His brother? "Down, *Ruso!*"

He let me slide down him, then pulled me around with my back to his front. He draped his arms over me, possessiveness in full force.

Aleksandr was as tall as Máxim and had similar features, that strong jaw and chin, the proud nose and broad cheekbones—though Aleksandr's eyes were amber to Máxim's blue. And Aleksandr had tattoos on his fingers and closer-cut hair. Definitely rougher around the edges than Máxim.

Aleksandr stared at his brother as if he didn't recognize him. "You look . . . changed."

Máxim's hair was ruffled, his skin tanned, his bright blue eyes hooded with relaxation. He appeared younger and was grinning—an authentic smile. His brother's shock clearly amused him.

Yet I could detect currents of strain between them, as if Aleksandr remained on guard.

"You brought a date." Aleksandr turned his attention to me. I must have looked like I'd just gotten jackhammered in a covered bridge.

"Katya, this is my brother Aleksandr. *Bratan*, this is my woman, Cat Marín." There was an undertone of *say something, I dare you* to his words.

"It's a pleasure, Aleksandr," I said. "I can't wait to meet your bride."

The man frowned down at me. "You're from Miami?"

Máxim laughed. "Yes, this is the girl I held prisoner. But as you can see, she's an overjoyed guest here. Aren't you?" He squeezed me.

"I'm here to keep Máxim in line. There'll be no mischief while I'm on watch, or I'll kick his Russian ass."

That got Máxim to laugh, while Aleksandr just looked baffled. Finally he said, "Natalie is going to like you very well. And please call me Aleks."

After another couple of stilted exchanges, Máxim and I started back to our room.

As we made our way up the stairs, I asked him, "Why was he so shocked?"

"He's never seen me like this."

"Happy?"

Máxim paused on a step, seeming as shocked as Aleks had just been. "Happy," he repeated, as if he were turning the word over in his mind, tasting it. "I suppose I am."

"You enjoyed his surprise. It amused you. Is my presence here solely to screw with people?"

"Though I was perversely pleased by Aleksandr's surprise, I brought you here because I want you with me. Simple as that." He leaned down to say, "And already, you're glad you came. In both senses of the word."

I was attending a Nebraskan dinner in a countryside lodge as the date of a Russian *mafiya* sex god. What exactly did one wear to an occasion like that? I hoped I'd picked the right outfit.

My simple black pencil skirt accentuated my ass without being *too* tight. But my copper-colored blouse was a work of art. It was a cold-shoulder design with a scoop neck and long blouson sleeves that were cut out to reveal my arms from my shoulders to my elbows. The back dipped low, almost to my racy new bra, and was held in place by a string (which I hoped Máxim would spend all night thinking about untying). My black, strappy heels were high—because of my date's height.

Saving the pearls for the ceremony, I wore the lock-and-key earrings. I left my hair down, curling loosely. All that time by the pool had highlighted strands to a caramel color, and I wanted to show them off.

My makeup was understated, a touch of tawny eye shadow, mascara, and a bit of shimmery blush. The burnished gloss on my lips picked up the play of light on my blouse. My black clutch had a small copper medallion in the center.

Holding my breath, I walked out of the dressing room to join Máxim. "*Te gusta?* You like?"

"*Me gusta*," he murmured, immediately frowning. "I'm usually smoother than this, but you have a habit of making my mind go blank." He crossed to me, wrapping an arm around my waist. "I could not be prouder to show you off."

I petted the lapel of his black suit. The lines were so classic and crisp, he looked like he'd stepped out of a magazine ad. "When you burn through all of your money, you can be a model."

With a grin, he said, "It's good to have a backup plan."

"How much did your suit cost?"

"The price of this one gave even me pause." And he would wear it once. Sometimes his wealth blew my mind.

He grazed his forefinger against one of my earrings. "The lock-and-key ones. Do they make you think of me?"

"Only every time they kiss my neck." Oh, I could tell he liked that.

He offered his arm. "Come, let's go. Before I say to hell with this and take you to bed."

His smoldering look made me very aware that I wore garters and stockings for him later.

I took his arm, and we headed downstairs toward the Grand Hall. As I'd dried my hair, I'd studied the fire escape plan to note exits, a habit born of self-preservation. I now knew the layout of the lodge.

In the reception area outside the hall, dressed-up people mingled. At the outskirts of the room, men in understated suits stood alone, near all the exits. I recognized two of them from Miami. I just stopped my-self from waving.

"I see your security, Máxim. Is Nebraska a hotbed of mob hits?"

"Better safe than sorry." He covered my hand on his arm. "The Sevastyans have much here that is pre-cious to them."

"Where's Vasili?"

"Overseeing everything. He excels at this."

We'd barely gotten downstairs before a redhead in-tercepted us, almost as if she'd been lying in wait. "So you're Maksim's mysterious date! I'm Natalie."

She was my height, with flawless pale skin, flame-red hair, and a sexpot figure. The green-eyed billion-airess PhD student was a knockout. Because that wasn't intimidating or anything. Her engagement ring had a diamond the size of a meteorite.

Aleks joined her. "This is Cat Marín. She's actually *with* Maksim."

I stepped forward, offering my hand: "Hi."

Natalie hugged me. "Oh, you're freaking gorgeous!" She was sweet on top of everything?

When my cheeks heated, Máxim appeared charmed. In social situations like this, I tended to be more demure at first—a far cry from how I behaved with him. "Thank you," I told Natalie. "I can't wait to see your dress. You're going to be the most beautiful bride." Having met her—and knowing her past—I hoped she had the WOTC, wedding of the century.

Another girl our age slinked over. Must be Jes-sica. She looked like a runway princess with her svelte frame and cropped black hair. She wore a clearly expensive outfit: a red miniskirt, thigh-high boots, and a silvery halter. No bra. The girl raked her blue eyes over me. "*OH-la,* fineness. I'm Jess. Why are you sober, hot *mamí*?" She shoved one of her *two* drinks into my hand. "This ought to take care of the issue. Don't say I never gave you anything."

I couldn't help but laugh. "I'm Cat Marín. Nice to meet you."

"What kind of name is that?" she demanded. "You and Pussy Galore hang out? You sound like a cat burglar."

"Thief of hearts, yo."

Natalie cracked up. Aleks half-smiled. Máxim chuckled, wrapping his arm around my shoulders.

Jessica's red lips curled, and she lifted her cup to me. "You and I are going to have rocking chairs next to each other. It's a done thing."

Máxim said, "Jessica, it's a pleasure to see you again."

She gave him a chin jerk in greeting. "Are you really keeping this one prisoner in a Miami penthouse?"

Everyone grew quiet.

"He did keep me against my will," I said airily. "Then he stopped being *un cabrón hijo de puta*, and I decided I'd let him hang out with me."

"No wonder you like her," Natalie said to Máxim. "She doesn't put up with your bullshit!"

His eyes were lively. "She lets me get away with very little."

Aleks said something in Russian that made Máxim

tighten his arm around me. Natalie murmured something to Aleks that made him incline his head. Ah, the interplays. What I wouldn't give to speak Russian!

Jess asked me, "Hey, *mami*, with an accent like yours, you speak Spanish?" I nodded. "I guess I'm the sole monolinguist. Which either means I know a single language, or I'm committed to eating one box. In any case, it's rude to speak another language in front of me."

I belly-laughed at that. Had I actually thought these people would be stiff?

An older couple walked up then. The woman had shining brown hair and glasses. The man had similar glasses. Definitely a married pair.

The lady said, "Dinner's about to start." Then she turned to me. "Maksim truly did bring a plus one? I'm Natalie's mother, Rebecca. And this is my husband, Tom, Natalie's stepfather." They both struck me as good-natured. "We're RVers."

I checked my mental acronym databank for *RVer*, came up empty. Good money said they must do RVing. "It's nice to meet you. I'm Cat Marín. And RVing sounds exciting."

Whatever I'd said was the exact right thing. "Oh, it is! I can't interest Natalie. But I have oodles of pictures."

"I'd love to see them."

Rebecca's gaze flicked to Jess, and she sucked in a scandalized breath. "Jessica! Where are the rest of your clothes? Must you?"

Completely deadpan, Jess said, "Becks, I *must*."

"Couldn't you slip on a sweater? This is why I

shouldn't have let you fire the wedding coordinator! She would have told you . . ."

"We'll see all of you inside." Máxim steered me away from that, and we headed into the spacious wood-paneled Grand Hall. Elaborate crown molding adorned the ceilings. And there were fireplaces. Plural. Big ones!

About a dozen tables had seven or so seats each. Máxim found his placard, with one that read *Guest* beside it. He rubbed his thumb over it. "I suppose 'guest' is as accurate as the name you told me. Give me one thing right now, *solnyshko*. Anything."

My gaze darted. "Um, I never expected to like you even half this much?"

Good humor restored, he said, "That'll do for now." He curled his finger under my chin, and I wondered if he was going to kiss me right there. Then everyone else started arriving inside.

Jess sidled over to me. "Since Natalie's getting married, she won't be able to give me all the attention I need and deserve. You'll pick up the slack." She moved her placard to my other side.

Natalie, Aleks, Tom, and Rebecca made up the rest of the table. When we sat, Jess tossed back an old-fashioned she was holding—drank it *down*. Whoa. I expected her to swipe her forearm over her mouth.

As Máxim made small talk with Rebecca and Tom, and Natalie teased Aleks about something, Jess said to me, "We need to discuss shoe-polishing the limo tonight." She ordered another drink and got me one too. "I'm open to dirty limericks. Any suggestions?"

"I'll work on it."

"So lemme give you the lay of the land." She hiked her thumb over her shoulder. "At that table, we have three bridesmaids. Polly's the corn-fed-looking blonde, and the only one worth mentioning. The other two are lame and their invites make me wonder where Natalie's head's at. The three uptight guys are Russian grooms-men. My charm is lost on them, so obviously they're nobodies—guys who did hits with Aleks or some such shit."

Whoa, she was talking about his hit man back-ground aloud? Just like that?

She continued, "I was surprised by the turnout, since Natalie gave us zero notice about this shindig. The rest of the crowd is extended family of Rebecca and Natalie's adoptive dad."

"Where is he?"

"He died. Natural causes. Not like her birth father."

Across the table, Rebecca said, "So, Cat, is your name short for Catherine?"

Máxim's gaze was lasered on me.

"They just call me Cat." I had a crazy impulse to stand on the table and shout to everyone, "I am Lucía Martinez! I was born and raised in JAX, baby!"

"Well, it's a cute name."

Jess said, "Your name doesn't suck too bad, Becks."

Rebecca ignored her, asking me, "Why don't you tell us about yourself?"

Máxim turned his chair and faced me.

Dodge and deflect? Bobbing and weaving was dif-ficult in the hot seat. "I'm about to finish college."

"Oh, where do you go?" she asked.

"It's a small private school." Máxim would think I was lying, believing I'd denied going to college.

"You and Maksim met in Miami, right? What brought you there?"

"I like the city very much. I'm keeping my eye out for new opportunities there." Not a lie.

"How long have you two been together?"

He smoothly interjected, "Not long enough. How could it be?"

Charming devil. I tasted my old-fashioned. Not bad.

"What's your major?" Natalie asked.

"Business. Economics major, finance minor." Too much information was flowing from me! I felt like a miser flinging away coins.

Máxim raised his brows, sipping his drink.

Natalie looked impressed. "I can't even do simple sums in my head. Business was forever out of my reach."

"But you're getting your PhD, right? Who needs simple sums when there are calculators?"

"That's what I've always said!"

Jess said, "Hey, if I sit between her and Natalie, will I get smarter? I guarantee they'll get sexier."

Rebecca spoke over her: "Tell us about your family, Cat." Such a "mom" thing to say. In an arch tone, she added, "It's like pulling teeth getting information out of any of these Russians."

Over the rim of his glass, Máxim said, "Yes, Katya, tell us *all* about them."

"My mom was from Cuba. She met my father

when he visited from the US." The weight on my chest was returning.

Servers approached with the first course, distracting the table's attention from me. *Gracias a Dios.*

Under his breath, Máxim said, "How much of that was true?"

"Whatever you *think* is true, multiply that by ten. Oh, wait, anything multiplied by zero equals zero."

"For future reference, a US citizen would have difficulty traveling to Cuba, especially twenty-plus years ago."

"Thanks for the tip," I said, instead of crying, "My father was an attaché there!" One day this boiler was going to blow. . . .

Over the next hour, the dishes continued to arrive. Some were Midwest Americana, some traditional Russian—both exotic to me. The cook in me relished the experience. When I tasted *pelmeni*, meat dumplings, I told Máxim, "This is really good."

At my ear, he murmured, "I'd much rather be eating Cuban."

I coughed and kicked him.

All throughout the meal, he kept his eyes on me. When he wasn't indulging in the courses, he rested his arm over the back of my chair. Protective, possessive.

He wasn't the only one studying me. Aleks seemed to be taking my measure. Even Natalie cast me a couple of quizzical looks over her wineglass.

After the dessert course—Jess inhaled her red velvet cake, then trespassed on mine—she rose, telling Máxim, "I hope you're ready with your best-man speech. We're doing our dog and pony shows tonight, while I'm still coherent."

Rebecca said, "What? You can't! Those come *after* the ceremony."

Jess blinked. "No. This works best for me." When Rebecca started to bluster, Jess said, "This is how they do it in Russia. Ask Maksim."

Rebecca turned to him. "Is that true?"

Máxim gave a measured answer, "The most prominent Russian families fairly much do as they please."

Jess cast her a *see?* look. "In any case, the wedding coordinator ordered that this happen tonight. And who is she? Oh, yeah—she's *me*. Relax, Becks. Remind me to get you a Valium."

Rebecca turned to her daughter to do something, but Natalie said, "Jess's coup to oust the coordinator *was* successful, Mom. We're slaves to her dictates now."

Rebecca faced Jess. "What are you going to do?"

"A vid." At that, she swerved toward the front of the hall, to a computer.

"A *video*?" Rebecca whispered, aghast.

"Listen up," Jess called as she queued up a video on a large screen against one wall. "Hey, *errybody!*" When the room quieted, she said, "I'd introduce myself, but let's face it, my reputation precedes me, and I've slept with half of you. As maid of honor and coordinator for such a rush-job wedding, I did a vid instead of a speech. You're welcome." She pushed play, then returned to her seat.

She'd put together a compilation of pictures from the last couple of months of Natalie and Aleks's relationship.

Leaning in toward me, she said, "Keep your eye

on Aleks in the pics. He fucking worships the ground Natalie walks on."

It was true. He always had his gaze on his fiancée. Such devotion! Also interesting was the evolution of his expressions. At first, he looked stern and uncomfortable. As time passed he loosened up, even giving tentative smiles.

There were pictures of an older gentleman with twinkling blue eyes—must be Natalie's birth father, Pavel Kovalev. As Natalie watched, tears welled. Even steely Aleks was moved.

The last frame was the date of the wedding with a message from Jess. "As you go about your married lives together, always remember: Dance like nobody's watching."

While there were a ton of *Aww*s, I thought that was kind of lame.

Then another line appeared to complete the message. "Dance like nobody's watching. Fuck like everyone is."

Oh, no she didn't! I turned to her. "There went the last little piece of my heart, Jessica."

She air-smooched me.

Red-faced Rebecca screwed her eyes shut, but everyone was laughing. Natalie had to hold her stomach; even Aleks chuckled.

Máxim laughed, telling me, "Like I said, colorful."

Rebecca pointed at her. "We will talk later."

Jessica belched into her fist. "What?"

Smoothing her hair, Rebecca addressed Máxim, "I suppose if you have a speech, you should go now."

Had he prepared one? As best man—and
brother—would he mention their family? Aleks and
Máxim hated their father. Their mother was dead. Natalie's family was full—an adoptive father and mother,
a birth father and mother, and now a stepfather she
clearly liked. How was Máxim going to handle that?

"Of course, Rebecca," he said, his tone casual.

As Máxim stood, Aleks grew visibly nervous. Did
he expect coldheartedness from his brother? Scheming? Natalie held his hand on the table.

Anyone else might have been tentative addressing
a gathering like this, but Máxim, the politician, was all
confidence. He gazed around with that *I command all
I survey* look, until the room quieted. Even Jess sat up
and paid attention.

In a self-deprecating tone, he asked the crowd,
"How am I going to follow Jessica's eloquence?"
Laughter sounded. Then he flashed a movie-star smile
that wowed everyone. I could have sworn I heard sighs.
One rapt server paused midserve, holding a plate in
the air.

Por Dios, could he be more charming?

"I make this speech on behalf of myself and Dmitri, the youngest Sevastyan brother, who sadly couldn't
be here." Aleks raised a brow at that.

With his deep voice resonating, Máxim said,
"First, I would like to say *spasiba*—thank you—to all
of you for your warm Nebraska hospitality. We from
Russia appreciate it deeply, as does my beautiful lady
from Florida." He winked at me as he said, "Who is
delighted to have come with me."

My cheeks heated, and I mouthed, *Devil.*

"When I heard that my brother was to marry Natalie, I marveled at his fortune. She is everything Aleksandr could hope for in a wife. In fact, my brother heartily recommends this great Husker State for finding brides and apparently for something called . . . *football*?"

Laughter and cheers broke out. Oh, he was *good.*

He continued, "I wish our mother Roxana Antonovna Sevastyan could have met his soon-to-be wife. She would have called Natalie her *dorogaya doch'ka,* dearest daughter."

Aleks's uneasiness deepened.

If Máxim noticed, he didn't show it. "Natalie is a credit to her family here: to the late Bill Porter—a guiding force in her life; to Tom Christianson—who'll proudly walk her down the aisle tomorrow; and to Rebecca"—he leveled his blue gaze on her—"the lovely and most gracious mother of the bride."

Thunk. I could all but hear Cupid's arrow hitting her heart. She rested her chin on her hand and *mooned* over him. Natalie grinned and bumped her shoulder against her mother's. Aleks narrowed his eyes suspiciously.

Addressing the rest of the room, Máxim said, "Across the world in Russia, Elena Petrovna Andropova, Natalie's birth mother, tragically passed away before she could know her daughter—but not before she loved her. Yet it was Natalie's birth father, Pavel Kovalev, who brought her and Aleksandr together."

Had I worried how Máxim would handle this

speech? Natalie was in raptures. Strangely, Aleks looked like he was bracing for an inevitable hit.

"I'd met Kovalev, and sometimes crossed paths with him socially." Máxim turned to Natalie. "As an aside, I *never* saw him so happy as he was in those pictures with you."

Her eyes glinted again, her hand tightening on Aleks's.

Máxim resumed his speech: "Though our mother started Aleksandr on the path to becoming an honorable and respected man, it was Kovalev who guided him the rest of the way. Kovalev was a gentleman of the old order who believed in the code: respect those who earn it, assist those who need it, and protect to the death all you hold dear. In his lifetime, he did *all* of these things." Máxim paused a moment, letting everyone in the know reflect on the sacrifice. "He raised my older brother by the code; over these last few months, I've recognized that Aleksandr Sevastyan has become the man his beloved mentor always knew he could be. So no longer do I say how fortunate Aleksandr is to marry Natalie; I say how fortunate they *both* are to have found each other." He raised his glass to the couple. "Katya and I, as well as Dmitri, wish all blessings upon you for a long and joyful marriage. *Schast'ya vam.* Happiness to you."

Cheers broke out, everyone drinking. Máxim had included me, like we were *together*, together.

Aleks gazed at his brother as if he didn't recognize him. Then, weirdly, he shifted that dumbfounded expression—to me.

Natalie mouthed "Thank you" to Máxim. Turning to Aleks, she gave him an *I told you so* look.

To the crowd, Máxim called, "*Vyp'em za lyubov!* Let's drink to love." This time he raised his glass only *to me*.

Jets. Overheating. *Mal funcionamiento*. My glass shook on the way to my lips.

He sat down nonchalantly, as if he hadn't just made a roomful of people claw out their hearts in tribute to him. Myself included. "How did I do?"

His speech had left me speechless.

He curled his fingers, buffing his nails. "I know, baby girl, I'm *that* good."

CHAPTER 29

$\mathcal{A}$s dinner wound down, Jess declared to the table, "Natalie, hot *mamí*, and I are late for the bar."

"I'm not a big drinker," I told her. "More accurately, I'm a very bad drinker."

Máxim raised his brows: *Understatement, then?*

Jess said, "I scheduled the ceremony for tomorrow night, because I could, and because I'm fucking brilliant like that. We'll have all day to recover." To Máxim, she said, "I'll get Cat drunk for you, so maybe you can get to first base."

As she dragged me and Natalie to the adjoining bar, I looked over my shoulder at Máxim. *Help!*

He held his palms up, a mischievous smile playing at his lips.

The barroom was as dark-paneled as the Grand Hall. Huskers memorabilia lined the walls. Top 40 country music played on a jukebox.

At the bar, Jess ordered a round of tequila shots. Natalie looked around. "Did you scare off Polly?"

Jess said, "She slipped out thirty minutes ago. One of the groomsmen slipped out thirty-four minutes ago. Polly ought to be choking on motherland tonsil right about now."

How had Jess noticed them leaving? She'd always been engaged with our table's conversation. Not for the first time tonight, I wondered if Jess's carefree attitude masked a keen intellect.

The bartender served up shots, salt, and lemon wedges. "Are we really doing this?" I asked, though I already had the salt shaker in hand.

Jess cried, "*Sí, sí, señorita.*"

Natalie added, "It's futile to resist her. *Trust* me."

Lick-shoot-suck-gasp.

Another round.

As the third round arrived, Máxim and his brother came over. Aleks wrapped his arms around Natalie, as if he'd missed her. She melted against him.

Máxim told me, "I'm going with my brother to smoke cigars: I'm supposed to separate him from the bride, right?"

"You are."

"Tequila? Should I be worried?"

Under my breath, I said, "You left me to the wolves. Now I'm trapped in their den."

"Take this." He slipped bills into my clutch, what had to be a thousand dollars.

"Aww. Did you give me pin money?" I probably should've brought my own, but I hadn't even thought about my purse in the guest bedroom closet—the one filled with ten grand.

"In case you leave the lodge and go into town. Call me if you need more, *moyo solnyshko*. Or anything at all." He seemed as reluctant to part as Aleks obviously was. "And if you see those farmers, you text me immediately."

I saluted him.

Jess told Máxim, "I'll take real good care of our hot little *mami*." She raised two fingers in a V and wiggled her tongue between them.

He cast me a look: *I can't even with this one.* He tugged me off the bar stool to pull me aside. "Is she hitting on you?"

"She's just having fun with me. I think she's got eyes for either the buxom barmaid or the burly barback, probably both. In any case, I would think a hobbyist like yourself would love to imagine me and—"

"*Nyet.* I—don't—share."

"Easy, Trigger. I wasn't planning on it."

Satisfied nod. "And I'm a *former* hobbyist."

I wished it were that easy for an escort to say grandly, "I'm a *former* paid sex worker." Life was so not fair. I canted my head at him and said, "You're done with that, are you?" He'd racked up enough hours with escorts to earn a dozen college degrees. Could a PhD of hobbyism quit cold turkey?

"That's in my past." He brushed his knuckles over my jawline. "It's my understanding that better things await me in the future."

I needed to fan myself. All day he'd hinted at a relationship with me. Just when I decided I wasn't imagining this, a stray thought arose: *What if he's only amusing himself—with me? Has he been broken of his scheming ways?* My withered trust wanted to know. "Your brother looked astonished by your speech. He must be relieved that you've changed so much toward him." *Have you changed toward everyone?*

Máxim nodded. "He feared I would go the route of Jessica, only not as well-meaning. Did you notice his apprehension growing? He suspected I was setting the room up, readying to deliver a blow."

"But you're not like that anymore?" As brilliant as Máxim was, I could see him getting bored without something to occupy his mind.

Another brush of his fingers. "I have other things to focus on now. Such as my *vigorous* plans for you later."

My breath hitched.

He brought me back over to the bar, assisting me into my seat. "Until later." He brushed my hair over to one side, then pressed a kiss between my shoulder blades.

I was trembling when Máxim strode off with his brother, my mind whirring. A relationship with a man like that? I'd always hoped my luck would turn around, but this was ridiculous.

Natalie said, "So, you and Maksim are clearly serious. How long have you been seeing each other?"

"I met him almost two weeks ago."

Jess's eyes went wide. "Holy shit! It's your two-week anniversary. We should *drink*."

Lick-shoot-suck-gasp.

Natalie pressed the back of her hand to her mouth,

then asked me, "How did Maksim know all those things he said in the speech?"

He's in the business of information, I thought. But I just shrugged. "Are you nervous about tomorrow?"

"Not at all. I'm ready for it to happen. Aleks is nervous though. He thinks something will stop the wedding or take me away from him."

Jess added, "She won't tell me all the details, but he, Maksim, and the other brother had a fucked-up childhood in Siberia." Did they know about the scars on Máxim's back? "So Natalie is pretty much air for Aleks." She acted like she was suffocating. "Must . . . have . . . air."

Natalie told me, "He's been uneasy about you, because he wouldn't put it past his brother to kidnap you permanently. And Maksim watched you like a hawk throughout dinner. I was surprised he left you."

He probably had one of his security detail spying on me.

Jess said, "You're about to bolt, aren't you? We'll totally help you! We can go to my parents' lake house."

"Are we scheduling a *mafiya* carefrontation?" Natalie asked. Then she tapped her chin. "I should warn you: I ran from Aleks twice. It ended in marriage."

"Why would you run?"

"The first time? Because he broke into my house, intending to abduct me back to Russia. The second time? Because he wouldn't talk to me about his past."

Máxim had shied away on the plane, but I knew I could get him to open up. If I did.

Natalie said, "Aleks kept all his emotions bottled up. Unlike his brother! When Maksim toasted love and held up his glass to you, everyone in that room knew he was lost."

For me. It struck me that if Máxim was legit, my whole life might turn around. I was making friends and had seen snow. I'd ridden a horse and gotten laid in a covered bridge. I possibly had a boyfriend who could help me fight for my life back. I couldn't stop a smile. "I wouldn't want to be anywhere else in the world right now."

Jess told Natalie, "That sounds like something a prisoner would say." To me, she said, "I can't let Natalie get nervous about anything the night before her wedding. So pony up the deets."

To distract them, I said, "Let's do one more round." Famous last words.

Lick-shoot-suck-gasp.
Lick-shoot-suck-gasp.
Lick-shoot-suck-gasp.

Sometime later, I patted myself on my back. I'd distracted them and was having serious fun in the meantime! I'd missed hanging out with people my own age so much.

And I loved watching the rapport between Natalie and Jess. Natalie was the most laid-back girl I'd ever met. Jess was absolutely the craziest. Yet they totally fit.

As we grew drunker, Jess turned philosophical. "Why do guys think I want to date just because I bounced their dick for a night or two? Men are so predictable, so boring! Especially compared to women. If you and the Russian don't work out . . ." She made a phone gesture against her head, mouthing, *Call me.*

Lick-shoot-suck-gasp.

Eventually Natalie admitted that Aleks had taken her to a masquerade at Le Libertin, an exclusive BDSM club in Paris. So both brothers had that interest? Did Dmitri as well?

Natalie would've been sparing on the sex club descriptions, but Jess, who knew the story, kept prodding her: "You left out the best part! The metal dildo! And the sexual circus."

The details of that night scorched my eyebrows—and fueled my curiosity. What else would Máxim show me?

Jess pouted. "For some reason, *I* didn't get an invitation to Cirque du Cock. So I have to live vicariously."

Natalie said, "The weird thing was learning Maksim is a member too." *You don't say.* "He'll probably take you."

"*Mamí* gets to go to Cirque du Cock? And not me? Now you two are just being twats."

Lick-suck-shoot-gasp.

Jess also grew more physical, seizing Natalie in a headlock. "Who's your wedding coordinator, now? Huh? Huh?" She rubbed her knuckles in Natalie's red hair until she'd created a huge rat's nest. "*I* am the wedding *coordinator*—the coordinated terminator. Say it."

Natalie just laughed. And she let the rat's nest stay.

Lick-suck-shoot-gasp.

"How did you meet Maksim?" Natalie asked me,

slurring. "He usually only 'dates'"—she made air quotes—"blondes."

Oh. We were back to me. My head swirled. *Bob and weave, Cat.* But I didn't want to with these girls. They were so nice and real. "Oh, it's not a big deal."

"Sure it is!" Natalie said. "I want to know how my future brother-in-law would meet a smart co-ed."

I considered telling them about my escort foray. They probably wouldn't find it a big deal. I didn't know if it was gut instinct or the tequila advising me to trust them, but at that moment, I felt like I could. To an extent. I would never tell them about Edward— apparently, I couldn't yet gasp out the words *husband* and *murderous sociopath* in one sentence—but I could put their minds at ease about Máxim.

"Tell us!" Jess shoved her shoulder against mine, nearly sending me off my bar stool. "We're all drunk, and it's obvious that you and I are long-lost sisters— which means I can't fuck you." Leaning in, she added darkly, "In certain states."

"Anything you tell us stays between us." Natalie hiccupped.

"Okay, well, um, I needed some money quick. So I . . . took my friend's place on an escort date. Máxim ordered tall and blond, but I went instead. He's my first and only client."

When I saw the disgusted look on Jess's face, I instantly regretted my admission. Then she said, "You mean I've been doing it all this time for free? Who's the chump?" She pointed a thumb at herself. "I'm the chump."

Natalie was more romantic about it. "If you hadn't gone that night, you never would have met him!"

Never to have met Maksimilian Sevastyan? The man steadily turning my world inside out?

"How do you feel about him?" she asked.

"I'm falling for him, but I try not to. I know he's a player. He's a gorgeous billionaire and could have any woman he wanted." Even with his *issues*. Maybe they were fixed now? "Yet sometimes I get a sense of déjà vu around him, like we've known each other before. Does that sound stupid?"

"It sounds romantic," Natalie said.

Jess nodded. "Totally romantic. Hey, do you read romance novels? Of course you do. I'm sending you some faves. Give me your addy when I sober up."

I smiled and nodded, though I had no addy. It was such a simple request. No one else would give it much thought. But I had no home. I wanted a home. And a Russian. And a dog. "I've only known Máxim for thirteen days. I can't be feeling what I think I'm feeling."

"I was half in love with Aleks after a single night." Natalie twirled her ring with a secretive smile.

"You mean after a single glance," Jess said. "I was there. I witnessed the whole thing. Love at first sight exists. What did you think of Maksim?"

"DDG. Drop dead gorgeous. Thought beyond that was impossible."

Natalie said, "He's got it so bad for you."

"If she tells you that, then listen," Jess said. "We call her the Manalyzer."

"I can read any guy. Except Aleks." Natalie waved

that away. "And Maksim is lost for you. He called you *moyo solnyshko*."

"Tell me what that means!"

" 'My sun.' It's a fairly common endearment, but for a guy like Maksim to say it? And it totally fits with what I heard him tell Aleks about you."

"What'd he say?"

"Just before they came over here, Aleks asked what he was doing with a nice girl like you, and Maksim said, 'She makes things . . . brighter.' "

Pang. "But can he ever truly get past the fact that I had sex for money? After he told me I was going to this wedding, he also told me he expected a heated negotiation for clothes and jewels."

"He doesn't know he was your first client?"

"He refused to believe me."

Natalie frowned. "Oh. That sounds not so good."

I couldn't disagree. "Now I want to see if he can love me despite my past."

Jess squinted at me. "Let me get this straight. You want him to love you even though you're an escort, even though you're really not?"

"Exactly!"

"But what was all this about you being a hostage?" Natalie asked.

"I got drunk, and we had sex without a condom at my peak time of the month and all."

Jess nodded. "As you do."

"He accused me of trying to trap him with a pregnancy and refused to let me go."

Natalie sighed. "It might have started like that, but

his feelings have deepened. Aleks told me he's never seen Maksim look so satisfied. Not even when they were young. Apparently, Maksim was an anxious kid who rarely cut up."

He'd told me he never laughed naturally. "It's so strange, since I love his humor."

My phone chimed from my clutch. I fished it out. M Sevastyan: having fun?

I told the girls, "Hold on, it's him."

Me: I loke natlie & jse! So fn!

M Sevastyan: ah, the tequila hits. are you being a good girl? or do i need to put you in chastity?

I moaned.

"Cat, did you say something?" Natalie asked.

"No. *Nada.*"

Me: fuck'g devillll!1 😊

M Sevastyan: little witch

With a shaking hand, I stowed my phone.

CHAPTER 30

"*I* wasn't going to come down here," Máxim snapped when he reached me outside the lodge's garage later that night. He looked more pissed than I'd ever seen him. "You're a grown woman. How much trouble could you and Jessica get into in a garage? Then I realized that I didn't know who was in the building *before* one of my men followed you here."

"I knew you had someone following me!" I was slurring. Weird. I wasn't even that drunk!

"What the fuck were you doing in there?"

"Had work to do," I said breezily.

With a thunderous expression, he loomed over me. "And by *work,* do you mean a blond *farmer*? If I go in there, what will I find?"

"The limo—and sheer brilliance!" I laughed, then covered my mouth. "There went the surprise!"

Voice like ice, he said, "You're wearing a man's coat."

"Jess bought it for me with most of my pin money."

I whispered, "I suspect she pocketed the money and stole it off a rack. I was coming to get you because I don't think she should sleep in the car, but she won't leave because someone might wash it."

Jess's cry sounded from the garage. I turned back. Vasili was exiting, with her over his shoulder in a fireman's carry. She wore the other coat she'd "bought."

Upside down, she yelled, "Faster! Fun!" She slapped his ass with both hands. "Run, bald Russki!"

Vasili said something in Russian that made Máxim's meany face fade, then the bodyguard toted Jess away.

Sevastyan exhaled a gust of smoky breath. "You were shoe-polishing the limo? I didn't expect that. You had me very worried, Katya. You didn't answer any of my texts or calls." He signaled someone behind me— probably more *mafiya* security—then started squiring me toward the lodge.

"Jess thumped me in the boob each time I tried to text, and accused me of being dick whipped. Natalie told me it's futile to fight her. Psst, it *is*."

He opened the lodge door, ushering me inside. As warmth washed over me, I frowned. "Did I have a curfew?"

He scrubbed a hand over his mouth. "No, it's not that—"

"You believed I was sleeping with someone in the garage?" My frown deepened. "Aren't I *your* date?"

"You are. I didn't know what to think when you wouldn't answer your phone. Worrying about my woman is uncharted territory for me. I feared I hadn't made things clear enough to you."

When we reached our room, I asked, "What things?"

He deflected. "Tell me about your night."

I had to gush: "The polish is the most brilliant thing I have *ever* seen in my *whole entire* life. We shocked ourselves." I hiccupped.

"You've got it all over your face and hair."

"A small price to pay." With a condescending pat on his chest, I said, "Máxim, I'm a *very* important person here. Basically the life of the wedding. But with great power comes great responsibility." Had I said that last sentence in Spanish?

He chuckled, all his anger gone. "Very important, hmm? What graffiti did you write on the limo? Do I need to go back and take care of it?"

"We settled on 'He offered his honor, she honored his offer; all night long, he's on her and off her.'"

He laughed, pulling me into the bathroom to start the steam shower. "Come, *solnyshko*. Let's get you cleaned up. Hold on to my shoulders." After he removed my heels, he rose, turning me around. He untied the string of my blouse, saying, "Been wanting to do this all night." He dragged the garment off and pulled me to face him, whistling low at my black see-through demi-cup bra. "I like this little number." Then he brushed a forefinger over one nipple. "You were good for me tonight?"

"Very good."

He carefully removed my jewelry. "Did Jess behave herself with you? Or did she hit on you?"

I cocked out a hip. "Of course she did. I'm a hot

mami! But I told her I was with you. And she and I got into a fight anyway."

"Why would you two fight?"

"She insisted we should write stuff on the *inside* of the limo too. I tried to explain the law of diminishing returns, and she told me to eat a dick."

Why did he keep laughing at me? He reached around to unzip my skirt. "And now I get to care for my drunken female. Still more uncharted territory for me." He pulled my skirt down, leaving me in only my new lingerie set.

"Drunken? I'm *fine*."

"Indeed." His gaze roamed over my garters and hose, my demi bra and tiny thong. "If I'd known you were hiding this, we wouldn't have made it out of the suite." He unclasped my bra and tossed it away, giving both nipples a sweet nuzzle. Then he unfastened my garters, kneeling to roll down my hose and peel my thong to my ankles. With a groan, he pressed a heated kiss to my bare mons, inhaling my scent.

I threaded my fingers through his hair. "Umm. I love your mouth." More slurring?

He made a sound of frustration, rising once more. "Despite your sexy garters, I'm going to give you a reprieve tonight, which means I'm a better man than I'd ever suspected. Come on, in you go." He led me to the shower, then stripped to follow me in.

The leather lead around his neck caught my attention. I sighed, "You had that on?"

"You wore those earrings, and I wore the key."

"It drives me crazy to see it on you."

He gave me his devilish grin. "I had an idea." He lathered up a washcloth and gently scrubbed my forehead and cheeks.

I raised my face. "You gave me the earrings, but I didn't give you the key."

"In a way you did."

Because I was participating in his kinks? "Hmm. Do you like me when I wear my belt?"

"Oh, I do." The washcloth descended to my neck.

"You like me when I cook and sing?"

"I like you very much when you cook and sing." He soaped up my breasts, his breaths coming quicker.

"Did you like me around your brother and your friends?"

"When you quipped that you were a thief of hearts, I would've sworn you are."

"Aww. I like you too. I've learned about you."

Had he tensed? "I wondered if others would speak of me to you."

"Huh? *Qué cosa?* I'm talking about during our two weeks." In a proud tone, I said, "If it's past twelve, today is our anniversary. We met two weeks ago." This was important—I wish I wasn't slurring so much!

"Ah, so it is. And what have you learned?" He washed my belly, making the muscles trip.

"I can tell your real smiles from your fake ones. When you *half*-smile, you always curve the left corner of your lips. You don't overpronate when you run. Your eyes get lively when you're amused but also when your brain is engaged. You need your brain engaged as much as you need sex. You write the number seven with the sexiest little slash. I make you happy, and you can speed-read."

"My clever Cat." With his free hand, he stroked between my legs.

I sucked in a breath. "Natalie let it slip that you're a member of a sex club in Paris."

His fingers roved. "That's true. Anyone who is rich enough and has those leanings is a member of Le Libertin. I'll take you next week."

"Can't go. Or I'll break rule number three."

"You have rules, do you? How many?" His forefinger tickled my clit.

"S-six critical ones. If you follow the rules you live to fight another day." He'd think I meant figuratively.

"Tell me about them, love."

"If I tell you about the rules, I'd break rule number one. Besides, I need to talk to you about something else."

"Of course. What is it?"

"You know how you said everybody wants something from you? I do too."

"Yes, but with you, I'm *very* inclined to give. What can I get for you? A horse? You want Chestnut, don't you? Easy enough."

I rose on tiptoe, pulling him down to whisper at his ear, "I want you to have anal sex with me."

He inhaled sharply. "I was already aching from the sight of you in those garters. And now bathing you? Don't tease me further. I'm not made of stone, Katya."

"What do you mean?"

"You're drunk. I'm not going to take advantage of

you." Yet even as he said this, his hand had wrapped around me to squeeze my ass.

"Jess said that being tipsy is okay for the first time, because I'll be relaxed."

"You discussed this with Jessica?"

"She said I was the only one at the wedding who hasn't done it. She said that made me Amish. I'm not Amish. *Yo soy católica.* Kind of."

A strained laugh. "I'm sure there are others who are . . . Amish at this wedding."

"Your brother did it to Natalie—"

"Do *not* want to hear about that."

"I used to have a friend whose boyfriend always encouraged her to go to girls' night out, because she'd come home drunk and they'd get *freaky.* Can't we be like that?"

"Katya . . ."

"I always do *your* kinks. And I've never asked you for anything. Do you realize that? Well, except for you to let me go."

His shoulders stiffened under my palms.

"You *did* promise me you'd do this to me." I grasped his hard cock, stroking as I whispered, "Please, *mi amor,* I know you'll make it good."

"I fear hurting you. I'd need to prepare you."

"There's bath oil on the ledge." My hand dropped to his heavy balls, kneading them the way he had the night of my persuasion.

He groaned. "You'll hate me in the morning."

"I'll hate you if you don't."

"Ah, Cat, you've just sealed your fate." His tone

reminded me of our first night, when he'd told me I was about to get fucked hard.

Soon, I'd fulfill a fantasy! Sizzling thrills coursed through my veins, from my head to my toes, clearing some of the tequila's fog. I wanted to experience every second fully.

He snagged the oil, then pulled me through the steam over to the shower's wooden bench. "I want you to straddle me." He sat, patting his thighs for me to join him.

When I stepped over one of his knees, he grabbed my ass, lifting me above his lap. "Hold on to my shoulders and lean into me. Wrap your arms around me."

I did.

"Put your feet flat on the bench. Trust me. I've got you."

When I did, my pussy pressed against his shaft. I rocked, just as he bucked. In sync.

Then I shook my head. "Eyes on the prize, Máxim."

He looped his arms around me, holding me upright. Behind me, I heard him squeeze oil and felt my first tendril of nervousness. I was so exposed like this. Vulnerable.

But when he said, "Now would be the time to tell me to quit," I didn't want to.

I trusted him to make this incredible. No matter what happened with Máxim, I'd have this memory forever. "I want this. From you. Only you."

He shuddered and his cock pulsed against my pussy. He poured oil at the small of my back.

I quivered as it ran down between my cheeks. "Oh, that feels *amazing.*"

He pressed a flattened palm over my back, easily keeping me in place, and leaving one oiled hand free. I felt a whisper of sensation as he circled the pad of his forefinger around my opening, teasing me.

A little more pressure. The oil began to feel hotter, more slippery.

"Take my finger, baby." He pressed, pressed; it inched inside me.

"Oh!" I bucked again, digging my nails into his shoulders.

"My God, woman. So tight." He nipped and licked my neck. "And it's all *mine.*" With that word, his chest heaved against my breasts, my stiffened nipples.

Despite how good his finger felt, my empty pussy yearned to be filled, so much that I almost told him to stop. To let me sit on his length and ease the ache. When he thrust his finger in my ass, I couldn't help grinding my clit against his shaft.

"You can't do that, Katya. If you use my cock to get off, it'll be over. It was bad enough our first night."

"I'll be good. Somehow." With our bodies pressed together, I could perceive all the latent power in his muscles, could feel the toll his restraint was taking. "Don't stop. Give me more."

He used his free hand to drizzle oil around his finger. Then I felt more pressure. He was wedging a second finger inside. "There you go. That's it. . . ."

When both penetrated, I moaned low, arching my
back.

"Ah, you like that." With this cue from me, he
delved deeper. "I'll make tonight pleasurable for you."
He withdrew his fingers almost all the way, pouring
more oil. Then he sank both inside. For what felt like
hours, he pumped them. Twisted them. Spread them.

"*More.*" I felt the invasion all over my trembling
body. How much longer could I take this? My pussy
was dripping against his cock. "I'm dying, Máxim!"

He eased his fingers from me. "Then you're ready."
He coated his shaft with oil, stroking it with a shaking
hand. "I could spill right now. I promise you, this will
hurt me, not you."

He needed to come that badly?

"Rise up." Holding his glistening rod upright, he
maneuvered me until I was poised over it. He tucked
the head between my cheeks, against my entrance.
Then, with a groan, he lowered me, the tip nudging.

I whimpered as the broad crown demanded entry.

When the head popped past my ring, he lowered
his chin to his chest, shuddering. "*Fuck.*"

"Ah! This is . . . don't stop." I felt him stretching
me, but no pain.

He shook his head hard, his determined look sur-
facing. "Relax now." He cupped my cheeks with both
hands, holding me in place. "I've got you."

I shifted my weight to his hands. He lifted me,
sensuously lowering me farther. "You're taking me so
good, *dushen'ka.*" His praise was like its own caress.

I was bombarded by pressure, fullness, even by that

sense of closeness he made me feel. Steam shrouded us, misting our skin and slicking our bodies.

"Am I hurting you?"

I didn't know if I was light-headed from drinking or from these new sensations, but . . . "No, need more."

Máximo shockeado. I leaned in to lick his parted lips.

He raised me up on his dick, then lowered me more. Up . . . down . . .

"Finger yourself for me." His accent was so thick.

One of my hands dipped down to my pussy. As he lowered me again, I slid a finger inside. "*Ay, Dios mío* . . ." My head fell back.

He leaned down to my breasts, his mouth seeking. He took a taut nipple between his lips and suckled. Against the peak, he grated, "Two fingers, baby." He turned to my other breast, tugging my nipple between his teeth.

When I wedged in a second finger, I could feel the pressure of his cock, pushing against my sheath. I was nearing the brink, but fought off my orgasm, wanting this to continue forever.

"You like being filled this way?" He went even deeper, making me accept more of the stretch.

And the stretch was *increíble.* "*Más!*"

"You're torturing me! I will outlast you if it fuck-ing kills me."

"I'm getting so close!"

He raised his head. "Keep your fingers moving and look at me." We met gazes. "I've claimed every inch of your body. You're mine, Katya. You're with me now."

My lids slid shut as pleasure pooled deep in my belly.

"Eyes open. Look at me." His words were a harsh rasp. "You're *with me* now. Say it."

"I-I'm with you." The double fullness below my waist made it impossible to focus.

"There's no one else but me for you. Do you understand me?" Lifted up . . .

"I-I think so."

Lowered down . . . "You know what you are now. Say it." Lifted up . . .

Lowered—as far as I could take him. "I'm yours! Yours!" For how long?

His jaw muscles bulged, the tendons in his neck straining more than I'd ever seen them. "That's right. You belong to me. Keep working your pussy, Katya."

"Oh, *yes!*"

As I finger-fucked myself, he glanced down and made that growling sound. "Just when I think you can't possibly be sexier . . . You're going to make me lose my mind before it's all through, aren't you?"

Up . . .

Down . . .

"About to *explode,* woman." He gave shallow bucks of his hips in time with my busy hand.

"Máxim, I'm close!" With each thrust of my fingers, my pussy contracted more. "Make me come . . . make me . . . *make me.*"

"Fuck, FUCK!" Fingertips biting into my curves, he wrenched me up to the tip of his cock.

Heartbeats passed as I hovered, as *he* hovered . . .

I descended, seated; his seed *erupted*. Grinding up into me, his head fell back and a bellow burst from his chest.

When I felt his first shot of heat, I whimpered, almost fearing the strength of my own orgasm as the pleasure quickened and quickened and blazed—

Rapture.

Scalding me.

My core clenched my fingers. I threw back my head and screamed, "*Oh, my God!*" I shuddered and quaked, ecstasy ruling me.

"I can feel you coming!" His thick cock jerked inside me, pumping his essence.

I met his lips, crying out against them. Our tongues tangled as he emptied himself, and my mind turned over from the searing bliss. . . .

I collapsed against him.

"My God, Katya." He brushed kisses all over my face, murmuring in Russian.

I adored his affection, shivering against him. "*Gracias, mi amor,*" I sighed.

"You thank *me*?"

I nipped his neck. "You like me when we get freaky?"

He gave a strained laugh. "You could say that," he muttered, squeezing his arms around me so hard, I thought I would break.

CHAPTER 31

*E*arly the next morning, I sat bundled in the window seat. Outside, snow fell like crazy.

Máxim slept on. I would get to spend the whole day lazing by the fire, snuggling in bed with him. With my wicked man. I shifted my position, feeling a twinge in my bottom, but it'd been so worth it.

He'd told me I was *with him*, that I was *his*—as in, we'd stay together! Maybe he'd gotten excited and said more than he should. Maybe he'd gotten as drunk as I'd been. Though now that I thought about it, I'd never seen him drunk. I shrugged. I'd know soon enough.

Before I crawled back in bed with him, I gazed out through the frosted panes, wanting to memorize every detail of this place. Two ice-covered twigs sparred—*ping ping ping*—outside the window. Winds began to blow, low moans that wrapped around the lodge and made it creak. Inside, the fire popped.

Such foreign sounds to me. This place was magical.

Being here with Máxim made me feel things so *deeply.* Apparently he did as well. I recalled his jealousy from last night with a dark thrill. . . .

Over the last few days, I'd realized that the reason I hadn't yearned for another relationship wasn't just because of my circumstances.

I hadn't yearned because I hadn't met Maksimilian Sevastyan. He *was* the yearning. I was in love with the Russian.

Done. Finished. *Terminado.*

And now that I loved Máxim, I recognized that what I'd felt for Edward had been pale and puny, informed by everything *except* my heart.

But Máxim was still a player. His longest relationship had lasted for fourteen days—and counting. If a man like him actually settled down with one woman, he'd want her completely in return. He'd expect her to be his. Legally, I still belonged to another.

Oh, me jodí. I was so screwed.

What I wouldn't give for a do-over. For Edward never even to have counted.

The winds picked up even more, buckets of snow coming down. A real live snowstorm. A gust rattled the windows, the lodge creaking as if we were in a hurricane.

Máxim woke moments later, blinking at me, then slowly smiling—so handsome my heart twisted. In a rumble, he said, "Hey, baby." He patted his chest for me to return to bed. I rose, dropping my blanket on the way and crawled in naked beside him.

When I laid my head over his heart, he grazed his

fingers up and down my spine. "How long have you been up?"

"A bit. I've been watching the snowstorm."

He reached down to lightly cup a cheek. "How are you?"

"I definitely feel what we did. And I regret nothing."

He resumed stroking my back. "You never do."

"That's not true," I said. "I just don't with you."

"Maybe you don't remember everything."

"My takeaway from the shower: *Is there anything Máxim can't do?* It was wonderful. You were."

"You, *solnyshko*, boggled my mind."

"Me? I just held on for the ride."

"You're passionate, and when you do something you leap with both feet." He curled a finger under my chin, tugging till I faced him. "You're *brave*."

I could make no claim on that. If I was brave, I'd fight for my birthright. I'd put a murderer behind bars. I cast my gaze down. Máxim deserved a brave woman. Wouldn't a man like him *expect* one?

"Are you miserable from drink?"

"Not at all. Natalie made me and Jess take her hangover preventative before she sent us off to paint the limo." We'd guzzled a bottle of Gatorade each, then took a few over-the-counter pills. It'd totally worked, but . . . "I have a sinking suspicion our shoe polish art wasn't as brilliant as I thought."

"I got up at dawn and checked it out, in case you two had written 'eat a dick' over and over."

I laughed.

"Luckily, the poem is in place, and it's passable. Definitely gives the wedding flavor. Did you forget you wrote 'yo' at the end?"

"You lie."

"No, it's there."

Nota personal: no tequila with Jess ever again. I made circles with my forefinger over his chest. "Did you enjoy spending time with your brother?"

"He still holds himself back. But I think I do too. I suppose it will take time."

"As long as it's happening. Will you please tell me why you two were separated?"

"You didn't learn anything from Natalie?"

"She was very closemouthed. I had to glean a lot. Will you tell me more?" I leaned up to lay my hands on his face. "I want to know you."

He gave me a brows-drawn look. "You ask me *today*, showing the interest I've craved—just when Aleksandr advised me last night to tell you my sordid secrets. I can't understand what this would accomplish. And I can't believe you would view me the same way."

"I will."

"How can you be so certain?" He sat up against the headboard, and I did too.

I drew the cover closer over us. "Because the only way I'd view you differently is if you were pitiless to another, hurting someone who wasn't as strong as you are." Edward, Edward, Edward. "And I know you would never do that."

"It's an ugly story. My father was . . . abusive. He was part coldblooded schemer, part drunken thug. He used to beat me and my brothers, break bones."

I just kept my eyes from going wide. "Go on, please."

"He was always worse in the winter. When I was nine, he killed my mother in a rage."

Oh, my God. "I'm so sorry, Máxim. Were you there? Did you see?" Witnessing Julia's death had done a number on me—all that blood everywhere—and I'd hated the woman.

"Dmitri found her body at the foot of the stairs."

"That's what's been haunting him?"

"I wish that were all. It gets worse. Are you sure you want to hear?"

"I'm sure. Please."

His chest rose and fell on a breath. "Two winters later, my father would've killed Aleksandr as well, but my brother defended himself, accidentally ending the old bastard. Certain he'd be sent to prison in Siberia, Aleksandr ran off into the night, leaving Dmitri and myself behind. We were eleven and seven, and believed he'd abandoned us. Only recently I learned that he thought we would be taken in by distant relatives, a thousand times better off."

"What happened instead?"

"Orloff, a middle-aged 'guardian' from the nearest town, was appointed. The way he looked at Dmitri gave me chills, but I didn't know why. I had no idea there were adults who preyed on children like that."

Oh, no, no.

"I didn't like how much time they spent alone. Dmitri never complained, told me Orloff was a good man. And Orloff *was* different from my father. The man didn't drink, never struck us, never even raised his voice. He never spoke inappropriately."

Just like Edward. Sometimes monsters pretended to be gentlemen.

"There was no reason to doubt his decency, but I couldn't shake the feeling. So I went to Orloff and asked him why he was so focused on Dmitri." Máxim hesitated. . . .

"What did the man say? Please."

"He told me that he only wanted to be a father to the boy, that Dmitri needed to lean on him to recover from the recent loss of both his father and his eldest brother. He wondered aloud, 'Why would you not want Dmitri to be happy? Are you that jealous?' The man lied so believably. I can't express how skillful he was. He made me doubt myself. I walked away, convinced I was petty and selfish."

Gaslighting. No wonder Máxim didn't trust.

"Over the years, Orloff slowly replaced all the servants, those who might help us, those who'd also raised their brows. By the time I was thirteen, we were without friends, trapped in our secluded home."

Sometimes, *friendless* was another way of saying *defenseless*. "Go on, please."

"Orloff continued to spin his tales. And again, Dmitri was his staunchest advocate. I later learned that he'd told Dmitri he'd kill me—the last of his family still with him—if anyone found out."

"How did you discover Orloff's lies?"

"On Christmas Eve, I sneaked into Dmitri's room to assemble a train set I'd ordered for him. He wasn't there. I found him in Orloff's bed, with this chillingly blank look on his face. The man had made my brother spend the night with him, because even a sick fiend believed he should be close to his victim—over the fucking holidays."

That was why Dmitri had been blowing up the phone that particular day. And why Máxim hated the holiday.

"I attacked Orloff, but he was so much bigger than I was. When I regained consciousness, I was locked in the basement, my back flayed."

His back. His scars. He'd carried them since he was a boy.

Máxim gazed past me. "Orloff wanted to break me, to silence me. The position was heaven for him—living in a mansion with so many luxuries—and Dmitri there for his . . . use. The man would've done anything to remain. So he kept me down there. I didn't see the sun for . . . some time."

"Wh-what? How long?"

"Half a year."

My lips moved wordlessly. This nightmare only grew more twisted.

Eyes gone distant, Máxim said, "He provided me little food or water, keeping me without light of any kind. When I wouldn't break, he revealed his buried rage, whipping me till his arm tired, reopening all my wounds. In that dark place, filth and blood caked my skin." He shuddered. "It burned, itched, tormenting me. I was starved for sunlight. The longer I went without it, the worse the affliction grew, spreading over my body. It got so severe, I would dream about not having skin at all."

My eyes watered as I imagined his pain. So many things made sense now. His words: *Thirty-one years of misery is lifted.* Abused by his father first, then by Orloff. For decades later, Máxim had been haunted by those memories.

"I sickened in that dank, freezing basement, and knew I'd die down there. So I attempted to behave as if he'd broken me, but I couldn't deceive as well as Orloff. I'd been sentenced to death at thirteen. As each day passed, my execution neared."

I barely kept my tears in check. "That's why you asked me those questions about my memories."

He nodded. He'd wondered what I'd been doing—while he'd been dying.

That was why he hated winter. That was why he always wanted the windows and doors opened.

And this man called me . . . *his sun*?

"Worse than anything was knowing that Orloff still abused my little brother. Everyone was gone. Protecting Dmitri was *my* responsibility. And I'd failed."

"There was nothing you could do. You were a boy."

"Aleksandr said the same, though I believe he could've come up with some way to escape and save his brother. In fact, it was Dmitri who saved *me*. The night of a bitter freeze, he woke from his haze long enough to comprehend I was about to die. He knocked the man out with a shovel. My brother knelt beside me, crying . . . as I strangled Orloff. I killed him before he could ever wake."

Máxim had been forced to do that? As a boy? My heart broke for him and Dmitri.

He gauged my expression. "My family is surrounded by death and destruction. Aleksandr killed young. As did I. Only I did it with my bare hands when the man wasn't able to defend himself. I crept out of that basement, some dark warped thing, desperate to kill. How can you not view me differently?"

"I do view you differently. I'm staggered by how brave you were to protect yourself and Dmitri from a monster." I wish I were so brave! I clutched Máxim's shoulders. "I can't feel more fiercely about this. I *hate* that the weight of this fell on you. But have you thought about the children you spared in that man's future? Or the ones you avenged from his past? And since Orloff was ready to let you die, why should we not believe he'd murdered before?"

My reaction took Máxim aback, but I needed to make him understand. "Sometimes people aren't courageous enough to do what is necessary—adults aren't." In my position, Máxim would've met Edward head on, fighting. "All they can do is dream about being brave. You did what had to be done when you were just a boy. So yes, I see you differently!"

"I didn't expect you to be so . . . vehement." Máxim's gaze flicked over my face, then slid to his right shoulder.

I was squeezing him? Self-conscious, I dropped

my hands and cleared my throat. "What did you do afterward?"

He frowned at my reaction, but continued, "Dmitri didn't want anyone to know what Orloff had done to him, so I got rid of the body in the woods. He was never found. We said he got drunk, went out before a storm, and didn't return. No one particularly cared. Years later, I learned he'd been suspected of abusing girls and boys from his own town. Afterward, an elderly woman arrived as guardian. She didn't hurt us, nor did she help us."

"How is Dmitri now?"

He scrubbed a hand over his face. "He was *displeased* to hear of my relationship with you."

Máxim had said he wasn't ready for his brothers to learn of me. "And I pretty much announced myself."

"He would have heard by the time of this wedding."

"So some of the angry phone calls have been about me?"

"It can't be helped." He exhaled. "Dmitri could not be more damaged. Every move he makes to get better seems to entrap him more deeply in the past."

"Does he have anyone in his life? A partner? Friends?"

"He's incapable of a relationship. We were alike in that, commiserating over it. While I had my script, he'd developed what he calls *protocols*. They are more far-reaching, even . . . absolute." He opened his mouth to say more, then paused. "You will meet him. I don't want to color your perception any more."

What more could there be? But I said, "I understand."

"He blames Aleksandr for abandoning us. As eldest, Aleksandr had been a father to Dmitri. Then he was gone."

"Is that why you said you resented him?"

"I used to hate him, imagining his carefree life under the protection of a good man like Kovalev. Yet I learned recently that Aleksandr lived on the streets before Kovalev adopted him. Among so many homeless children, he was an outsider. He'd been raised with privilege—abused, yes, but wealthy—and he talked little by nature. Being alone meant he also had . . . trials, was in no way freed when he left us. In fact, he used to believe he'd been singled out for torment. After finding Natalie, he believes he was tested so he would become strong enough to protect her—that the purpose of his life was always to safeguard hers and ensure her happiness. What do you think of that?"

I softly asked, "How do we know that isn't true? If you believe everything happens for a reason . . ."

He seemed to mull this over. "For decades, I could see no reason for my own trials as a boy. Insomnia plagued me. My appetite was deadened; I could take or leave food, deriving no enjoyment from it. My hypersensitive skin made touch unbearable. For years, I had to grit my teeth just to wear a shirt. Even when I improved physically, my mind wasn't ready to let go. If anyone got close to touching my skin, I'd feel as if my chest was caving in."

Just like mine did when I practiced revealing my past. "But things are different with you now. You have a sweet tooth. You sleep soundly." I whispered, "I touch you."

"I told Aleks of these developments, seeking his opinion."

How odd to hear a man as self-reliant as Máxim getting another's take. But then, Aleks was his big brother, newly reunited with him. "What did he say?"

"He believes a man knows his woman because he begins to evolve for her, to become what she needs. You told me if the incentive was strong enough, some men could change. Aleksandr wanted Natalie more than he wanted his old ways, so he cast them aside. Isn't that what you believe?"

"Yes."

"I sensed something was different about you *before* we touched, *solnyshko*. When you grinned over your wineglass and told me the view from the Seltane penthouse was 'adequate,' I got a chill—because I had the impulse to grin. I responded to you as I never have to another, and it unnerved me." Máxim grazed his fingers along my cheekbone. "All those years ago, when I was down in that basement, I wish I had known that on the other side of the world, there was a bold little girl fighting for her pride. And that she would come into my life one day to make it brighter."

With a press of my lips to his forehead, I said, "Now I know that in the snowy north of Siberia, a boy was becoming a man under the harshest possible conditions." How could Máxim have grown so confident? So at ease with power? So remarkable in every way?

He said, "You told me it happened, it hurt, and better things await me. Do they? Am I becoming what you need, Katya?"

I drew a shaky breath. "Maybe you can move on now that you're different? Maybe you want to move on?"

He was silent for long moments, seeming to make a decision. Finally he asked, "Was this too much for you to hear?"

"No. But I hurt with you." For the scared boy he'd been. For the man dealing with his brother's anguish. And his own.

"I do feel . . . better. Lighter. Aleks was right. It's a burden lifted. I would've had to tell you eventually, so I'm relieved it's done."

Because he was that certain we'd be together? My heart clamored. I wanted this man so much! He *was* the yearning.

"If I'd known you'd react this way, I wouldn't have dreaded the telling so much."

"Thank you for trusting me."

"And you'll give me yours in return. So we can move forward."

Dios mío. I swallowed with nervousness. How could I not trust him?

I might have told Máxim even now—or tried to utter the words—but the look in his eyes said he needed something completely different from me. He wanted to lose himself inside me. To know pleasure and bury pain. I wanted to give him whatever he needed.

As he took me in his arms, I decided that once we got back to Miami, I was going to trust him too.

My heart skipped a beat when I realized, *I'll have to tell him eventually*.

After the wedding, I'd tell him everything.

CHAPTER 32

*W*hen I kissed Máxim good-bye that afternoon, he blinked open his eyes.

After making love twice, he and I had ordered room service, then fallen asleep again. I'd gotten up and dressed before he'd awakened.

Jess and Natalie had told me to join them at three to get my makeup and hair done with the bridal party, but even after last night, I hadn't wanted to impose. Now that it was closing in on five, I figured it wouldn't hurt to show and see if Jess could use some last minute help.

Máxim took in my appearance.

I'd knotted my hair in a high, loose bun and looped my pearls around my neck to make a choker. Matching pearls adorned my ears. I wore minimal makeup. Against the color of my unforgettable dress, my eyes appeared amber, so I played that up with a smidge of soft tawny eye shadow.

But would he approve of my gown? "Well?"

When the designer had first suggested yellow to highlight my tan and my eyes, I'd scrunched my nose, predicting a more conservative crowd here. Then I'd tried on the simple, strapless sheath dress and fell in love.

Máxim's gaze turned heated, his lips parting. "You are . . . exquisite, *solnyshko.*"

Seeing his reaction and knowing his past, I was glad I'd chosen vibrant and bold.

He met my eyes. "And you're *mine.*"

I swallowed. He'd meant every word last night.

Just when I got excited, he said, "Give me ten minutes, Miss Marín." *Miss.* "Let me grab a shower, and we'll go down."

"I thought I'd go see if Natalie and Jess needed anything."

Tension stole through his body. "Are you . . . are you avoiding me after what I told you?"

I leaned down to cup his face. "*No.*" I kissed him, brief, hard. "They asked me to be there two hours ago, but I held off. Then I started getting worried about Jess's wedding coordination today. I need to make sure that Natalie has a wingwoman. After all she's been through, she deserves to have the most fantastic wedding."

"Ah. I see." He stretched his arms over his head, making my mouth water. "I'm glad you hit it off with them. Go. I'll see you soon."

Out in the lodge, I headed toward the pavilion. I found the bridal party in an adjoining drawing room by following the sound of laughter. Inside was crowded. I skirted past bridesmaids and friends, hair stylists, makeup artists, photographers, and a videographer to get my first look at Natalie. My jaw dropped.

Her ivory gown must've been taken straight from a fairy tale. The dramatic, backless work of art had a skirt of flowing silk chiffon, with tints of pink that made her pale skin shimmer. She wore her long red hair up, loosely pinned and dotted with pearls, wisps curling around her beaming face.

I exclaimed, "*Dios mío, tan guapa!* You're so beautiful!"

She blushed and waved me over. "You're one to talk—you should always wear this color! I'd hug you, but Jess has forbidden me to touch anyone wearing makeup. Or to follow anything shiny. Or to sweat."

"Is there anything I can get for you?"

"It's all good, just as long as Jessabel doesn't catch me eating."

I saw Jess then. She wore the same soft pink dress as the other bridesmaids, only hers had a plunging neckline to reveal cleavage.

She pointed at me. "You are smokin' hot in that dress, *mami.* Come give me sugars. That limo's walking as bowlegged as Polly, amirite? Fucking Russians. Grab some bubbly. Catch up."

I guessed we'd smoothed over our tiff. One day, though, I *would* make her understand the law of diminishing returns.

I snagged a couple of flutes off a server's tray, handing one to Natalie. After a sip, I knew champagne remained a no-go for me.

"Were you eating a pastry?" Jess demanded of Natalie. Stern Jess was a force of nature. "Don't you *dare* touch that gown with your grubby Natalie paws. You might have no appreciation for couture, but I spent tens and tens of thousands of your dollars on this! You could at least be appreciative." She turned to snap her fingers at Polly. The girl tripped over herself and everyone else to get to Jess—who promptly tugged her bodice down to a sexier height. "What are we? Fucking Amish, like Cat?"

No longer! I stuck out my tongue at her.

Rebecca wended through the packed room to reach Natalie. Her eyes watered at the sight of her daughter. "My little girl." She sniffled.

"Oh, Mom," Natalie said in an aggrieved tone, but she was grinning widely.

When Rebecca's tears began to fall, Jess snapped, "She's not walking the plank; she's merely getting married—to a shady Russian mail-order groom. Did you take the pill I gave you? Take the pill. And I will tongue-check you."

Rebecca rolled her eyes behind her glasses. "Just to stop you from haranguing me, Jessica!" She plucked something out of her clutch, holding it up with a defiant look.

Jess's eyes went wide. "Hold up—"

But Rebecca was already washing it down with champagne. "It's just a Valium, right?"

Jess shook her head *no* as she said, "Yes, absolutely. In theory." *Oh, Dios mío.*

Rebecca thought she was joking. "Now can I cry over my little girl?"

"Ask me that again in twenty, Becks. . . ."

After that, we all chattered about nothing in particular, everyone excited, spirits high. I wished I could have had an experience like this, surrounded by friends and family for such an important event.

"All right, ladies." Jess clapped her hands. "T minus fifteen. Bathroom? Anyone? Speak now—or forever hold your piss."

Polly dashed out like she was taking fire, Rebecca followed her, unsteadily. Jess was right on her tail.

Shortly after, Jess returned to pull me out into the hall. Rebecca was leaning against the wall with a dreamy expression on her face.

"What's up?" I asked.

In a hushed voice, Jess said, "Natalie does *not* need to know this, but I might've accidentally given her mom the molly I was saving for tonight. You're officially on Rebecca Is Rolling duty." She turned to the woman. "See, Becks? Doesn't everything feel *softer* now?"

Mierda. "It's not a problem." My mantra. On the bright side, the woman's tears had dried right up!

"Can you take her to the pavilion?"

"On it."

As I was leading Rebecca away, I heard Natalie say, "Has anybody seen my mom?"

Jess loudly said, "Hot *mami*'s with her. They're already on their way."

I smiled up at the starry-eyed lady. "We're almost there, Rebecca. Here we go. We're turning left—our *other* left. Okay, *muy bien*."

The pavilion was spectacular with its sky-high pitched ceiling, arching rafters, and gleaming wood floor. Peonies, lilies, and lavish orchids graced the area, scenting the air. Past the immense plate-glass windows was a lit courtyard with hanging lanterns reflecting off the snow.

When I found Tom, he took Rebecca's hand with a frown. She petted his tie.

"Everything okay?" he asked me.

Bob and weave. "She had some champagne?" As I said that she licked his face like a stamp.

Baffled, Tom said, "Uh, Cat, will you please stay with her while I walk Natalie down the aisle?"

"You got it. Not a problem. Rebecca, we're over here." I tugged her to the front pew, eventually getting her to sit. I gazed around for anything to keep her attention—or possibly a pacifier and a glow stick. Coming up empty, I pointed at her dress hem. "Oh, look, Rebecca. It's the end of your dress! It's frilly frilly frilly."

She grew *fascinated* with it.

This whole weekend was turning out surreal. I was at the wedding of a Russian mobster's daughter to a cherished hit man, sitting next to a mother-of-the-bride who was tripping balls.

My . . . boyfriend (shivers) was in the *mafiya* as well. Oh, and a billionaire.

Aleks and three groomsmen entered then from another drawing room, taking their places at the altar.
They were supposed to line up and wait for the bridesmaids. So where was Máxim?

Natalie's groom was dashing in his crisp tux, yet he
still looked dangerous with his tats and close-cropped
hair. He was also clearly nervous, pulling at his collar,
craning his head, trying to get a look at Natalie.

His nervousness made me go *aww*. A man who
ate bullets for breakfast truly was afraid—that she'd get
away.

Then . . . Máxim entered.

When I got my first look at him in a tux, I sucked
in a breath, my arm flying out to the side, as if I'd been
in a car wreck.

Un hombre magnífico. He could not have looked
more gorgeous.

When his eyes found me, he gave me a cocky grin,
knowing he looked fucking magnificent—knowing I
was *floored* by him. The dark promise in his eyes made
me melt.

He took his place beside Aleks, both men so tall
and strong. The strain I'd sensed between the two had
eased a little more. He clapped his brother on the back,
razzing him about something.

As the wedding song began playing, I helped Rebecca to her feet. One by one, the bridesmaids walked
down the aisle. When Jess traipsed by, she winked and
blew me a kiss. My gaze slid to Máxim; he scowled
at that. Rebecca pointed at the ceiling and whispered,
"*Ohhh.*"

Then Tom escorted Natalie down the aisle and everyone sighed at the beautiful bride. Except Aleks. He adjusted his stance, as if he'd just caught himself from reeling.

Natalie looked totally at ease, ready to be married. To start a new life.

Even after Tom had given Natalie away and we'd all sat, Aleks still appeared awestruck by his bride. I thought his hand shook as he took hers.

I could hear Natalie say to Aleks, "You turned up hot, Siberian. I think I better put a ring on it."

His brows drew together, and he nodded earnestly.

As I tugged Rebecca to sit, I tried not to stare at Máxim. But my eyes only wanted to look at him.

Going to a wedding like this, with a man like him, was dangerous to my heart. At every turn something reminded me of a fairy tale; how long would it be before I started yearning for one of my own?

Once the bride and groom began to exchange their heartfelt vows, Máxim pinned me with his piercing gaze. Everything else faded until I could swear we were the only ones in the room.

His expression made my breath hitch, as if he was making his own promises to me. After his confessions this morning, I knew he wanted more from me—and he was willing to *bare his entire soul* to get it.

But the fact remained that as of right now, I was a married woman—and I'd let him believe I wasn't. I'd let *everyone* believe that.

No, I didn't speak lies.

I just lived them.

◆

Por Dios, don't let Máxim catch the garter. I adjusted my sweating grip on the bride's bouquet—the one *I* had caught.

Earlier, Jess had forced me into the crowd of single women vying for it. Though Polly had all but warmed up for the event and more than one girl had a fervent glimmer in her eyes, I'd been standing off to the side, feeling like an imposter, with no right to be there.

The flowers had hit my chest, dead center. If I hadn't caught the bouquet, it would've fallen to the ground.

All the girls congratulated me, some more believably than others. (*Really, Polly, sour grapes? Here. Take them.*) Natalie had hugged me, while Jess had declared herself my wedding coordinator: "Dibs, bitches!"

Máxim had wrapped his arms around me, eyes lively. "How *interesting*."

I'd plastered a smile on my face for all of them, never more aware that my life was a lie.

Everything had been going so well until then. On a back bench, I'd sat in Máxim's lap, with our fingers intertwined. We'd talked about Rebecca's recent drug use (about four more hours to roll, Becks), and how little I'd had to drink (champagne was dead to me), and how little he'd had to drink ("I'm a wingman. I hear these positions are to be taken seriously"), and how much his brother had relaxed now that Natalie was officially his.

Well, for a while, he'd been relaxed. Yet as the night

wore on and Natalie continually teased her groom—
with little glances and not-so-secretive touches—it
became clear that Aleks was ready to get to the con-
summation of his marriage.

Now, as he knelt before Natalie to remove her garter, the desire between the two could be measured on a
Richter scale. His hands shook with anticipation as he
tugged down the creamy lace band.

Máxim and other single men had gathered. The
swaggering devil winked at me. If I'd been single with
no worries, I probably would've swooned. Now it was
everything I could do to smile back.

When Aleks slingshot the garter over his shoulder,
I watched it as if it were a Hail Mary pass. Slo-mo . . .

Máxim caught it—because of his height advantage.

Jess bustled me to a chair. "Come on, *mamí* and
Maks!" I sat with the bouquet in my lap, and he knelt
before me. Everyone crowded around, clapping and
laughing.

All too happy to place the garter on me, Máxim
appeared very lusty himself.

"Look at that, he's about to get to first base," Jess
said. "You won the girl this round, Russian. But you
better take care of her. I have a Taser, and I don't know
how to use it!"

When he smoothed my dress up my legs, his gaze
darkened even more, and his hands began to shake
no less than his brother's had. As his touch ascended,
Máxim murmured, "Do you think fate's trying to tell
us something?"

Heart. In. Throat. I stiffened against him.

He could read me so well, and knew something was up. He secured the lace above my knee, then smoothed down my dress. As would be expected, he smiled at me.

For the first time ever, he'd given *me* his fake smile. . . .

CHAPTER 33

"*W*ill you please talk to me?" I asked Sevastyan shortly after we took off for Miami.

After we'd made love last night, I'd basically passed out, exhausted from maintaining a happy façade. I awakened briefly in the night and found him at the window, staring out into the dark, seeming to look at nothing. But that muscle had ticked in his jaw, and I could swear he'd looked . . . wounded.

I didn't think he'd slept at all. At the breakfast reception, tension had emanated from him. He'd been distant and stiffly courteous, that fake smile in full force.

"You've hardly spoken to me today, Máxim."

"I have a lot on my mind."

His phone rang, and without a word to me, he answered. I gazed out the jet's window, waiting for another chance for us to talk. One call turned to two, and then to five. I couldn't understand the words, but I had an uneasy feeling he'd been talking about me.

I retired to the cabin, lying down. Instead of making love on this bed again, we stood on opposite sides of a new rift.

My body was still exhausted, and my mind felt sluggish, as if I were shaking off the effects of one of Jess's drugs.

Maybe all this new stimulation had been too much for me. For three years, I'd lived as a social hermit, then I'd been thrust into a crush of new people. I'd gone from broke and scraping pennies to a shopping spree worth half a mil. I'd been abstinent, then glutted with sex. I'd been convinced I might not live to see my thirties—much less remarry—then I'd fallen in love with a man who wanted everything from me.

Confused, I slipped off to sleep. Nightmares of Edward overwhelmed me.

In one, he was covered with blood—*mine*—creeping closer to me. I stood frozen in place, unable to force my body to run—my only defense. In the background, I heard those ugly, wet sounds Julia had made as she'd strangled on her own blood. Again and again, I struggled to escape, begging Edward to leave me alone, but he kept stalking closer, vowing to me, "*I will BUTCHER you! I will cut you into pieces while you live!*"

My body jolted on the bed. I shot awake, sucking in breaths. Had we just landed? Why hadn't Máxim awakened me?

Once we began taxiing on the runway, I went to the lavatory. I'd never had nightmares about Edward this bad. Had I flown right back to him?

I washed my face, peering into the mirror. The relaxed woman I'd beheld days ago was gone, replaced by the Cat I'd seen for years.

When I rejoined Sevastyan in the cabin, I drew back at his expression. His tension had morphed—into seething anger.

I'd never seen him so furious. "What's happened? What's going on?" He could hardly look at me. That fury was for me?

I was in love with him, and he couldn't look at me.

He shot a vodka, saying nothing. His knuckles were white on the glass, that muscle in his jaw ticking.

In a daze, I followed him off the jet into the limo, though he acted as if he could've left me there on the tarmac.

We hadn't even gotten under way before he'd downed his first shot from the Bentley's bar. Here we were, back in sunny Miami—and it felt like the Arctic in here. He took another call, his tone clipped. We were closing in on the hotel before he hung up the phone.

"Máxim, I don't know what's happened with us, and I need you to explain it to me," I said. The divider was cracked, and Vasili could hear everything, but I didn't care.

"I told you I have a lot on my mind. We'll discuss it later." Everything about his demeanor said: *Back off.*

"You're putting walls up between us. Please *don't*. Talk to me."

"Very well." He poured another steep vodka. "Marry me."

"*Qué?*" I couldn't get enough air.

"I want you to marry me. Today."

I was about to throw up. This wasn't *happening*.

"I'll take that as a *yes*. We'll go directly back to the airport and fly to Las Vegas." He said something to Vasili, and the man began to slow the car.

To turn around.

I shook my head. "G-go to the hotel."

"Give me a reason."

"I've only known you for two weeks."

"Are you sure there's no other reason?" he demanded.

"Why are you being like this?"

He snapped something to Vasili, and we resumed our course to the hotel.

Sevastyan turned his infuriated gaze to me. "You didn't even consider the possibility of marrying me. Not for the briefest second, did you? Last night, when you caught the bouquet, you looked miserable about it. When I placed that garter on your leg, your body stiffened against me as it *never* has before."

"Everything was too . . . it was a lot to take in over one weekend. As of Christmas Day, I thought we would be parting on the twenty-eighth."

He gave a bitter laugh. "You've got your claws all in me, and you're looking for the door! You have never even imagined a future with me."

"No, that's not what I meant." How to explain? I'd known I was going to have difficulty revealing my past to him. Now, freaked out and emotional, I could barely find words. "It's just that . . . things are complicated."

"I'll bet they are."

"What does that mean?"

He waved that away. "I just told you I'd marry you. A woman in your position should've been *tempted*."

"My position." As someone who sold sex.

"But then, the problem with all my wealth is that I come with it!"

This argument had taken me completely off guard. Because I'd *lowered* my guard with him.

"What the fuck was I thinking? I told you there'd be no one else. That you were with me. I confided things I've never told another soul." The pain in his eyes rocked me. "And I don't even know your real name. I expected things from you I shouldn't. I can't force you to change."

"You want me to change?" I couldn't disguise the hurt in my voice. "How?"

"For instance, when I inform you that I'm a *former* hobbyist, you might mention to me that you are a *former* escort. Just a thought."

I rubbed my temples. "I don't understand any of this. I don't know where it's coming from." Maybe he regretted revealing his past. I believed talking to me *had* eased something in him—but it still would've had to hurt, to leave him raw. Was I getting the backlash from that? "Why are you coming at me like this?"

"You shouldn't have let me believe you were attainable if you aren't. You let me believe you could be won."

"What are you talking about?"

"You lied about that and so many other things. You looked people in the eyes, and the words danced from your tongue. You deceive better than a politician."

My confusion was turning to anger, my foggy mind

clearing. "I get your mistrust. I have reasons not to trust others too. But you need to understand something."

He shot his glass. "Can't wait to hear this."

"I have never—from the first sentence I uttered—lied to you."

The fury in his eyes almost had me shrinking back into my seat.

"I told you never to deceive me! I've revealed why I will never tolerate it. Yet you keep doing it."

"When? Name an instance!"

"I nearly believed you when you told me you had no other man! You met my gaze and assured me you didn't—yet you told your friend that you were involved with another."

"What friend?" Had he misunderstood something I'd said over the weekend?

"Last week, I bugged the penthouse for my meetings. I quite enjoyed your conversation with Ivanna."

I gasped, reflecting over what I'd said. I'd talked to her about the belt, about walking around in this lust-fueled haze, fantasizing about his body. That conversation had been private—and humiliating! My face flushed with embarrassment, which just made me angrier.

"Did you think I wasn't aware a phone got to you? I allowed it in. Later that night, I listened to the recording."

"Then you knew I never tried to trap you with a pregnancy! And you didn't tell me? Just like I thought! You *wanted* to keep me there—to keep treating me like a deceitful *prostitutka*! So you could do whatever you wanted with me. You amused yourself with me. You played with me. With *my* life."

We pulled up to the hotel. Vasili hurried out of the car around to the door, but then he just stood there.

"Just like you played me!" Sevastyan snapped. "You made me believe you felt something for me. So I decided I would win you from him—I would spoil you, immersing you in my world, while removing you from his. I thought I'd had success until your reactions last night. Now I know that I can't simply *will* this to happen. Your heart's taken. By *Edward*. You're in love with him."

I could feel the blood leaving my face. Sevastyan had said Edward's name out loud. I had the impulse to cross myself. "H-how?"

"On the plane, you said his name in your sleep! Moaned it!" He knocked back another vodka. "I now know what you sound like when you fuck the man you actually do give a damn about."

Had I said anything else? The need to run overpowered me. My gaze flitted to the door handle.

"Even before the recording confirmed it, I knew you had another. I knew every time you stared off at nothing that you were thinking of him. When you took that goddamned picture for the escort site, you were thinking of him."

Sevastyan was right. I had been.

"When you were *with me*—you fucking moaned *for him*." He was about to shatter his glass. "But then you warned me all along, didn't you? You told me I wanted you more than you wanted me."

He inhaled, as if to rein in his rage. "All of this is moot. I don't have to trust you or win you. I merely have to *pay* you. Shouldn't we settle accounts before you come up?"

"Don't do this." He was breaking my heart.

"Do what? Will a 'donation' of fifteen thousand a day suffice? Or twenty?" He popped open his briefcase, revealing stacks of wrapped hundreds. With a snide look, he said, "Perhaps Edward is expecting you to return flush with cash? Do you two have that kind of arrangement?"

Some invisible force was punching me in the stomach, like a fist. It had to be, because I couldn't breathe.

"Come now, ask me for your payment, little girl."

When I thought about how close I'd come to revealing to him all my secrets—breaking the rules that kept me alive—I grew queasy. I *hadn't* learned the lessons I'd paid so dearly for. "I was planning to tell you everything today, to trust you! *Gracias a Dios*, you showed your true colors—yet again—before I could say anything. You're the only one here who's betraying trust! Go back and review your creepy tapes. I— never—lied."

Shaking with fury to match his own, I took off my string of pearls and threw it at Sevastyan. "You *don't* want me more than you want your old ways. You aren't ready to cast them aside for me. So I've got no time for you. I'm leaving, and this time you won't stop me."

In a bored tone, he said, "Enough with the theatrics. You won't leave."

"Oh, I won't?" I nearly ripped my earlobes to get the earrings out. "You are always so wrong about me. Do you know why? Because you have never given me the benefit of the doubt. Not from the first minute I met you. You always expect the worst of me. ALWAYS." I threw the earrings and almost flung my purse at him but somehow had the presence of mind to stop myself. I'd need what was left of that pin money to get a cab back to my apartment.

I would use the seven grand in my safe and get out of town, as I'd always planned. After my exam tomorrow, I'd take the first bus heading west. I'd put this man behind me—just as I had my husband. I reached for the door.

My leaving seemed to baffle him. "All you have to do is ask for your gifts. Hundreds of thousands of dollars' worth. No escort would walk away from that."

As I exited the car, I said, "Watch me, *cabrón*."

"Fucking ask me, Katya, and they'll be yours." Just like that first night, he kept talking, still engaging me. "Or is your pride going to get in the way?"

I glared at Vasili standing next to the car, then leaned down to tell Sevastyan, "You have no idea about my pride, Russian. It burns so bright, I hope it fucking blinds you." I slammed the door and strode away. With each step my shoulders went back, my chin up.

Going forward? Rule number seven would be never to fall in love.

CHAPTER 34

On the long ride home, I hardly registered the glaring sun, the swaying palm trees, the warmth after Nebraska.

The second I'd gotten into the cab, I'd taken out my phone and stared at the screen, wondering if he would contact me. To kill time, I'd sent Ivanna a voice message and then a text. I needed to tell her good-bye anyway.

That had been a while ago—strange that she hadn't tried to call. Shouldn't she be dying for scoop?

What would I tell her about Sevastyan? Was I making the right decision with him?

During my time at the hotel, I'd worried that I would grow used to hooded blue eyes and mind-blowing sex, and my infatuation with him would spiral out of control.

Check. Check. Check.

I might put Sevastyan behind me, but I was never

going to *get over* him. Though I'd easily shed my re-
gard for Edward, it wouldn't happen with Máxim.
With a sinking feeling in my belly, I recognized that I
was always going to love him.

Me jodí. I was so screwed.

Was I ready to write him off totally? How would
I feel if he'd groaned another woman's name in sleep?

Now that I'd had some time to cool off, I wasn't
as outraged about him playing me. He'd never *lied*
to me per se, and he had started treating me better
after eavesdropping on my conversation. He'd tried
to win me.

But nothing could excuse how callously he'd
treated me today. *I merely have to pay you.* Clearly, he
hadn't gotten over the fact that I was an escort.

As I closed in on my dismal neighborhood, my
need for survival rose to the fore, drowning out my
spiraling emotions. I never would have taken Sevastyan's gifts (not even my red scarf), but I shouldn't
have left my ten grand in the closet. *Mierda!*

Wait, Anthony still owed me! I pulled up his
number and rang him. An assistant put me straight
through.

"Cat! Great to hear from you!"

"Hey." We'd never actually spoken, even in the
midst of his selling me to Sevastyan. "I need to come
by and get the money I earned."

"What money, darling?"

Was he joking? "For all my outcall hours. Plus the
twenty-five hundred I'm due for my phone number."

"Oh, honey, I've already invested it for you! Got you lined up with a photographer! A legit one. He'll make you look like a million dollars."

It is not *a problem.* "Anthony, you can get my pay back, a quick refund. I need it now."

"No can do. But if you're short of dough, I've got a French millionaire in town who loves Latinas. He's a huge tipper. A shade raunchy, but he pays for his raunchy ways, you know what I mean—"

"You son of a bitch! Get my money back!"

His voice dropped. "You better be nice to Uncle Anthony, girl. Especially since the Russian's well ran dry. At least for you."

"What are you talking about?" He couldn't know Sevastyan and I were over.

"He just got done scheduling someone else."

"Wh-what?"

"Five minutes ago. He booked the one he'd wanted in the first place."

Ivanna. Stunning, glamorous, sensual Ivanna. Who ticked every one of Sevastyan's boxes.

"The Russian was as determined to have her as he'd been with you. He's definitely through with you, darling."

I didn't know whether to scream—or cry. Sevastyan *had* gone back to his old ways, the PhD was at it again. Former hobbyist, my ass!

Did I believe he had felt something for me? In his own way, yes. He'd probably requested Ivanna just to hurt me, or to amuse himself at *my* expense. He *was* still scheming and coldhearted! Fuck him!

Oh, wait, that was Ivanna's job. No wonder she hadn't called me back. Would he stick to the script with her? Or would they enjoy the pool and champagne?

Anthony said, "So let's talk about the French guy—"

Without another word, I hung up the phone. That invisible fist had returned, punching me even harder. I doubled over, gasping to the cabbie, "Stop here."

Anthony called back. Then he texted about that date. And again! He thought he had the right to burn up my line? The asshole was using my dire straits to lure me deeper into hooking!

As the cab rolled to a stop, I glared at my still buzzing phone. It'd been in Sevastyan's possession for over a week. Business of information? He'd probably placed some kind of tracker in it.

This town was done for me; I had no one to call. Decided, I stuffed the phone under the cab driver's seat as I paid him.

Under a winter-bright sun, I stumbled across the parking lot. Too late I realized that Sevastyan would have to give a damn to use my phone against me. He'd be too busy tonight with Ivanna.

I'd worried that he was setting me up for a crash landing. Oh, he had. I felt like there were parts of me scattered all over the pavement, my heart shattered like glass.

Once I reached my apartment complex after being away so long, I grimaced. I hadn't remembered how horrid it was. I climbed the stairs, feeling a hundred years older.

Inside my studio, I peered around, thunderstruck. How had I lived here for half a year? *Only one more night, only one more night.*

Over the weekend, I'd started to believe I would have a future with a guy who could help me stand up to Edward. A partner, someone on my team. I'd lowered my guard. I'd gotten caught up in that life, that *man*. I'd gotten soft.

Never again.

I crossed to my safe. I'd count up my loot. That would make me feel better. I unscrewed the AC vent and removed the grill—

My thoughts blanked. My safe was . . . empty. I blinked in bewilderment. Empty?

EMPTY?

My money was gone. My own meager savings, plus what I'd earned from Sevastyan. Who the hell could have taken it? Who would've known?

I had only Sevastyan's pin money to my name. After the cab, that left me two hundred and forty dollars. Would that even pay for the bus fare out west?

Tears welled. My hopes of leaving Miami, of reaching safety, were gone. I had no expectation of help from Sevastyan; the well *had* gone dry—right when I'd been robbed.

I threw back my head and yelled.

Once I'd finished primal screaming, I realized that my ID and my mother's rosary had been filched as well. What kind of fiend would steal a rosary? Even Sevastyan's money clip was gone.

Who could have gotten in? I had a dead bolt on

the door. I gazed around, fear trickling inside me. I stilled, only now detecting a smell that shouldn't be here: a mix of sweat and cigarettes.

Shadwell.

He'd been in my apartment. He must've stolen everything! But how had he known where my hiding place was?

Following some instinct, I crossed to my underwear drawer. All of my thongs were gone. That sick fuck! He knew I couldn't go to the cops. My first impulse was to go throat-punch him. No, he probably *wanted* me to confront him.

Yet again I would be the shrewd coward, unable to do a damned thing. *Stole my dinero, Shadwell? Don't spend it all in one place. My ID? I didn't need to work—that's not how I roll. My mother's rosary? Vaya con Dios.*

When the import of what I'd lost truly hit me, I was sure I'd lose my ever-loving shit as well.

Block it out. For now, survival. How the hell was I going to get money? I weighed options. Maybe I should call Natalie? But she was in St. Bart's for her honeymoon. Jess? Oh, wait. No phone.

Fuck. *Me jodí.*

My eyes went wide. Mrs. Abernathy! I'd confirmed with her. In a private jet, I'd told myself the joke was on her. I almost laughed.

I could clean tomorrow before my exam at two and get another one twenty. It wasn't a lot, but I could increase my net worth by 50 percent.

Three hundred and sixty dollars.

Three-sixty.

How fitting.

Still, it'd be enough to get me out of town. But how to make it through the night? Shadwell had a key, could waltz in here at any time. If I nodded off, I could wake up to his leering face.

I'd gone from strong arms to hold me and body-guards protecting me to imminent attack.

CHAPTER 35

As I scrubbed the floor of the blue bathroom at Mrs. Abernathy's, I stared at the tiles until they ran together. Only a few more hours to my exam.

Last night, I'd held vigil at my violated apartment—inside my own bathroom, with the door locked. I'd gotten little sleep, but I'd been able to steal out early, eluding Shadwell and kissing that place good-bye forever.

Now to blow this city.

On Mrs. Abernathy's computer I'd looked up the Greyhound bus schedule. My three-sixty would take me to San Diego, barely. A bus left tonight, not long after my exam. I located a women's shelter in Cali not far from the terminal. Maybe they could help me until I got back on my feet.

Until I could get another ID.

Here I was—totally screwed—and yet I couldn't stop thinking about Sevastyan and Ivanna. This morning, I'd vomited after imagining them together.

While I'd fallen for him, his preferences had re-verted to tall, slim, blond, and European.

Of course, I hadn't been able to study last night, what with the continual crying and fear of Shadwell. What if I was so tired and despondent that I couldn't think? What if I flunked? For years, my goal had been to make a perfect 4.0. If I failed right at the end, why should I believe I could succeed at other goals?

My grail, my college credit odyssey, my penance and atonement. All jeopardized because of Sevastyan—

"What the hell are you doing?"

I jerked around with a scream, stunned to see him at the doorway of the blue bathroom. "H-how did you find me?"

"I knew you were going to be at a Mrs. Abernathy's on this day. There are only so many in Miami that made sense."

When I'd confirmed with the woman, he'd recorded it! "You have no right! If I get caught with you here, I'll get fired." Not that I was ever coming back.

"And that matters?" His tie was loosened, and his hair was unruly, as if he'd been stabbing his fingers through it. He looked like he'd slept less than I had— and I'd been in my bathtub.

Because he'd been with stunning Ivanna all night? The invisible fist paid me a visit.

"You appear . . . different," he said.

Even in the midst of my emotional turmoil, I hated the fact that I looked like hell. My hair was plaited in two braids, and I wore a faded bandana on my head.

Bright yellow gloves, clunky running shoes, frayed jean shorts, and an old T-shirt rounded out my ensemble. No makeup, naturally.

And I was kneeling in floor cleaner. I sponged it up. "You have to leave." What did he want from me? Did he regret his snide cruelty to me? Did he regret screwing my friend?

Too late, Russian.

"Here." He offered his hand.

I slapped it away, standing on my own, tearing off my gloves. I stuffed my supplies in a cleaning caddy, then shoved past him.

"I'm not leaving until you tell me what's going on." He followed me as I stowed the caddy in a closet.

"I'm at work. You're stalking me."

"You know I'll pay for any income you lose, however modest it might be."

I whirled around on him. "Don't you dare! You don't get to insult me for being an escort, then turn around and insult me for cleaning houses. You can't have it both ways!"

He pinched the bridge of his nose. "You're right. But yesterday I offered you more than you could make at this in years. You know economics. This is not the highest and best use of your time."

"I don't want *your* money! And I damn sure don't want to beg you for it." I hurried down the grand staircase to collect my pay and my backpack.

He was right beside me. "I was angry. That was uncalled for. I would not do that again."

In the kitchen, my gaze flicked to the envelope on the counter; his did too. He lunged for it before I reached it.

"That's mine!"

He flipped through the bills, then surveyed the spotless mansion. "Are you fucking kidding me?" He finally handed my pay over.

Stuffing the envelope into a pocket, I headed to the back entrance. At the door, I grabbed my pack and snapped to Sevastyan, "Get out. *Now.*" I punched in the alarm code. If only I'd armed it before my stalker had arrived.

With raised brows, he exited. "To be given the code for a place like this, you must've been cleaning it for a while."

The clock on the alarm panel said one! *Mierda!* I'd lost track of time. My bus stop was half a mile away. If I missed my ride, I'd miss my exam.

"I just want five minutes, Katya."

"I don't *have* five minutes and wouldn't give them to you even if I did. Sevastyan, consider this a *scarcity* situation. As far as you're concerned, my ass just got scarce." I hurried outside, rolling my eyes to see Vasili parked on the street.

Forbidding clouds gathered overhead. Getting to school in the rain; perfect. When I hustled toward my stop, Sevastyan kept following me! "*Déjame en paz!*"

"Leave you alone? Not until you talk to me."

Would he follow me onto the bus? If he did, he could find out where I went to school. Maybe I should try to put him off. I stopped, telling him, "If you go now, I will meet up with you later. I'll swing by the hotel."

"Oh, really?"

"I can be there at five, and we'll talk all of this out."

He blinked down at me. "You're . . . lying." A breath left him. "And you're fucking *awful* at it."

"Ugh!" The bus was already at the stop. I took off running to catch it, careening inside the doors. I wanted to scream when the bastard climbed in right before they closed. So much for a period of calm to get my mind straight for my last exam in college. "Isn't public transportation beneath you?" I demanded, tapping my card pass.

He gazed around at all the eyes on him. With his expensive threads, he stood out like a Russian billionaire on public transportation.

"Where's your pass?" the driver barked.

Sevastyan looked at a loss. "I don't have one. But I'm not getting off this bus."

"If you pay in cash, you don't get change."

Pulling out his full money clip, Sevastyan peeled off a crisp hundred. "I hope this will suffice." He'd just handed away almost as much as I'd made slaving over a huge mansion.

The driver said, "Enjoy the ride."

I hastened toward the back, wishing there were more people. I sat by a window, putting my pack next to me.

He moved it to his lap and sat. "I need to speak with you—in private."

I yanked my bag from him. "And I need you to *not*

be here. We both crapped out." Rain began to patter the roof, then pour.

"You're not even interested in what I'm offering?"

"Go. To. Hell."

"Please talk to me, Katya." Determined to ignore him, I stared out the window. "So stubborn. You'll find that I am too."

For the rest of the way, I refused to speak to him. When the bus slowed, my face fell. At the stop for my next bus, the one that took me close to campus, everyone was crowded under the shelter. I'd have to wait in the rain.

I rose and trudged through the doors to the street.

He followed me into the downpour. "You're waiting for *another* one of these?" he asked, aghast.

The temperature had dropped. I began to shake from the wet cold. "F-feel f-free to leave."

When the bus pulled up, he said, "Enough of this." He waved for his Bentley, because apparently Vasili had been following us—

Sevastyan snagged my upper arm, forcing me toward the car.

"Nooo, I need to get on that bus!" Though I kicked at his leg, he was dogged, and in seconds, I found myself in the backseat.

The divider was down, so he told Vasili, "Follow the bus." To me, he said, "See how much easier this is?" He turned on the heater.

"You can't do this to me!" At least we were heading in the right direction. Once we closed in on the campus, I'd dart out of the car. "Y-you kidnapped me off the street?"

"You forget I'm in the *mafiya*. Taking people off the street is a matter of course." Was that a joke? Or a threat?

I hit my limit. I was *sick* of men threatening me, manhandling me, ignoring my wishes, stealing my life's savings—and my underwear—and planning to kill me. "Stop this car."

"I'll take you wherever you want to go. Tell me the address."

I screamed, "*Stop this motherfucking car!*"

Undaunted, he said, "Where are you so desperate to get to?"

"What the hell is this, Sevastyan? You were cruel and disgusting to me, not twenty-four hours ago! So why are you stalking me now?"

"I made a mistake yesterday." Did he think he could just erase it, and we'd go back to the way we were? "Katya, I was in your apartment."

"*What?*" I couldn't be more horrified. I pictured the pots on the floor and the pitiful cot. "How?"

"We canvassed out from where the cab dropped you, paying people for information. It led us to Shadwell. For a price, he let us in." *I bet he did.*

Wait, I'd walked blocks from the Seltane to catch that cab—specifically for this reason! "How could you know which taxi drove me?"

"By tracking your phone all over town. You were smart to ditch it, but ultimately it led us to the cab you'd taken."

Burn. Foiled by my own attempt at cleverness. "You had no right to be there."

"No wonder you knew about those shithole apartments. You're living in one yourself. You would prefer to be there? Instead of with me?"

"Yes! Because I paid for it. Because I didn't have to beg some sick Russian hobbyist to give me my 'donation.'"

He seemed to stifle a wince at that. "You had money. Thousands. Why not find a better place? An extended-stay hotel? Anywhere but there?"

"You're really going to do this? Then listen up, Sevastyan. I couldn't stay in a hotel because Shadwell—the guy you paid for entry to my apartment—stole all my money out of my hiding place. Seven grand. Gone. My mother's rosary too. Even your money clip. Oh, and my thongs! He's been shaking me down for months, shaking down everybody—making a fortune, and using the women as his personal harem. And now he was coming and going in my place as he pleased?" I leaned in, drawing my lips back from my teeth. "Even so, I stayed the night in my locked bathroom—rather than ask *you* for help."

That muscle in Sevastyan's jaw ticked overtime. "Did he . . . you . . . ?"

"I wasn't weak enough—yet. I paid him to leave me alone." But my rosary and ID were gone for good.

The full import of what I'd lost was starting to hit. I *was* about to lose my ever-loving shit.

"You'll have your rosary and your money back." He said something in Russian to Vasili, but I heard

"Shadwell." Oh, the plans going on behind Sevastyan's eyes.

I could almost feel sorry for Shadwell, that preying, stealing serial rapist—

No. Actually I didn't feel sorry for him at all. Maybe I was an ideal match for a mobster. My supe was about to get a horse's head in his bed. *Okay, muy bien.*

To me, Sevastyan snapped, "You could've been raped last night! Or killed! You never thought about calling me?"

I gave him a palms-up shrug. "Oh, so sad, no phone. I didn't toss it solely because I was suspicious of you tracking me. Uncle Anthony wouldn't stop burning up my number. You see, he stole even more of my money and was trying to coerce me into a date with some French businessman, so I could—as you so eloquently put it—suck and fuck."

Sevastyan grated more Russian to Vasili. Anthony gets a horse head too!

"You're never going back to that apartment, Katya. I'll burn it to the goddamned ground first."

"Wasn't planning on it."

His gaze flicked to my full backpack. "You're about to disappear." He swallowed, as if I'd just presented him with a ticking bomb. "I'm asking you for one conversation. Or simply give me the honor of assisting you now." He opened his briefcase, revealing stacks of bound bills. "I *owe* you money. Please collect what is already yours."

"I don't want anything from you. I'll take my three hundred and sixty dollars, and I'll start over. I will go round and round and fucking round!" I knew I wasn't making any sense, but I couldn't focus my thoughts. "I'm so sick of men! I was nothing but good to you— for you—and you drove me away!"

In a low voice, he said, "You group me with Anthony and Shadwell?"

"You're *worse*! I never believed in them!" I couldn't stop shaking. "I'd made the decision to tell you everything, but you would rather be cruel and hurt me than listen!"

He leaned forward in his seat, fists clenched as if he was barely preventing himself from touching me. "Let me help you, please. I want to protect you. I understand that I handled things badly. But I don't know my way around a situation like this."

Gazing past him, I said, "Like what?"

"You told me your pride burned bright. It should. Yesterday, mine took some deserved hits. I comprehended that I loved another more than myself—and that I want her far more than she does me. She'd given her heart to someone else, and it made me crazed with jealousy—an emotion I have limited experience with. I didn't know how to handle it, so I lashed out and hurt her."

Love?

He stabbed his fingers through his hair. "I thought I'd treated you well. I thought I'd pleasured you and indulged you—but you still wanted Edward. Then last night, I realized it didn't matter if you loved someone else. I *need* to protect you. You could tell me to go to hell, but I would still do it."

And all it'd taken for him to have this epiphany was screwing Ivanna. Something in me snapped.

With a screech, I dug stacks of money from the briefcase and threw them in his face. "Maybe you should've thought of that before you booked my friend!"

His lips parted on a breath. "You're jealous, finally! You *do* give a fuck about me! Now you know how I felt when you cried out for another man!"

Out of the corner of my eye, I saw the water tower near campus. "*Stop!*" We'd passed my classroom! "Stop here!" I could still run and make it on time.

"Tell me what's here."

"I will—just stop!"

He called for Vasili, and the car slowed.

I lunged for the door, but Sevastyan snatched my hand. "Where are you running?"

Eyes wide, I cried, "To get the grail!" I yanked open the door, stumbling out into the rain, almost falling before I righted myself. Money flew out after me, crisp hundreds flying on a stormy breeze.

Without a look back, I ran to finish my degree.

CHAPTER 36

Get it together, Cat.

As I waited for Ms. Gillespie in her classroom, I gazed out the window, catching my breath after my frantic sprint here. The clouds were so dark, the day looked more like night.

My thoughts raced. Too many things had happened to process. Over the weekend, I'd recognized that I loved Sevastyan. I'd been happy with him, happy to make new friends. He'd basically proposed. Last night I'd been barricaded in a bathroom, all my hopes in ruins. And now my whole life was in turmoil. What did Sevastyan want from me? Did he expect me to contact him—

My jaw dropped. His car pulled up and stopped across the street! How the hell did he find me? I'd hauled ass over more than a mile, skirting between buildings and over the quad.

He stepped out into the drizzle, scanning for a moment before his gaze settled on me. From his vantage, he could see into my second-story classroom. Could see *me* under bright fluorescent lights.

What must he be thinking about this? Would he bust in? Or would he hang out while I took my test?

He took out his phone and texted someone. A instant later, a chime sounded. I stilled.

That was *my* text chime. From *my* bag.

I opened the pack and fished it out. He'd slipped the phone in so he could track me! Maybe when I'd been looking out the window on the bus? Sneaky Russian!

He was giving me a brows-drawn look. I must like pain in all its forms, because I pulled up the message.

M Sevastyan: I don't know what you're doing. I hope you do well. I would never be unfaithful to you.

Damn him! Did I dare believe him? Maybe he'd booked Ivanna to get information on me. But why hadn't she called me back? I checked the rest of my messages. Several were from her number, not two hours after I'd ditched the phone. *Mierda!*

Despite her long red nails, she'd attempted to text: takked ti Sev!!1 U lnded hom!

Landed him? Even if he hadn't been with Ivanna, Sevastyan and I still weren't good. Not in any way. He'd been horrible to me. Because of him, I'd nearly lost my mind last night—and today.

I texted him back: you broke my heart yesterday

When he read the message, his head jerked up, disbelief in his expression. Without looking away from me, he replied: let. me. mend. it.

We stared at each other as my chest twisted and twisted.

"Hi, Cat, are you ready?" Ms. Gillespie said as she breezed into the room.

I turned from the window. "Ready as ever."

"You'll have forty-five minutes." She handed me the exam.

I settled into a desk. I could do this! Yet as I stared down at the page, the text swam before my eyes. Were my eyes watering again? I never cried in front of other people.

"Are you okay?" she asked.

"I-I'm fine." *Get it together!* "Ready to get started." My gaze slid to the window again. Sevastyan was still out there, watching me. *Hey, no pressure.* If he caused me to tank my grade, I would have to murder him.

I read, "Question number one," and I thought *Rule number one*. I was at the end of my odyssey. Would I choke at the finish line . . . ?

Forty-five minutes later, Ms. Gillespie said, "Time's up."

I gathered my stuff, then trudged up to her. I couldn't remember my answers. I wanted to go back over the test—and make sure I hadn't written MUR-DER over and over—but she looked expectantly at me.

"This is your last class, right?" When I nodded, she said, "I could grade the exam now, if you'd like."

"That'd be great." As she began to read my answers, I peered out the window. Sevastyan leaned against his car, phone at his ear.

Again, I wondered what I would have done if I'd heard him groan a woman's name—after overhearing him tell a friend, "I'm involved with another woman."

"This looks wonderful, Cat," Ms. Gillespie said, drawing my gaze. "An A. Congratulations on completing your courses!"

I'd finished.

I'd atoned and kept my promise.

One day, I would transfer all these credits to get my degree.

One day, it would say summa cum laude on it.

All this time, all this work, and I'd done it! When I'd first started college, I'd pictured myself celebrating with friends upon graduating. What would I do now? My eyes only wanted to look at Máxim. He'd said he loved me, but could I believe that? Should I give my flawed mobster another shot?

Maybe. Since he'd kind of ended up being the love of my life and all.

Our relationship wasn't pretty. The heavy lifting still needed to be done. But the foundation was there. "I really appreciate the makeup, Ms. Gillespie."

"I had something else I wanted to talk to you about. Last week, there was a man looking for you. But he wasn't from around here."

I gasped out, "What did you tell him?"

"Though I knew this was your last class, I told him you'd be here when the spring term started."

Next week. I still had time. "Why would you lie for me?"

"I didn't like the looks of him. It's none of my business, but he seemed . . . unwell."

Deranged. "Th-thank you so much, Ms. Gillespie."

I was crying before I made it down the hall. Edward

had *already* been called down upon me. Ready to break every rule and swallow all my pride, I rang Sevastyan. "*Ruso?*"

"Katya, what's wrong?"

I hurried down the stairs. "I need"—my voice broke on a sob—"help."

"Anything. Name *anything.*"

"I-I'm in trouble." When I reached the quad, I spotted him in the distance.

He'd already started across the street to come for me. "Whatever it is, we'll figure it out." The skies opened up even more and rain poured. Winds gusted, palm fronds battering each other. Lightning jagged across the sky.

Comprehension struck with the intensity of the bolts above. *He* is *in love with me.* He'd said he wanted to protect me. If there were ever a time I would need him to . . . "The dream I had on the plane was a—"

An arm snaked around me. Searing pain exploded.

I stared down in horror. At the blade jutting from my chest.

Blackness.

CHAPTER 37

A guttural bellow woke me. Sevastyan's? My eyes crept open.

Edward had stabbed me. He'd actually done it.

I lay on the ground. The bastard had my head in his lap, his pale, haggard face above me. The knife hilt was rising and falling with my wheezing breaths. The *pain* . . . every inhalation was a new anguish. My fingers clawed at the grass, my legs uncontrollably writhing. Dots swarmed my vision.

I didn't want to die by his hand. I wanted out of his repulsive arms—

He tore the knife from my chest; I needed to scream, but I couldn't.

The ugly sounds were now mine.

"And who are those men, wife?" Edward put the knife to my throat, but he wasn't looking at me. His crazed eyes were focused on Sevastyan as he ran for me, Vasili in the distance behind him, gun raised.

"Stop where you are," Edward yelled over the rain, pressing the knife harder.

Máxim and Vasili went motionless.

"Your man needs to drop his gun," Edward called. "Then you both back away. Or I'll show you my wife's throat from the inside."

If Sevastyan was shocked to hear him call me wife, he didn't reveal it. He'd probably put so much together. "Release—her—now." He looked lethal, his big body tensed to attack. Rage blazed from him, his eyes filled with it. His wet hair whipped over his face in the wind, his fists clenched.

Edward had no idea who he was dealing with. "This doesn't concern you, stranger."

Máxim told Vasili something in Russian. Vasili put his gun down, backing from it by a step.

Never looking away from Sevastyan, Edward told me, "I didn't expect you to make friends, Ana-Lucía. You never did before, not in any of the six cities you hid from me. It would've made finding you so much easier. Not that I would ever have stopped. I will get revenge for Julia, and I'm prepared to die for it."

He'd been to all the places I'd lived? Between wet coughs, I bit out, "H-how?"

"I overheard your vow to your mother to finish your degree. For three years, I spent your money to comb every school in the country. You used family names— your first and only mistake." His chin and jaw were slack between words. "I hunted you here. When I suspected your bitch of a teacher was lying for you, I knew I had you trapped."

Máxim grated, "Get the fuck away from her, *Edward*. This is my last warning."

"You almost won, Ana-Lucía. You almost got the best of me. For someone like you to rob me of Julia . . . it seethes inside me every second of every day. Because of you, I had to bury her like trash in some fetid marsh—"

Máxim told Vasili something else in Russian, then started forward.

Edward jerked his head up. "What are you doing, stranger? I'll kill her if you come closer!"

Máxim kept coming, six foot four inches of towering, enraged Russian. "She'll bleed out if I don't."

"I didn't expect her to have friends, but I wasn't unprepared." Edward dropped the knife, pulling a gun from a holster under his coat. "Now you and the other man leave us, or I will shoot you down."

He was going to kill Máxim! "*Don't.*" There was nothing I could do to stop him! Frustration welled inside me.

Máxim was fearless. "I know gunmen. You're not one."

Edward cocked his weapon. "I *will* shoot!" This close, he couldn't miss.

"And when you do, my man will retrieve his gun and take you out." Máxim was *planning* to get shot? For me? "There is no scenario where she doesn't live."

Need to help him. Gritting my teeth, I patted the ground for Edward's blade. So dizzy. *Stay awake or Máxim dies.* For all these years, I'd wanted to be brave. Now was my chance.

There! The knife. I curled my fingers around the hilt.

"Stop where you are!" Edward squinted one eye—to take the shot!

No, no, no! I lifted the knife. With the last of my strength, I screamed and struck, stabbing his arm. But the gun was going off! The deafening blast boomed beside my ear.

Máxim's shoulder jerked back. Edward yelled, "You bitch—"

Another shot followed? Edward was thrown back from me. My head slammed into the ground, and the angry sky spun.

A second later, Maksim pulled me into his arms. "*Katya*," he rasped. "I've got you."

CHAPTER 38

As the car started moving, I tried to wake up more, to make sure Máxim was okay and to tell him that I'd be fine.

He had one arm wrapped around my back, his other hand pressing down on my wound. "Stay with me, *solnyshko*! You need to stay awake!" He yelled at Vasili. Our speed increased till I felt like we were zooming.

"Máxim . . . you were *shot*."

"Flesh wound. You fouled his aim—or I'd be dead."

I pried open my eyes. "Is he?"

"He's taken care of. Please stay awake for me!" Máxim looked like he was about to lose it. "Talk to me. Tell me about this."

"I finally *can*."

"You've been running from Edward for three years?"

"Never stay in a place . . . longer than six months." My voice sounded so far away. "Rule number three."

"You were about to leave Miami for good?"

I tried to nod. "I clean houses. Ivanna's. But Shadwell . . . I had no money. Thought I saw Edward here. . . ."

"Keep talking. You thought you saw him, then what happened?"

"Scared. I could take Ivanna's date with some Russian . . . I figured one guy, one night. Couldn't be worse than Edward." I lost track of what I'd been saying. My lids felt so heavy.

"You told me I was your first. I refused to believe you. No, no, stay with me! Keep talking. When did you marry him?"

"Eighteen. After my mom died. H-he killed her." My voice broke. "I was so stupid. Got swindled out of everything."

"Swindled? What did he want from you?"

"He and Julia . . . wanted my beach. Planned to kill me too."

"Your *beach*?"

"Martinez Beach. Worth one fifty."

Sevastyan's brow furrowed. "They targeted you for a hundred and fifty thousand dollars?"

"Million."

I heard Vasili gasp from the front seat. "Is Vasili shot too?"

"No, he's surprised, as am I."

"It's in trust . . . couldn't sign it over." I needed to close my eyes for a second. "Edward's a lawyer. I signed everything else over to him. *Idiota*. . . ."

"No, you were so young. Keep talking. *Wake up!*"

My lids flashed wide.

"Eyes on me, baby. Then what happened?"

"He framed me. Couldn't go to police . . . I got a gun. *Accidente.* Shot Julia and blood was *everywhere* . . . He swore he'd kill me. I ran and ran. Probably going to jail."

"Nothing will ever happen to you again! Never. Look at me. Talk to me. About anything. What were you doing in the classroom?"

"Last exam. Máxim, I-I finished college today."

His brows drew together, as if I were breaking *his* heart. "Congratulations, little love. We will celebrate when you are better." He barked something to Vasili, who responded just as tersely. "You must've had a laugh when I asked you why you didn't go to school."

"I never lied. I bob. And weave."

"You're very good at that. But you're an atrocious liar."

"The worst," I agreed. "Anthony told me . . . you booked Ivanna."

"Fucking *kill* him. He likely said that to convince you to take the date you spoke of. I only called for her number to try to find out more information about Edward. I decided on the plane that I would discover who he was and pay him to give you to me."

"You did?"

"When I comprehended you were really leaving me yesterday, I let you—so I could track you and find the man I thought you loved."

"Sneaky."

"I knew he wouldn't possibly leave you for less

than a billion, so I decided to give him that and make the better bargain."

"Are you telling me this . . . because I'm dying—"

"*NO!* You are not dying, *solnyshko*. We're almost at the hospital. I'm telling you this because I will always tell you everything in the future."

"I saw the blade . . . but my chest doesn't hurt at all."

Immediately, I perceived even more pressure from Máxim. He snapped at Vasili, then asked me, "With all that happened to you, how could you not scream at me when I accused you of entrapping me?"

"Rule number one. Don't tell . . . anybody anything. I wore a muzzle . . . nice to lose it."

"You were leaving last week, weren't you? You rescheduled your final. I forced you to stay in Miami, then drove you right to him. You would've told me, trusting me with this."

Numbness was stealing over my body, but I still felt his fingers biting into my arm as he said, "I could have taken care of him while you slept soundly last night."

I lifted my hand to his face, frowning when it fell limp. I'd streaked blood across his cheek. "I'm really dizzy."

His eyes were glinting. "I know, but you have to be strong, Katya. You cannot leave me." His body kept tensing up against mine, like the invisible fist was paying him a visit. "Though Katya's not your name. You're Ana-Lucía."

"Just Lucía."

His breath shuddered from his lungs. "Did you know that your name means . . . *light?*"

Light. Sun. I was his sun, and he was my Russian. He'd taken a bullet for me. He'd never booked Ivanna. He loved me.

Máxim rested his forehead against mine, rocking me in his arms. "I'm begging you not to leave me, Lucía."

Needed to tell him . . . "*Te quiero tanto, Máxim.* I love you so much."

Those black dots swarmed again. The last thing I heard was his anguished roar.

CHAPTER 39

*B*eeping sounds. The smell of disinfectant. Hushed tones.

In some hazy twilight, I knew I was in a hospital. I heard Máxim's voice, and others' as well.

Over what felt like days, conversations filtered through my mind to the beat of a heart monitor. I clung to threads.

In one, Aleks was angry with his brother: "We had to fucking hear about this from Vasili?" Aleks and Natalie had come here? They'd left their honeymoon?

In another, Natalie had asked Máxim, "Is your chest going to be okay?"

"Thanks to Lucía." *He's out of danger, gracias a Dios.* "That fuck actually had a bead on my forehead." *And Máxim had kept charging forward??*

In another thread, he told them about his fight with me, ending with: "This is all my fault. When I thought she would leave me for another . . . I imagined life without her, and I lost my fucking mind. Couldn't think or see reason." He asked Aleks, "Did you know jealousy before you met Natalie?"

"Maks, I didn't know *anything.*"

One time, I'd heard Máxim outside the room in a heated conversation with someone. Inside, Aleks had asked Natalie, "Why do these things keep happening to our family?"

"Oh, no, no. The Sevastyans do not get to shoulder this one. Cat—Lucía—never would've met Maksim if she hadn't already been in danger. And I jeopardized *myself* when I searched for my birth parents. When she pulls through, everything will be better."

Whenever Máxim was alone, he pleaded for me to wake up, promising me that I was safe. "You lost a lot of blood, but you've already started healing. When you wake up, you'll be as good as new. Please come back to me, Lucía. . . ."

He also took the blame for everything: "You told me 'don't do this,' but I kept hurting you. I drove you away." Now I sensed he was beside me, alone. I could feel his warmth, even before he took my hand in both of his.

He sat on the edge of my bed with a ragged exhalation. "*Solnyshko,* you must wake. It's been four days."

En serio? I'm here! I could hear him perfectly, but I couldn't speak. Or move. How frustrating! Why couldn't I clasp his hand?

Voice thick, he began talking, about everything and nothing. He described the weather and wondered aloud what kind of dog I would like. He talked about trips we would take to fill up my passport. He relayed how awful Vasili felt for his suspicions about me.

I wished I could tell Máxim that I would take the ugliest mutt I could find out of the pound, one with street cred, one no one else would bring home. I'd like to see Cuba and Russia. I wished I could tell him that I understood and appreciated Vasili's concern. I'd had no identity, could've been preying on Máxim. All the man had wanted to do was look out for "boss."

How could I fault him for that? When I wanted to as well?

Máxim continued, "How will you forgive me? Anything I could possibly do wrong, I did."

You took a bullet for me, Ruso!

"You can do anything now. You'll have your life back. You're so young, and you wanted your freedom. If you choose to leave me, how will I let you go? I couldn't before."

I wouldn't choose to! I needed to tell Máxim that we could work through this, that I was ready to do the heavy lifting in our relationship—but I couldn't even lift my lids.

"Will you please wake for me?" He raised my hand to press my palm against his face, as if he were starved for my touch. Stubble covered his jaw. Was his cheek damp? "Better things await you, Lucía."

I was ready for him. I wanted my Russian. I wanted to claim my name again and start a brand-new life. If I could just wake up. I fought to lift my lids.

The heart monitor began to speed up.

Beep . . . . . . Beep . . . . . Beep . . . . Beep . . . Beep

I felt my free hand clench the sheet. Hey! That was new.

Beep . . Beep . . Beep . . Beep . . Beep . . Beep

He exhaled a gust of breath. "Are you about to wake? Come back to me! You can do this!"

If I could move, maybe I could talk now. I struggled to grate out, "*Máxim.*"

His hands clenched mine as he snapped, *"STAY AWAKE!"* then he bellowed for a nurse. To me, he said, "Keep talking! Please, Lucía!"

I cracked open my eyes. Once I got used to the brightness and could focus, I gasped at his appearance. He hadn't shaved in days, and his hair was a mess. His eyes were so red, the blue of his irises appeared indigo. His suit was rumpled, his shirt collar unbuttoned. I could see the edge of his bandage.

"You look like hell." My voice was scratchy.

That made him smile. He raised my hand to his stubbled jaw. "Good of you to notice." His eyes were glinting.

Damn, I loved this man. "What happened?"

"The blade missed everything major, but you lost too much blood. You went into shock. After surgery, you didn't wake up."

Surgery? I glanced down, saw the edge of my own bandage peeking out from a hospital gown. "Are *you* okay? When you were shot . . ."

"I'm fine now. It will take more than a bullet to keep me from you."

My voice was weak and my throat felt like it was on fire, but I still teased, "Do you like me when I pull through?"

He laughed without humor. "I *love* you when you pull through. Everything's going to be better now."

"Edward's dead?"

"You're a widow. You're free." The door opened behind him. "They'll need to check you, now that you're awake."

A doctor came in, also rumpled. Behind his glasses, his eyes were bloodshot too. He warily glanced at my Russian. The man swallowed, then told me, "I am very, *very* relieved that you're better." He sounded Australian.

Had Máxim been scaring people? He reluctantly let go of my hand.

The doc fussed over me, a nurse too, but my eyes only wanted to look at Máxim. He had his gaze locked on me, even as he called Aleks and Natalie.

I heard her squeal on the phone.

The doc said something about my vitals looking good, but I'd probably get sleepy and that was okay. "You're fortunate," he told me. "A hair's width to the left and we would not be having this conversation."

Once we were alone again, Máxim sat beside me on the bed.

"Did you scare that poor doctor, *Ruso*?"

"A bit. He didn't want to travel here from Australia. At least not at first," he added darkly.

"You brought in someone from across the world?"

"Of course. I wanted a second opinion on your surgery, and he is the best." He hiked his shoulders, stifling a wince. "Aleks and Natalie are coming right over. They'd gone to the hotel to change. They've been here each day."

"They don't have to return. I can't believe they left their honeymoon."

"They want to make sure you're okay. You have friends who care very much about you. Jess would be here as well, but we've kept your location secret for your protection. That one is chaos embodied, no?"

"They all know what happened?" So strange. My marriage to a murderer had been my burden. Now, out in the world. "I can't believe Edward's dead."

"He was married six times." In a grave tone, Máxim said, "Lucía, you are the only one to survive him."

"S-six?" If my race hadn't been canceled, would I have been his next victim? "Have the cops been here? When will I have to talk to someone?" I dreaded having to spill the entire story, to dredge up so many painful memories.

"Talk about what, love? Edward Hatcher was found shot in a public restroom in Atlantic City. A drug deal gone wrong."

My lips formed an O. "No one heard the shots on campus?"

"Few people were there on New Year's Eve, and the storm brought a lot of thunder. We left quickly afterward."

"Why Atlantic City?"

"He lived there for a while, and I didn't want him connected to Miami, in case you wish to stay here. I burned to punish him for hurting you, but if he were found tortured, there would be even more questions." Máxim's gaze grew even more intense. "He wouldn't have been found at all, but . . . I wanted to make you a widow."

I swallowed. So Máxim could marry me? "I'm Lucía Martinez again?" My eyes watered.

"Yes, love. Now you have nothing to worry about except getting better."

"There's a case, Máxim. It's in a safety deposit box—"

"It's already been collected."

"How did you know?"

"Before Hatcher died, he confessed to things."

They'd taken him alive. I thought back over that crazed car ride. Had something thumped in the trunk?

The trunk of the Russian mobster's Bentley.

Máxim said, "He admitted to profiling you for months before he ever approached you. He knew everything about you."

He had? "No wonder we had so much in common."

"Hatcher also recently *signed* things. You own your home again, and we've recovered about half of your money, with more to follow. If you want to make his actions public in the future, you can, at your own pace. But nothing can hinder your recovery."

"How did you access the box at the bank?"

Máxim appeared somewhat affronted, raising his brows as if to say *honey, please.* I suppose he knew the type of guys who could've gotten into the Pentagon if I'd needed them to.

"What about Julia's death?"

"She'll never be found. That often happens to women in Hatcher's presence. He was wanted for murder in other states, but you've kept him so busy, he hasn't been able to target another. I can't find evidence of more crimes."

That made me feel better. But still . . . "He was a monster, and I invited him into our lives. Now *your* life. You were shot."

"A predator picked you. He studied you. You were a teenager. As for myself, I deserved nothing less." He raked the fingers of his free hand through his hair. "I fucked up at every turn, and you lie here because of it. You almost . . . you nearly died." He visibly shuddered.

I couldn't stand to see the guilt in his eyes. "I guess we could blame ourselves. I have an idea—let's blame him." I was starting to get sleepy.

"We could do that. We have time to discuss all this. You already look tired, love."

"If I'm going to be out, you could go to the hotel and rest."

"Not a chance." He pressed a kiss to my forehead. "I'll watch over you. Right now, just concentrate on getting better."

"Then what happens? I need to know something before I pass out."

His Adam's apple bobbed. "Whatever you wish to happen will. I'll see to it." I read a question in his gaze. Was I keeping him?

"What are my choices? I like things settled, *Ruso.*"

"You know what I want from you."

I bit my lip at the fierceness in his expression. "You want everything?"

A slow nod. "Everything." The man was a *goner*. Done for. *Terminado*.

"What if you get jealous again? And stop talking to me?"

In a hoarse voice, he said, "I have learned—in the harshest possible way—to talk to you. I want to spend my life making up for the way I treated you. But I won't rush your decision. For now, you need to rest and heal so you can go home."

I couldn't stifle a yawn. "Home?" In Jacksonville? I didn't want to go there, not for a while. Not until the pain had faded more.

"You have a brand new house in Miami, *moyo sol-nyshko*. It has spices in need of organizing. When you're better, you'll have a discerning dog. And I'll bribe him to like me."

He got me a Miami house? "Is my place big enough for me and my dog and even you?"

"Indeed."

I yawned again. "You wanna share it with us?"

He swallowed. "Are you certain? You have your freedom now. You're young and wealthy and can do anything—can *have* anything—in this world."

I was drifting off. "I want my Russian. Come live with me and the scrappy mutt we pick out at the pound. *Mi casa es su casa*."

"Ah, my Lucía wants a scrappy mutt. I should've known you'd prefer a dog who's been on the run." As I drifted off, I heard him say, "I'll live with you, then. Until I can convince you to marry me. . . ."

CHAPTER 40

$\mathcal{I}$ sat on Máxim's lap as Vasili drove us to my new place. The day was a Miami stunner. I raised my face to the sun coming in the window, starved for it after so long inside.

At the hospital, Vasili had opened the door to the (new) Bentley, literally hat in hand. He'd mumbled fervent Russian to me.

I'd asked Máxim, "What's he saying?"

"That he's very happy you're better. And sorry for his suspicions."

I told the man, "You took care of Máxim. How could I hold a grudge? You get a lifetime supply of *turrón*."

Now we were slowing to turn onto a bridge. "I recognize this! We're going to Indian Creek Island?" The tiny Miami eden for the ultra-rich was home to only fourteen families, yet the enclave had its own police force and mayor. "I always wanted a cleaning job here, but the security was crazy."

"In lieu of a job, would you accept owning the best house on the island?"

I gazed back at Máxim. *"En serio? Sí.* Let's do that." I craned my head to look at everything, squirming over him. My eyes widened when I felt him harden. Máxim had definitely recovered from his gunshot wound. I slid him a smile.

The left corner of his lips curved. "And I'd been so good the whole way here."

The doc had told me I couldn't have sex until I got the all clear. I leaned back against the uninjured side of Máxim's chest. "This chastity is going to be the worst of all, isn't it, *Ruso*?"

"I'd prefer another bullet wound."

As we pulled into a driveway lined with majestic palms, my jaw dropped at the enormous mansion. Máxim hadn't been kidding about ours being the best.

The design was modern, with an abundance of oversize windows, the stucco tropics-white. Lush landscaping abounded.

Inside, I turned in circles. The décor was warm and inviting. Tasteful art adorned the walls. The ceilings soared, giving the rooms an airy feel. Plush rugs softened the acoustics.

In the living room, an entire wall opened to the outside—and a breathtaking pool. A green lawn sprawled down to a beach and lapping blue waves. A cigarette boat hung in a lift.

"Te gusta?" he asked.

"We can live here today? It's *krasavitza.* Beautiful!" I crossed to him.

He smiled at my Russian word. "You're already moved in. I wasn't joking about the kitchen spices. For the future, there's a treadmill and the yard is fenced. Though maybe you'd like somewhere else better? We could stay in Jacksonville, or the North Pole, or wherever St. Bernards serve brandy."

I grinned up at him. "I like it here. But don't you need to live in Russia?"

"Aleksandr wants to go into business. He has totally changed his mind about me. He could take over things in Russia, and I could expand here. In fact, you and I could start operations in this very house."

I was already heading into phase four of my life plan? "How many briefcases of cash did this place cost?"

"Many. But the markets were good—today we are billionaires. We should reward ourselves."

"Okay, but when do I get to visit the motherland?"

"Once you're fully recovered. Our estate there is beautiful in the spring." He grazed his knuckles along my jawline. "I want you to meet Dmitri as well."

I smoothed the lapel of Máxim's blazer. "Won't he hate me?"

"He called when you were in surgery, and I was out of my head with worry. I didn't bother trying to hide how frantic I was. When I called to tell him you were better, he said, 'You love her. I will meet her.' This is huge for him."

"Then count me in."

"I let him know that I will always be there for him, but things have changed. My focus will be on the future." Máxim's eyes were full of promise. "Come, I want you to see some things in your closets."

The spaces weren't *closets*—they were *rooms,* each one with new swag and clothes! He leaned against the doorway, content to watch me explore. When I found my red scarf, I closed my eyes in relief.

"You should look at that new wallet as well." He pointed to one of several.

I opened it. Credit cards filled all the slots. "Aww. Did you get me pin money?"

"Only in the checking. The savings is yours."

Wait . . . I looked at the ID. "This is *me*!" The picture was from my former license. Oh, I looked so young! "You got the Hatcher taken off so quickly! I'm officially me again."

With that gleam I loved so well, he said, "Maybe you can still be Cat and Katya—on occasion."

I traipsed closer to him. "This kitten will want *a lot* of toys. Let's dedicate a room."

He inhaled sharply. "*Sí,* let's do that. For now, you have more exploring to do. Your jewelry."

All my previous bling was organized, along with tons more. Among my pearls and gold was my mother's rosary. "Oh, Máxim, you got it back?" When the import of what I'd regained truly hit me, I would surely lose my shit. In a way, that rosary had been on as wild a trip as I had.

"Of course." He took my hand. "When you feel like it, you can decide what you want to do with your home in Jacksonville as well."

"I wish the place would be the same, just minus that one room."

He raised his brows, as if to say *challenge accepted.*

As we strolled toward the pool, I said, "I got the strangest text from Ivanna this morning. From what I could decipher, she wrote that her family would be in the States by the end of next week. And that her new place was amazing." (hus s amzasng!1) "You know anything about that?"

He shrugged. "If she hadn't sent you to me . . . I am very beholden to her—and to Botox in general."

"She was a little pissed that I hadn't asked for help, but she understood too." I already had a friend in Miami! "She also texted that Anthony closed up shop and is on the run from the *mafiya.*"

A raised brow. "I will prolong that for as many years as it pleases you." Beside the pool, he sat on a lounge chair, then gingerly pulled me into his lap. Sun bathed us in light, dappling the blue water beyond.

"When do you think we'll christen this chair, *Ruso?*"

He groaned. "Unfortunately, not for a while."

"I understand, baby boy. After all, you *were* shot. And at your age too?" I fake-winced. "But I'm sure they'll clear you for duty"—I wriggled over the growing bulge in his lap—"eventually."

His voice was husky. "Little witch."

"I guess I'll give you a reprieve because you took a bullet for me."

"I'd do it to eternity to have this moment. Though you know I won't rest until you're mine in every way."

"It's you for me, *Ruso.* You are stuck with me. But what if I want to wait awhile before thinking about marriage?" Even with the man of my dreams, I didn't want to rush things.

I had this feeling that I'd know when the time was right.

"Then I'll propose to you weekly."

I found that fair, since we both knew he could use a magic wand, rope, and the strategic application of a chastity belt to get me to yes.

I twirled my finger over the left side of his chest. "You aren't done with me yet?"

He pinned my gaze with his own. With a surprisingly smooth accent, he told me, "*Nunca voy a terminar contigo.*" I'll never be done with you.

EPILOGUE

"*Y*ou can't be late, Lucía," Máxim rasped in my ear as his body worked mine. "How did you talk me into this?"

"It's your own fault for looking so hot in that suit," I told him, my nails digging into his shoulders. "When your woman needs it, she needs it. We'll be quick."

I was getting it on with a Russian sex god. In a closet on campus. In my graduation robe. Because I could.

Life was sweet.

"Am I hurting you?" He was asking me that after what we'd done last night?

Though I was totally healed up, he *still* asked. My scar wasn't even that bad. But as Máxim had said, "I can *see* how close I came to losing you." Sometimes, he would shudder and kiss it. Well, no more than once a day. He'd also said the mark was much "daintier" than his own "rugged" bullet-wound scar.

His was on the right side of his chest; mine was on my left. Whenever Máxim and I kissed, so did our scars.

Because we were intertwined. In sync. Lock and key. Our bodies, our lives.

"Hurting, Máxim? I'm in agony here." I rubbed my face against his, purring Spanish in his ear—that I needed him, I needed every inch of his gorgeous body, and every inch of his magnificent cock—which made his hips surge, because the devil understood it all.

In Russian, he told me he wanted to fuck me forever, that my body was his heaven and my skin tasted like sun—which made me rock my hips on him in a frenzy. Because I now knew more than four words of his language.

He had to muffle my screams with his palm, and his own yells against my neck.

Forehead to forehead, we caught our breath.

"You like me when I graduate, *Ruso*?"

A sound of satisfaction rumbled from his chest. "Woman, I *love* you when you graduate."

We made each other presentable, then hurried to the auditorium, hand in hand. Beside the stage, he gave me a lingering kiss. The man could not possibly look prouder of me. "Behave up there, *moyo solnyshko*."

Behave? Just for that, I mussed his hair before I ran to take my place in line.

The dean was moments away from handing me my holy grail! All it'd taken was half a decade, a near-death experience, and teaming up with a Russian mobster.

Natalie, Aleks, and Jess were waiting for Máxim in the audience, saving him a front-row seat. They all laughed at his disheveled appearance.

I'd begged the three of them not to come, but they wouldn't be dissuaded. Because I was family.

Jess had been on her best behavior, because she wanted to coordinate hot *mamí*'s wedding, the one everyone knew would eventually happen. Organizing two billionaire weddings would pretty much set her up in the coordinator biz.

After this, we were all flying to Russia to see Natalie and Aleks's estate and vacation at Máxim's own—which he insisted was half mine. Which meant every horse was half mine!

I was also going to see Dmitri. I was nervous about that, but optimistic since he'd wanted to meet. Máxim remained committed to reuniting his brothers, and thought Dmitri visiting with someone who was a big fan of Aleks and Natalie could only help.

Also going to Russia? Scrappy Miami mutts. Máxim and I had kind of gotten *three* discerning dogs. At the pound, I hadn't been able to pick between a trio of bad-ass brutes. He'd frowned. "Why choose, *solnyshko*?" He bribed them as shamelessly as he spoiled me.

I hoped the pack didn't trash the jet (as they had the Bentley and Vasili's shoes!).

After our visit to the motherland, I planned for Máxim to take me to Paris—so I could experience the infamous Le Libertin club. I'd become an ardent and aggressive fan of my Russian's kinks. Late last night, I'd still been primed after our earlier marathon session.

I'd woken him by trailing the end of a rope along his torso. "You like me when you tie me up?"

He'd groaned, "I love the fuck out of you, woman, but I think I've created a monster."

Sigh. I loved the fuck out of him too. He was the man I was always supposed to be with. *Muchas gracias, Botox.*

Ivanna would've been here for my ceremony, but she was overseeing the reroofing of my old apartment building. Máxim had given me the property for our second month anniversary. I'd asked Ivanna—a seriously savvy businesswoman—to manage it.

Yes, Máxim had set her family up financially, but she'd needed something to do. As she'd told me, "There's only so many times I can take my mother and sister to Disney World. The song 'It's a Small World' gives me hives."

Shadwell had lined his pockets so heavily, the apartments had turned a profit from month one.

I'd finally learned how the man had discovered my hidden "safe." The perv had secretly *filmed* me and other female residents.

But the strangest thing had happened—Shadwell had . . . disappeared. Never to be seen again! I'd asked Vasili if he knew anything about this. The man had said, "Al-ee-gahtor accident?"

Now the name of the game for that apartment complex was repairs. We planned to turn it into the neighborhood's oasis. Already people's lives were so much better.

In the meantime, Máxim and I eyed our next acquisition. We'd been working together every day, plotting to take over Miami. As we read reports and evaluated holdings, the dogs lazed at our feet.

He and I took plenty of time off for *cafecitos*, and each night we jogged and cooked. On weekends, we'd go boating, exploring islands and keys. Often he would use *persuasion* to make me shop. Well, when the vendors just showed up, I guessed I could.

For my birthday, we'd visited Martinez Beach and my childhood home. It'd been emotional, but I'd gotten excited when Máxim found an architect—who could actually take that one room off the house. Why the hell not?

I thought my dad would've liked Máxim. Would my mother? I didn't know; it didn't matter. Though Máxim's endowment to my college in her name couldn't have hurt things. . . .

Shortly after our move to the island, he'd made a formal proposal (with an obscenely large marquise-cut diamond ring). I'd asked him to give me more time. True to his word, he'd proposed every week.

He'd asked again yesterday.

I glanced from behind the curtain at my Russian. His gaze found and locked on mine. *Look at him.* I sighed.

Only one more person was left before the dean called my name! I blew Máxim a kiss, then ducked back behind the curtain. With a grin, I peeled off the cover I'd affixed to my graduation cap, revealing the hidden message I'd written. I would tip it to Máxim, make the man's day and all.

"*Ana-Lucía 'Cat' Martinez. Summa Cum Laude.*"

As I strode across the stage, I canted my head so my Russian could read . . .

YES YES YES

ACKNOWLEDGMENTS

*M*any thanks to Carmen S. for all your translation help! You helped make Cat into one of my favorite heroines to date.

And as ever, I'd like to thank the talented team who help me get books to readers in the best shape possible.

To Dr. Bridget, for making sure all of my medical details are on point. Though I did run with the contraceptive shot (there could be one in the U.S. soon, right?).

To Dr. Beth, for your psychological insight into character motivations. You floor me every time.

To the production department at Simon & Schuster. I know this one was a doozy. Chocolate AND booze TK.

To Elana Cohen, for somehow keeping me on track as we published six books in three genres over nineteen months. This project alone should get you a promotion and a crazy raise (your move, S&S, your move).

To Robin Rue, for your invaluable guidance during these exciting times in publishing!

To Lauren McKenna, this is our twenty-fifth book, baby! You give each and every one flavor and heart.

And to Swede, you scrub through manuscripts like M-O from Wall-E. Only you're cuter.